Glenda & Arlene,

Happy reading!

The Whipping Post

a story of oppression, enlightenment and redemption of those who tied and were tied with ropes seen and unseen

JuliAnne Sisung

JuliAnne Sisung

ISBN-13: 978-1985757240
ISBN-10: 1985757249

This is a work of fiction. Characters and incidences are the product of the author's imagination and are used fictitiously.

Published March 2018 by JuliAnne Sisung

Books by JuliAnne Sisung

The Hersey Series

Elephant in the Room
a family saga

Angels in the Corner
a family saga

Light in the Forest
a family saga

Place in the Circle
a family saga

The Idlewild Series

Leaving Nirvana
an account of love and oppression
race, gender, honor

The Whipping Post
a story of oppression, enlightenment and redemption of those who tied and were tied with ropes seen and unseen

Ask for the Moon
a tale of love, growth and acceptance
as Idlewild comes of age

Acknowledgements

Thank you to the residents of Idlewild and neighboring towns for sharing stories with me. Their rich past makes historical fiction possible and meaningful. Thank you to Cila Cochran for sharing a little of her knowledge with me in a fascinating tour of Idlewild.

Thanks to the activists who gave their time and lives to change the future for black men and women and, especially, Charles Waddell Chesnutt who chose to be black and wrote profound novels and short stories about the experience. His words about building blocks made of esteem pierced my heart in a way I will not forget. He was a gentle man.

Mark Jessup read and guided my work, created the cover image and helped with the title. His words of wisdom were instrumental in maintaining the intent of the novel.

To Larry Hale: I appreciate the intense editing and search for continuity. My books would not read as well as they do if not for you.

No words of credit would be complete without mentioning my mom, Esther Mathia, who turned ninety-two this year and danced at Idlewild long ago. She directed my reading since the day I began bringing books home from the school library and made sure I read real literature and the classics. Thanks, Mom.

Chapter One

Spring 1920

"You're not going anywhere, yet," Abby shouted and tossed her auburn braid back over her shoulder. "Wait just a minute."

She pushed the drink tray toward Jackson and moved to stand in front of the handsome man.

"Kind of pushy, Abigail," he said, the devil dancing at the corners of lips that weren't really smiling. "What do you want?"

"You know everything in this town, Samuel. You must have heard something."

"Why don't you ride out to the farm and ask your beloved in-laws where their son is?"

She tossed a damp towel at him and scowled.

"You know they don't want to see me. Probably shoot me on sight."

"I don't know where he is, Abby. I just know he's gone."

An unconscious frown furrowed his brow. Samuel didn't crinkle his face for anyone and wouldn't like knowing a scowl marred his perfection, but it irritated him she wouldn't give up trying to track down her useless husband.

He suspected Frank had done one selfless thing in his entire life, and that single honorable act probably kept him from his wife. Because he feared the consequences.

Samuel sat at the end of the hotel bar nursing a drink and watching Shorty and Bear eye him from the other end. They didn't like him much, and the idea quirked his lips in an attempt to force a smile. They didn't *dislike* him or have anything concrete against him, but he was friends with Abby, and that served as plenty.

Shorty, a bald giant, couldn't speak above a whisper, and Bear was all hair, including a black bushy beard crisscrossed with white scars created by an actual bear. The ex-lumberjacks were draped in Abby's cats, Cleo and Phantom, who believed ownership of humans was a feline right and a serious responsibility. People weren't as smart as they believed and needed guidance.

Shorty and Bear had followed Abby and her father, Patrick, from Nirvana when they left the dying lumber town to help build the Idlewild Resort a few years back. They were her family, the brothers she never had, and they'd put her in a protective bubble if she let them.

Samuel enjoyed poking *the Bear* and his friend just to watch the smoke curl from their ears when he'd get too close to Abby. He lifted his glass to them, nodded and smiled, trying to stir the warm ashes of their angst.

Jackson Parker shouted a drink order, and Abby lined up glasses to fill with whiskey they weren't allowed to sell. Prohibition had tried to shut down their bar business, but, like all the others, they found ways to serve the alcohol everyone wanted. If anything, consumption had increased.

Abby scrutinized Samuel as she moved the bottle from one glass to the next and poured a continuous flow of the brown liquid without spilling a drop.

Immaculate, as always – his crisp white shirt peeked from under a black vest and matching jacket. His russet skin shone satin in the light of the oil lamps, and a pencil-line mustache perched between nose and upper lip. Samuel pulled a watch from its vest pocket, and it caught the light and shimmered as the gold chain stretched.

Abby's eyes roamed the noisy bar, but the faces of Idlewild patrons didn't register. Her mind was on Frank and his family. She imagined his brother, George, in a jail cell for what he'd done to her friend. He sat there because she'd forced the issue when Betty would have hidden it. If she hadn't, he'd be at the family farm, milking his father's heifers, eating his mother's meals, and following Betty through the woods, waiting to attack her again.

She hurt for the Adams family, but couldn't feel bad for George. In her mind, he and the Tatum boys earned their jail cells and received proper payment for a job done way too well and way too often.

They didn't see it, though. Bullies and tyrants never did. Nothing was ever their fault, and they felt entitled to take what they wanted – especially from a young, colored girl.

"Gotta go, Abby. Stay out of trouble," Samuel said.

"I try, but Sheriff Hicks says it follows me. I'm a beacon." She stuck her hand in the air and waved it around. "Here I am. Come get me."

Patrick tottered into the bar from the kitchen and took a stool by Bear and Shorty. He ran a knobby hand over his face, and Abby smiled at her father and held up a glass. He hadn't bothered to shave again, and gray stubble covered his cheeks and chin. Red-gray curls flopped over his forehead and bounced when he nodded to her. She filled it half-way and brought it to him.

"Irish?" he asked before taking a sip.

"Course. Ratty and Del are looking for you."

"Why didn't you send 'em in?"

"They wanted to see Jesse first." She pointed to the corner table just as they saw Patrick and stood to move in his direction. "Dang. Couldn't they give you a minute?"

"It's alright, lass. I'm content."

Ratty and Del Branch were two of the four men who started the Idlewild Resort. It had been their brainchild, and, although property was selling well, they still owned much of the twenty-seven hundred acres around Lake Idlewild. They'd always intended to build a club and hotel on the island and wanted Patrick to be a part of it. This year they were going to make it happen.

"Told you this day would come, my friend. You want in?" Del grabbed Patrick's hand and pumped it up and down.

"You want to be a bit more specific, Del?" He yanked his hand back and rubbed at the red knuckles. "Sweet Mary, but you don't always have to crush my hand."

"Sorry. Guess I'm a bit eager. The island hotel. I figured you might want in now you got your feet wet with this one." Patrick crossed his arms and straightened his back.

"Guess I'll need a wee bit more information, but tonight me brain is mush. Can ye come by tomorrow?"

"Sure. Kind of sprung this on you, didn't we?" Ratty patted his shoulder and ruffled his curls with affection. He liked the little Irish leprechaun. That's how he always thought of Patrick. "While we're here, though, maybe we can convince Shorty and the Bear to give some thought to running a construction crew for us."

"Run it? Not work in it?" Shorty asked.

"That's what Del and I thought. We've watched you work and think you're the men for the job. You've got a way of taking no guff, and men respect you. Give it some thought, and we'll talk."

Del slapped his back, and a wide grin showed the Branch family charm which bought and sold real estate all over Michigan.

"You both did a fine job catching those Tatum boys setting fires to the resort cabins. And those damned KKK cross paintings! They'd still be doing it if it hadn't been for you two."

He thumped his glass on the wooden bar, remembered anger infecting his humor. Peace hadn't been in the air long enough to be an accepted fact, but, with the Tatums in jail, folks in Idlewild were beginning to breathe without fear and walk without looking behind them in the dark.

"We'll give it some thought, Del. Appreciate your offer," Bear said. "Right, Shorty?"

The big man nodded, finding it easier to remain silent much of the time rather than try to raise the decibels of his whisper so people didn't ask him to repeat himself.

While Abby wiped down the gleaming bar, Shorty and Bear piled chairs on the tables, so Betty could sweep in the morning. They helped where they could, partly to pay for their permanent rooms at the hotel and partly because they were Abby's adopted family.

"Want another on the porch?" she asked her da as she finished up.

"Can't walk on one leg, lass," he said. "You pour and I'll carry."

They went to their favorite wooden rockers lining the covered front porch. They each had their own, as if their bottoms had formed permanent indentations in the seat and any other backside wouldn't fit. When another person joined them, one who didn't understand the rules, they were forced to try a different chair. They sat gingerly, wiggled around to find some small, unfamiliar comfort and waited for the interloper to leave.

Tonight, all was as it should be, just the four of them, and contentment hummed in the exhale of their breath, soft and sweet like a lover's sigh or a baby's lullaby.

Two moons held court. A sliver hovered in the sky, and a matching slice shimmered on the water. It wiggled and dipped in a circle of rippling glass as the nose of a small mouth bass or speckled trout broke the surface.

Spring had come early to Michigan, and the summer-like night erupted with the sounds of nocturnal prey and predators testing the boundaries of their power.

Abby sighed with pleasure on the tail of the loon's wail. It had returned from a winter hiatus, and she'd missed it, missed their nightly conversations. Its haunting song reclaimed the territory, and his mate yodeled back in response to his vocal demand.

In the distance, visible at the edge of a sliver of moonlight, Cassandra and her clowder of cats poked along the edge of the lake. As always, the felines followed her single file, looking neither right nor left as if their entire focus should be, could only be, on the witchy woman, their mistress. Without looking back toward the hotel porch, Cassandra lifted her walking stick into the air in a gesture of acknowledgement, and Abby felt honored.

Rockers clicked on the wooden porch, a rhythmic companion to their thoughts.

"You gonna build a new hotel, Irish?" Shorty asked without interrupting the moderate tempo they'd adopted.

Abby waited for his answer, hoping it wouldn't be *yes* but knowing she'd be there to help if it was.

Frank hadn't liked that about her, and she understood. Husbands and wives should be sidekicks, not fathers and daughters. But Abby and Patrick were. They were a team, as they had always been, the leprechaun and his lass.

"Tired tonight, so it doesn't sound like the best idea. In the morning, though, you never know. I could feel a mite better."

"Night comes every day, Patrick," Bear said.

"Now isn't that profound," Shorty said. "You sure got a way with words, my friend."

"I know what he means." Patrick bumped Bear's arm with an elbow. "I'm no wee lad anymore. What do you think, Daughter?"

"If it's what you want to do, Da. I like where we are, though."

"You want to run his building crew, boys?" Patrick asked.

"I might." Bear was a man of few words, and they all knew those two meant he'd take the job.

"You couldn't talk to me about it first?" Shorty asked. "We're partners."

"This is me talking. You in?" Bear stroked the white Phantom draped over his shoulder and clicked an invitation to Cleo to climb on his lap. He was happier covered in cat.

"Guess so," Shorty said. "What'd that Samuel want tonight?"

"A drink. Why?" Abby tried to circumvent Cleo's path to Bear with her own snapping fingers, but the cat ignored her. "Did you bathe in catnip?"

His chortle charmed the night. If she had to lose her cats, she couldn't find a better person to lose them to.

"Don't know what to do about liquor. We're living one day to the next. Any ideas, boys?" Patrick asked.

The thought of bootleg whiskey prompted an imperceptible break in the rhythm of their rockers before the melody resumed.

"Southern edge of the forest has a place where men play big stakes poker, the Hess Hotel. I could check it out, cuz gambling and booze come from the same mother," he offered.

Shorty stilled his chair to look at him.

Al left her room before the sun rose and headed for the kitchen. She had the hotel's secret blend of chicory coffee percolating and sausage sizzling when Abby entered.

"You don't need to get started so early, Al."

"I know," Al said without looking up from the bacon she was laying in even rows on the giant cast iron griddle.

She was a tiny thing, blonde haired and milky skinned. When Abby hired her, she questioned whether or not Al could lift one of the giant soup pots from the stove. Al had said she'd been doing it since the age of five – for her father and four brothers. Her glare and the way she'd said it made Abby believe her.

"How are you feeling?" Abby asked. "Did you sleep well? Is Cassandra's chamomile helping?" She knew Al wouldn't respond with more than a grunt, but she couldn't help asking.

All of Al's brothers were incarcerated, and she'd been beaten bloody by her monster of a father when the boys were arrested. Abby found her tied to a whipping post and had tended to her wounds, sitting by her side night and day until she healed enough to eat, sit and move on her own.

"I came across a ribbon in my clothes chest. For your hair. It's deep blue," Abby said, hoping for a response.

Al turned her head and raised her eyebrows as a signal for her boss to get on with cooking breakfast for the guests.

"Okay. I'll get the potatoes," she said, irritated at herself, but chuckling. Abby didn't know why she continued to try to change the young woman. A mission, a higher calling, compelled her beyond logic. Al brought out the urge to nurture, which was Abby's burden and her fault.

Al became *Strange Al* when Abby felt peevish, and she felt like calling her the nickname now. Sometimes it slipped out.

Bear sauntered in with Shorty close behind. Cleo and Phantom followed and climbed Bear's legs as soon as he sat. Abby poured coffee and waited in silence while Shorty gulped his. She watched him from the corner of her eye while she sliced potatoes and waited for the caffeine to work its magic. No one spoke to him before his first cup, or the foolish person risked being picked up and placed on the high cupboard, legs swinging in limbo, until he wanted to put you down. Patrick had learned that lesson the hard way.

"Where you off to this morning, my friends? You building today?" she asked, after seeing wakefulness settle in the big man's eyes.

Shorty's shoulders moved up to his ears as he stretched and rolled them back, groaning in pleasure. He rubbed his head and smiled – a cherubic look for such a giant of a man.

"Nope. Looking for whiskey. Newaygo county. Across the forest like Robin Hood."

"I thought Da was going?" Abby said.

"That's what he said. But I'm thinking we are. You tell him so when he pokes his scruffy head out of his room." He didn't mind talking to Abby in his papery whisper. She always understood and never asked him to speak up.

Abby dried her hands, filled the plates and set them on the table. Twisting the towel around her arm, she leaned her back against the cupboard and watched them eat, studying her friends.

"Why are you two going instead of Da? Is there going to be trouble?"

"Hope not. Never know," Bear said and moved his plate from the hazard of Phantom's paw and scratched his bearded jaw. "If there is, Abby, better with us than Irish. You know that."

"I don't want trouble for you two either. Go somewhere safe for whiskey, or we'll sell lemonade instead." Their guffaws helped ease her fears but not entirely. While they ate, rumbles of disquiet messed with her mind.

"Any place they peddle bootleg is gonna have trouble, Abs. It goes with the territory," Shorty said.

"I know." She tugged her braid and looked for assurance. "But . . . I've heard some things about that area."

"Like?"

Abby glanced at Al. How much could she say in front of her – or should she say? She'd been hurt enough, and Abby didn't want to put her at risk with knowledge she didn't need to have.

When they picked up their empty plates and took them to the sink, Abby followed as they ambled out the front door, not in any real hurry to get where they were going. She stopped them on the porch with a hand on their shoulders.

"The Ku Klux Klan is there. I've heard that. Quite a few. Not like Grand Rapids, but . . ." she said, turning her head around to see if she'd been overheard.

"We're not immigrants, Catholic or colored, Abby. They won't even notice us," Shorty said.

"What does the KKK have to do with bootleg whiskey?" Bear asked.

"It's . . . they support prohibition, so . . . I don't know. They scare me." Her last three words came out in an explosion as Jesse came up the stairs to the porch behind her.

"Who scares you, Abby?" he said, and squinted like he would seek out the culprit and take care of him.

"Nobody." Abby squinted back at him.

"We're going to Newaygo today, looking for supplies. She thinks the KKK is going to cause us trouble."

Jesse's smile warmed his dark brown eyes. He was the first friend Abby made after leaving Nirvana and making a home in Idlewild. Between Abby and his wife, Edna, pushing him all the way, he'd created the town's first Chautauqua and built a town pavilion.

"Jesse's a lawyer. You probably shouldn't tell him everything you're doing," she said with an impish eye. "Talk in pig Latin around him."

Jesse squeezed her.

"Ou yay on't day ow knay e may."

Abby slapped her thigh and snorted. "You're amazing. Can't get a thing by you."

"On a serious note," he said. "Be careful. I hear a guy named Capone is trying to make Lake Michigan his own. Newaygo is already one of his towns."

"Thought that crook was in Chicago," Shorty said.

"He is, but he likes to gamble in the basement of the Hess with a bunch of thugs. Stay away from him. Maybe from Newaygo completely. I hear lots of gossip about that pretty little place – true or not."

"Oh, jeez. Don't go there," Abby wailed, throwing an arm around both men.

"We'll be sure and keep an eye out." Shorty winked at Abby and stepped off the porch. "Don't worry."

They walked off, Bear shuffling along with his fingers stuffed into his front trouser pockets, and Shorty in a rolling gait with muscular arms dangling at his sides. Abby watched and mumbled a prayer they would stroll back up the steps later – all intact.

"They'll be fine." Jesse punched her arm with affection.

"Sure. Why are you here?"

"Waiting for the Branch boys. They here, yet?"

"Del and Ratty? No. Why?"

"Hotel business. Maybe build you a new one. Patrick in the kitchen?"

She scrunched her face and Jesse laughed.

"For a pretty girl . . ."

"What?"

"You say a lot with that face. Not happy?"

"Seems things can't stay the same for five minutes. I wish they would. Maybe just for ten or so." She opened the door and pulled Jesse through to look for her father.

Chapter Two

"I think we'll forget Newaygo and head west," Bear said as they rounded the corner of the hotel and entered the stable. He tossed his saddle over the mare's back and cinched it down. "And I think we ought to invest in an automobile. We wouldn't have to mess with all this. Or feed it."

"You think those things run on air? You see any food in Idlewild we can put in that hungry, metal belly?"

Bear put a foot into the stirrup and threw himself into the saddle with a grunt, and Shorty put a leg over his seat on the tall gelding and smirked at his friend.

"Maybe so," Shorty said. "Could be we should. I'd hate to think I'm wearing out this old boy with my heft. An auto might stink, but it wouldn't have feelings. None I'd care about, anyways. West, you say?"

He let his horse amble and tried to enjoy the countryside's morning symphony. He'd read all about bird songs and could name most of their refrains if people would shut up long enough for the birds to be heard. But folks weren't quiet much, and he wished they were.

"Yup. West. I'm thinking to leave Newago to the Chicago boys. Least ways for now."

"You been doing an awful lot of thinking this morning, Bear. Hear the Black Cap?" Shorty said.

"I give. What the heck is a black cap?"

"Chickadee. Sounds like a high-pitched *see-saw, see-saw* to me, but the so-called experts think he's saying *fee-bee, fee-bee.*"

Bear grinned, and the white paths gouged in his beard flamed pink in the sunlight. He wore them like a badge of courage, an Ursa-awarded purple heart. The scars kept strangers at a distance or brought them in close for an inspection. He didn't care either way. He had survived the bear, and life was the important thing.

"Thanks. Now, I know all about chickadees." He turned to glance at Shorty. Humor played in his eyes before turning serious. "I don't believe we ought to bring bootleggers to Idlewild."

"You know how we're gonna get whiskey then?"

"I don't. I guess we'll ask around. Can't put a man in jail for asking questions."

They passed through Baldwin, and just inside Mason County, at a place called Logan Township, they stopped at Lucy's diner.

Fried onions, fish and other oily aromas assaulted them when they entered, but the tables were shiny and the floor clean. A rosy cheeked, full figured woman they thought was most likely the advertised Lucy bounced over chewing on the end of a stubby pencil. She exposed three teeth in a wide grin and let them know they could have anything they wanted – in the way of food, too.

"Special is meatloaf and mashed potatoes or beans," she said and waved them to a table.

Lucy shouted their order at the kitchen and plopped into one of the empty chairs at their table.

"What you boys doing in little old Logan?"

"Just passing through," Shorty said, trying raise his voice so she could hear him.

She ran a chubby hand down his arm and winked.

"Ought to stay a spell. Logan could use some new blood. Specially a couple of healthy boys like you two. Where you coming from?"

"East of here," Bear said. "And we're not looking to relocate."

"Too bad." She hummed a flat note and thrummed on the table. "I hear there's lots of colored folks over that way, not too far. I go west, myself, for shopping and such."

Neither responded to her comment, and she heaved herself out of her chair and headed for the kitchen.

"Ask her to sit with us when she brings our plates," Shorty said. Bear raised an eyebrow like Shorty had lost his mind. "She probably knows everyone and everything in Mason County. These places hear it all," he added. "Be nice."

"I'm always nice."

She brought two cups of coffee without asking if they wanted any and went back for their food. When her hands were empty of plates, Bear patted the chair next to him and said, "Sit. Rest your feet, Lucy."

"How'd you know my name?"

"Some folks know things. I'll bet you do, too."

They were hungry, and the gravy slathered meatloaf filled their bellies. She watched them scoop food into their mouths with pleasure. Nothing sweeter to her than a man who eats with gusto. When Shorty rubbed a hand over his stomach, she grinned.

"Pie?" she asked.

He leaned in to her.

"What we could really go for is a shot of whiskey. Been a dusty ride."

Lucy pulled at her ear and frowned.

"Sorry," he said. "Didn't mean to put you on the spot."

"I'd pour you both one if I could. Prohibition, you know," she said as if they might be ignorant of the law against the selling of booze. "Can't sell. I could give you some if'n I had any. But I don't."

"You're a sweet woman, Lucy. If I had any, I'd give some to you, too," Shorty said and looked at Bear. "Wonder where we could find us some whiskey to share with our new friend?"

He mumbled along, speculating and brooding out loud, and watched Lucy's eyes bounce from the door of the diner to the table in front of her. She tried to twist a ring around, most likely a habit from the past because it wasn't budging. It rested stuck in between the white rolls of skin puffed up on either side of it.

Bear had to look away, but Shorty put his hand over hers and patted like it was one of Abby's cats or the head of a favorite beagle. He caressed it until he heard murmurs from her.

"Shouldn't say this, but I heard some boys in Custer been getting bootleg brought into Ludington from across the lake. Probably wrong, though. You know how people talk nonsense just to hear themselves say something."

"Do you have names, Lucy?" Bear asked. "We'd be grateful if you did."

"And beholding," Shorty added.

Lucy flushed a pretty pink from neck to hairline in the first stages of gray. Sweat beaded her upper lip, and Shorty's heart broke. They were using the poor woman, and he didn't like it. He swallowed and opened his mouth, but nothing came out. He tried again with no better success.

"What Shorty means is he wants to thank you for the wonderful lunch, and if you have a name or a place where we could find this person in Custer, we'd be forever grateful. Isn't that right, Shorty?" Bear stared hard at him until he nodded in agreement.

"He gets tongue tied when he's happy," Bear told her.

They paid their bill and left with a name, Hank. No last name. Just Hank, and he could be found in the only bar in Custer. Maybe. They figured they were lucky for that much and rode west.

"That was more words strung together than I've ever heard out of you. Mighty pretty, too," Shorty said. "Didn't know you had it in you. You sweet on her?"

"Too much woman for me," Bear said with a chuckle. "Sides, I think she's sweet on you. She was blushing like a girl while you were caressing her hand."

"Means to an end is all. I don't like means to an end. No justice in it for her."

"We needed a name, Shorty."

"I know that. Don't have to like it."

"Think of it this way. You made her smile for a while."

Hank wore a straw boater hat and sat with his legs crossed at the knees, long leg hanging down, an affected, superior position. One elbow rested on the table, and a hand bent like it held a cigarette in a long holder between two fingers.

He played with a mustache which had made a valiant effort to sprout under his nose and bounced his foot. Two others at the table, normally dressed and positioned, listened attentively.

Bear raised one eyebrow Shorty's way and tilted his head toward the man.

"What do you think? Hank?"

"Likely bet."

They stood sideways at the bar, facing each other so they could talk and watch the man with the hat. Hank, if that was his name, affected nonchalance, but it didn't work – or it worked about as well as his mustache.

"He can't even grow hair on his lip and here he is wearing a ridiculous hat and sitting like he owns the place," Shorty whispered.

"What's your pleasure?" the bartender asked.

"I'll have a *near beer* if you got it. And if you're giving whiskey away to your friends, I'm a friend," Shorty said.

The bartender stepped back and looked up at Shorty – all the way up. He nodded, said, "Sure thing. Friends share," and nodded at Bear who nodded back.

Bear thought they were doing too much nodding and not enough talking. It made him nervous.

"Name is Shorty, and this is Bear. We're looking for Hank."

"Friend of yours, too?" he asked.

Shorty shook his head, and the bartender cracked his first grin. "Good thing you said so. He's right behind you."

"Let me guess. Boy with the pretty hat?" Bear said.

"Be nice, Bear."

"Why have you been saying that to me all day? I *am* nice. Always."

When the bartender brought their drinks, they tossed back the shot of whiskey, picked up their beers and took three steps toward Hank who tilted his straw-hat way back. The closer they got, the further his head tilted until the hat fell off and he grabbed for it. Bear got there first and whipped it out of the air before it landed on the grimy floor.

"Thanks," Hank said, eyes wide with a comical combination of awe and fear. "I . . . I like that hat." He ran a hand through thinning, sandy colored hair and slammed the hat back on as soon as he could grab it from Bear's hand.

"Welcome. You Hank?"

They danced around the introductions with inane words like *Who's asking?* and *Could be* until Hank waved his friends away and invited Bear and Shorty to sit.

"Who gave you my name?" Hank asked.

"A friend," Bear said.

"Of mine or yours?"

"Doesn't matter. This does. Know where one could buy whiskey?" Bear asked.

"One can't do that. Prohibition, you know, Mister Bear."

"We're asking nice and polite, Hank, so a real honest answer would be a good thing," Shorty said.

Hank toggled his head back and forth like processing a thought made for movement, but he took too long.

"Cut the crap, Hank." Shorty stood, and Hank's head followed once again. His hat fell, again, and this time nobody moved to pick it up.

Shorty bent, put a gentle hand under Hank's arm and lifted. They moved to the door in a choreographed tango, Hank's feet barely touching the floor.

"My hat."

"Later," Bear said.

They danced around the building until they were far enough from people to not be seen or heard. Custer was small, but the bar stood in the middle of town, and it felt to Bear like all its two hundred sixty residents were on Main Street watching Shorty shuffle Hank behind the bar.

"What makes you think Custer even has that many people?" Shorty asked when Bear complained about them.

"Sign at the edge of town when we rode in. Boasting like a proud papa."

"Hmmpf. You're sure something."

"Aren't I?"

"Boys," Hank said, trying to remove his arm from Shorty's grasp. "My hand is getting numb."

Shorty released him, apologized and warned him to stay put. Hank kicked at the sparse grass under his feet and mumbled while trying to replace his battered self-esteem with some dignity. Shorty crossed his arms and waited.

"Ready?" he said, and when Hank lifted his shoulders, he repeated Bear's earlier question, their reason for being in Custer. Hank responded this time, and even sounded eager. Perhaps he didn't like to tango.

"Boys in Scottville bring it from Ludington. Take it wherever anybody wants it. Or bring it to me, and I take it. I told the truth. I don't sell whiskey. I just deliver it. Don't think there's a law against being a delivery boy."

He grew petulant as he spoke, and Bear interrupted before his peevishness turned belligerent. His feet hurt, and he didn't feel like tracking down another *delivery boy.*

"So how would one get a load, and how would one pay for it?"

"Let me know what you want, and I'll get it. Where does it go?"

Shorty stepped back to let Bear make arrangements. The kid seemed less afraid of him and more willing to talk with some sense.

Bear told Hank they'd pick up the whiskey themselves. They wanted bootleggers away from Idlewild, away from Abby and Patrick. They'd heard the stories, too.

They watered the horses at the trough and left for home with the sun high in the sky and warm on their backs.

"Glad we avoided Newaygo," Bear said. "Could be tricky business."

"Agreed."

Miles down the road, Shorty voiced what bothered him.

"How we gonna keep them from finding out where the whiskey's going?"

"Probably won't be able to. Depends on how bad they want to know."

Bear slouched in his saddle. His mare turned to look at him, wondering if she'd missed a cue, decided he was just being lazy, and walked on but with a slower gait. Two could play at this game.

Bear chuckled.

"Not yet, Gertie. Keep the pace up a little."

Thought you were asleep. You try hoofing it fifty miles.

"No. Not today."

Joe Foster, owner of the town's only grocery store, flagged them as they were passing. They pulled up but didn't get down. Neither man could stand Joe. Not only was he cantankerous and mean as a cobra, but his scent made your eyes water.

Folks said he hadn't bathed since his wife died - or ran off. There were bets her body didn't take up space in the coffin he'd buried. Some said she'd had enough of him and left. Someday, somebody would say they'd had enough of Joe, too, and dig that coffin up for a look, just to try and send him to jail for fake burying. Send him anywhere, as long as his address didn't include Idlewild. Maybe put *him* in the empty coffin.

"What?" Bear said, thinking about finding a shovel.

"I see you didn't bring any back. Couldn't find any?"

"What are you blathering about, Joe?"

"Booze. Don't pretend you don't know."

"I can't see it's any of your business. Move aside, now, before Gertie gets a foot."

"You can't sell whiskey, Bear. I'll turn you in. It's against the law, and it's about time. Fools people make of themselves with the stuff."

"But not you, Joe? I don't see you pushing your glass away. Now move."

Joe had a hold on Bear's stirrup and refused to budge, but Shorty had heard enough, clicked to his gelding and walked him around. He squeezed the obstinate man in between the two horses until he squeaked and danced.

"Gonna let go, Joe?" Shorty asked.

He held both hands in the air and turned purple.

"You'll see," he grumbled. "You just wait."

He waved his arms, mouth still moving when they rode into the driveway of the hotel.

Jackson Parker, was the second-best hire Abby had made. The first was Betty Gerard who helped clean and prepare rooms. She'd hired her on the spot and hadn't regretted it for a moment. Now, as she saw Jackson dashing around the room, taking orders on the way and passing out drinks and smiles, Abby thought he'd worked his way nicely up the appreciation ladder.

She shoved a stray hank of auburn hair out of her eyes and pushed a tray of drinks his way. Patrick wiggled his glass at her from the end of the bar. He'd closed his kitchen and now squatted on his favorite stool where he could people watch and keep his eyes on them all.

Abby brought his bottle of Irish and held it to the light to see how much remained. She'd not like to run out of her da's favorite drink. He deserved a couple after the long, hard days he put in. Patrick tipped his head toward the doorway as Bear and Shorty walked in.

"Mayhap we'll have good news. The boys are home."

Abby's eyes lit. She hadn't realized she'd been worrying all day until she ran around the bar to hug them both.

"I'm so glad you're back. I was afraid."

"Of what?" Shorty asked, taking a seat beside Patrick.

"That you'd be hurt in Newaygo by some giant Chicago thug with a big gun and scars on his face."

"Face scars aren't so nasty," Bear said, turning his lips down in a pout.

"Oh, I didn't mean . . . damn . . . oops. Um, you know I love your face, Bear. You do, right?" Abby blushed, and he chuckled at her stuttering. Nobody stuttered as well as she did.

"Big isn't so bad, either," Shorty said.

"Come on, guys. You're having me on. My imagination was running amuck while you were gone."

"We're joshing you, Abby. And what we saw today was a long stretch from scars on anybody's face," Shorty told her.

"What? What'd you see?"

"A pretty straw hat on a man who couldn't make a mustache without coal to draw it. No scars on that boy."

"Men wear straw hats in Newaygo?"

"Didn't go there," Bear said. "And you don't want to, either, Irish. We set up some things in Custer. Tell you about it later."

"Thank you, boys. I know you made the trip to save this old leprechaun from trouble. I'm appreciative. It gets you an extra glass on the porch tonight."

"You learn anything from the Branch boys or Jesse today?" Bear asked.

"I did. I might let them build me a hotel," Patrick said. "Not sure yet. But they're talking my language. Use their money and save mine."

Bear and Shorty glanced toward Abby, trying to gauge her response to the news. Used to be, thoughts showed on her face like a twitch she couldn't control. But events had changed her over the last couple of years – only some of them good.

Patrick noted his daughter's eyes and knew them well. "I'll tell you my tale, too. Later."

When they retired to the porch, Abby served nighttime drinks and went inside for her afghan, the one her mother made for her with flowers the color of spring crocheted along the edge. She chuckled on the way back, thinking about what creatures of habit men were. When she pushed the screen door, silence dropped like a hammer on an anvil.

"You think that wasn't noticeable?" she said.

"What?" her father said, doing his best to make his impish eyes look innocent.

"That you stopped talking about whatever you were talking about before I came out."

"How do you know that's what we did?" Shorty said. "We could've just been done talking."

"You done rocking, too?"

Patrick stomped a foot and hawed.

"She gotcha, Shorty. We did that, Lass. What you said. We were talking about the new hotel and prohibition and general things that don't make for a nice night."

"I'm not fragile, Da. Tell me what you're thinking."

Patrick resumed his rocking, and the chair tilted back and forth at a tranquil rate. He looked comfortable in his thoughts, and somehow the soothing, gentle movement of his chair eased her mind.

"Guess we're gonna build a hotel, lass. On the island."

She wondered how she'd run two hotels and tried to keep her chair in rhythm with theirs, but it felt contrived – not at all relaxed.

"Alright. When?"

"Gonna start soon as surveys get done. The IRC is buying."

She'd have to hire more help. Maybe put Betty in charge of the room cleaning. Hire a cook and a helper. Another bar person. Be cold in the winter time out on the island. Windy.

"Hey, lass. You okay? Your eyes are kinda far away and glassy-like."

"I'm here. Thinking about everything I need to do for the new place. I just got used to this one."

Patrick let his hand lay on hers, and they rocked together.

"I wouldn't do this, but I'm afraid we need to. Another hotel coming in – especially over there, surrounded by beautiful water. Well, we don't want all our customers leaving us for the fancy new place."

"I know, Da. We'll manage." She turned to Shorty. "You want to tell your tale?"

"Not much to say. We'll pick up our first load in Logan Friday night."

"That's your story?"

"Yeah. Oh, and old Joe stopped us on the way into town. Thought to tell us we can't bring whiskey to the hotel. Had a hold on Bear's mare like he could keep that horse from moving."

"What happened," Patrick asked, getting a kick out of the picture. "Joe's a scrawny old fool, but he doesn't know it. He keeps getting himself into situations where you'd think he was a big man. Every once in a while, I have to admire the crotchety old goat. But then I remember his mouth."

"And his scent," Abby said with a puff of air.

Bear explained how Shorty had made a baloney sandwich out of Joe, squeezing him between his big gelding and Bear's mare until he turned an abnormal color.

"He's an unnatural person," Bear said. "And speaking of unnatural persons, here's your favorite, Abigail."

Cassandra stopped at the lake's edge, halting the progress of her long line of cats following behind. She poked in the mud, peered at the hole she'd made, pulled something from the muck and stuck it in her sack.

Abby smiled. She had affection and respect for the strange woman. Cassandra had healed both Betty and Al when they were hurt and helped Abby when she didn't even know she'd needed it.

Abby had called her *witchy-woman* before she knew her name. She still did sometimes, just for the fun of it.

Cassandra waved her stick at the group on the porch, the long, wide sleeves of her gown flowing with the movement, and a loon wailed. In response to her? Abby didn't know but thought it a possibility. Maybe even a likelihood.

"I'm going up to bed, boys. Have you heard anything about Frank lately?"

All chairs stopped.

"Me neither. Night."

Chapter Three

A thunder storm burst with a gust of wind, blew her hat from her head and tossed it over the railing. Abby grabbed her skirt to keep it from whipping around her legs and raced down the steps. Every time she got close enough to her hat to grab for it, another drenching gust picked it up and flung it further away.

A long roll of thunder rumbled, and she looked up to see streaks of lightening fracture the sky. She waved goodbye to the lost hat and scampered back onto the porch and into the lobby. Her hair hung in limp, dripping strands, pulled from its ribbon by the squall. She stomped her soggy shoes and waved her arms, shaking rain water onto the entry rug.

Hearing the din, Patrick stuck his head out of his room, and his eyes grew round.

"Ye look like a wee, wet gremlin, lass. You out playing in the puddles?"

"I was waiting for Jesse, Edna and Daisy. Going to church with them."

"So, while you waited, you couldn't resist the puddles?"

She glared at her witty father and shivered as the wet seeped through to her skin.

"I need to change. Will you watch for them for me?"

The door opened before she got to the stairs and Samuel entered. He stopped in his tracks when he saw Abby, his lips drawing back in a quirky, controlled grin.

"Playing in the rain?"

Abby whirled around.

"Everybody's a comedian, today. What are you doing here on a Sunday morning, Samuel?"

"Picking you up for church. I was with Jesse last evening, and he asked me to come for you. They're staying home. Daisy is sick."

"You didn't need to come. I could have driven myself."

"I know that. But I'm here. You going like that?"

She shivered and clutched her arms.

"Nice hair," Samuel added with a smirk.

Abby twitched at the well-placed barb and ran up the stairs, yelling back at him.

"Give me a minute."

It took a few of them to repair the damage, and Abby wondered why she felt strange riding to church with Samuel. It wasn't because of the color of his skin. She went about with Benjamin and Edna. Sue and Sally, too.

She huffed and pinched her cheeks to put back some of the color the cold rain had stolen.

"Ready," she said to the mirror. "Best I can do."

When she reached the door to the outside, she stopped walking and stared through the glass pane in shock.

"It's an automobile."

"Yes, it is. Very good, Abby. Fine observational skills you have there." His mustache twitched when she put her hands on her hips and glared at him.

"More comedy. It's Sunday. We're supposed to be nice."

"Hard to do. Wait here. Let me get the door open first."

The automobile sat close to the porch steps. He opened her door and held an umbrella in his other hand to keep her dry as she climbed in, cranked the engine and got in, folding and stashing the umbrella as he settled.

"You spoil me, Samuel," she said after they started down the road.

"Didn't want you drenched again and don't want a wet, grumpy companion all the way to the Gerard's. That's where we met, I think. Wasn't it?"

"You know it was. You were insufferable and told me you weren't an Uncle Tom. As if I thought you were or should be."

"You've put me in my place since then. Many times, if I recall correctly."

"You do." She settled back into the comfortable cushioned seats and took her time inspecting the interior. It smelled like oiled leather, and she ran her hand over the black, buttery smooth surface. The brass door handles glowed golden. Samuel took good care of it - or paid someone else to do it. She hadn't known he owned one.

The engine noise inside the enclosed space comforted. With the rain coming down hard, beating on the roof, and the wind still raging, it felt cozy. Even peaceful.

She'd assumed people choked from the gasoline fumes as they drove, but she inhaled easy air along with a clean, masculine scent. Her eyes rolled his way, and she craned her head closer to sniff.

What smelled so good? She sniffed again.

"I took my morning bath, Abby."

"What? Why, of course, you did. What makes you say that?" Abby's cheeks colored sunset, tulip, holly berry, and nothing she could say or do would un-paint them. "Sorry. That was dumb. But something smells really good in here, like new leather and cinnamon."

"It's us. The auto and me. We're a team."

She had no response, so she tried to relax and enjoy the ride and the wild storm whipping around them. She was glad not to be in the buggy – sides or not.

Halfway there, Samuel removed one hand from the wheel and looked her way. She reacted with a jolt of fear and automatically grabbed for the wheel.

"Don't! What are you doing?" he said.

"Sorry. I thought we might go off the road."

"We might if you grab the wheel like that again. I can drive with one hand, Abby. Quite well, in fact."

"Sorry. I'm not used to these things."

"I know. By the way . . . Frank was in town."

"Frank?"

"You know. Frank. Your husband?"

She felt her eyes grow wet and blinked, mad he could so easily turn on her tears. Abby wasn't letting Frank upset her today. Absolutely not. She stared out the side window and slowed her heart. He'd left. They thought differently – about nearly everything. There's the beginning and the end of the story.

"Where did he go?"

"Not sure where he ended up. I saw him walking through town. Didn't look intent on heading anywhere in particular. He didn't come to the hotel to see you?"

She shook her head, a slow movement, like a heavy weight dangled from her chin.

Samuel saw and damned the man for hurting her. Himself, too. Why couldn't he just shut up?

Betty met them at the door looking beautiful in her pale-yellow dress. Her bruises had healed, leaving clear, unblemished, mahogany skin. She looked so much like her father, James, they could be twins, but one was every inch a man and the other the embodiment of femininity.

For his own safety, James had deliberately been kept in the dark about the assaults on his daughter. He would have retaliated, and someone would have died. If James survived, he'd have lived the rest of his life in prison because a negro could not kill a white man, even a rapist. Lincoln may have removed their shackles, but his death had tied their hands with a hundred years of bias.

When Betty finally spoke out against her rapists, she spoke first to her father, gaining his promise to take no action and leave their punishment to the authorities. He gave his pledge, unwillingly, and kept it.

"You look lovely, Betty," Samuel said.

"You do, like spring sunshine," Abby said. "And I'm a drowned rat, especially next to you."

Betty's eyes traveled up and down Abby.

"You're not drowned, cept your hair. What happened?"

"I had a fight with a storm. My hat and me. The storm won, but I gave a good battle."

Mildred Gerard hurried everyone to their seats, and, without warning or invitation, the reverend's baritone sang out in deafening praise, competing with the thunder God was producing outside. Reverend Jenkins expected his sheep to be in their seats with hymnals open to the correct page when he wanted them there.

His sermon spoke of forgiveness, and he used the Tatum boys to stretch imaginations, to dig deep within the souls of his flock to find their personal wells of compassion.

"It's in all of us. It's in *you*," he shouted, "and you're not getting that potluck dinner that's smelling so fine till you find your peace. Do it now!"

When half the congregation rose like they'd done what he asked, he shouted them down again.

"I'm not done. I want that little blonde girl at church next Sunday, and I'm holding you all responsible. Hear me? Al Tatum needs to be under our wings. Protected by us. Blessed by the Lord."

Reverend Jenkins squinted meaningfully and searched the room, stopping at each set of wary eyes to cement his words. Heads nodded, afraid of him or fearful the loud grumbling from their stomachs would never be satisfied.

Samuel poked Abby in the side.

"I gotta see this. Can I drive you and Al to church next Sunday? Please?"

She couldn't respond because the reverend chose that moment to focus on *her,* awaiting a formal nod of acceptance. She gave it and poked Samuel back as soon as Reverend Jenkins looked away.

"No. You can't, and didn't you see the reverend looking at me?"

"Yes, I did." He chuckled, enjoying her precarious position – the only white face in a sea of brown. They were all used to her by now, but he knew she didn't know it and was still looking for acceptance.

Betty watched the interplay and stifled a grin. "You two remind me of my brother and me, back when we were little and before we knew better than to bicker in church. Did nobody ever spank you when you were young?"

"Course not," Abby whispered, watching for the reverend's eyes to flit back to her again.

"Never. I was a perfect child," Samuel said.

"Well, you're making up for it now," Betty told him.

"It would be good if we could bring Al to church," Abby said. "Do you think you could talk with her, Betty? You two have been getting along since she's been staying at the hotel. She could use a friend. Probably never had one."

Betty grunted, not happy with the job Abby asked of her. Sometimes Christian charity began with yourself, a lesson Betty had learned a long time ago.

She'd spent years hating the Tatums. Changing her mind about them might weaken her, diminish the wrath that stiffened her spine. Some loathing was justified, and hating those boys felt good – felt right. Whatever they'd thrown at her, done to her, she'd turned into stones. And those stones made of hate formed the foundation that kept her sane. She stood on them now, used them to stay firm and strong.

"Please?" she heard next to her.

Abby flipped a wet braid over her shoulder, and a drop of water left from her drenching landed on Betty's cheek.

"You gonna throw me in the lake next if I don't be nice to Strange Al?"

"Sorry, Betty. But you've become friends lately. Right?"

"I don't hate her, Boss. That doesn't make us friends." Her arms were crossed, her chin high. "You gonna fire me if I don't make a friend out of her?"

"Of course not. I'd never force a friendship on you." Recognition dawned. She tucked an arm through Betty's and patted it. "That was wrong of me."

"Yes. It was."

"I was being thickheaded."

"Yes, you were."

Samuel smirked, and Reverend Jenkins' baritone signaled the final song. Satisfied his flock had understood the command to forgive the unfortunate Tatums, he would now allow food to be served. The song seemed to pick up in speed with each verse, and, like a runaway train, the pace was frantic by the end. There were a lot of empty stomachs in the crowd.

Abby and Betty, along with most of the ladies, went to the kitchen to prepare for the potluck and set out the casseroles, pile plates and utensils on the table. The aroma of smoky ham and beans, sweet and sour greens, and yeasty fresh bread tantalized the senses. Abby's mouth watered, and her stomach rumbles added to the din.

"What else can I do, Mrs. Gerard?" Abby repeated it when she got no response, raising her voice to be heard over the noise. Nothing.

She tilted her head to look into Mildred's face. It was blank, harsh, and Abby put a hand on the woman's shoulder, bringing her out of her daze. She'd been somewhere other than the warm and inviting kitchen and bitter lips signaled her thoughts.

"Are you alright, Mrs. Gerard?"

"Sure. I'm fine."

Her eyes strayed to the corner where her husband stood talking with Samuel and the reverend. His face wore the same look as his wife's, and his eyes were unyielding granite. His jaw muscles bunched, jumped and bunched again.

James and Mildred Gerard were not having a good morning and didn't ask folks to tarry after the meal. They led them to the door and waved them away like they wanted their home to themselves.

Betty and her mother flanked James with arms wrapped around him, eyes sliding furtively to his face. Abby watched until the door shut and worried.

The rain slowed to a drizzle on the ride home, and Samuel drove around the deepest puddles. Still, mud splashed up the sides of his automobile, and he scowled each time it sprayed. Steam coated the glass windows, cocooning them in an unnatural and spectral world where no one existed but them.

"Should I wipe the glass so we can see?" she asked.

He pulled a white handkerchief from his pocket, handed it to her, and she wiped circles on the glass in front of them. She sat with her hands in her lap until the glass needed wiping again, becoming uncomfortable with the long stretches of silence.

"Have I done something?" she asked.

"Probably. But what this time?"

"I don't know. Don't be a brat, Samuel. You're very quiet, even for you."

"Just thinking, my friend. That's all."

"Okay. I like quiet. A lot, actually."

Moisture thickened the air and collected on her clammy skin. The confined space smelled of damp wool, instead of leather and cinnamon like before, as if it had rained so hard and long the water had penetrated all the nooks and crannies of auto and people. She wiped the dash and windows again, including the one at her side, and her heart lifted.

Half a rainbow peeked around the clouds where the sun pushed against them and nudged them aside. White fluff settled next to the black, heavy storm clouds. The heavens wore a day of complications, too, a day of running into snags and overcoming obstacles.

"I'm betting on the rainbow," she said.

"Excuse me?"

"The rainbow will win the sky. It's only half finished, but it has the sun on its side. It will win."

"So, you're a romantic."

Abby didn't know if he'd asked a question, made a statement or a denunciation, but she answered anyway.

"Yes. I'm quixotic."

"You're hoping I don't know what that means, aren't you?"

"Why would I do that?"

"I don't know. Why did Frank leave you?"

Stunned, Abby crossed her arms and swallowed, her smile wavering.

"You think it's because I'm quixotic?"

"Which definition of the word? Idealistic? Unrealistic?"

"I don't like this game, Samuel. I'm not having fun, and I'm not going to play it with you."

When they pulled up to the hotel, Samuel turned in his seat instead of getting out and put a hand on her arm. She was ready to open the door and bolt.

"I'm sorry, Abigail. That wasn't nice of me. Idealism is good. Romanticism is, too."

"What does all of this have to do with why Frank left? Which, by the way, is none of your business."

"Nothing, and you're right. It's not my business. I apologize for my uncivilized behavior. I saw him wandering around, and . . . my curiosity overruled my civility."

"Apology accepted. Is that how you win cases in court – by springing questions on your witnesses?"

"Sometimes. It works."

They stared at each other, waiting. For what, they didn't know. "Don't suppose you'd let me drive you and Al to church next week."

"No. And if weather permits, service will be at the pavilion, and I'll walk."

Samuel got out and ran around to open her door before she let herself out. He stood at the bottom step while she crossed the porch and went inside, wondering if she knew why Frank left town.

Did she know about old man Tatum? He wasn't positive, himself, but he was ninety-nine percent sure and didn't know how to get to a hundred without getting people in trouble.

He turned to leave and saw she was right. The rainbow had been victorious and spread all the way across the sky, brilliant primary colors against a blue background.

Chapter Four

"Morning," Abby said in a chirping, spring-like tone that sounded outlandish to Al's ears.

She nodded in response, flipped a pancake and stacked it on a tall pile in the warming oven. Two plates sat side-by-side on the table with sausage and bacon piled on one side of each.

Making breakfast was getting easier for Abby every day because Al got started before she climbed out of bed and headed downstairs. She'd given up telling her she didn't have to start so early. Al wanted to do it, so she did. Among a bunch of other things, Abby liked her firm independence.

"For the boys?" Abby asked.

"Yup. Told me to make it early."

"Wow, Al. You gave me a seven-word answer. I'm proud of you."

Al turned to look at her boss, not sure if Abby had made a joke or not. She knew people kidded around because she heard the laughter, but humor was hard to discern. She didn't know funny, didn't understand the art of conversation, but she knew herself, which was legions more than most folks did. Abby felt Al's confusion and regretted her flip words. The day deflated with her insensitivity.

When are you going to get it, Abby? You're the misfit, not Al.

The kitchen erupted in noise as somebody's fist banged on the swinging door, accompanied by a male voice shouting for Abby.

"Get out here now, woman!"

Abby shoved the door open and stomped through, ready to tongue lash the noise maker, but threw herself into his arms instead.

"Micah! Maggie! Where's Benjamin? So glad to see you."

"Benjamin is following. He traveled by himself this time," Maggie said.

"Are you staying at the hotel?"

"No. The cabin. But we were hungry and knew breakfast would be about ready."

She pushed the door open and shouted back to Al.

"You okay by yourself for a minute?"

Al raised her eyebrows and didn't bother to respond. Abby poured coffee and sat with them to catch up.

"Micah wanted to be here to help with the Chautauqua," Maggie said, her eyes warm as she glanced at her husband.

"I did. It was great fun the last time, and I have some ideas I'd like to share."

"Your work with the 369th soldiers was pivotal to that Chautauqua's success," Abby said. "Jesse will be happy to have you back, Micah."

"What? Only Jesse? What about you, girl? You haven't left all the work to that old scallywag, have you?"

Micah's eyes lit as he talked about possible Chautauqua events and a few speakers he'd been in touch with, especially Marcus Garvey of the famous Universal Negro Improvement Association and African Communities League. Garvey had unofficially agreed to keynote, and Micah's awe of the Jamaican who'd traveled the world and built powerful organizations single handedly flooded his eyes.

"He knows I'm just a lot owner here and have no official right to put him in as keynote speaker, but we've been in a few different meetings together, and the subject came up."

"Had he heard of Idlewild before?" Abby asked.

"Yes, and he liked what little he knew. It seems this fledgling town roughly follows his communal ideal. Even though it's not in Africa," he said with a chuckle.

Abby thrummed her fingers on the table as if she played a piano – which she couldn't.

"Something wrong, Abby," Maggie asked.

"No. And you're right about Idlewild, Micah, except *we're* here."

"We? We who?" Micah's big hands lifted as he looked around for the illusive 'we.'

"Me, silly man." She pointed to her chest. "White Abby and Patrick – and Shorty and Bear and Al. Lots of others, too. Well, not lots, but some."

"And that means what?"

"I don't know much about Garvey, but I thought he promoted separatists' ideals. He wants colored people to have their own state – away from white people." Abby's eyes clouded. For the second time in an hour, she felt like she'd grown scales and flopped around like a fish out of its element. "Am I wrong about that?"

"He talks about those things, and about going back to Africa, but he also talks about a lot of other ideals, like justice to all."

"Can we put that aside for a moment, Micah?" his wife said, pulling on the sleeve of his white shirt to get attention. "Let's let politics go and have a little gentle conversation. Please?"

Maggie shifted in her seat and let her spoon clink against the side of her cup. She was clearly unsettled, and Abby tried to calm the waters.

"How is Benjamin doing? Are his wounds behaving?" Has Bradley gone back with his unit?"

Benjamin, one of the revered Harlem Hell Fighters, had been wounded in France, and shrapnel still made its home near his spine. Doctors thought it safer to leave it in than risk use of his legs.

"He's good. You'll see in a few minutes, I'm sure. He wasn't far behind."

Al pushed the swinging doors open carrying a huge tray of bacon, sausage and pancakes just as guests came from the lobby looking for breakfast. Abby excused herself to help.

Most of the guests knew each other from past stays and shoved tables together so they could eat and catch up at the same time. As Abby went back and forth between the kitchen and the buffet table, she smiled at the backslapping conversation between them.

They acted like family who hadn't seen each other for a long time but came together as if it had been yesterday. 'How's that grandbaby?' 'You still running the grocery store?' 'How's your leg? You try that salve I gave you?' Conversation flowed like it hadn't been interrupted by the months of winter.

However, when the names Marcus Garvey, W.E.B. DuBois, and Charles Waddell Chesnutt were spoken, she also heard stress. Disagreement. She didn't want tension in her dining room. When people were eating breakfast, she wanted them enjoying her food and themselves, not talking politics. On that point, she and Maggie Chambers agreed.

Patrick came down to take over the kitchen and she went upstairs with Betty to clean rooms.

Abby was a tornado with a broom and dust mop, and Betty kept up. Like Al, she knew what to do and did it well.

"You going to a fire, Boss?"

"No. Baldwin – with Sue and Sally."

Betty planted a hand on a hip and gave Abby *the look*.

"Why you doing that? You trying to get yourself in trouble?"

"They wanted to go, and I said I'd take them. I've done it before and it wasn't a problem. I need supplies anyway."

Abby shoved the dust mop under the bed and brought out dust bunnies and a cat. White Phantom hugged the fluffy mop head and wrapped his clawed paws around it as Abby pulled. He howled and Cleo, his black buddy, leaped from under the bureau onto his back.

"Out cats. Go find Bear."

"They're prostitutes, Abby."

"My cats are prostitutes?"

Whenever Abby played ignorant, Betty gave her the one-eyed-Betty-stare in a frightening friendly way, and she did so now.

"If they were, you'd have a sweet little litter of mixed race cats. I believe they're segregationists."

Abby cocked a leg out and leaned her chin on the dust mop. "I know what Sue and Sally do for a living, and they're nice. I like them. And my cats aren't dogmatists. They're just slow." She took a moment, and her eyes lit. "Hah! Get it? My cats aren't dog . . . matists. I'm a hoot!"

Betty couldn't help but chuckle.

"That's funny, Abby. I like it. And I like Sue and Sally, too, but . . . never mind. You know what you're doing."

"No. Not usually. I know just enough to get myself in trouble."

They were dressed in red and purple, one tall and thin as a sapling and the other less than five feet and as many around. Abby brought Marie to a halt and got out to help push Sue up onto the seat. The buggy rocked, and Abby cringed as the springs creaked and groaned. Sue settled herself in the middle, and Sally climbed up beside her.

"Good thing I'm thin or we wouldn't all fit. Don't put on any weight, Abby."

"Going to try not to."

The mare trod down the road at a somber pace, not in a hurry to get anywhere.

"Can't you make her go any faster?" Sue fluttered pudgy fingers at the horse.

"I think she's enjoying the sunshine. You in a hurry to get there? Got a boyfriend waiting for you?"

Sue shined a grin and poked Abby's arm.

"Might could be. Never know."

"Sue couldn't stay true to a boyfriend. She likes all the men," Sally said. "I kinda do, too."

"In a good line a work, I am, considering all the good-looking men around," Sue said.

When their conversation leaned toward the male anatomies they'd seen in their chosen profession, and which ones they preferred, Abby tried to steer the conversation in a different direction.

"Am I taking you to the same saloon as before?"

"It's a club, Abigail." Sue lifted her chin.

"Of course, same club?" Abby grinned at Sue's effort to elevate the little bar.

"Same one, yes. It's the best in the area."

"The only one we can go into," Sally said, facing facts more readily than her cousin. "Excepting yours, that is."

"Is Gus still there?"

Both ladies turned round black eyes on her and fired off questions.

"What do you want with Gus?"

"How well do you know him?"

"He's a colored boy. You know that?"

"Aren't you still married?"

Abby laughed and was tempted to lead them on with a tall tale, but they looked too horrified by her interest in the huge bartender.

"He played a little prank on me the last time we were there. If I could think of a way to pay him back, I'd do it."

"Gus did? What'd he do?"

"He let me think you were in the back somewhere . . . You were . . . uh . . . Never mind. He laughed at me."

Sally slapped her leg and hawed.

"He's a pip, that one. You thought we were with some men, didn't you?"

Abby's red face bobbed up and down, acknowledging her thoughts.

"So how long before he told you we were playing cards?" Sue asked.

"Long enough for me to order a drink, finish it and make a fool of myself."

"Now that's one I'd consider being true to," Sally said. "He's a real man, got arms as big as me."

"I recall," Abby said. "I almost set mine next to his just to see the difference. Stopped myself in time. Thought he might believe I was looking at the color difference. I've never seen skin so dark."

Both ladies roared.

"Would have liked to see that," Sally said, her tone one of regret. "Surely would have liked that. I'd even pay."

Music blared from the open door of the small building, still bright purple and yellow, like before. They repeated the loading process in reverse, and Abby breathed a sigh of relief when Sue landed without breaking anything or anyone.

"Two hours, right?"

They agreed, and she waited until they were safely through the door and left to do her shopping. She finished in record time because she wanted a few minutes with Gus. She had some questions on her mind.

Abby stood silhouetted in the doorway of the dark room, unable to see until her eyes adjusted to the shadows. Her name boomed above the music.

"Miss Abigail. It's about time. Miss Sue and Miss Sally said you'd be coming. Whiskey with your water?"

"Thank you, Gus. That would be nice." She moved toward the bar when she could do so without bumping into chairs or tables and saw him put a glass in an empty spot. Every head turned her way, and all eyes scrutinized her white face as it grew red. Gus ignored them and clasped her hand when she reached for his.

"Good to see you, Gus. Are you well?"

"I am, Abigail. How bout you? Hotel good?"

"Sure is." Abby sipped and blinked back tears. The drink was either a robust mix of whiskey and water or bad whiskey. She didn't know and didn't ask.

He crossed his arms and leaned forward, resting them on the bar. His eyes were bright with laughter, his lips resisting the urge to make a wide grin.

"So, Abigail. The ladies tell me you kinda like my arms a little bitty bit."

"What? I . . . What did they say?" Abby's brain stuck on hearing the words *little bitty bit* come out of this huge man's mouth. It was incompatible. She created defiance with two hands fisted on her hips.

"Do they lie?" He flexed the massive muscles of his biceps.

"No, they don't lie. They're fine arms. But I didn't say that I *liked* them. I merely mentioned them."

Gus made a sad face. "Aw, and here I thought . . ." He didn't finish because laughter bubbled to the surface, and he couldn't keep the pretense of sorrow any longer.

"Just what did they tell you, Gus?"

He pushed the short sleeve of his shirt all the way to his shoulder and laid his arm on the bar.

"Now you do yours," he said.

"I can't do that. That's crazy, Gus."

"Of course, you can. What are you afraid of?"

"Nothing. I'm not scared of you."

"Well, then?"

The grin on his face was made by the devil, and it danced in his eyes, too. Abby took a deep, long breath and tried not to look around at the watching eyes. She unbuttoned the cuff, rolled the sleeve up to the elbow and placed her arm next to his. A gasp huffed and fluttered across the room.

"Wow," she said, in whispered awe.

"Different, huh?"

"I'll say. Look how big it is? It's like a leg."

Gus' laugh came from his bass drum chest, loud and booming.

"Told you he'd do it," Sue said, coming up behind Abby and stuffing bills down the front of her dress all the while.

Sally handed Sue a few bills of her own. "You were right, Sue. You and Gutsy Gus win."

"Gutsy Gus, hell. Abby's the one showing off her pasty white arm in a colored bar."

Abby jerked it from the counter and buttoned the sleeve, face ruby red. She tossed her drink down without choking and remembered why she'd wanted to see Gus.

"Could I have a glass of water, please."

"No whiskey?"

She shook her head. "But I do have a question. We're making arrangements for bar provisions, and I wondered where you get yours."

His eyes grew wary, and, for a moment, Abby feared she had crossed some invisible line. Was talking about bootleg booze forbidden, even more so than comparing bare arms?

"It's that . . . uh, we don't know anyone, and I'm afraid to have my friends blunder into harm . . . and . . ." She didn't finish because Gus tapped her hand and told her to be quiet. In a nice way.

"Who's looking into it for you?"

"My almost brothers, Bear and Shorty – who's almost as big as you." She lifted her shoulders in apology, trying to come back to where they'd been before.

"Tell your Bear and big Shorty to come see me. We'll talk."

"Thanks, Gus. You're not mad at me?"

"Hell no. You got moxy, girl. That's for sure."

"You, too. See you next time."

Sue stood on the step with both feet and bent forward at the waist, waiting to feel four hands on her bottom. She grunted, pushed off with her toes while the hands shoved, and landed full body on the seat, her legs pumping to find purchase on the floor of the buggy to help her roll over.

"Sit up, Sue, so I can get in," Sally said.

"I am."

"Then why are you still laying on your belly?"

Abby went around and climbed in. She pulled Sue upright after she'd turtled herself over.

"You good?" Abby asked.

"Perfect." She patted her purple hat and yanked at the skirt of her dress, pulling it back down over her knees. Sue wheezed with the exertion and fanned her sweat beaded face. "Could use a drink, now."

"Want me to go get some water?"

"Thank you, Abs. That'd be nice. You can see your boyfriend again." Her cheeks moved up to her eyes, almost squeezing them from sight in the wide grin she gave Abby when she gasped.

"Behave yourself, Sue," Sally said. "And you can get water when we get home."

Sue and Sally had cleaned out the men at the poker table and made new friends who would visit them in Idlewild at their *establishment*. They'd learned where the newest *Klan* had sprung from the marshy bogs of distrust and bigotry, and deluged Abby with the details, details, details.

Her mind filled with visions destined to haunt her nights. Abby told them they should write a book. They were rich with the gift of remembering the smallest particulars.

"Is there anything you two didn't learn about in that backroom? Wait . . . maybe I shouldn't have asked that."

"Yeah. We didn't find out where Frank is staying. Nobody knows. Did he go to see you the other day?" Sue asked.

"That's none of our business." Sally pursed her lips but her eyes were eager.

Abby shook her head without a verbal response. She didn't want to talk about Frank. Everyone in town knew he'd been in Idlewild. They had all seen him. All but her. And she was the one person who wanted to, or thought she wanted to.

"Know where he's living?" Sue asked.

"Sue! Stop." Sally slapped a hand on her arm and squeezed to keep her quiet.

Sue twisted it away. "I'm not doing anything wrong. Abby needs to talk to us. It's good for her. For her psychic."

"You mean psyche," Sally said.

"That's what I said. I just put an ick on the end of it. Like it's *icky*." Sue laughed at her own joke, and Abby glanced over the top of her head and caught Sally's eye.

"It's okay, Sally. She cares about me. Right, Sue?"

"Exactly. See? Abby knows." She gave her cousin a know-it-all, satisfied look.

"I don't know where Frank is staying, and I don't know why he left town. I wish he would talk to me and let me know he's okay."

"Well, he was strolling down the street the other day, looking alright and heading your direction. Maybe he went on to Foster's store. Sorry I mentioned it." Seeing the sorrow in Abby's eyes, Sue finally quit talking.

The sun had drifted behind the tallest trees when they pulled into Idlewild, and Abby worried Jackson would be swamped at the bar without her. She hurried the ladies from the buggy and thanked them for keeping her company. Sally glanced back at Abby, and the deep pools of her brown eyes were damp.

"You deserve more, Abigail."

Abby gaped at her. "More what, Sally?"

"That's all. Just more."

Abby watched Sally's tall frame glide to the door of their colorful house and smiled. The ladies were always interesting, always good humored.

She liked that about them.

Chapter Five

Betty tended bar, and Jackson raced from table to table with a smile and a word for everyone he passed. He'd learned how smiles translated into coins and sprinkled them liberally.

"Thanks for staying, Betty. I'll take over as soon as I wash the dust from my hands and face."

Her eyes roamed the room, making sure faces wore satisfied expressions. Happy customers returned and didn't make trouble after two or three drinks. Her gazed stopped at a stranger, one of two in the room. He was tall and thin with cropped blond hair and a cigar hanging from his mouth. He lifted a coffee cup, sipped, and put it down to say something to the man next to him.

Hairs prickled on the back of her neck when she saw his eyes. They were the palest she'd ever seen. In the dim light of the bar, she couldn't tell the color, or if there was any. She forced herself to turn from his locked gaze and walked past him as she went to clean up and change.

When she returned, the man was standing and talking to a room full of amazed customers who weren't used to being harangued in the hotel bar. They came to relax and have food or a drink with friends. Abby stayed by the door, out of sight, and listened. She didn't know what she'd missed, but what she heard infuriated her.

"It is for the protection of our society – above all else," he said, his words sure and distinct, as if he'd been trained at public speaking. "The demon is in your glass, and, when you drink it, it is in you! You carry the devil in you!"

Abby had heard enough. She moved into the room and stood in front of him.

"I don't know why you are lecturing our guests, but if you don't stop, I'll ask you to leave."

"This is a free country. We believe in free speech. I have a right."

"Not here, you don't. This is a private hotel. Owned by a private citizen."

"Have you not heard of prohibition, young woman? These people are breaking the law." One pale eye had a tic, and his cheek jerked in time with it. It mesmerized her.

Abby found it difficult to look him in the eyes. She wanted to put a hand on her cheek to make sure it held still and didn't jump around while she watched his dance. She came close to tapping a toe and mentally slapped herself.

"We didn't ask you, Mister . . ."

"With prohibition," he proclaimed in a formal, grating voice, "the state will advance morality, stop sinners in their tracks . . . all through law, laws made by the government for the people of this country." He was wild eyed, elated. His arms raised to the ceiling, and he turned away from Abby to include any drinkers who might be ignoring him.

"Alcohol is a temptress!" he shouted. "The demon drink goes hand in filthy hand with prostitution! Your children will be tainted by sin!"

Abby took his arm, ready to drag him to the door, but he jerked it from her hand. She looked around for help, wishing Bear and Shorty were there, Jesse or even Samuel, but they weren't. When the kitchen door opened, she saw her father moving in their direction with a coffee pot in his hand and renewed her efforts.

She grabbed his arm, tighter this time, and began moving toward the door. Abby was big footed and tall for a girl but much shorter than her opponent, and her slender form didn't drag him far before they both came to a halt.

"You cavort with sinners! Prostitutes! I can smell them on you!"

Abby stopped, stunned. Did Sue and Sally have a scent all their own? Could he smell them? She jerked on his arm, furious he'd made her think of her friends that way in his ranting mania.

"If you don't come with me right this instant or sit down and shut up, I'll be getting the sheriff." She didn't know how she'd make that happen, but that didn't matter at the moment.

Abby gritted her teeth, determined her father wouldn't be forced into a fracas with this man. The fevered look in his eyes scared her. They screamed zealot, and she didn't trust a fanatic to think before acting. She prayed he'd sit before Patrick rolled across the room and got to them.

Her prayer went unanswered. Patrick stuck his hand out to the man and introduced himself.

"I own this establishment. And who would ye be?"

The man shoved his chin in the air. "Darnell Rumford."

Patrick turned to the man still sitting at Darnell's table.

"And you?"

"I'm just passing through." He stood and reached for Patrick's hand. "Don't know this man. I sat in an empty chair, and now I'll be leaving."

"There be a drink for ye at the bar, *Passing Through*. Ask Betty who's bartending.

Passing Through nodded and moved away.

Like lightening, Patrick grabbed Darnell Rumford's ear and pulled until it was an inch from his own lips. He tried to twist away, but Patrick yanked him back and whispered. If the man could turn whiter, he would have. When Patrick let go, Darnell sat, and Patrick refilled his coffee cup.

Abby watched, her eyes wide, her lips tight, and went behind the bar to relieve Betty. Patrick went to the end of it and sat next to *Passing Through.* When Bear and Shorty came in from work, they joined them.

Patrick looked at Darnell Rumford and pointed to Bear and Shorty. His smile held a barrel full of meaning and menace. Abby's brain ran rampant wondering what her father had said to Mister Rumford. She hadn't known he had that kind of power. What else didn't she know about her father?

The little leprechaun she'd known her entire life had changed in the span of moments.

Darnell kept his mouth shut unless it opened to sip coffee. He looked like he wanted to speak, but when he glanced Patrick's way, his lips clamped together. In half an hour, he put some coins on the table and left.

Passing Through joined them on the porch that night. He hadn't been entirely forthcoming about a couple of things. He intended to stay for the week, instead of leave right away, and his name was Charles.

He followed Shorty outside, who pointed to a chair that didn't belong to the regular porch-sitting group. They all knew Shorty would share the porch, but not the *family chairs,* and Charles was quick to pick up on the dynamics. He grinned as it became clear he'd been put in his place via seat selection, and life landed in his eyes as a sparkle, like the first star in a dark night sky.

He was enjoying Idlewild and this hotel. He'd heard about it, but hearing was a long way from seeing.

Abby brought a tray of nightcaps that grew heavier with each addition to the group. Samuel, coming up the steps, took it from her.

"Don't suppose there's one here for me?" he asked.

"Do I look like Cassandra?" With a frown, she twisted around to see if the soothsayer hovered nearby and could catch her in a witchery blasphemy – if there could be such a thing.

"Not at all. Not nearly enough color in your clothes."

"Drag a chair over, Samuel. What would you like? This is Charles or *Passing,* whichever you prefer."

Samuel's eyebrows raised, but he let it go and pulled a chair close to the group, but not in it. He settled in the rocker and matched its rhythm to Patrick's, a steady but unhurried motion that agreed with the night and the call of lake critters. A loon wailed, and he heard the long intake of Charles' breath.

"Nice," *Passing* said.

Soon, all the rockers danced together, a measured waltz that left the tango of the day behind. Abby returned with Samuel's drink and took the leftover seat.

"Where you from, Charles?" Shorty asked.

"South of here."

"Whole lot of land between here and the Gulf of Mexico," Samuel said, and they were quiet as the loon's mate answered his call. A coyote broke the silence with a steady yip across the lake, looking to find his own mate.

"That there is," Charles said. "I'm finding the north to my liking."

"Is the name *Passing* what I think it is?" Samuel asked.

Charles laughed, a light sound that fit the night. "Depends on what you think it is."

His words were pleasant and cool, not antagonistic, but Samuel patted his pocket until he found his gold watch and pulled it out. He didn't have anywhere to be, but the action said, 'your time is about up, Mister.'

"I got that moniker today when I told Mister Riley I was just passing through. That's all. What did you think?"

Samuel's brow creased. He wasn't sure he believed the man, but let it go.

Picking up on the bit of tension between them, Abby diverted their thoughts and asked Charles if he came to buy a lot at the resort.

"I don't know. It's a possibility."

"It's a resort for colored people," Bear said. "You know that, right?"

Charles nodded. "Does that mean white folks can't buy in?"

All the chairs went motionless.

"Damn," Bear said, stroking Phantom who draped over his shoulders and Cleo curled on his lap. "I never gave it any thought."

"Me, either," Patrick said. "Shorty?"

He shook his head. "Never had anyone bring it up before. Not until now."

Charles tipped his head back and laughed, his white teeth gleaming in the moonlight.

"What's so funny?" Samuel asked. His nerves were on edge, and he couldn't put his finger on why. Something was going on, something off kilter, and Samuel didn't do well with off kilter, unless he owned it. So, he set out to put it to right. "Want to share with the rest of us?"

"Sorry," Charles said, and meant it.

He had an intelligent, narrow face and close-trimmed salt and pepper hair. His hands were slender and well groomed, proclaiming he didn't do manual labor for a living. Abby watched him straighten the collar of his tweed jacket and wondered where he'd come from. Where he was going.

"Ever hear of *The House Behind the Cedars?"* Charles asked.

All but one head shook, and Samuel's his eyes lit. "So that's it. I've read it. A book about two people passing as white in a white world." He brushed at his mustache with his thumb and middle finger while he watched the lake. "Thought you said you weren't passing – just passing through." Edginess came flooding back.

"I'm not."

Samuel's eyes widened. "Wait. Are you *that* Charles? The author?"

"I am."

"Then you're not white."

"Correct. Although at the time I was born, the south claimed me legally white because my paternal grandfather was a white slaveholder. But I said no."

"My God. Charles Waddell Chesnutt. In Idlewild," Samuel said, and reached to shake the hand of the famous writer, lawyer, activist. "I am in awe, sir."

"Don't be. Please."

No rockers moved. Bear, Shorty, Patrick and Abby were frozen, listening, heads moving back and forth as they tried to make sense of the conversation. In moments, Samuel's voice boomed in laughter.

"*Passing*. They called you *Passing*. That's funny and prophetic, and they couldn't have known."

"It is," he said. "I had a difficult time not laughing, but I didn't want to offend."

Samuel looked pointedly at the others.

"Here's your Chautauqua speaker, Abby. This man's short stories rocked society, changed contemporary ideas about slaves looking for freedom. He is a hero to a lot of people. He could have chosen to be white and privileged but chose to be negro, to help change society for all negros."

"Well, the one-drop rule has changed all that. Now, I'd be considered as black as you."

"But . . . you look white," Abby said, and clapped a hand to her mouth. "Sorry, but you don't look like . . . um . . . Samuel."

She raised her hands in the air looking for common sense, trying to grasp some wisdom. Hers had flown. "Sorry. Really, I am."

"Nothing to apologize for, Miss Riley."

"I'm a Mrs. I mean, I'm Abigail. Just call me Abby. I'm going in for a small refill. Anyone else?"

Charles had had enough of the spotlight and turned it on Bear and Shorty, curious about their place in this cozy circle. "Are either of you the Mister to Abby's Missus?"

Bear grunted, and Shorty said, "No. More like brothers. Been around since she was a squirt."

"Work here?" he asked.

"Construction for the resort. We'll be building a new hotel soon. On the island," Shorty said. "Can't talk 'em out of it."

Abby returned with the drinks in time to see Cassandra at the lake's edge. She came toward the hotel and stood in the road like the Statue of Liberty with her stick as the flame. Her eyes were riveted on Charles, and she was flanked by a dozen or so cats. He dipped his head at her, and she bowed hers.

"Thank you, Cassandra. Nice clowder."

"They watch over me. Come for tea, Abby. Tomorrow."

Voices stilled as she headed back to the lake with her single-filed felines.

"Amazing," Charles said.

"She is," Abby said. "She is a healer and . . . other things, as well."

"I meant the cats. Cassandra, too, but the cats are spectacular and so well trained."

"I don't think they're trained." Samuel laughed. "I'm not even sure they're awake. Probably hypnotized."

"How do you know her?" Abby asked.

"Hmmm." Charles scratched a forefinger at his temple. "How do I know her? I guess I don't."

"But you called her by name."

"I did, didn't I?" Charles' brows drew together. Her name was easy on his tongue, but he hadn't met her before. He knew it.

"She bewitched you," Bear said. "She's powerful. And you have an appointment with her tomorrow, Abby. Be careful," he teased.

"I'm going in. Good night all. You know where your room is Charles?"

"Yes. Thank you and good night. I'm going to listen to the loons for a while longer."

"The ones on the porch or on the lake?" Abby gave him a smile and went inside.

Patrick followed his daughter as the rest listened to Charles tell them of his experiences with the NAACP and other activist groups.

"You'll want to meet Jesse Falmouth," Samuel said. "He's a lawyer, too."

"Too, as in we both earn a living from that nefarious but lucrative line of work?" Charles asked.

"No, as in you, Jesse and I are all licensed arbitrators of the . . . law." His lips pulled back into a grimace, leaving no doubt as to what he thought of his chosen profession.

"If you don't like it, why do it?" Shorty said, and Charles leaned in trying to hear the big man's words that grew more whispered as the night progressed.

"Do you have a throat problem?" he asked Shorty.

Bear answered for him. "He likes to irritate people. That's all. He makes us move to the beat of his drum."

Samuel leaned back in his chair and tapped on the arm, his pose relaxed, but the attitude didn't fool Shorty. He raised his hands like he warded off an attack. "Didn't mean anything by asking, Samuel."

"I can answer your question, Shorty," Charles said, "at least for me. When I began practicing law, lofty ideals filled my brain. I thought I'd be helping folks, negros who needed my skills. It's all I wanted to do. But they didn't trust me. They wanted a shark – a great *white* shark who knew what he was doing and could get them out of whatever kind of trouble they were in. And even though I looked white, they thought I wouldn't be any good because I was *black*."

Charles paused and looked out at the moon on the water. The creamy white circle undulated with the ripples of some night feeder's motion and played with the diamonds scattered around it.

"That doesn't make any sense." Bear swatted as if a gnat had buzzed his ear.

"I thought so, too. But it's real. Years of prejudice and lack of knowledge have created a deceptive image of who we are, what we're capable of. A demeaning vision. Not only on the part of our white brothers and sisters, but by our own."

When Charles turned from the lake, a glaze of water coated his eyes, and he sunk his chin onto a hand propped with an elbow on his knee.

"I realized the truth, and it remains the most defeating day of my life. I can handle white bias; it just makes me angry. It's my own and my brothers' mistaken presumptions of our ineptitude that eat from the inside out like gangrene."

Shorty nodded. He didn't have any words to comfort, no words to move the conversation away from this man's obvious anguish and onto a positive plane. He picked up his glass, still half-full of whiskey and tilted it toward Charles. Then to Samuel.

Heads moved back and forth, and each man sipped. Words weren't needed. The night held commentary in the owl's hoot and crickets' chirp. A determined coyote's yip grew more fevered as he impatiently called for the mother of his kits. The runners of their rocking chairs gave muffled taps on the wooden porch, and the lawyers and the lumberjacks were in sync, at least for this night.

Chapter Six

She filled two plates with bright heaps of scrambled eggs and sausage for Shorty and Bear, refilled their coffee cups, and put a plate of flaky biscuits in the middle of the table. Breakfast scents made someone's stomach growl. She heard it and smiled, happy to be making them happy.

"Need anything else for now?" Abby asked and scooted Phantom away from Bear's legs. He'd sunk claws into the man's pantleg in preparation for the leap to his shoulder. "Don't let him do that, Bear. He'll scratch you."

"He pulls the claws in. He's smart."

"Where are you headed so early?" she asked.

"To the building site and then to Baldwin to see your friend, Gus."

"I'd forgotten already. I can't keep up. Seems like the days all blend into one another and scoot by, or each one is a year-long, all at the same time."

Shorty tweaked her arm. "That's you getting old."

Abby scrunched her face and tugged her long auburn braid. "You're both older than I am. Yeee-aaars older." She drew the word out for emphasis.

"Not so much. Al, here, is the baby of our little group. How old are you, Al?"

She scowled at the potato she was peeling, and Abby noticed a pink flush at the collar of her dress.

"Al?" Shorty said thinking she hadn't heard his whisper.

"Twenty," she said to the potato.

"You are not!" Abby said, shock making her words harsher than she intended.

Al looked up but didn't respond. If Abby didn't believe her, she couldn't do anything about it. She tossed the naked potato into a pan of water and grabbed another.

"I mean, are you really twenty, Al? I never would have believed it. You're so . . . young looking and tiny."

"I'm twenty."

Shorty saw the young woman's blush and came to her rescue. "I've got close to a decade on you, Al. Not quite but getting there. Guess that makes me an old man. Bear, too, but he won't say so."

Abby put an arm around his shoulder and squeezed. "You're not even close to thirty. But you and the other old man be careful out there today."

"You think your buddy might do us harm?" Bear asked.

"No, not Gus. But you never know. Things aren't like they used to be. People are . . . strange. They're antsy-like."

Betty halted conversation as she pushed through the swinging doors like a fresh breeze, confident, happy and vocal.

"Morning, all. Beautiful outside, isn't it? I love spring." She turned in a circle, aware all eyes were on her and waited, one leg stuck out as if she was modeling. "Well?"

Al peeled her potato as the men stared, wondering what she expected of them, and Abby scrutinized.

Hair's the same. I recognize the blouse. Skirt? That's it, cuz it certainly isn't the scruffy shoes.

"I love it. A new skirt. Great blue for you," Abby said on a relieved puff of air. Betty's hands went to her hips in mock irritation.

"It's an old skirt, boss. Come on."

"Sorry. Then, I don't know."

"Look how tight it is at the waist. I finally put on a couple of pounds. I'm almost fat, now. Surely you can see that. Right?"

The room, except Al, of course, burst into guffaws. Betty was as scrawny as they come, a broomstick. A puff of air would pick her up and drop her in another county if tough cookie wasn't her middle name.

Shorty left his chair and patted Betty on the head.

"You should probably go on a diet soon." He pushed at the door and Bear followed.

Abby waved them away, and Patrick came through. It was a circus with a revolving door, people coming and going, stopping for a chat or a bite to eat and leaving again.

She kissed her father's cheek and left to clean rooms with Betty. She paused at the linen closet to grab a pile of sheets and dragged the dust mop in the other hand.

"I'd have thought you'd notice," Betty said. "Really."

"Well, given some time, I'm sure I would have. I was preoccupied thinking about the boys going to see big Gus."

"Gus? Who's big Gus?"

Abby followed Betty's broom around the room, scooping up left over dust with the mop and hissing at Cleo when she attacked it like a big mouse.

"Gus is the bartender where I take Sue and Sally in Baldwin, and . . ." Seeing the wide eyes on Betty, she went clammy and broke off. "Uh, never mind. He's just a man. That's all."

How can this young girl make me feel like such a fool? It isn't right. I'm the boss.

"What you doing with Gus?" Her round black eyes bored into Abby.

"Stop looking at me. I'm not doing anything with him." But she giggled when she thought of his bare arm next to hers – in front of an entire bar full of patrons. "Bear and Shorty are going to see him about business."

"Bar business?"

"How'd you get so smart, Betty? Would you consider being in charge of room cleaning when I move to the new hotel? We'd hire another woman – or maybe a man. I suppose they can clean, too."

"No, they can't." Betty gave her a look of curious wonder that Abby had come to expect.

"Okay. You're right. A woman."

Abby wiped out the washbowl and hung new towels while Betty stripped the bed. She dusted the bureau and polished smudged fingerprints from the walnut armoire. Betty flipped the crisp sheet in the air and tugged it by two corners. The rectangle of white floated to the mattress and landed in perfect uniformity. Even bed linens toed the line for her.

"You're amazing, Betty. I've been making beds all my life, and I can't throw a sheet like you do."

Betty's grin was proud, could even be considered haughty – in a pleasing way. She knew her strengths. One was making a bed, but she'd like to do more than flip sheets her entire life. Her mind spun back to Abby's comment about the new hotel. She could be a boss.

She'd like that.

"Your father's really gonna build a hotel on the island?"

Abby stood at the window and saw Bear and Shorty heading to the stable. She wished they didn't have to be involved in bootlegging. It made her nervous just thinking about it, and she jerked when Betty tapped her shoulder.

"Wow! Pretty jumpy, boss. Where were you?"

"Nowhere. Here."

"So, you didn't want to answer me?"

"Sorry. What did you want to know?"

"Never mind. Nothing important." Betty knew how much she loved Bear and Shorty. She squeezed her arm in empathy. "Boys'll be fine, Abby."

"I know. They're capable."

But something didn't feel right, and she teased herself with the idea of asking Cassandra about it. She knew everything. Maybe she'd know about the itchy thing going on at the back of her neck.

When they finished the last room, Abby checked the bar to see if Jackson was on the job, told him she'd be gone for an hour or so, and stepped into the sunshine. The fresh air, the chickadee's fee-bee song and the sun on her face took her breath away.

Spring was her favorite time of year – along with autumn and winter and summer. When she lived each season, *it* became her favorite. She was fickle.

Turning down Cassandra's lane and out of sight, her arms stretched out as if to embrace the weather, the sky, the sun. She skipped like a child playing hopscotch and laughed at herself. Thoughts were rampant.

Can you smell spring? Taste it? I'm surely sniffing it now. It's on the back of my tongue, and it tastes yellow, like a dandelion. And green like the tall weeds lining the path.

"Of course, you can. Think of all the natural scents and tastes in the world," Cassandra said from behind her.

Abby whirled around, startled.

"Why did you answer me? I didn't say anything, and I wish you would quit doing that."

"What?"

"Sneaking up on me."

"I don't sneak. I happened to be going in this direction behind you."

"And reading my mind."

"I can't help that. Your thoughts fly off your fingertips like projectiles. Tea?"

Abby took the unconventional woman's arm and held it close to her side while they strolled to Cassandra's home. A shack on the outside, it hadn't changed since Abby first saw it and had refused to walk onto the porch because she believed it wouldn't hold her weight. The boards were broken, rotted, decrepit. Cassandra had scoffed at Abby's hesitance and dragged her in by the sleeve of her dress.

She'd been shocked when the interior of the shack registered. Beauty and tangible tranquility cloaked her exterior and buttered her insides like a hot biscuit. It was warm and fluffy in soft pastels. Abby's gaze wandered the room in random fashion, taking it in with pleasure.

She roamed the bright room, inhaling flower arrangements and admiring satin pillows while Cassandra lifted the lid of a flowered teapot and dropped in the prepared tea basket. The scent of hibiscus and lemon balm filled the room.

"What kind of tea are you brewing today, Cassandra?"

"No evil brew."

"Of course not. I know better."

"Today you do," the woman said with a chuckle. "But I threw in some sage and St. John's Wort just for you."

"Why?"

"Calm your nerves and relieve the thistle at the back of your neck. You did want me to fix that, yes? Sit."

Abby shook her head in curiosity but obeyed, and Cassandra poured the tea. With her hands wrapped around the cup, Abby let the steam rise and inhaled deeply.

"Feeling better?"

"I am, thank you. I needed this. I've been so worried about my friends. Tell me they'll be okay."

Cassandra sipped her tea and ignored the request, causing Abby to search her friend's eyes for answers.

"Charles Chesnutt mixes a strong potion of heart and brain. He is a gentle soul. He would be good for Idlewild, but Idlewild may not be good for him."

Abby sat back in the chair, wondering what made her think of Charles and why she'd mention him to Abby.

"I think he's just passing through." She laughed when she said the name her father had given him.

"Maybe."

"Do you know where Frank is, Cassandra?"

Her eyebrows lifted.

"Will you tell me?"

"No. He will. He's coming. Are you ready for him?"

Abby drained her cup before answering because she didn't know. How could she be ready? What could she do to prepare for what it takes to make marriage work with a man you felt was abusing you – even if he didn't know it. And he had chosen to leave her. He'd made the final choice.

But he didn't carry the blame for their failure alone, and she knew it. She should have said something, done something.

Cassandra went silent, and it bothered her. Abby needed her to say something, anything. She was used to her help, not silence. Well, silence, too.

"Maybe I'm ready," she said. "He *is* my husband. We vowed for better or worse. I have to help him change if he wants to.

"Brain and heart must meet."

"Do you think mine don't?"

"Yours do much of the time. Sometimes more heart than brain."

Abby knew Cassandra had meant Frank. Sometimes he didn't use both. He lived in a bubble – a Frank bubble. But he wasn't an evil person. He wasn't mean spirited, just thoughtless, kind of like a toddler who sees a toy and wants it. Now. She knew that.

"Tell me this, Cassandra. Will Bear and Shorty be okay? I'm really worried, and I can't even say why – just a feeling."

Cassandra smiled, the creases in her weathered skin deepening, making her appear angelic and satanic at the same time. She put her hand on Abby's and left it there, opposites. One black, one white, one gnarled, one smooth, one warm in knowledge, one cold in anxiety.

"Quit having a feeling," she said. "They will live."

"Thank you, Cassandra. I don't know what I would do without you."

"As you do now. Change is coming. If change didn't happen, we'd all be bacteria and parasites living in a stagnant pond, anachronisms in a universe filled with transformation."

Abby stood to leave and laughed. "You and your 'isms' will be the death of me. I lay awake at night and try to figure out the meanings."

"Maybe there aren't any. Maybe I just say weird things to confuse you. Tantalize you into visiting me."

She got back to the hotel in time for the Friday crowd to check in. They were in full-blown good humor, getting ready for the spring Chautauqua. She asked Jackson to carry bags for a bit and signed people in, joking with those she hadn't seen since last fall, happy they'd returned despite the fires and troubles they'd weathered. She'd feared some might stay away.

Abby heard Benjamin at the piano through the open doors and the laughter of folks already in the bar celebrating the week's end.

"Glad he's here," she said to Jackson, and several people waiting in line agreed.

"Those fingers can sure travel the ivories," a stranger said. Abby smiled at him. He was a wide man. Not overweight, but broad shouldered and big boned. His cheeks were stretched with clear, russet skin and his intelligent, high forehead met a full head of black hair. He exuded energy and confidence.

"You like piano music?" she asked.

"Yes, ma'am, I do. Any kind of music, really."

She turned the registration book his way and read upside-down as he signed his name.

"Oh! You're the keynote speaker Mister Garvey sent. I've saved a special room for you. I'm Abby." She extended her hand and he shook it firmly. "I can't wait to hear your talk."

He smiled. "If you let go of my hand, I'll go to my room and prepare for it."

She jerked her hand from his and blushed. "I'm so sorry, Mister Bradford." She wiggled her hand like it stung and called for Jackson to take his bag.

"Don't bother, young man. I can get it if you'll just tell me where to go."

"Is anyone meeting you, Mister Bradford? Do you need someone to show you around?" Jackson asked, awe shining in his eyes.

"Thank you, son. Jesse Falmouth is meeting me here in about an hour, but I appreciate your offer." When he turned away, Jackson wilted.

"Do you know who that is?" he said, eyes following the broad back.

"I do. He's a man with a magical dream. At least, Marcus Garvey is, and I'm sure Mister Bradford thinks like he does. I hope Charles gets a chance to converse with him. The two believe in different paths."

"Charles?"

"You know. Charles Chesnutt. *Passing Through.*"

Jackson laughed and looked ten, not twenty.

When the last person had registered and the rooms were full, she donned her bartending hat and Jackson his waiter's apron. Benjamin's music kept time with her movements and lifted her spirits. Abby glanced his way with clouded eyes. She could love him for his music alone.

"Do you know how many important people are coming to Idlewild now?" Jackson asked, in between serving drinks. "I can't believe it."

Abby grinned and wiped the bar as he walked over to a table of guests without glasses in front of them, returning with drink orders and growing enthusiasm.

"Think about it. Dr. Dan, Buddy Black, Mister Chesnutt, Mister Bradford, W. E. B. Dubois . . ."

"Don't forget the women. How about Leila Wilson, daughter of C. J. Walker? She's an amazing lady."

He nodded and took the tray, delivered the drinks, stopped at a table with empty glasses, and came back.

"Three short shots. You're right. And we're just beginning. We can really *be* something. Something great. The whole nation will know who we are."

"We're something already, Jackson." She lined up three glasses and poured brown liquid from a bottle.

"But this is different. We're colored. Well, not you."

"Really? I hadn't noticed."

"Real funny, boss." He toward the lobby. "These people – they're famous. My head is spinning."

"Keep it on your shoulders, Jackson. Feet on the ground. They're people, just like us. Help Da put the supper buffet out, please. Carry the big stuff if he'll let you."

Jesse Falmouth showed up about the same time Harrison Bradford came downstairs. Abby waved them to the buffet, offered drinks and didn't notice them again until she saw them leaving for the pavilion.

She eyed the stragglers in the bar, wishing they'd leave so she could, too, when Bear and Shorty walked in. Abby's heart thumped in happiness seeing them with all their parts and pieces intact, and she ran around the bar to wrap arms around them.

"Missed you, too," Bear said, and Phantom flew from the bar to his shoulder. Cleo opened her mouth to make a meow that rarely became a full-fledged sound.

"Hungry? Let me get plates for you. Sit. Want a drink first? Of course, you do. I'll get that. You're fine, yes?"

"Abby. Slow down," Shorty said. "What's wrong?"

"Nothing. I had the creepies all day, and now I don't."

"Well, I'm glad. Nothing I hate worse than creepies. Specially if they come with crawlies," Shorty said. "I'll take a beer to wash the dust from my throat before I eat."

Patrick came from the kitchen and climbed on a stool next to them. "Good day?"

"Yup. Good."

"Can I get a drink, lass?"

She brought his Irish and stayed, thinking about the prohibition issue they'd been skirting since January. "Have you given thought to how we'll run the hotel bar now that selling's illegal?"

"We may have to give it away."

"What? That's not a very good business plan."

He chuckled. "Tis true. Or they bring in their own and we sell water or colas."

"Why has no one shut us down? Sheriff Hicks knows what we do."

"I wondered that, too, lass. Probably cuz we're small potatoes. Some states don't recognize prohibition at all. Things go on as they always have. Others are ruled by bootleggers. That may be the case here. Low profile is what we need, Abby girl."

She didn't like going against the law, even if it was a stupid one. "I'd like to go hear Harrison Bradford talk. I think we're pretty much done here til the end of the Chautauqua music. Would that be okay?"

She filled a glass with Irish and hung an arm over his shoulder. "You good, too, Da?"

"I'm dandy, lass. You scoot outta here and don't worry."

She did, waving as she left.

Chapter Seven

She heard Buddy Black's blues as soon as her feet hit the porch, and her heart entangled in the strings of his guitar. He could bend a note longer and further than anyone she'd ever heard, and, as far as she was concerned, blues wasn't blue until Buddy Black played it. Heart and guitar strings became one.

She slowed her walk to the pavilion to enjoy the music and looked around at the mass of humanity gathered. It amazed her. Like Jackson, she was in awe of the people who came to play in Idlewild.

A short time ago, days after she and her father moved here, she'd gone to Jesse Falmouth's office to offer her help in making Idlewild a place to be proud of. The Chautauqua had been her idea, and, in truth, she needed it. She needed the intellectual stimulation, the music, and the people who came to participate.

She'd said it was for Idlewild, but a good part of her motivation had been for herself. She'd never wanted to feed chickens and milk cows all her life without philosophical discussions in between or read books and never deliberate over what they meant. Chautauqua fulfilled her.

Honesty came to her in a harsh realization on the way to the pavilion. She hadn't been fair to Frank. Even if her da hadn't needed her at the hotel, she'd want to be there. It rewarded her in ways being a farm wife couldn't.

It's good for all of us, for Idlewild, for our children.

When Buddy Black left the stage, a new group set up, and their ragtime music brought dozens of people to the makeshift dance floor under the pavilion. Abby hadn't seen ragtime dancers before, and her mouth hung open as she stood at the back and watched.

They were all doing different moves, energetic moves that included wiggling and strutting and even cuddling. It was silly, fun looking, and their ankles showed! She wanted to do it and jumped as if guilty of blasphemy when a voice spoke in her ear from behind.

"You're moving to the music, Abby. I can see it."

"Was not, Samuel. I was switching feet. They're tired." He stepped beside her and crossed his arms.

"What are they doing?" she asked.

"Dancing."

Abby gave him a quirky grin. "I could tell that much."

"It's called the One-Step. Started in the cities almost a decade ago, and that's where most of Idlewild came from. Tonight's visiting crowd, anyway."

"But they're doing more than stepping once. They're hopping and skipping and . . ."

"Fox Trot, Turkey Trot, Camel Walk. Animal dance variations of the One-Step. Want to give it a try?" He held out his arm, but she backed away, eyes wide in fear.

"No. I can't."

"Course you can. Come here," he said, taking her arm and walking her toward the outer edges of the mass of people, off the pavilion and onto the grass.

"Now do what I do."

"No." She giggled an anxious titter. "I could probably do a Cat Walk, or maybe a Bunny Hop, but . . ."

He put his hand on her back at the waist, grabbed her hand, pulled her toward him, and took a long step. She had to follow or tumble. He took another, and her foot automatically followed. Soon they were turning in a wide circle doing a quick One-Step. When the song ended, Abby struggled for breath and giggled.

"How'd you learn to dance these, uh . . . animal things?" she asked, catching her breath.

"I'm an amazing man, Abigail. Truly remarkable."

His grin was slight but visible in the growing darkness, and she returned it.

"Thank you for the dance, Samuel."

He nodded once in response.

"I'm going to move in closer to hear Mister Bradford," she said. "As soon as the band finishes, he's due to speak."

"I'll join you. I'm interested in what he has to say – as Garvey's mouthpiece."

They inched forward through the crowd, closer to the band, dodging other like-minded folks who were advancing for the keynote address, as well. Samuel took an arm to maneuver her through several tall men and felt eyes follow them. He glanced around, but it was hard to detect a single ogling person in the middle of the throng.

When they made it to the edge of the dance floor, he let his eyes roam the faces circling the open space in front of the podium. A first perusal revealed no one he'd consider threatening. On a second, however, he stopped at a pair of eyes squinting and glaring at him and Abby. He nodded.

"Didn't know Frank Sr. attended Chautauqua events." His cynical humor gave the words a harsh edge.

Abby twisted toward him. "Frank's father is here? Where?"

"Right next to Joe Foster. You look like a rabbit caught in a live trap." He chuckled, a short burst cut shorter by her obvious fear.

Abby's heart pounded. Her head spun back and forth, searching for her father-in-law in the crowd.

"Stop it, Abby. What are you afraid of?"

"Nothing. I'm not frightened."

"You're doing a good job of faking it. You've done nothing wrong." She straightened her shoulders and flipped her hair back, lifting her chin in defiance.

"Yeah. You show him, Abigail," he said with another chuckle. "Do you want me to stand somewhere else?"

"Of course not. Why should we not stand together?"

"Why ever not?" he said, but not out loud.

Applause thundered when the last ragtime note faded, and the dancers left the floor. Jesse Falmouth climbed the podium and held his hands in the air for quiet.

"I know you've all heard of Marcus Mosiah Garvey, President General of the Universal Negro Improvement Association and African Communities League. Mister Garvey could not attend today, but we are fortunate to have his second in command, Mister Harrison Bradford."

He waited for the clapping to die down and continued.

"In 1917, there were thirteen members of Garvey's organization. Three months later, over 3500 folks were due-paying members. It was with Mister Bradford's help the UNIA has been so successful. Please give him a warm welcome."

Harrison Bradford stepped up to the podium and looked at the variety of faces staring back at him. His stomach clenched and twisted. He should be used to it by now, but wasn't, so he did what he always did – picked out the friendliest face and smiled in greeting – then picked out the meanest looking and began talking. He talked right at Joe Foster.

"Marcus Garvey believes in 'One God! One Aim! One Destiny!' and so do I. We believe in justice for all mankind and in the preservation of our noble race."

Cheers from the crowd forced him to pause, and minutes passed before he could begin again. They listened for ten more with interest and respect that grew vocal when he left the podium and went to stand directly in front of Foster.

It appeared as if Harrison spoke only to Joe, his sole purpose – to convince him and only him. He thought if he could persuade the meanest person in Idlewild, in any town, the most hateful to his race, he'd win. They'd win, because he could triumph over anyone. He could bring peace. His voice rose to carry to the back over the heads of the large crowd.

"Mister Falmouth said 3500 people followed Mister Garvey, but this year more than four million negros have faith in the ideal of industry, education, and community for our race. If you consider conditions of life for ethnic Africans both at home and abroad, you will agree with the plan for a permanent, peaceful home! We would live far from the foolish, hateful race riots such as occurred in East St. Louis, Chicago, and Tulsa where black and white people died without reason. We would live as a united community – in Africa. Our dream will safeguard our race through education, home and industry. In our community, there will be no more victimization of the negros who broke their backs for this country!"

"Then go home!" Joe screamed and flung a haphazard punch at Harrison. "Go back, go back, go back," he yelled.

The crowd went deathly silent, until murmurs began at the back and moved forward like a wave. Harrison held up a hand to stay the crowd that looked about to come to his rescue. The last thing he wanted was a brawl.

Frank Sr. pulled Harrison away from Joe and held his arm. His face turned blotchy in rage, and the pulse at his temple pounded.

"Mister, you need to go home. All the way home. It's coloreds' fault my family is broken." He wheezed and clutched his chest like he needed air.

"I got one son in jail, another who left town because of a woman – I won't say wife, cuz she ain't – but she loves coloreds more than her own in-laws. And her own husband. You've turned this town into a joke. It ain't fit for nobody. Not fit for a Christian, anyway."

He stood directly across the dance floor from Abby who tried to back away and out of the crowd when he started ranting, but she couldn't escape. She was trapped, forced to listen to his hate.

Terry Adams shoved his way through the stunned crowd to his father's side and seized his arm. He turned and stared directly into Abby's eyes. Anger seethed from his. She could feel it burning in the cold atmosphere.

"You're making a fool of yourself," Terry growled under his breath, and dragged him across the floor, moving near enough to bump Abby's arm.

"There are better ways to make a point," he said to his father, but he made sure Abby heard, and his eyes never left hers as they walked by.

Samuel followed Terry, close enough he could have kissed the back of his head. There was no kiss, but when Terry's head spun around to respond to words Samuel had spoken, his eyes were lit with fire and his hand fisted.

"I wouldn't," Samuel said.

"You're a son of a bitch."

"I am. Remember it."

Tears formed in Abby's eyes, but she refused to acknowledge the desire to weep. What had Terry meant – 'other ways to make a point.' What did he plan? What point did he want to make?

As she turned to head for the hotel, the ragtime band played *Jelly Roll Blues,* and a line of costumed girls took the stage. Abby's eyes grew wide watching them kick their feet, skirts rising clear to the knees, and she forgot her brother-in-law.

The dancers hugged each other, linked arms, hopped and jiggled. They'd obviously left their corsets at home, and Abby's rosy skin burned with embarrassment, but she couldn't turn her eyes away.

Their joy was tangible. She wanted to join the frivolity, kick up her heels and twirl around the dance floor with the abandon they exhibited. The smile on her face matched the girls', and she ignored the arm around her shoulders until he whispered in her ear.

"Want to be a dance girl, lass?"

She laughed. "I do, Da. I think I do. It looks like so much fun." Her foot tapped, and her shoulders moved with the syncopated rhythm of the tantalizing music. The distress brought on by Terry and Frank Sr. washed away in the river of melody and brightly clad dancers having a good time.

"You'd be a good one, Abby. You've got your mother's light feet. Music set her to dancing, too."

Abby turned to her father. "Did the two of you dance when you were young?"

"Does a rainbow have a pot of gold?"

She snorted. "I've never seen one."

"Did ye look?"

Shorty and Bear came up behind them, and she heard Shorty's intake of breath when he saw the dancers wiggling around the floor. She watched him as he watched them and laughed at the expression on his face.

Bear poked him. "Have you never seen a woman dance, Shorty?"

"Not like these girls. They're . . . uh, something."

His face turned sunrise red down into the collar of his shirt, and he turned away from the dancers toward Abby.

"I saw Frank's father and brother heading away. Were they here at the pavilion?"

Remembrance punched her, and she flinched before speaking.

"Everything okay?" Shorty asked.

"Yes. They're gone. They were screaming at Mister Bradford near the end of his speech."

"Frank and Terry? Why?"

"No. Frank and Joe Foster. Joe was yelling 'Go home' and Frank said . . . some stupid things. I don't know exactly, but Terry took him away. Samuel followed."

Surprise registered in all their eyes.

"Whatever for?" Bear asked. He didn't think Samuel had much to do with those men. Didn't think he liked them at all – nor they him.

"I don't know," she fibbed. "I think maybe he wanted to be sure they left. They were pretty angry at some things Mister Bradford was saying."

"Like?" Bear shifted closer, an automatic closing of ranks around Abby to protect her. He didn't believe anyone could hurt her here in this crowd of people, but the maneuver made him feel better. It was instinctive, an unconscious act of love.

"At the time, Mister Bradford was talking about all the race riots that happened a while back. A short while ago, actually. After the war."

Her words melted off rather than ceasing, and they stared at the dancers, mesmerized, as if the movement of their bodies had hypnotized them. Abby shook her shoulders, stretched and whirled around.

"I think I'll go on back to the hotel, get ready for the rush, maybe find Benjamin and ask him to play some soothing music to cool everybody's fiery blood."

"Who has fiery blood?" Shorty asked.

"You for starters."

"Nah. That's crazy. I'll walk you back," he said.

Bear flanked her other side, and Patrick said he'd be up in a while. He was going to get a wee bit fiery first.

"You didn't tell me how it went today. What did you think about my friend, Gus?"

"He seems a good man. We talked."

"Is he going to help with liquor deliveries?"

Bear snuffled, a sound Abby had come to associate with sardonic laughter, and she got a queasy feeling in the pit of her stomach. But Cassandra told her they would be fine – her makeshift brothers – and she believed in the woman's prophecies. She shifted the unease to the back of her brain where it could do nothing more than keep her up at night.

"Why do you snuffle, Bear?" she asked.

"I'm thinking we may be the helpers," he said.

"You're going to help big Gus? I thought he had everything figured out."

Bear's burly head swung from side to side, and Shorty's gleamed in the moonlight. Both men didn't want to burden their friend with the ugly news. And it was ugly because Gus, who bought his booze from Newaygo, was being shaken down, forced to buy at ridiculous prices, forced to pay for their protection. When they told Abby the gentle version, she was livid.

"What do you mean shaken down? He's too big to shake. He's even bigger than you, Shorty, and that's why I suggested he work with us. He's fierce, my friend, Gus."

Bear smiled at her enthusiasm. "Yes, he is fierce, Abby."

Her head jerked back, and her hands balled into fists.

"You're placating me! Stop it!" She flipped her braid, and it curled around the back of her head and slapped her cheek. "Damn thing. I should cut it off."

Both men guffawed at the Irish elf turned grizzly.

"Settle down. We're working together, your Gus and us," Shorty said. "We're including him in our pick-up this week. He can decide if he likes the situation for himself. He'll ride along."

"Three's better, anyway," Bear added. "How'd you find this guy, Abby?"

"Um . . . I'm sure I mentioned meeting him. Long time ago."

"That doesn't tell us much, Abs," Bear said.

Abby dropped her voice and head. "In a bar in Baldwin."

"What were you doing in a bar in Baldwin?" Bear's words were curt, like he'd restrained himself from punching something.

"You remember, Bear. I told you about going there with Sue and Sally, and you already scolded me. And I told you it was not your business, and I was a grown woman able to make my own decisions."

But when she thought about the *arm thing* she blushed and hoped they never heard about it.

"I remember. Sorry. I know you're capable."

Abby hooked a hand around his arm, letting him know her affection remained, as they climbed the steps of the porch. She heard the tinkle of piano keys before they opened the door and knew Benjamin already entertained himself and whoever listened.

Her spirits lifted.

Jackson, behind the bar, had a foot propped on something she couldn't see. He looked at home, chatting with customers, leaning an elbow on the gleaming wood.

Charles Chesnutt sat next to Samuel, and Sue and Sally flanked them. Sue's feet wiggled back and forth, swinging with childlike abandon, and her eyes squinted in laughter. Sally's tall frame sat erect and immobile, the only movement her slender hand on Samuels arm, patting it with affection. The women had something Abby admired: grit, fortitude, an indelible attitude mixed with voracious confidence.

I'd like some of what they have. Just a wee bit. That's all.

She ran to her room to wash up and shrieked when she saw a man stretched out on her bed. Bear, Shorty and Samuel heard her alarm and raced to the stairs, sounding like a herd of cattle pounding on each step. When they reached her, she was frozen in place, staring at Frank who had awakened with her scream.

He lay in the dark and gazed at the door opening. His wife had been silhouetted alone for a moment, and in the next instant, three men surrounded her – the bodyguards – her friends. In a flash, he wondered what he'd been thinking coming here. Nothing had changed. Their lives wouldn't be any different. She liked her life fine the way it was . . . without him. He threw his legs over the bed and reached for his shoes, noting the silence in the doorway. No one moved. No one spoke.

"I'll be going," he said.

"No." Abby turned to shoo the men away. When they'd gone, she entered and closed the door.

Frank had one shoe on and held the other. He looked it over as if he'd not seen it before and dropped it to pat the bed beside him. Abby was motionless, hardly able to take in enough air to sustain life. Her heart pounded.

She was terrified and wanted nothing more than to wash her hands and face and go back to the bar. Make drinks. Talk with friends. Be happy. Be safe. Water tried to leak into her eyes, but she fought it, sniffed it back.

"What are you doing here, Frank?"

He tilted his head to look at her.

Was that hope in his eyes?

"Wanted to talk. That's all."

"Where have you been?"

He shifted his shoulders like he didn't know or didn't want to say. "Around and about."

"Are you here to stay?"

"I don't know. That depends."

"On what, Frank? Has anything changed?"

"I guess I'd like to know, Abby. Can we talk about it?"

Now he wants to talk?

Abby sat next to him, not touching. Her back stiffened; her hands twisted in her lap. She was afraid and didn't know why. The bed started shaking, and she wondered about the trembling of her legs. She knew Frank wouldn't hurt her. He would never hit her.

So, why did she tremble? Why did she wish he sat somewhere else rather than in her room.? Yes, *her* room. It had never been theirs, and she knew it and felt shame.

It *should* have been theirs.

"I know you'll hate me for this, Frank, but a crowd will be in the bar in minutes, and I need to be there."

Frank's head did a quick, theatrical drop to his chest. She looked at the cowlick sticking up at the back of his head and wanted to smooth it down. But it had a mind of its own and wouldn't change. Nothing did.

"Of course. The bar. What's the matter with me?"

"Will you stay so we can talk? It'll only be a couple of hours."

"Probably not, Abs. But we'll see."

"Please?"

"We'll see."

"You hungry?"

He shook his head, and Abby stood. She rinsed her hands and face in the cool water and watched him between her fingers. She brushed her hair and tied it back. All the while, he watched her, and she questioned what traveled through his mind.

What motivated her husband? What made him think as he did? Who the hell was he? This Frank. This . . . man.

He didn't speak until she said she'd see him later. When he did, the curl of his lip didn't fill her with confidence.

Chapter Eight

Her sister-in-law pushed through the swinging doors to the kitchen early next morning, saw Al and pasted on a smile.

"Cecily! Whatever are you doing here? Good to see you." Abby dried her hands on her apron and hugged the black haired, curvy woman, mother of the nephews she hadn't seen in a while.

"Just visiting. I miss you."

"Coffee?" Abby asked. "Pull up a chair. I have to keep peeling these things cuz I can't get them to do it for themselves." She chuckled at her lame humor, but saw Cecily found it difficult to smile, let alone laugh.

Abby poured a coffee and glanced around the kitchen, assessing how long she could be gone if she left for a few minutes with Cecily. Al met her eyes and tilted her head sideways toward the door. Abby wondered for a moment if she had psychic powers.

"Thanks, Al. I'll just be a few. Grab your coffee, Ceci."

"Can we go to your room?" She pushed at the door she'd come through a moment before.

They covered the amenities of family, health, happiness, and all the miracles her two boys might have performed while they meandered up the stairs. Words were stilted, and they were glad to be opening the door to Abby's room. She pointed to the chair, indicating Cecily should sit, and Abby perched on the edge of the bed – in the same spot she'd sat next to Frank.

Had it just been last night? Had he really been there?

Silence stretched, and Abby tried to find a reason for Cecily's strange behavior. She looked for words and settled for those that addressed their common bond – the brothers they had married.

"Why are you here, Cecily? Did Terry send you?"

Her head bobbed up and down, and Abby saw tears at the corners of her eyes.

"Why? What does he want?"

"Frank. He wants his brother."

Abby shifted on the bed and smoothed a hand over her mother's afghan; a finger traced around the rose crocheted into the pattern.

"So why come to me? I don't have him. I'm not hiding him under the bed."

The tears she'd seen gathered in the corners of Cecily's eyes were now flowing down her cheeks. Abby's eyes watered, as well, but anger kept them from falling. They'd sent this sweet woman to do their dirty work rather than confront her on their own.

"I know you don't have Frank," Cecily said, her words a bare whisper. "Terry thinks he was here."

"He was, Cecily. Last night."

"And now?"

"Now, I don't know. He was gone when I got off work." She pulled the afghan to her lap and fingered the rose. "I wanted him to stay, but he . . . I guess he didn't. I don't know where he is," she repeated.

Cecily left her chair and went to stand at the window. Abby followed and put an arm around her shoulders. She liked her sister by marriage. Cecily was a good woman and slavishly committed to the Adams family. Many times, Abby had wished to be her, to be in the fold of the family arms. That had never happened, and she blamed herself.

"Did you come alone?"

She shook her head and pointed. Abby saw the wagon down the road. It stood between the hotel and Foster's store, and Terry paced in a circle around it.

"Did you know Terry was at the Chautauqua last night? He was with your father-in-law who was screaming his head off at our keynote speaker."

"They talked about it."

"He was yelling about a broken family. He looked right at me, Ceci. He scared me."

"He scares me, too. I don't know what to do about it, though. Since George went to jail, he's been . . . I don't know what to call it. Just off."

At the window, they watched ducks and geese landing on the lake and boaters rowing across it. Some folks held fishing poles, long bamboo rods that stuck out of the small crafts. Others lay back with their legs over the sides, letting the cold water of Lake Idlewild cool their toes and the rising sun warm them.

"Remember when you wanted to make pate` out of the mallard who almost flew in this window?" Abby pointed to the flock soaring over the hotel roof. She heard a chuckle, and her heart warmed.

"It was a goose, not a duck."

"Was it? Of course, it was goose pate`. What are they doing, Ceci? What do they want from me?"

She leaned her head on Abby's shoulder and took a moment to breathe in the water's tranquility.

"They don't know where he is or why he went away, and they're afraid. That's what they say. But I think big Frank knows more than he says, and that's why he's afraid. And *that's* why he hates you, and it scares me. I think . . . I think he's a little crazy now." She twirled her finger around her temple to clarify.

Abby patted her shoulder, the only comfort she could give. She didn't have to live with them, and she felt deep gratitude for the family she had: Da, Shorty and Bear, her chosen family. Strange but sane.

"I don't understand any of what you just said, Ceci, but that's okay. Stay clear of him if he scares you. Hear me?"

"Hard to do living in the same house with him. And Terry's all he has for help now. Besides me and Ma Adams. Pretty soon, my boys. They do what they can now." She jerked from Abby's arm and fled to the door as if she'd seen a mouse. "I gotta go."

Abby followed her down the stairs, told her to visit more often, and knew she wouldn't be allowed to unless they sent her to spy. She pounded her fist on the frame of the door after Cecily quick-stepped through it and skipped off the porch. Terry's gaze fixed on his wife as she ran in his direction.

Bear and Shorty were in the kitchen with Al when she returned to the potatoes Bear was peeling in her stead. She smiled at him, taking knife and bare potato from his hands.

"Nicely done, Bear. Want a job?" She flinched and glanced into Shorty's cup to check the coffee level – the barometer indicating whether chatting would be tolerated.

"Almost gone. We're good." Bear shook his head, seeing her flinch, fearful of a seat on top of the cupboard. "And I got more work than I need right now."

"Construction's booming, isn't it?"

"Tis."

"New hotel?"

He nodded and moved to his regular seat at the table, lay Phantom over his shoulder, picked up his cup, cradled it and stared into the brown liquid.

"You looking to read your fortune?" Shorty said.

"That's tea leaves. And I'm pretty certain of my future. You?"

Shorty grunted, and Bear cleared his throat.

"We fixing breakfast for Frank this morning?"

Abby's paring knife slipped, and she watched red well in the nick on her finger. She stuck it in her mouth and held it there while Bear got a clean towel, led her to the sink and ladled water from the bucket. He pulled on her wrist and took care of the wound.

"It's just a scratch, Bear. It'll be fine."

"I'm sorry," he said. "Let me wrap it for you. Keep it clean while you cook. I'm sorry."

"You said that. And no, we're not feeding him. Is that why you two are here so early? Avoiding Frank?"

Phantom yowled as he shifted his shoulders, answering without words.

Al put filled plates in front of the men, all but the potatoes that were still raw, and Abby got busy slicing them into a sizzling pan.

"Thanks, Al. Sorry I messed up the process today."

Al gave no indication she'd been spoken to. Abby didn't expect a response; after all, she hadn't asked a question.

Breakfast went to the buffet in haphazard fashion this day, but it was there. Abby's head spun to the door at every footfall, wondering if Frank had returned. She shivered, and the little itchy hairs at the back of her neck stood at attention. Laughing at herself, she thought she might have to visit Cassandra again to get the *itch* taken care of. She moved the platter of sausages to make room for pancakes, straightened and sniffed.

"Grab a plate, Sheriff," she said to the man behind her and heard him groan.

"I can't ever sneak up on you, Abigail. Don't say you smelled me again." His eyes were light and sparkling with affection. They'd become friends in the last couple of years, and he liked her pluck.

"Not you, Sheriff Hicks, your pipe. If you want to sneak up on me, you'll have to change your tobacco." She held a hand out for a shake, but he took it and pulled her in for a hug. "Good to see you, too," she said. "What are you doing here? Not that you're not always welcome."

"You and your Chautauqua shenanigans. Got a couple of complaints and thought I'd check them out."

Abby's hands fisted on her hips.

"Really? Complaints? It was a wonderful event. Great music. Enlightening speech. Dancing girls."

He held his hand in the air. "You've outlined the whole issue. Idlewild should make you the keeper of the law." He grinned and rubbed his chest.

"You still having trouble with your heart, Sheriff? You need to get that fixed."

"Not my heart Abby. You already broke that being a married woman." He smirked at her, knowing her response. "A little indigestion and job tension. That's all."

"So, why are you here?"

"Dancing girls for one. The ladies of the county heard about women kicking up their heels. They didn't like it."

"Pshaw." Abby whirled away from him. "People will find something to complain about if they want to grumble. There wasn't anything wrong with the dancing. I danced."

His eyes widened, and he wiggled his eyebrows. "Wish I'd been here to see you kicking up your heels."

Abby handed him a plate and stepped aside for guests who'd been drawn to the buffet by the scent of breakfast and growling stomachs.

"Mister Chesnutt. Mister Bradford. It's nice to see you both again. I enjoyed your talk last night. Help yourselves, please."

Harrison Bradford nodded, not looking at all pleased, and scooped a few eggs onto his plate, adding a biscuit and cup of coffee.

"Not much to sustain a busy man, Mister Bradford."

"I'm a little off my game this morning, Abby. And please call me Harrison."

"Same here, Abby," Charles Chesnutt said.

"You want me to call you Harrison, too?" she teased. "It's strange, but I aim to please."

"No, Charles," he stammered, turning red.

The sheriff came to his rescue. "She's a brat, but she makes a good breakfast." Putting his plate on a nearby table, he reached for a hand to shake.

"Sheriff Hicks, and you are?"

The sheriff joined their table and learned of the night's interruptions by Frank Adams and Joe Foster. Abby watched his scowl grow but let him eat in peace. She wanted to know the names of the women who'd complained about the dancers, but she'd ask him before he left.

As it turned out, she didn't have to. The women came to him. Mrs. Darnell Rumford, Mrs. Reverend Evans, three women Abby didn't know, and one she knew well – Emily Adams, her mother-in-law.

She knew they were trouble as soon as they walked in – three abreast, close together in a double line. They could have been a well-trained infantry the way they marched, shoulders thrust back, chests and chins thrust forward. They moved as a single entity up to Sheriff Hick's table and waited for him to look up from his plate. He took his time, savoring the last of his syrupy pancake and making them wait. When he pushed his chair back, they swooped.

"What are you going to do about this filthy nonsense, Sheriff? It's outlandish, wiggling and shaking," one woman said, her voice shrill and angry.

"Showing legs. It's inviting men to . . . well, ogle and worse," another complained. "It has to be stopped before our children are tainted by their promiscuity. Strippers. That's what they are. Might as well be prostitutes."

Abby stood in the lobby just outside the door and listened.

"Eavesdropping?" her father said.

She jumped, startled, and had the sense to acknowledge his accusation. "You should hear them."

"I think I did, all the way upstairs. What's their problem? What do they want?"

Abby scratched her head. "The dancers to go away? I'm not sure."

Patrick ambled into the room, sure he was about to make a nuisance of himself.

"Top o` the morning to ye, Sheriff." He bowed to the ladies. "And to you Mrs. Reverend, Mrs. Adams, and all the rest of you lovelies I haven't become acquainted with yet."

The two he named had the good sense to appear uncomfortable, and the rest shuffled from foot to foot, unable to form an answer.

"Patrick," he said, ruffling his curls and grinning in the way he knew charmed women. "I would offer ye a wee nip if it's not too early for ye." He peered at the sheriff. "On me, of course, and from my private stock since we can no longer buy it or sell it. What do you say, lasses?"

His Irish brogue blossomed when he turned on his charisma, and it was blooming like warm summertime at the moment.

A stocky woman pushed her way to the front of the group, taking over as spokeswoman from Emily Adams whose tongue had tied in knots.

"We do not imbibe. The demon drink leads to immorality, the disintegration of family and society. And prostitution. You will all find your eternal home in hell. Mark my words, Mister um, Patrick."

Her arm flailed in a dramatic sweeping motion to indicate everyone in the room would land in purgatory, and beads of sweat formed on her brow and upper lip. She yanked on her collar, pulling it from a fleshy neck, and stopped speaking to wheeze for air. Patrick was beginning to feel sorry for her and a couple of the other ladies who had begun to inch away from their new leader.

Emily took advantage of the lull to retake her position.

"Sheriff, I understand there was a scuffle at last night's Chautauqua. Not everyone in this community wants festivities and revelries such as loud music and dancing going on in their town. I do not."

Sheriff Hicks stood, and the ladies were forced to back away. He made sure of that.

"I'm here to listen to legitimate complaints, from anyone, but I haven't heard any. From what I understand, no law was broken. Two men acted out, disrupting events. I might have arrested them had I been there. One was Joe Foster. The other was your husband, Mrs. Adams."

Sheriff Hicks gave a thoughtful pause, dropped his chin and eyed Emily over his glasses. "He ought not to do that."

"What about selling liquor? That's not legal. We saw to that," one of the women screeched.

"If illegal activities are occurring, I'll look into it. Anything else?"

"What about the prostitutes dancing and showing their legs? Aren't you gonna do anything about them?"

Sheriff Hicks rubbed his chest. "We can have that conversation when they stop dancing and start prostituting. Right now, ladies, you're interfering in this man's right to run his hotel. I suggest we move out of his dining room."

"Dining room my Aunt Bertha's rear end."

"Gertrude! For shame."

"Well, come on. It's a bar. With booze. Let's go talk on the porch like he said."

Charles Chesnutt tried to maneuver around the ladies, but a hand on his arm stopped him.

"I'd like to pass," he said, and was struck by how often in his lifetime that word popped up, how often it had unintended meaning. At the moment, he'd like nothing better than to pass by these angry ladies. White women scared him, especially when they were too near or touched him. They were trouble.

"Say," she said, holding onto his arm with a grip he'd have been proud to own. "Aren't you Charles Waddell Chesnutt?"

"I am. And you are?"

She batted her eyes a couple of times and watched for the expected reaction. It didn't come.

"Charity. Charity Evans." She leaned into him. "Ma made me come. I didn't want to. I think it's stupid. Nothing wrong with music and a little dancing." Blond eyelashes flickered again in invitation, and her shoulders swayed.

She was lean and angular, her hair bobbed and cheeks rouged. He could see them up close as they were inches from his eyes. He wanted nothing more than to loosen her claws and flee.

"I've just come from university. I've read your work and love your stories. We should talk. Anytime."

Patrick noted the trouble his guest was in and moved in to give assistance. Charles grinned appreciation and quickly left the room, not waiting for his new friend, Harrison. He was on his own.

Sheriff Hicks led the ladies outside and let them go on about the dancing, music, drinking and prostitutes. He nodded, rubbed his chest, and nodded some more.

Gertrude Evans stuck a bony finger in the air as if pointing the way to heaven and poked it into the sheriff's chest. He stepped back, nearing the limit of what he would take as a public servant; enough was about enough. He held a hand up, palm out, to keep them from closing in and backing him up further. He felt a hand on his back and twisted around thinking a new assault came from behind, but found Samuel, a friendly face.

"Just keeping you from tumbling off the steps, Sheriff."

Gertrude's finger swung to Samuel, and Hicks laughed, glad to share the woman's fury . . . with anyone.

"Mrs. Evans," he said. "Ladies."

He tried to walk by, but Gertrude had other ideas. She glared, renewed the vigor of her pointed finger and hissed at him.

"This sinner was dancing! With Abigail Riley! A married woman."

Samuel's black eyes sparkled when he said, "A *white* married woman."

She sucked in a disgusted snuffle and pinched her lips. "Well, I never! See Sheriff? What are you gonna do?"

"I'm going to thank Samuel for keeping me from breaking a leg falling down the steps backwards because you, madam, keep sticking your knobby finger into my chest and pushing me. You've had your say. There's been no law broken that I'm aware of, and it's time for you to leave. This is private property."

Gertrude's eyes squinted, and her mouth opened, but no sound came out. She flung out an arm like she was calling her troops and trod down the stairs. Charity lagged behind, looking for Charles. When Gertrude saw it, she huffed back, grabbed her daughter's arm and tugged her along.

"You stay away from sinners, girl. You hear me? Dancing leads to no good. Coloreds and whites dancing together . . . You stay clear of that Chautauqua garbage. Vulgar iniquity. That's what it is. A den of vulgar iniquity."

"You sound like a preacher, Ma," Charity said, her shoulders slumped in defeat. She should have stayed at college. This town had nothing for her. Then again . . .

"I'd do a darn sight better than Reverend."

"Why don't you call father by his name? Why Reverend? It's like you don't even know him. Like you don't sleep in the same bed at night." Charity turned to her mother, eyes flashing in delight. "You do sleep in the same bed, don't you?"

Spittle gathered and moved in projectiles from Gertrude's lips. Her face mottled pink and purple.

"Charity Evans, you stop having immoral thoughts. Tisn't proper. And, by the way, I'd likely do a better preaching job. Men are too easy on the sinners. That other one baptized the town prostitutes, for heaven's sake. I was mortified."

"Maybe he was saving them, Ma. Did you never think of that?"

"Harrumph. Not everyone belongs in heaven. That's all I'm going to say on the subject. You get on home. I'm gonna talk with the ladies." She released her daughter and turned back with a scowl when she heard, "Ladies my derriere."

"Charity Evans! You will stay in your room until I tell you to come out."

"That isn't going to happen," she muttered. "I'm just beginning to have some fun."

Chapter Nine

Sunday morning sun streaked through dark clouds and painted an eerie sky. Breakfast over, hotel guests gathered near the windows to watch and wait. Abby listened to homilies about weather, remembrances of storms past and nor'easters that ripped homes apart and made rivers rise high enough to carry away milk cows.

Faces turned upwards to watch jagged, red spears playing with mere mortals who were below envying the power of the threatening storm. They waited for rain or breeze sharp enough to blow away the clouds, thinking they didn't want the pavilion to be their only shelter during a spring squall.

Abby knew Betty was upstairs getting started on the rooms, but she left her alone a while longer so she could watch the panorama unfold from her porch rocker.

She liked a good storm, liked to sit on the covered porch and watch the wind bend trees and gaudy, miscreant lightening streak to the ground. She enjoyed loud thunder and the way it trembled the earth, its supremacy manifest as vibrations skidded into the wooden planks of the porch, through her feet and on up to her heart. Abby swore she could feel its tremor in the beat of her pulse. A good storm was exhilarating in its tyrannical authority.

The air had changed, and she shivered in the chill but didn't want to go in. It smelled wet, clammy, and a single drop had yet to fall, but the atmosphere had prepared. Thunder crashed like heaven tumbled from the sky, and Abby gasped when a shawl dropped over her shoulders.

Phantom leaped to her lap from Bear's arm, his green eyes ablaze with awareness of the elements. She could feel his muscles tense in preparation for the next roll of thunder. Bear sat next to her with Cleo tucked inside his shirt. She didn't have the same appreciation for weather Phantom did.

"Hope it comes and goes soon," Bear said. "Shorty and I have things to do."

"What? Stay here with me and enjoy the show." Abby couldn't drag her eyes from the sky. It had hypnotized her.

"Got a shipment to haul. Just waiting for your buddy, Gus."

"You going if its storming?" The words registered, and she sat back in her chair. "Oh! *That* shipment. You'll be careful, right?"

He rubbed his burly beard. "Likely won't melt in the rain. And I'm always careful."

"But you could be struck by lightning, and no you are not."

"Look who's sitting outside in a storm preaching."

"Sorry. And careful isn't tangling with a mama bear."

"Yeah – that did happen."

Abby sighed, not wanting to leave her chair and the view, but rose and handed Phantom to Bear.

"Gotta get to work or Betty will fire me or quit. Let me know before you take off." The sky broke open before she got to the door.

"Thought the storm got you," Betty said when Abby found her already flipping a sheet in the third room.

"Sorry. I was on the porch watching it."

"Why?"

"Why?"

"Is there an echo in here?" Betty said, her black eyes flashing a look Abby didn't understand. "Why – as in why were you watching the storm? What was it doing?"

"Nothing different. I just like them."

"You are strange, boss." Betty shook her head with a look of pretend sorrow on her face. "Clean the bowl and dust mop the floor, and we're done in this room."

In the eighth room, she surprised Abby by saying she'd like to be done by the time Al left for the day.

"You can go, Betty. Even if we're not done, I can finish by myself. You've done it often enough. And while we're on the topic, I need to hire more help. Can you think of anyone?" Abby ran the mop under the bed and asked, "Why when Al leaves?"

Betty gave a quirky grin, knowing she'd be surprised. "She's going out to the farm today, and I'm trying to be her friend like you asked by going with her. Al wants to move back home."

Abby's face fell. "No. She can't. I mean, she can but she shouldn't. She needs to stay here. Safe."

Betty grabbed the broom and linens, heading for the door. "Bring the dust mop and bucket."

In the next room, she pulled the sheets from the bed and flipped a clean one on. Abby swept the floor and wiped out the wash bowl thinking about Betty who'd been raped and beaten by Al's brothers, repeatedly.

And I asked her to befriend Al. I have some nerve.

She filled the water pitcher and dusted the bureau while Betty finished the bed and ran the dust mop. They worked in silence, each wondering what the next words should be. They found them together.

"I'd want to go home."

"I'd go. So would you."

They giggled and moved to the window together to watch the storm break into a fury. Rain pelted the pane along with small hail pellets. In between blasts, they could see white caps on the lake and ducks riding the crests like they were having fun.

"It'll be hard for her to get here on days like this. And in winter."

"She did it before. Weather didn't stop her from coming to work."

"Since when are you Al's champion?"

"I'm trying to make you see some sense. I'm nobody's champion. Never. Don't want to be." Betty blustered and grabbed the work tools. "Let's go."

"You're a good person, my friend. What about that girl – Charity? The blond bob?"

"What about her, boss? I swear," she said, dragging both the broom and mop down the hall to the next room. "Sometimes you don't make any sense. You surely don't. Bring the bucket."

"To hire. Here at the hotel," Abby added.

Betty's face went blank, eyes wide. "You're not serious. The college girl? White college girl who has manicured fingernails and bats her eyes?"

"Her eyelashes. You can't bat your eyes – unless. Well, you can't. And what's wrong with her? She seemed okay – sort of."

Betty's hip came out, and her hand went on it, her fighting stance of choice.

"She's been at *university,* as she tells everyone she meets. Why would she want to make beds here?"

"What's wrong with here?" Abby asked.

Betty's head dropped as if exhaustion had set in, and she released a long, intentional sigh.

"You ask her then, Abby."

Before she could respond, loud voices drifted up the stairway and into the room. Both women ran to the door in time to hear the first refrain from *I Shall Be Whiter than Snow* coming from the bar, now called the dining room in honor of prohibition. The irony made Abby smile.

Both ladies went to the landing and joined the choir. *Now wash me, and I shall be whiter than snow.*

Shorty's head poked out of his room, eyebrows climbing his forehead and eyes wide.

"Church?"

Abby's shoulders rose and all three tripped down the stairs, eager to see the people singing praises to the Lord in the hotel dining room in the middle of a thunder storm. The space had filled. Standing room only. Benjamin sat at the piano, and Reverend Jenkins stood at the far end, in front of the buffet – now empty of food.

She spotted her da at the end of the bar and raised her hands in question. He did the same while shaking his head and lifting his shoulders. Most of the folks in the room she sat with every Sunday, except for five or six she'd never seen before, white men in dark suits.

A shiver tickled the back of her neck, and she thought of Cassandra, but turned to Shorty.

"Who are they?" she asked.

"Don't know."

"They came for church?" Her voice was strained, hopeful but skeptical of her own suggestion.

"Doubt it."

"Have you seen them before, Betty?" Abby asked.

"Nope. Never."

"Maybe they came for the Chautauqua last-day events," Abby suggested, and Betty rolled her eyes. Abby wondered how Betty knew things she didn't – just knew things.

Shorty shifted and looked around for Bear who came in from the front porch with a wet cat. He signaled Shorty to follow, and Abby went along. Upstairs in his room, Phantom leapt from his shoulder to the bed, and he pulled Cleo from his damp shirt and set her on his pillow. She made a nest of it and closed her eyes.

"Well? Do you know who they are? Why they're here?" Abby asked.

"According to Jesse, they're from White Cloud, the businessmen's association or some such nonsense."

"What do they want here?" Shorty asked.

Bear's scowl said it wasn't good.

"What? Tell us." Abby said.

Shorty's boot toe kicked at the dresser leg, and he made a sound like a warthog. "Damned busybodies. Can't leave folks alone."

"Will you explain before I go downstairs and ask them myself what they're doing here?"

"What group do you know who advocates America being restored to a white, protestant nation and is against race-mixing, immigrants, alcohol and what they perceive as immorality? Ring any bells, Abby?"

Her breath caught in her throat. Fear turned her face white and her eyes into round saucers.

"KKK?" It was whispered, the vile letters that brought brutal visions to her mind and remembered nightmares to others – of killing and lynching, of fire and hate. "It can't be. From White Cloud?"

"I believe so. Jesse does, too," Bear said.

"But the Branch brothers are from there. The founders of this resort," she said, questioning their facts.

"Several cities in Michigan have Klan populations, even small northern cities," Bear said. "I think the Chautauqua weekends and the popularity of the resort brought us to their attention."

Abby dropped onto the bed, her chin in her hand. It didn't seem real. They hadn't had to worry about the Ku Klux Klan back in Nirvana, or bootleg booze and thugs from Chicago. She wanted to go home, and it made her think of Al.

"I have to find Betty. Are you still going to – wherever it is you're going?"

"Soon as Gus gets here," Bear said.

She left the room and looked down from the landing. There he was, standing with his arms around two ladies dressed in evening gowns. All three stood just inside the door between the lobby and the dining room and, with pure heart and great volume, were singing *I Shall Be Whiter than Snow*.

Abby stared, stunned, and, when the words connected with the picture, she giggled and couldn't stop. She wobbled down the stairs and sat on the last step, put her face in her hands and tried to choke back the laughter until tears ran down her face; the tension and the joy of the day had become too much. The KKK. The thugs. Bootlegging. Al.

On a particularly loud, laughing sob, Gus turned and saw Abby in apparent distress. Believing she was hurt, he ran and picked her up by the shoulders until her toes dangled off the floor

"Who did this? Who hurt you? I'll kill him."

"No one, Gus," she choked out, but her neck had turtled into the shoulders she hung by, and she couldn't speak too well.

"Put her down, Gus," Sue said. "She's trying to talk. I think."

By this time, the congregation had heard the commotion and gathered in a tight crowd in the lobby: regular church goers, KKK, friends and prostitutes who were friends.

"Let's praise the Lord with *I Shall Be Whiter than Snow.* Sing it, now," Sue shouted.

"Stand on the third step so they can see you, Sue," Sally said. "You look lovely, today. Now say it again."

Sue repeated her words, and Abby choked again, a continuing sob-giggle, and Gus put her down but wrapped an arm around her, pulling her into the protective shelter of his massive arm.

"Who is he?" whispers flowed across the room. "Who's the giant colored? Haven't seen him before."

"Let's sing. Could it get any better than this?" Sue begged, her beautiful face glowing with religious fervor.

When the refrain ended, thunder cracked louder than most had ever heard. Everyone jumped, and faces turned heavenward, some in fear, some in passion.

The clouds parted, making a path for a sliver of sunshine, and the rain ceased.

Reverend Jenkins' hands went up in praise, and Abby slipped from Gus' one-armed embrace to go in search of Betty and Al. She found them in the kitchen at the table.

"What are you two up to? Concocting trouble?"

"Waiting," Betty said. "Don't want to drown."

"I think it's safe to go now. I'd like to go with you, but too many people are in the bar – I mean dining room."

"Give it up, boss. You'll never get it right."

Abby's head bobbed back and forth sideways, looking foolish but agreeing.

They walked in silence, cutting through the woods and along the edges of fields belonging to the Adams family. Betty's feet quit moving at the end of the rutted Tatum driveway, and she stared at the broken house. Weeds had grown tall around the rickety porch, and vines covered the posts and climbed to the roof. The door hung at an angle from one hinge, and a window pane was shattered. She wondered how many more had been the object of stones slung from a neighbor boy's sling.

Al ignored Betty and kept walking, head down, eyes on the dirt in front of her shoes. When Betty realized she'd been left behind, she double-timed to catch up.

"Wait. I'm coming."

"I didn't ask you to."

"I know. I didn't ask you to ask me."

Al picked up a foot to climb the steps of the porch, and Betty grabbed her arm, pulling her back. "You think it's safe?"

"Been this way forever."

"Will it hold me? I'm bigger."

"Put your feet where mine go."

Al stepped, and Betty followed.

Together, they pulled at the cocked door and wedged it open, stepped over the threshold without mishap and stopped. A dust covered cast iron kettle sat on the stove, and dirty dishes were heaped in the dry sink. More were on the table, some with bits of dried food stuck to the insides. Critters had taken any worth licking up or hauling off.

It smelled of animal urine and feces, and Betty pulled a kerchief from her pocket to hold over her nose. Skittering noises from behind the stove made them turn their heads, and, when she spotted the long gray body, Betty moved to stand on a chair while mama opossum led four of the cutest ugly babies out the door. She glared up at Al, who wouldn't be bothered to move out of the way, as she waddled by her immobile feet.

They walked through the single living space and up into the sleeping areas. Betty wouldn't have called them bedrooms. They weren't rooms at all, just four walls and lots of beds with ratty curtains hanging from ropes. She speculated where Al had slept, where she'd found any privacy in a house full of men. She tried not to think what it had been like for her, but the frown on her face was fixed.

"He hasn't been here," Al said.

"Who hasn't?"

"Pa."

"How do you know that?" Betty did a little hop-skip when a mouse scrambled out of the way. Clearly it wasn't happy about the intruders in its house.

"It looked like this before."

"On the night . . ."

Al didn't let her finish. "Yes."

"Where would he be then if . . .?"

"Don't know," Al said, interrupting again.

She seemed ready to leave the house, so Betty followed. They secured the door by wedging an old chair under the knob, and Betty again traced Al's steps to get off the porch without breaking through the rotted lumber. They stood side by side, gazing at the rope swing hanging from an old oak, the dog house that no longer had a whole roof, the chicken coup barren of chickens.

Al had enjoyed taking care of the hens. They gave eggs in appreciation, and she didn't have to wring their necks for dinner. She'd saved them from her father and brothers with the threat of no breakfast. They were her friends. She talked to them, and they had responded with gentle clucks. She hoped Samuel had found good homes for them. He'd said he would.

"You okay?" Betty asked as Al moved toward the barn.

"Course."

At the door to the barn, she tried to turn Al back. Betty knew the horror contained in those dusty gray walls, the pain and suffering, and didn't want Al to see it. *She* didn't want to see it.

Betty put a hand on Al's arm, but the tiny blond jerked it away with more strength than she should have.

Al walked in and ran her hand down the center post where she'd been tied and where her brothers had always taken their punishments. They'd wrap their arms around it and hold on, to their tears and screams, their pain and fury, and to each other. It's what kept them alive – along with their hate.

After, she had bathed their wounds, salved and bandaged them, knowing they'd taken beatings in her stead, kept him from her until they couldn't – because they'd been taken away for arson . . . and for raping the girl standing next to her.

She knew about it, though she didn't want to. They said what they'd done was okay because Betty was colored, and Al had shut her eyes and ears and pretended it wasn't hers to care about because she needed her brothers to keep her safe.

The ropes her father used to bind her that night still hung from the post, and the breeze from the open door blew them round and around. She frowned, thinking it sounded like something she'd been forced to do in school – dance around the May pole. She hated dancing, stepping and hopping and doing what somebody else said. But that school May pole didn't compare to the one in the barn.

She'd passed out at the end, hoping death would come for her. But she remembered the leather whipping across her arms, chest and face, the belt buckle smashing against her spine and legs. And the blood . . . all the blood.

She knew why her father hated her so much because he'd screamed it at her in his drunken rage - *You killed her! You killed your mother! You killed her!!*

It burned into her brain. Tears gathered, and she blinked them away. Angry.

She grabbed a rake and swept the dirty straw from around the center post and into the barn yard. Seeing Al's hooded eyes, Betty found a second rake to help. They shoved the barn doors wide open, and the sun streamed in, dancing with the dust motes and warming the space with light. They gathered the rest of the straw, all the way from the corners, and pushed it into the yard to let the wind blow it away. Their muscles were tight, and their clothes grimy, but the room was clean.

"Let's go, Al. I'll walk you back to the hotel."

"I'm not a dog."

Betty's eyebrows came together, and her forehead furrowed in confusion.

"Why'd you say that?"

"I don't need walking. Like I'm tied to a rope."

"Well, of course you don't. I don't . . . oh. I get it." Betty chuckled, and Al kept walking toward the Adams farm.

"You can go on home," she said. "I know the way."

Betty nodded, but Al wouldn't know because her eyes were intent on where her feet would go next.

"Your skin is the fairest I've ever seen. Do you sunburn easy?" Betty asked, trying to find something to talk about with the taciturn girl.

"Yes. You?"

Betty's feet stopped moving, and she watched Al get further from her. She was stunned, and her shoulders hunched with tension. Was Al being nasty? Funny? She didn't have a funny bone.

Al turned around with a smirk on her face before long. Her eyes rolled up and to the right, and Betty knew. She had made a joke!

"That was funny, Al. Really funny. Got any more?"

She caught up, and they strolled side-by-side listening to the birds' twitter overhead, enjoying the warmth of the sun and the scent of damp loamy fields.

"Where do you think your pa is?" Betty asked, breaking into the silence.

"Dead."

Betty's feet stopped again, but she skipped forward knowing Al's would keep on moving.

"Why do you say that?"

"Cuz he'd be there."

"Maybe he's hiding? Maybe he's afraid somebody will arrest him for what he did to you."

Al's silky blonde hair flipped in the breeze as she shook her head.

"He could be somewhere else. He doesn't have to be dead." Betty listened to Al's silence, waiting. "Are you sad?"

"No. He never went back into the house. I know."

Betty wasn't sure how to respond to Al's certainty and acceptance. "You still want to move back to the farm?"

She nodded. “I’m cutting through the woods now. You don’t have to.”

Chapter Ten

"Don't serve drinks to the strangers in suits," Abby told Jackson after dragging him into the corner for a quick conversation. "And ask if they'll be staying for lunch and would like a coffee or soda."

Jackson scratched his head. "What's going on?"

"I don't trust them. For now, only the guests living on the premises will be served alcohol, and we won't take their money at the table. I'll put it on their room charges. Drinks will be included in the fee. Prohibition."

"What about Samuel or Jesse or the ladies? Or the other regulars?"

"I'll take care of them at the bar. In coffee cups."

"The world's going crazy, Abby."

"That's for sure."

She moved to where Jesse and Edna sat with their daughter, Daisy.

"Maybe we should have church here every Sunday," Edna said. "Fills up the bar. Good for business."

"The *dining* room," Abby said, glancing toward the strangers.

Edna's eyes widened. "Yes. That's what I meant."

And she was unfortunately right. But Abby would have preferred everyone to leave. She needed bit of peace and serenity, but the place overflowed with customers.

Waiting in the corner, Sue and Sally surveyed the room, shrugged to each other and sashayed over to the strangers' table. They knew the type and were ready to have some fun.

Sue took the vacant chair and leaned forward, breasts spilling from her dress and onto the table as she deliberately smoothed the fabric downward. All eyes watched as she displayed the voluptuous bounty never more than barely held in check by red satin.

Her eyes moved from one man's face to the next, assessing the red creeping from their collars, the spittle gathering at the corners of their lips, the hitch in their breathing. She'd bet dollars at least two of these had visited their house in the dark of night.

"What you looking at, boys?" she said in her smokiest voice. She ran a finger down the nearest hand and nipped the end of his finger. He jerked, and all eyes flicked away from her breasts to stare at each other, embarrassed at their own lust and accusing the rest.

Sally draped an arm over a shoulder and bent to tweak an ear with her full lips, causing him to shove backwards with a horrified grunt.

"Not very friendly. What's a matter, sugar? Loving embarrass you?"

He wiped at the side of his face as if a mosquito had climbed into his ear, and Sally stiffened.

"You don't like brown sugar, do you sugar?"

Samuel, watching the interplay, wondered if he should intervene or wait to see how it would end on its own. He loved Sue and Sally, and, if any winners would be named, he'd bet on them. But he didn't know these men.

"Join me, ladies," he said. "I've been waiting for you." He patted stools on either side of him, and they left the strangers' table with a show of reluctance.

"See you tonight," Sue said to the man with the nipped finger. She winked, and he gasped and sputtered as she shuffled away.

Reverend Jenkins shared a table with Harrison Bradford. Charles Chesnutt sat on a stool next to Jesse and Edna. Several others milled around the room or found seats at other tables – Maggie and Micah Chambers, Ratty Branch with his brother Del, and the strangers.

The white men in suits tainted the atmosphere.

Charles understood when Abby asked what he would like in his coffee. His eyes twinkled in sympathy to her dilemma.

"If it weren't for prohibition, I'd be having whiskey in it, but I'll take it however you make it."

Jesse chuckled, said he'd like the same, and Edna grinned. With careful questions and answers, they maneuvered through the problem, but Abby wondered how they would continue or even if they should. Walking on hot coals would be easier. One misstep could mean more trouble than they could handle.

Patrick came from the kitchen with Irish stew in a big, black kettle, and Abby helped carry bowls and platters of soda bread to the buffet table. People became too intent on food and their stomachs to care much about the strangers, and the noise was restricted to the clatter of cutlery and clink of the spoon against the bowl along with groans of satisfaction.

Benjamin serenaded lunch with a peaceful tune, and Abby swayed back and forth in time to its rhythm. For the first time all day, she felt the tension easing from her spine and chastised herself for imagined tragedies.

In the semi-quiet, one of the strangers stood, pulled a stack of flyers from his pocket and began to read from one. "We are here to invite you to join our society, a social order dedicated to maintaining white supremacy, to preserving our homes and the chastity of womanhood, to . . ."

Patrick sailed through the kitchen doors like a tempest had tossed him. He'd been waiting. He reached up, grabbed the speaker by the collar and twisted it until the man's throat constricted and he had no air left for words. Patrick turned into an Irish dervish, and he moved toward the rest of the strangers with the collar tight in his hand, glaring.

"What is this man doing?" His voice thundered.

"What every conscientious white man should do," another said. He, too, stood and faced the crowd, finishing what his friend had started.

"You make a mockery of womanhood by welcoming prostitutes into your midst. You make a mockery of white supremacy by the mixing of the races. You make a mockery of America by your allowance of . . ."

Patrick snatched at his collar, but the man grabbed the fliers and leaped out of reach. He ran to throw a stack in front of Charles Chesnutt, more at Abby, several on the Branch men's table and startled Charity with a handful as she came in the door. They had targeted every white person in the room – they thought.

Patrick lost his grip on the first man's collar and fumbled to get it back, but Samuel took over, relieving him of the responsibility.

"Divorce, adultery, alcohol, Catholicism, immigration, evil . . ." a third man screamed, but Jesse's fist interrupted his tirade.

He hit the floor and stayed there, but two more headed toward Jesse. Charles led one to the exit and Reverend Jenkins the other. Harrison Bradford grabbed the last one by his earlobe and gently removed him from the hotel.

"You're white," he screamed at Charles and Patrick. "For shame."

"I could have been had I chosen to," Charles said with sincere calm. "I didn't."

"And I am simply Irish," Patrick said and led the man across the porch and down the steps. "And you are an arse. An evil monster. Get off my property."

The man brushed his hands over his suit and puffed his chest. "You'll regret this. Mark my words. You are bringing about the downfall of this great nation."

He ran when Patrick stepped toward him, fists out and ready, all the way to the road where he waited for his friends, out of reach of the mad Irishman. Every time the man opened his mouth, Patrick stepped his way, and he closed it. It became a game, and Patrick was enjoying it. He nudged Charles.

"Watch." He took three long strides toward the road, and the man ran. Patrick stopped, and he stopped. Patrick stepped. The man ran.

Charles' laugh resonated. He clapped Patrick on the back when he returned to the porch.

"Thank you. You took the sting out of this idiocy, this pestilence of ignorance."

"You, *Passing*, are welcome. I am ashamed of my race."

"Thought you were just Irish," he said, a sparkle shining through the weight of generations of sorrow in his eyes.

The strangers walked away – all the way down to Foster's store where Joe stood outside watching, his arms folded across his chest. He shifted his weight and waited for them to get nearer before shaking his head and calling them *nambies*.

"I saw you running away from that Irish runt. What mamas' boys, running away like little girls. Didja cry, too?"

He jerked on his shirt like the point had been made and agreed upon. The movement said he wouldn't run like they had.

"We did what we set out to do," the tallest man said. "They're on notice."

Joe sneered. "Do they know that, Longstreet?"

"Pretty sure they do." His voice was low and slow, and he stepped toward Joe who backed up, but shoved his chin out trying to maintain his fragile position within the group. "Thought I made it clear there would be no names."

Joe made a show of looking first one way down the road and the other. "Don't see anybody listening. Do you?"

"You can be a real smartass, friend. Could get yourself in trouble that way."

"You got nothing without my information, and you know it. You need me, so back off . . ."

The man's name started to slide off his tongue again, but the fear in his brain caught it and dragged it back in time. Beads of sweat popped on his brow, and Longstreet smiled. He knew Joe had only brief moments of bravado, and they melted into sweat with a well-aimed glance in his direction.

"We're expecting to hear from you, understand?" he said, moving in so he could tower over the shorter man.

Joe yanked on his droopy pants, hauling them up to his chest, trying to salvage some dignity.

"When it comes in, you'll know."

"We could have met you in Baldwin, Gus. Told you we'd meet you there," Bear said.

"Know that. I wanted to see the place I'm working with."

"Well, you saw it. Feel better now?"

Bear rode with Gus, but Shorty rode his gelding, not wanting to add his weight to the load they'd be coming back with. And he liked the advantage of altitude on top of his large horse. He was used to height.

"I do. Nice place. Wanted to see that little Abby again, too. She's something, she is."

Bear and Shorty looked sideways at Gus, warnings darting from their eyes.

"You don't mess with Abby," Shorty growled.

"He's got that right," Bear said.

Gus opened his mouth in laughter, making both men glance at each other, back at Gus and each other once again.

"Wish you could see your eyes," he said. "Look like you seen ghosties."

"What're you doing, Gus? Testing my mettle?" Shorty said.

"Just having some fun. Gonna be a long ride. Want to tell me a story, or you want me to tell you one?"

Shorty and Bear looked at each other, a long hard look that said, 'What the hell have we gotten ourselves into?'

Gus took their silence as a yes.

"Here's one you'll like. Way back when I was just a lad, my ma found tobaccy in the pocket of my trousers. Well, she lit out after me, and I ran off into the woods smack into an old grizzly bear right near the pond, and he chased me into it. I was running so hard, I stood atop of an old bull gator afor I knew it. I balanced myself like a tight rope walker in the circus while he paddled us to the other side. I didn't have any shoes, and it was a good thing cuz it made standing on him real easy. When he bumped into the marsh grass, I leapt off and ran some more. Back on solid ground I kept my feet moving. It started to get dark, and I'd got pretty lost, but a big ole gray wolf came sniffing around thinking I was his supper, and I was pretty hungry, too, by that time, so I stuck my fist in his face and shook it at him. He came at me, so I bopped him in the nose, and he left, saying if I followed, he'd lead me home."

"Now you're just lying, Gus. That could never happen," Bear said.

"Why you say that?"

"Cuz it didn't. It couldn't. That's just crazy."

"You think I didn't have any tobaccy, don't you?" Gus said, slapping his leg and snorting in delight. "Well, you're right. That part was a lie."

Gus told stories for the next twenty miles, some of which made sense, and Shorty found himself wishing he was the one sitting next to him. Sometimes he had to lean in in order to hear everything and told Gus to speak up. Gus raised his eyebrows.

"Really? *You* telling *me* to talk louder? Hah. Good one."

They saw Lucy sitting outside her diner and paused to say they'd be back. She eyed Gus when they introduced him, and Shorty figured she really liked big men, remembering how difficult it had been to get away from her the first time.

"She's gonna love you, Gus," Shorty told him when they drove off.

"Why you say that?" he asked.

"You just wait."

They pulled into Custer and drove behind the bar where they'd found Hank. Bear went in, and the other men waited with the horses and cart.

The back door opened, and out Hank sauntered, straw boater still squarely on his narrow head, face still sporting the wispy mustache. He came to a halt midstride when he looked at the cart. Bear, who followed close behind, made introductions, pointing like a good host should.

"Gus, Hank. Hank, this is our partner, Gus."

Hank's eyes took in the biggest, darkest man he'd ever seen, and he turned white. He fumbled with a handshake in which his small hand disappeared. Gus smiled at the man's discomfort but felt bad and tried to modify it.

"Seems I startled you, Hank. Sorry about that."

"No, not at all. It's just, I never . . . nothing. Everything is fine."

Bear was losing patience. "Point the way, Hank."

"I call it *the store*. Follow me."

He led them to another building behind the bar and opened the doors. Inside were stacks of crates full of bottles, hundreds of crates.

"Jeez," Gus whispered. "Now this is a store." He slapped Hank on the back, who stumbled and fell face first to the floor.

"Sorry, man. Didn't mean to do that."

Shorty picked him up and dusted him off. He scooped his hat from the floor, shook it, and plopped it back on Hank's head.

Darkness claimed the night by the time they pulled behind the hotel, taking the back way to avoid going by Foster's store. Shorty slid from his horse and threw open the door to the stable. Gus drove straight in, happy to find room for his two geldings and the cart.

Shorty unloaded half the bottles, stashed them in the corner and covered them with straw while Gus and Bear rubbed down the horses. They worked in the dark, but their eyes had adjusted to night on the ride home, so it was easy work. They watered and fed the horses and stepped back, arms crossed, pensive.

"Thanks for taking me along. Should last awhile," Gus said.

"It's a long haul, but worth it not to invite trouble here," Bear said. "Leaving them harnessed?"

"Yeah. I'll be going."

"Sit a spell and get some food first," Shorty said. "I know Abby will have some waiting."

They went in through the kitchen where Abby had a fire under leftover cabbage soup.

"Heard you," she said. "Sit. Want a drink first?"

"Absolutely." Shorty held a full, uncorked bottle in the air like a trophy.

Patrick pushed through the swinging doors when the first glug of whiskey splashed into the glass.

"You have your ear to the door, Irish?" Shorty asked.

Patrick's lips curled in an elf-like smirk. "Was protecting the front porch while you boys did your deed. Thought you might need to tell me all about it now you're back safe and sound."

"You were guarding, huh?" Bear said. "Keeping the wolves from the door?"

"That's right. Keeping the family safe. Any troubles on the road?"

Gus laughed. "Only one. Thought I might not make it outta Logan. Lucy appeared determined to chain me to the chair."

"Better you than me," Shorty said.

"Better either of you," Bear said. "But I think you malign the lovely lady. And I'd pay to see it again. When she came to the table and threw her arms around your neck, Gus, I thought you actually turned white."

"Now that'd be a trick I wish I could perform. Make me a million dollars in the circus."

Shorty clapped him on the back and thanked him for taking Lucy's attentions while Patrick and Abby's head spun back and forth trying to follow the banter. She finally threw her hands in the air and shouted.

"Stop! Who is Lucy, and why would she keep you prisoner?"

"Amorous intentions," Bear said. "She was infatuated with Shorty last time through, and I think his feelings are hurt now that Gus stole his girl."

The door swung open and Al came to a halt halfway through.

"Sorry," she said, backing out of the kitchen. Abby stepped toward her and took her arm.

"Join us, Al. You don't need to hide in your room. Come on in and have a seat."

"I don't hide."

Abby looked crestfallen. "I didn't mean it like that. I meant . . . Come on in."

Shorty stood and pulled a chair closer to her, between the table and the door, and stared at her until she sat. She was far enough from the rest of the group to be separate but close enough to hear the conversation and not feel like she had to participate.

Al wondered how Shorty had known exactly where to seat her, and she watched the group with well-disguised interest. She thought they'd be on the porch when she came to fetch water for washing up. Normally that's where they were. She didn't like interrupting them. It was one of the reasons she wanted to go home, that and the fact that it *was* home, hateful memories and all.

When they introduced Gus, he made Al stand up so he could position himself next to her. She looked like a young child by his side, and it brought a twinkle to his eyes.

"You're so tiny, girl, you could fit in my pocket. You're so damned tiny, you could be a kewpie doll I'd put on my shelf. I could break you in two just by giving you a hug which I'm gonna do right now, but I'm not gonna break you."

Gus bent for the hug and picked her up around the waist, his arms wrapping all the way around and back to him. Her feet and arms dangled like the doll he'd called her. Most faces in the room lit in grins.

"Put her down," Shorty said. "Leave her be."

"Yes, sir, Mister. Shorty. Gotta set you down now. Thanks for the hug."

Al hadn't said a word, but her eyes flamed with something close to happiness.

Abby ladled soup into bowls and sliced soda bread, putting it all on the table for whoever wanted sustenance. While their mouths were full and chewing replaced talk, Abby asked about Al's trip home, hoping she didn't offend the girl with her interest.

She never knew for sure.

"It was fine."

"The house hadn't been taken over by critters?"

Al shook her head.

"I understand your desire to be in your own home, Al, but I want you to know you're always welcome here, too. You know that, right?"

"Yes. I know."

Shorty stopped spooning soup to stare at the young woman. "You moving home?"

When she nodded, he frowned.

"You wait for help. I mean it. I don't want you moving in there until we check it out." He paused and lined his spoon up next to the butter knife, inching it over to be parallel and even at the bottom. His eyes flickered back to Al. "You hear me?"

Abby thought she saw the hint of a smile curve Al's lips, but it escaped in a flash, so she wasn't sure.

"I hear you."

Chapter Eleven

"Take the buggy," Abby said.

"We don't need it. Our legs work just fine."

"It'll be quicker and you'll get more done. Just do it. Don't be so stubborn, Betty."

"Alright, okay. Gee whiz, boss. Sometimes you are really . . . bossy." She said it with a frown, but an arm went around Abby's shoulder, and she squeezed.

"Are you making progress out there?" Abby asked. "I wish I could help."

"Yeah. That'd be nice, but then you'd have to hire Charity Evans to fill in, and I don't know how that'd work."

Abby walked her to the front porch where Al waited. "She might be a perfectly nice person. You don't know."

Betty's eyes rolled. She batted her thick black lashes and tilted her head at Abby.

"We're taking her buggy, Al. She beat me til I agreed."

The kitchen and living area plank floors gleamed, and the room smelled like lavender and pine. They'd spent days scrubbing the cook stove, walls, cupboards and, finally, the floors. The windows sparkled, and the sun poured in, making the room look comforting as it never had before, not in Al's memory. They paused in the doorway, gazing at the space, and Al almost smiled.

"Looks nice, doesn't it," Betty said. "It's alright to say so, Al. Where to now? Upstairs?" She had helped every smelly, dirt-filled step of the way and thought Al was beginning to accept her presence. While Betty might not admit it to Abby, she kind of liked the girl.

Never, not ever, would she have believed liking a Tatum a possibility. Even if Al wasn't one of the sons, she bore the name Tatum, and that was a tall mountain to climb over. But Strange Al was okay.

"That's fine," Al said.

Upstairs, they sneezed as they pulled down the dusty blankets hanging between the beds. The air grew thick as Betty moved the broom across the ceiling, stirring up dust and spiders. She shivered as they fell to the floor and cringed as she stepped on them. She didn't like killing, not even spiders, and hoped they and God understood.

"Open a window, Al," she said between choked coughs. "I can't breathe."

Al opened two and threw the blankets outside to the ground. All the ticked mattresses followed. She pulled apart the bed frames and tossed them out piece by piece. All except one.

Betty swept with one eye on Al and the other on the spiders. When she finished the ceiling and walls, she started on the floor.

"I'm gonna sweep you up if you don't scoot, Al. Just for a minute."

She swept around and under Al, retrieved a bucket of water heavily doused with lye and went back for the mop. Her eyes watered, and she blinked back lye tears until she could see.

"Wait a minute," Al said. "Almost done with this one."

Betty went to the open window to cleanse the odor of lye from her lungs with fresh air and watched the birds in a nearby tree. A robin's nest tucked into the crook between two branches was filled with noisy young. While she watched, an adult female flew to the nest's edge, and small mouths opened wide awaiting their meal. The bright male followed with more.

A brood of nestlings this late meant the first hatch had probably been destroyed, and the adults had tried again. Critters don't give up on each other, she thought. They keep doing what they're meant to do, and the parents take care of their young. Moisture clogged the back of her throat, and she cleared it, irritated at her instant sorrow.

Birds, for crying out loud.

But she didn't mourn for lost winged critters at the top of an oak tree. She grieved for lives no longer lived in this house. Or more accurately, for the people who hadn't made this house a home. She could feel despair seeping from the walls like liquid heartache. It eased with the cleansing they were giving it, that and the absence of intentional malice.

Al dragged the pieces of the last bed frame to the window, and Betty helped her toss them to the ground. She smacked her hands together, ridding them of dust and drawing in a breath of satisfaction.

"Look at the babies," Betty said, pointing to the nest.

"They always nest there."

"Do you think it's the same robins each year? The same Mama and Papa?"

"Maybe."

They watched them feed. Back and forth the adults flew, and with each return, the little mouths opened wide in confident anticipation of nourishment.

"It's nice, isn't it? Right outside your window. You gonna be okay in this big room all by yourself? Doing for yourself?"

Al drew back and looked at Betty, eyes wide and eyebrows raised in surprise at the question.

"Course. I've always done for myself."

"But they were here. Your pa and . . . brothers." She didn't even want to utter the word, as the thought of them filled her with repugnance. But there it was, hanging in the air between them.

Al glanced sideways at Betty, knowing how she must hate the boys who had beaten and violated her. She understood, and there was no way to explain her feelings about them to Betty, or to anyone. But in a bizarre way, they had loved their sister, and she both loved and hated her brothers for who they were and what they'd done – the good and the bad. Except for Marcus, who had a kind heart, and she held on to that.

"I'm gonna scrub the floor," Al said and grabbed the mop.

"What do you want me to do while you do that?"

"Wash the windows so I can watch the birds grow up."

"You plan on moving back here while they're still in the nest? That's gonna have to be soon then. Hold that mop water a minute."

She dampened a clean rag and rubbed at the pane. When it sparkled, she moved to the second one.

"Guess you could be here sometimes," Al said.

Betty kept on wiping at the window, pondering her words, not sure she'd heard them correctly. The mop swished across the floor, moving Betty toward the stairs as it went. They stood side-by-side at the door looking back at the large, clean room. Empty except for a single bed frame with sagging ropes, it seemed bigger than it had a couple of hours earlier.

"It needs a chest of drawers and an armoire," Betty said.

"I don't have any."

"Doesn't mean you can't get them. People buy things. You know – with money."

Al didn't feel the need to respond. It wasn't a question. She turned and went down the stairs, carrying the bucket and mop. Outside, she dumped the water, rinsed the mop head at the pump and took them both into the barn. When she came out, Betty had the pieces of a bed frame under the pump, rinsing the dust from them, and Al watched, perplexed.

"I'm going to store those in the barn," she said.

"Not this one."

Al raised an eyebrow.

"This one goes back up when it dries. It's where I'll sleep . . . sometimes. What'll we do with these?" Betty pointed to the dusty, almost flat mattresses lying on the ground where Al had flung them from the window.

"Burn pile."

"Now? What'll you sleep on?"

"Nothing would be better."

Betty shrugged and retrieved one of the filthy things. She held it gingerly away from her, not wanting to catch any bugs that might be hiding inside, and dragged it to a spot safe for flames. When they were all in a pile, Al dumped kerosene in the middle and lit the fire.

As soon as the fire burned through the ticking, the dry straw and feathers inside went fast, and a gray cloud spiraled into the sky. They watched from a short distance holding rakes in case errant sparks tried to escape and burn something unintended. Al snorted at the idea. Little here was of use. Just the four walls of the house and the barn.

"Does it make you sad, Al?"

The blond head swung back and forth, eyes forward, never leaving the waning fire.

"It'd be okay if you were a little sad. I might be."

"I'm not. Leave it alone."

"Okay. Sorry. Are we done here? Should we water down the area?"

Al nodded and took the rakes into the barn, returning with a bucket. She filled it and dampened the ashes while Betty retrieved the borrowed mare and buggy from where she happily munched on grass. It was a quiet ride back.

Betty got out at her house after handing the reins to Al. "Sure you're okay to drive this thing by yourself?" she asked, standing with one hand on the buggy, ready to leap back in if it tried to take off.

"Course."

Al moved to the center of the seat, unintentionally flicking the leather in her hands and making the mare dance and turn to look at her. Betty noted her stiffened lips, and it occurred to her Al had never handled a horse from this position, not on the ground feeding or grooming it.

"You sure?" she asked.

"I said I'm fine."

"Okay, but I wouldn't mind driving back with you." Al made the clicking sound she thought would move the mare forward, and her shoulders relaxed.

"Thank you, Betty," she called back, surprising the worried girl she'd left behind. She wouldn't have admitted her nervousness to Betty – or to anyone. What lived inside her was no one's business. She didn't feel the need to explain or hang her thoughts out like laundry on a line for everyone to see and talk about. They were hers.

They'd had one horse at home, and, like his wife and children, it was her father's property. She and her brothers were never allowed to ride it or use the cart.

"That's what you got legs for. Use 'em," he'd say.

Holding the reins to Abby's mare made her think about her father's horse. Where was it now? Where was the man who had ridden it? Holed up somewhere thinking he'd killed her? Afraid he'd go to jail? Dead?

She couldn't care. Unless he came back. She'd care then – and she'd not let him beat her again. One way or another.

The wide doors were open, and Bear and Shorty were inside putting their own horses up for the night when Al pulled up to the hotel stable. She managed to halt the horse, get down and look over the harness trying to figure out how it came off. Still holding the reins so the mare wouldn't run off, she went around to the other side looking for a buckle or fastener of any sort. She was lost, and the mare seemed bigger than ever.

"It's a breast collar harness, Al," Shorty said from behind her. "You're probably not used to this type. Let me get it for you."

In no time, he unbuckled the traces to relieve the mare of her harness.

"Yours done?" she asked.

"He's done and happy. How about you? Good day?"

"Yup."

"Cleaning again?" he said.

"Upstairs."

"You must be about finished by now, right?"

"Yes."

"Moving soon?"

"Before the robins fly."

Confused by her words, Shorty lifted the harness, and Bear led the mare into the barn. He poured a bucket of oats into her trough and grabbed a brush.

"I should do that, Bear," Al said.

"I will. I like doing it."

"I don't understand," Shorty said, still wondering about Al's plans to move back home. "Is that like 'before the snow flies' or something?"

"What?" she said.

"The robins flying thing."

Al chuckled and both men stepped back to look at her, their mouths open wide. They looked at each other and back at Al.

"You laughed," Shorty said.

Al pulled at her collar, feeling heat climb her neck, and turned to leave once more.

"Wait Al. Didn't mean to hurt your feelings. Sorry," Shorty said. "We don't hear you laugh often enough. It's nice."

"It is," Bear said. "It's very nice."

She stopped walking, looked back at them and stuffed her hands in her dress pockets.

"Baby robins are in a nest outside my window. I want to watch their parents feed them while they grow up."

Shorty patted his chest and grinned at her.

"I get it. I'd like that, too. I'll walk you in. See you in a few minutes, Bear."

From behind the bar, Abby saw Shorty and Al move through the lobby. When Al headed toward the stairs, Abby shouted to her.

"Don't go up. Come in here for a minute, please," adding, "Bring her in, Shorty," before he strolled into the bar. He climbed on his favorite stool and patted the one next to him indicating Al should sit.

"Did you want me?" she said to her boss.

"I did. I want to know how the cleaning went and . . . well . . . everything. Do you need things? Are you excited? When will you move back? Not that I want you to go."

Shorty laughed. "Before the robins fly," he said.

Abby's head tipped, eyes quizzical. "Excuse me? I must have misheard."

"It's a little joke – sort of."

"Hmmm. Okay." Abby nodded understanding, but she didn't, and for a moment she felt left out. She brought Shorty his drink and stared at Al. She'd never offered her a drink at the bar and wondered how that had happened.

"Can I bring something for you, Al? On me, a house warming drink," she said, smiling and hoping she'd say 'yes' and stay for a bit. "It doesn't have to be alcohol if you don't drink it."

"I drink it."

Shorty's head swiveled toward Al, and Abby's eyes grew round.

"Really?" he said. "What?"

"Moonshine."

When Abby brought her a small glass of wine, Al sipped and began to answer Abby's earlier questions. She thought there were too many, but she answered them to be respectful and be allowed to go to her room sooner.

"It's all cleaned. I need new mattresses, a chest of drawers, and something Betty called an armoire. I'm content but not excited, and I want to move back before the robins grow up and leave the nest outside the bedroom window."

She'd added that last part to avoid misunderstanding and more questions. Abby stepped back in surprise and Shorty choked on his beer.

"Don't you ever forget anything, Al?" he asked when the coughing stopped.

"No."

"Then you remember me saying Bear and I want to check everything out before you move in?"

She nodded.

"What are you looking for, Shorty?" Abby asked.

"Anything that doesn't look right."

"Like?" she probed.

Shorty shifted on the stool, uncomfortable saying what he thought. Al helped him out.

"He wants to make sure my pa's gone."

"Is that right?" Abby asked.

"Uh . . . partly. Just want to see for myself. That's all."

"He's gone," Al said.

"How do you know for sure?" Abby asked.

"Everything looked exactly the same as before he . . . as before. I know how it looked."

Shorty smiled.

"If you say so, I believe it. It's that big brain of yours. But I still want to see. You let me know when."

Phantom chose that moment to saunter down the bar. He stopped next to Shorty and sat sphinxlike, waiting. Moments later, Bear appeared, and Phantom crawled his arm to perch on a shoulder.

"How did he know you were on the way," Abby asked.

"He's my alter ego."

"You need a cat, Al," Bear said. "Keeps you warm at night."

"I'll add that to my list."

Abby knew a smile lurked behind her lips, maybe even waltzed in her eyes.

"Speaking of your list, I have a Sears Roebuck Catalog you can look through. Sears has everything you want – except for the cat, but you never know. Maybe one will show up like mine did."

Benjamin came through the door and went directly to the piano. Soothing notes filled the room in a soft melody you didn't hear as much as feel. It entered through your pores rather than your ears and became a part of you. Abby lost the conversation to the music for a while. Bear brought her back.

"He's leaving soon, too. I'm sorry he's going."

"How do you know that?" Abby asked.

"He said. By next week he'll have your old place ready. Nirvana is lucky."

Abby's eyes clouded. She didn't want either of them to go. Even though she'd see Al almost every day and Benjamin frequently, it felt like they were leaving her.

At the end of the bar, Samuel smoothed his mustache and clicked his empty glass on the wood. She gathered herself and went to him.

"I'm really sorry I've neglected you. I wanted to hear about Al's move home."

"Which is when?"

Abby's lips curved in a half smile. "Apparently at a particular time before some particular robins fly."

"Are you being deliberately opaque?"

"I could be. You bring out the worst in me. And Benjamin is going, too."

"So I hear."

She threw her shoulders back in pique. "Does everyone know but me? And I don't have to like them going."

"You can't keep collecting people like they're figurines, Abby. You'll run out of rooms for your guests and end up with a boarding house instead of a hotel. Besides, people aren't porcelain dolls you put on a glass shelf and dust once a week."

"I'd dust them more than that," she mumbled as she moved to rejoin her friends, but he tapped his glass again to get her attention and raised his eyebrows.

"What?" she said.

"Could I trouble you for a refill?"

"Sorry." A smile insisted on curving her lips. Samuel sometimes irritated, once in a while acted kind, and always peaked her interest. But she'd like to slip up on him while he slept and trim his mustache to make it crooked, make something out of place on his perfect person.

"Thank you, Abby."

Jesse and Patrick joined him, and Jackson came up with a drink order. She gave thanks for work, needing her mind occupied.

Bear and Shorty left their crew working on the new Oakmere Hotel, saddled their horses and headed for the

Tatum farm. Al was at work making breakfast, so they figured they'd have the place to themselves.

They flung the reins around the porch rail and took in the area: the barn, the woods, the fallow field. They looked inside the barn for signs a horse might have recently been there, anything that might indicate a presence other than Al. When they were satisfied, they checked the house, careful not to mark up the clean floors.

"Nice job they did in here," Shorty said.

At first glance, nothing appeared out of place, but they weren't done. Something niggled at Bear, made him nervous about Al being alone out here. He couldn't make her stay in town, so checking the farm was the best he could do.

"Let's see what's out there," he said, pointing to the thick forest behind the house.

They rode through the woods, winding around trees and stopping now and then to look at the ground when something looked askew. It had been months since the old man disappeared, and they hadn't really expected to find anything. The area appeared undisturbed and peaceful.

Bear listened to the tranquil voice of nature as he walked through the forest, letting his mare follow at her leisure. He knew it didn't reflect the angst that lived and burned when the old man was here. This serenity couldn't coexist next to the evil that existed in Tatum.

He shivered, shaking off the aura of his thoughts. Something wasn't right, but he didn't know what, couldn't pinpoint what bothered him. He had no concrete reason not to give an all clear.

Two weeks later, Al moved back to her home. She washed the blankets and linens tossed from the windows, hung them on the line to blow in the sunshine breeze, and put them back on the beds. They smelled like the lilacs blooming at the corner of the house. In fact, lilacs scented the whole house from the vase full of purple in the middle of the table.

She had poured over the pages of Sears and Roebuck, counted her savings, and purchased two mattresses with pillows and a tall armoire. It sat majestically in the middle of the far wall and separated the two carefully made beds.

The telltale chirps of baby birds clamoring for dinner came through the open window. A tie, like an umbilical cord, bound her to those birds, and she watched as the adults flew off for more food. She waited at the window until they returned and repeated the process.

Al stood mesmerized by them and didn't notice the swirling dust from travelers on the road until they were almost in the yard. Betty and Abby climbed down from the buggy flanked by Bear and Shorty's horses. They reached into the back and filled their arms with packages.

"You sure it's safe?" she heard Abby ask about the porch. "Were you really on it, Shorty?"

"It'll hold you, promise, but I'll fix it if she'll let me."

They knocked on the door, and Al flew down the stairs to open the door for her first guests. Her heart thumped, and her eyes sparkled, but she didn't know it.

Abby hadn't been in the house since the night she'd frantically searched for Al, afraid her father had killed her. He nearly had.

When she looked around the room, she couldn't believe it was the same place. It was cheerful and pleasant, clean and bright – a place one could be happy.

"It's beautiful, Al," she said. "I love what you've done."

"Betty helped."

"These are for you," Abby said, putting the pile of string wrapped packages on the table.

"Why?"

The question surprised Abby, and she didn't have a ready answer. She was stumped.

"Because . . . um, well, it's kind of like a housewarming gift for a new house owner."

"But I lived here before."

Feeling like a kid who hadn't done her homework and didn't know the answer to the teacher's question, she turned to Betty and back toward the men.

"Help me here?"

Bear shrugged and unbuttoned his shirt while eight eyes stared at him, wondering if he planned to remove it. He slid his hand in along the side of his belly, and a mewling began and grew louder. He pulled out a puff of orange and handed it to Al whose eyes were large round orbs with liquid at the corners.

She blinked and held out her hands to take the little orange tabby, cuddled him to her breast and felt the intense love a mother might have for a child, the love her mother might have had for her – had she not killed her.

"I love him. Him?"

"Yes. And I brought milk and some kibbled stuff Cassandra gave to me. 'Feed him of your spirit,' she said and figured we'd know what that meant. I don't. Do you?"

Al took her eyes from the kitten to look at Bear. "I do. And so do you, Mister Bear."

A clatter from the yard took their attention from the cat and them to the door. Samuel rattled along in a farmer's cart. He pulled up to the barn and dipped his head in an imperial hello. They left the kitchen one by one and went across the front porch, still not trusting it to hold all of them at once.

"What are you doing, Samuel?" Abby asked. "You look funny in that wagon."

"Thank you, my dear."

"I'm not your dear."

"I know, but I like the term. I am simply returning Miss Al's belongings. Sixteen clucking chickens and an old dog."

The hand without the kitten went to cover her mouth. Al swallowed, and swallowed again as she watched Samuel remove crates from the cart, open the tops and pull out chickens – her hens.

Her friends.

Lives she had cared for every morning and night and lives that had cared for her. She'd missed their soft clucking and cooing in answer to her voice and had feared they'd been somebody's Sunday dinner.

When he'd finished pulling the chickens from their crates, he picked up the old dog, who could no longer leap from the cart, and put him on the ground. He peered up, looked around and ambled over to Al. He sniffed a foot and then sat on it.

She smiled and bent to pat his gray head, "Hi, Dog."

"What's his name?" Samuel said.

"Dog," she repeated, and laughter filled the air.

Samuel hefted a sack of feed from the cart and asked where it went. She led him into the barn and the rest followed. It seemed like the thing to do. He stashed the bag in the corner and turned to see Abby staring at the pole where Al had been tied and beaten. Her face blanched white in remembered horror. Samuel moved to her side and nudged her shoulder.

"She's better now. Better than ever," he whispered.

"I pray he's really gone."

"I'm pretty sure you can count on it."

Abby tilted her head to look at him, eyes smoldering with anger at Tatum. "How can I?"

He pulled his gold watch from its pocket and flipped it open. "Gotta go."

"Thank you, Samuel," Al said. A simple response, but the light in her eyes said more, and he was glad he'd taken them all home and cared for them.

"Have you had them all this time?" Al asked.

"Course not. I don't much like critters."

"Then, where were they?" Abby prodded, thinking he likely fibbed.

"At a place. Being cared for. Figured she'd want them back some day. Gotta go. I told you that," he said, moving to the cart. He didn't need anyone knowing any more than that. It would ruin his cold and calloused reputation.

"Uncommon man," Abby said when his dust began to drift away.

"Nice to see him come around now. Used to be he kept to himself and frowned all the time," Betty said. "I think you're a good influence on him, Abigail."

Abby pointed at herself, eyebrows raised. "Me? I don't think so. We get along like oil and water."

"Sure. Let's go see the rest of the house. I want to show off all my hard work. I mean, Al's too. Our work."

She glanced at Al to see if she'd heard, but the girl was busy letting the dog say hello to the kitten. She called to her and went in.

Abby had brought a blue checkered table cloth, and they spread it on the table and replaced the flowers. Al shifted, uncomfortable with presents. Betty showed her the copper kettle she'd brought from her mother's cupboard. It gleamed in the sunlight pouring through the open door.

"Want it to hang by the stove, Al?"

"That's fine."

"Our gift to you," Bear said, "will be porch repair and a couple of shingles that need fixing. Right, Shorty?"

Shorty glanced at Al. "I could start now."

They were being nice, and she didn't know polite protocol. Should she give them something? Say something other than thank you? She'd like them to leave so she could talk with her chickens, find a bed for her cat, ask Dog if he was okay.

Betty stepped in, saving her from saying something she shouldn't and making a stupid mistake. "Want to see upstairs? We worked hard up there, too."

"Sure, we do," Abby said, and followed her to the stairs.

Betty let them all go up first and followed, listening to the *oohs* and *ahs* and wondering why they were sounding so impressed. When she reached the top, she understood.

Two beds with bright patch-work quilts and *Betty-like* squared corners shouted 'welcome' from the sides of the room, and a walnut armoire stood like a monument against the wall between them.

"It's really nice up here, Al. But two beds?" Abby asked. "Who's the other one for?"

"My friend," she whispered. "Sometimes."

All eyes showed surprise and curiosity. Betty moved to Al's side and bumped her with a fist on the shoulder.

"That's me," she said, lips open in a wide toothy grin. "Why you so shocked. You think I'm not a good person for a friend? Well, I am. Right, Al?"

"I didn't say that, Betty," Abby stammered.

"She didn't mean anything," Shorty added.

With all the clamor going on, no one noticed Al had gone to the window. When they stopped talking, they heard the chirps and joined her.

"Ah. Nestlings in the saga of 'before the robins fly,'" Shorty said. "Look how they wait. They know."

Chapter Twelve

Spring had worked its way into summer, and Idlewild bloomed like a bright flower, its petals made of colorful cottages scattered over the grassy landscape. Children's laughter sang out from sunrise to dusk as they splashed in the water of Lake Idlewild. Father's tossed them head first and beamed at their screams of delight. Mothers watched from shore or waded out to swim nearby, counting heads to make sure little ones were all accounted for.

It was a playful dream, unheard of for colored families. Some accepted the bounty and gloried in it, but others had long ago quit believing in dreams.

They blinked in the sunshine to confirm the vision, poked and prodded at the apparent reality to reveal its chinks and cracks, looked at the faces of strangers, listened for harmful intent buried in innocent greetings, and touched the silky wet skin of their children and smiled – tentatively, protectively. They were well aware that dreams had a way of dying, of turning to cold ash.

In the night quiet of their cabins and tents, husbands and wives whispered.

"This time, it's real. We can relax."

"Seems like."

"Enjoy yourself, honey. Go fishing and stop worrying."

"I'm fine. You quit worrying about me."

The kisses came more easily, the loving effortless in the freedom of Idlewild.

More people came to play. They came in buses and automobiles, on horses, in buggies and trains. They filled the hotel and littered the island and the perimeter of the lake with tents, not caring where they slept. They ate at the hotel or cooked over campfires, played music in small groups, and danced to music brought in by Jesse, Edna, Abby, the ILO, and others who planned weekend events.

On Sunday under the pavilion, Reverend Jenkins preached tolerance, redemption and forgiveness. Abby thought he must have heard about the ruckus made by town's women who thought music was created in the soul of the devil. He raised his hands in the air and then pounded a fist on the makeshift pulpit and demanded sinners not judge others unless they were sinless themselves.

Amens proliferated, and, at the back of the congregation, Abby craned her head to see the sinless people voicing their loud approval of Reverend Jenkins' exhortations. When she noted who they were, she decided they couldn't be the sinless, so they were likely opting for less judging. She decided to try that, too.

The choir sang them to the lake where the Reverend waited to baptize those wishing to be washed clean. Some folks lined the dock and kept dry, and others waded right in, enjoying the cool water and waiting their turn.

Abby envied their dip in the lake but headed back to the hotel. It was a work day for her, and people would be checking out as soon as the service ended. While some would spend the week with them, others would be heading back to the cities where work, home, and a different kind of life waited.

She ambled, her eyes still on the lake and enjoying the sunshine and fresh air, relishing every stolen moment. As the hotel got closer, she heard the voices of her father, Shorty and Bear, and . . . she quit moving forward.

Her husband perched next to them, looking like he belonged there. Like he'd never left. He held a cup of coffee with two hands, and his eyes were on her.

Everyone's was.

"Hello, Frank," she said, the quiver in her voice betraying her nerves.

"Abby."

"I . . . Good to see you. How are you?"

"Good. You?"

Abby saw his tongue run around the inside of his cheek, like a trapped hamster looking for an exit, a habit of his when he was nervous. He didn't even know he did it.

"I'm okay."

This is ridiculous. We sound like strangers.

She glanced at her father, who watched with more than casual interest, and at Bear who stroked Phantom hard enough for him to squirm and make a *Mrow a wah wah*. Shorty made no effort to look friendly at all.

"Well . . ." she said on a puff of air. "I'm going in for some coffee. Anyone for a refill?"

"Sure. Bring the pot," her father said.

"Need help?" Bear asked.

She shook her head and walked off, glad to be away from the noose tightening around her throat. In the kitchen, she leaned back against the door frame and tangled her hands in her hair. She growled, sounding much like the feral cats who had once made a home in her barn. "What now?"

Abby grabbed the cream and sugar, the pot, an extra cup, and dragged her feet back to the porch. Silence greeted her. Not one word was uttered while she refilled their cups and poured one for herself.

She tried to think of something to say, something easy, something nonchalant. Nothing came to mind, so she sipped in silence and watched folks as they left the pavilion and the baptism in the lake. Some dripped lake water, some still sported jaunty hats and crisp dresses and jackets. They smiled and talked, had things to say and places to go.

She wished she did. If she'd been baptized today, she'd still be there instead of on this porch sitting in dreadful silence with her husband, father and two best friends. Abby waved in response to Samuel's hand flapping out the window of his shiny black automobile and regretted it in an instant.

Things had just gotten worse.

He turned in the middle of the road and pulled up to the hotel. With the engine off, silence grabbed the air until he broke it by slamming the auto door. He took the steps two at a time, slapped Frank on the back, said hello to the other three men and gave Abby a shoulder hug.

"Think I could get some of that coffee?" he said, pulling a chair from the other side of the porch and placing it next to hers.

A hug? Since when does Samuel hug?

"Sure. I'll go get you a cup."

"Beautiful day," he crooned as he sat and put one ankle over the other knee. He leaned his head against the chair back and gazed at the silent group. "Reverend Jenkins outdid himself today. Should have been there. We can all use a little redemption."

Samuel watched Frank grow agitated and tried not to smile. Abby came back with a cup, poured his coffee and handed it to him.

"Wouldn't you say so, Abby?" he asked.

"I don't know what you're talking about, Samuel."

"Redemption. The reverend's sermon."

"I recall him talking about forgiveness and tolerance."

"He did, but most people don't deserve forgiveness, so I dismissed that part. Almost all of us could use redemption, however. Improvement, a little renovation. At least some redecorating of our souls."

He laughed at his own joke, and Abby wondered what was going on with him. He rarely talked, and today his mouth chirped on like a magpie. She tilted her head and saw his black, slender mustache quiver.

"You okay?"

"Couldn't be better." He sipped his coffee and glanced over the rim of the cup. "Here for a spell, Frank?"

"That's not any of your business, Samuel. Butt out."

"Not real friendly today, are you?"

"I was."

Abby said she had work to do and left without looking back. She didn't know if Frank would follow, but he either did or didn't. She couldn't do anything about his choices.

Patrick went to the kitchen to stir the lunch soup, and Bear followed. Soon they were all inside, bringing the noose with them, but guests started returning to eat lunch or check out, and Abby got too busy to feel it around her neck.

When it slowed down, she asked Bear and Shorty to cover for her in the bar, found Frank and dragged him upstairs. He stood in the middle of the room looking around, investigating the space as if it had changed since the last time he'd been in it. Abby sat on the edge of the bed and folded her hands in her lap.

"Where have you been, Frank?" she asked, breaking the long silence.

"Different places. Newago, Grand Rapids."

"Doing what?"

"Just living. Picking up work here and there."

"Sit down, Frank. Would you like something? More coffee? A drink?"

He sat in the chair by the table and stared at her but didn't answer. "Should I gather that's a no, then?" she said.

"No. I mean, yes, a drink might be needed, I think. A whiskey." She left, shaking her head and pondering the identity of the man in her room. At the bar, Bear's eyebrows rose when she asked for a tall whiskey and a coffee, but he poured them without comment.

Shorty, on the other hand, said, "Pretty early."

"Shut up, Shorty," she said.

"Want him to go away, Abby?" he asked.

She teared up and ran across the room and up the stairs, spilling only a little of the whiskey. Frank grabbed the drink from her hand and took a gulp, swallowed hard and started talking.

"I want to come back, Abby. I need to come back. I'm not the same man who said those terrible things to you."

She didn't respond, didn't know what to say. She wanted to save her marriage, but not as it was. Could she even talk about everything that had been wrong?

"Guess you don't want me back. Is that it?" he asked.

"No. That isn't it. I want us to be together. But things haven't changed. Things you hate. I still work here, Frank. It's what I do, and you don't like that. You never did. I live here, too. I can't live at the farm, and your family would hate it if I did."

"Guess I'll have to get used to us being here. Have to change my ways."

Abby moved from the bed to the window and looked out at the lake she'd come to love, at the people playing in it – neighbors and visitors she'd also come to love.

"We're really different, Frank. And Da is planning to run the new hotel they're building on the island. I'll be helping him."

Frank rubbed his forehead and left it in his hand. Abby saw the ruffled hair and the cowlick at the back sticking up as it always had. She wanted to smooth it down, to run her hands over his hair and tell him everything would be all right. But she didn't know if it would. She feared it couldn't be.

"I think Pa needs me at the farm. I'll ask, and if he does, I'll work there and live here – with you." When she didn't answer, he got up and stood next to her, not touching.

"It's what you wanted, Abby. It'll be just like you wanted."

"That's not all of it, Frank. I . . . I don't know how to say the other things."

"What do you mean you don't know how? Just say it." Frustration was making him edgy, and Abby moved away to sit on the bed again. He followed and wrapped an arm around her.

"I need you, Abby." He ran a hand down her cheek and turned her face toward him. When his lips met hers, she stiffened. Her mouth wouldn't cooperate. Her lips were hard, unyielding, and her heart thumped in fear. She felt the noose tighten.

"I need to think," she said, pulling away from him. "Please."

"About what? What is there to think about? Unless it's somebody else. Is that it?"

"No! It's not that." She put a hand on his arm, trying to connect with him physically without sexuality. "Why did you leave, Frank? What made you so angry you left? And why leave town?"

He made circles with his shoulders and twisted his head around like he ached from the tension in the room.

"It seemed like everybody got more of you than I did. I got angry. Nothing worked out the way it was supposed to."

"Because you thought I'd give up the hotel and move to the farm even though I said I couldn't long before we were married?"

Frank had the good grace to look embarrassed at being caught in a truth he'd rather not own. He *had* believed he could talk her into being a farmer's wife. Patrick would have survived, and the old man wasn't his problem. His wife was. And the farm.

"I guess. But I know better, now. I get it." He tried again to wrap her in his arms, but Abby stood and walked away.

"I'm not ready for that, Frank. I told you, I need to think. We have . . . more to discuss."

"Well? When?"

"Go talk to your father and stay at the farm for a bit, please. He's missing you. I'll be here thinking. We'll talk again in a few days. Is that alright? Can we do that?"

"Guess if that's the best I can get, it'll have to be. Can I get a kiss at least?"

She pecked him on the lips and backed away before he could make it into anything more. He shook his head and rubbed the back of it.

"You're a hard woman, Abigail Riley Adams."

"Am I, Frank? Am I really hard?" She didn't think so, but hurting him was. She was a patsy with a heart made of warm oatmeal. Soft, pliable, and easily consumed by scoundrels.

She grimaced at her unruly thoughts and reached for his hand in apology, changed her mind and went for her coffee cup instead. She sipped and peered at him over the rim.

He drained his drink and walked out the bedroom door, leaving the hotel without stopping at the bar, not wanting to meet up with anyone he'd seen on the porch. He'd been certain he would sleep in Abby's bed this night. That he wouldn't was a thorn in his side. And it pricked.

She removed her Sunday dress and hung it, splashed water on her face and brushed her hair. By the time she put her work dress on, she felt stronger, able to stare down the looks she'd get from her friends when she went downstairs.

Charity Evans' blond bob winked across the room like a lighthouse beacon flickering in the night. With each flip of her head, her platinum hair called to every eye in the room. It was hard to look away.

She sat between Samuel and Charles Chesnutt, alternately batting her lashes at one before moving to the other. Samuel didn't appreciate the fine art of flirting. Its calculated and deliberate dishonesty irritated him. He peered around her at Charles and tried to take the temperature of his engagement with the woman. What he saw was a reflection of his own thoughts.

He knew Charity's parents had no knowledge of her whereabouts or they'd be here dragging her out by her fashionable bob. The visual made him smile.

Abby's eyes widened when she saw her, and Samuel wondered what the next few moments would bring.

"You back," Shorty said from behind the bar, "or just visiting?"

"I don't know. Do I need to be back? Do you want to relax or go fishing or something?"

"I can stay if you have somewhere to be," Bear said. "Like if someone is waiting for you." He ran a hand over Cleo's haunches hanging down his chest. Phantom perched at the end of the bar, glaring and waiting his turn to ride his shoulder.

"No. Nobody's waiting." She shifted feet. "I miss Benjamin. It's too quiet in here."

"Maybe you should ride out and tell him. Offer him money," Samuel said.

Abby perked up, and her eyes brightened.

"I'm going to do that. Is that okay, Bear, Shorty? I need some Nirvana, anyway." Patrick came through the swinging doors from the kitchen in time to hear her last words.

"Some Nirvana? How you going to get some? Shovel up dirt and bring it here in a bucket? Treat it like it's your very own pot of gold?"

His Irish eyes danced because he loved his own wit almost as much as he loved his daughter. And he loved holding court, too.

"Nirvana is like a bit of gold, Da. It's idyllic, and if you have a pot, I'll fill it with some today – unless you need me here. I was about to find you and ask."

"Some would say *Idlewild* is the pot of gold," Charles said, surprising the others who turned to hear his words of wisdom. "Like Harrison talked about. This could be his *mecca*, the center of his new world with streets of gold."

Charity swung her head around, and Samuel moved quickly to avoid a face full of bob as she leaned back to look at Charles.

"Why? Why would this . . . this hick town be anybody's mecca? There's nothing here."

"There's more to life than gold in the streets, girl. There's freedom," Charles said.

Charity put a manicured hand on his sleeve to draw him closer, and, from behind her, Samuel winced.

"But you could have had freedom. It was handed to you, from what I understand. You could have been white."

Silence struck like thunder. And like watching the approach of a violent storm, everyone in the room waited for the second clap.

Charles picked up his drink and sipped. His eyes darkened, and his nostrils stiffened. He tried to be silent in the exhalation of air, tried to let it out slowly so he wouldn't have to inhale in the next moment. The air grew thick with false stillness, and it seemed breath would soon be impossible, like trying to breathe under water.

Samuel watched him from around the bobbed head, and thought he'd never seen such anger not already balled into a fist and ready to strike. His fury was still, quiet, contained.

Charles turned to her, his face inches away, and her pale blue eyes grew round, the flirtatious expression gone. When he spoke, his words were measured.

"What exactly do you think I might gain in naming myself a member of your race, Miss Evans? What do you have that I could possibly want?"

She blanched, and her lips formed a pout. She didn't respond.

Samuel's shoulders straightened. A smile twitched his lips that broke into a full-fledged chuckle when he saw Mrs. Gertrude Evans storming through the door.

"Oh, Lordy," Abby said.

"Ye might wanta pray a bit harder than that, lass," her da said, a grin on his face.

The stout woman stomped up to the bar and planted herself behind her daughter. She spun the stool, and, when Charity's knees slammed into her ample belly, Gertrude emitted an embarrassing *oomph*. She stepped back, but only for a moment.

"What are you doing here, Mother? Is Papa with you?"

"Of course not. I would not have him know you're in this den of immorality. Who brought you here? Who has corrupted you? This man?"

She jabbed Charles in the shoulder, not for a moment believing Samuel could influence her daughter. He was colored.

"No one corrupted Charity, Mrs. Evans. She came here of her own free will." Abby turned toward her father and made a face, crossed her eyes and turned down her lips. Patrick took her antics as a sign he should take over.

"Can I pour you a wee drink, Mrs. Evans? Ye probably could use a refreshment after your hard work this day helping sinners find their way to the Lord and all."

Gertrude's spine went straight, and her chin lifted. "Just what are you suggesting, Mister Riley?"

Patrick took her elbow and walked to a table, pulled out a chair and waited until she plopped into it.

"A medicinal tonic sure to put a little sunshine in your day. That's all, my good lady. We Irish know about tonics."

"I guess a small tonic might do me some good. At least somebody appreciates all the work I do. It isn't easy you know." She wiped her forehead with the back of her arm like perspiration might be sitting there waiting to drip.

Patrick danced back and forth from heels to toes, the sprite in him having a great time. She sighed and put a hand on her breast, the martyred matriarch.

"You know I don't hold with the demon rum."

"Oh, but of course. There is no rum in the tonic."

"But I meant that simply as an example, Mister Riley."

"Of course, you did. I understand completely."

Her head wobbled, causing the double chin to flop like a rooster's wattle, and Patrick flew to the bar for her tonic. Shorty raised eyebrows and shoulders in confusion.

"Tonic?" he said.

"Sure. The same that I use every night for my health."

"Uh . . . Oh. *That* tonic."

He poured a healthy tot and one for Patrick, too, thinking the man would need it before Charity and her mother left.

Patrick joined her at the table, and Shorty, Bear and Abby watched as Gertrude grew more talkative by the moment. She waved her arms as she spoke, grabbed Patrick's arm and began to laugh, a high-pitched cackle that turned every head in the room.

"Are ye feeling better then, Mrs. Evans?" Patrick asked, thinking he might need to get her out into the fresh air soon. "Should I get yer daughter to walk you home?"

"I'm feeling perfectly fine. Dandy." She stood, threw back her shoulders and moved to Charity. "I still want to know who brought you here. Who did this?"

Charity hadn't recovered from the lashing Charles had given her. In fact, she hadn't spoken a word since. She'd seen his fury and Samuel's glee over her discomfort. She was humiliated and angry.

"I don't need an escort to come into a bar, Mother. I'm perfectly capable of corrupting myself, and I'm sure these fine folks will be happy to see my backside."

"Charity! Language!"

"Let's go." She slid from the stool and headed for the door, leaving her mother sputtering and scurrying after her. No one knew whether to laugh, cry, or groan in relief as the door closed behind them.

"You good?" Samuel asked Charles.

"Just fine. Why?"

"No reason. You going to Nirvana?" he asked Abby.

"Yes. I need to. And I want to."

"Come on. I'll drive."

"Don't you have anything better to do than drive me around? You don't need . . ." She stopped mid-stream, threw her arms in the air and blew out a puff of exasperation.

"Oh, what the heck. Let's go."

Chapter Thirteen

They heard piano music before they reached the porch, and the sound instantly soothed her soul.

"God, I've missed that. I want him back at the hotel."

"It's not that far. Hire him," Samuel said.

A vase of lilacs greeted them at a front counter lustrous with fresh wax. The whole room glowed with care. Benjamin had obviously used elbow grease on the place.

"Hello," she called out, not wanting to interrupt his music but wanting to let him know he had company.

He played to the end of the familiar verse and turned with a smile. "Hello back. Nice to see you."

"You sure? Seems like you moved here for solitude and here we are busting in on you." Abby wrapped an arm around his shoulder and squeezed.

"I'm sure. And you just missed a couple of customers. That's right," he added when she drew back in shock. "I had customers. I've had several, in fact."

"Who?"

"The Avery brothers. Said they used to be regulars."

"John and James? Darn. I would've loved to see them. They used to come in at least once a week for supper and a couple of drinks." Abby's eyes misted with memory tainted by longing. "I miss them – and this."

"How are you, Benjamin? You and your friends keeping out of trouble, keeping your noses clean?" Samuel tinkled a couple of high notes back and forth. It had an eerie sound, like a prelude to something jumping out to say, 'Gotcha!'

"Trying," he said, 'but it follows sometimes."

He'd said it as a joke with meaning, and Samuel understood. If Abby left them for a few minutes, he'd have some words with him. Reassure him. His friends hadn't been named and it seemed they wouldn't. Samuel was as certain as he could be given the circumstances.

"You've done wonders here. It looks great," Abby said. "You'd never know it sat empty for so long – empty except for critters and dust bunnies, that is."

"It kept me busy for a while, but it's home now."

"Don't you get lonely, though? Lots of hours in a day."

"Alone doesn't mean lonely, Abby. If I need people, I can always drive to Idlewild. Or Baldwin. And I have this," he said, running a hand over the piano keys, "and an occasional person wandering in wondering what the heck is going on in the old Aishcum Hotel."

"What do they want?" Samuel asked. "Rooms, food?"

"To satisfy curiosity, usually, but, you're right, strangers to the area are interested in food and rooms. It's a bit odd. I seem to be in the hotel business without meaning to, but only as much as I want. When I don't feel like having people here, I put out the no vacancy sign."

"That's funny. I love it, but I want you to come play for us in Idlewild. We miss you."

"I don't know, Abby. . ."

She tugged her lip and pouted. "You going to make me beg? Okay, I can do that. Pretty please? One evening a week?"

Benjamin swung his legs over the piano bench and stood. His lips twisted, and Abby remembered his wounds, the shrapnel still in his back and the reason he was in Idlewild instead of back with the 369th, his unit that served in France during World War I.

"I don't like to commit to it, like it's a job. That's not how making music works. Let me think about it."

"Do you mind if I look around? You can think while I see what you've done with the place." She grinned at him, hoping charm would work.

"It's still yours, Abigail. Feel free."

"But it's your home, Benjamin. I don't want to intrude." He waved her away, and she wandered through the kitchen she'd grown up in and the upstairs where she'd learned to make beds and clean rooms.

She ran a hand over the banister she'd slid down when guests weren't around and remembered the many times she'd been caught with skirts flying over her backside.

Here is where she'd met Frank when he came for supper and drinks with his friends. He'd courted her on the porch on warm summer evenings. She thought of the last night here before moving to Idlewild and of Yancy, the lumberjack who begged her not to marry Frank.

He had proposed just to keep her from him. *Marry me, Abby. I'm telling you, that man ain't good for you.*

"Yancy," she said. "Where are you now? Did you know things I didn't?" She pasted on a weak smile and told herself to buck up, get on with life.

Coming down the stairs, she heard their voices and peered into the bar to tell them she'd be outside. They sat shoulder to shoulder, talking in undertones. When she drew near, the voices went quiet. She tilted her head and raised her eyebrows.

"Keeping secrets, boys?"

"We're quiet men, Abby. Loud is obnoxious and plebian," Samuel said, his mustache twitching.

"Did you know your mustache jiggles when you tell a fib?"

"It most certainly does not. That was me smiling."

Her eyes twinkled with mischief, and she exchanged a knowing look with Benjamin.

"He fibs. Be careful my friend. Only the hair over his lip can be trusted. I came in to say I'm going out."

"Did you hear your words, Miss Riley?" Samuel said.

"Mrs. Adams, sir."

"Of course. My apologies."

Benjamin, his back leaning against the bar, crossed his arms and looked around as if he'd not been in the room before. "Does being here make you feel like a young girl again?" he asked.

"Sometimes it does. Other times, it makes me feel old, like the young girl happened a long, long time ago – or she never lived at all. Not in me, anyway."

Abby faced away, afraid she'd said too much and turned the air in the room to maudlin syrup. Or worse, self-pity. She waved herself out the door and called back to them. "I'm leaving now. You can start whispering again."

"They're all doing time, one for arson, one for assault, and three for both, but none for rape," Samuel said after Abby left. "The prosecutor wouldn't believe her over four white boys who said she'd been giving it away. That son of a bitch . . . He couldn't ignore the evidence of her beating, however, and he charged them for it. They took a plea deal rather than go to trial, but George Adams had a lawyer, so his sentence was months in jail instead of years."

"Monsters," Benjamin said. "I hate it for Betty. They raped and brutalized her – more than once. They should pay for it."

Samuel put a hand on his shoulder and looked him squarely in the eyes. "You saw to it that they paid for raping her. No trial meant no opportunity for the unconventional payment to come into the light. Only Cassandra knows for sure. And so far, your friends are in the clear. They come around at all?"

"When they're on leave. Some still serve." Being a careful man, he pondered his next words. "I would enjoy seeing her again. Maybe I'll come play for Abby after all."

Samuel's eyes lit. "Betty? Bet she'd like that, too." He saw Abby about to come into the bar and put a finger over his lips to hush Benjamin.

She stomped her foot from the doorway, put her hands on her hips and scowled.

"Really? Again? What can't I hear? Why are you keeping secrets from me? I don't like this at all!"

Samuel's mustache jiggled, but he couldn't hold it together. The laugh came out and Benjamin joined in. She crossed her arms over her chest and tapped a toe.

"I'm not giving up until you tell me why you're laughing at me and keeping secrets."

"Will you at least smile if I say I'll come and play one afternoon a week – on a week day in case my hotel has guests on the weekend?" He winked at Samuel as she threw an arm around him like they'd known each other since childhood. It felt like it.

"Thank you. Thank you so much. I've missed you and your music."

"Aren't you giving me the grand tour?" Samuel said. "I'd kind of like to see the place."

They left Benjamin to his piano while Abby dragged Samuel from the kitchen to the upstairs rooms and, finally, to her living space at the end of the hallway.

Several windows looked out on both the front and back yards. She used to sit at the window and watch birds and critters and pretend they were the same ones her mother had cared for when she was alive, before she'd been born.

"I spent a lot of time here as a young girl, before Da put me to work and taught me how."

"You didn't emerge from the womb knowing how to change bed sheets?"

"Sometimes it feels like it." She leaned a shoulder against the window frame and took it all in.

"Da and I shared this room before I was old enough to have my own. I still think of him as the young man he used to be. He was a handsome devil. Full of the Irish blarney. It must have been hard for him, caring for an infant and running this hotel."

"You were worth it, Abigail."

Where had those words had come from? Abby was used to his sardonic mockery and expected it – even his humor had caustic hues. But kind words from Samuel's lips brought sudden tears, and she blinked them away and turned to him.

She studied his face with its smooth skin, close-cropped hair and deep brown eyes.

"I'll show you our path in the woods."

"*Our* path?"

"Yes. We both used it, my mum and me. Not at the same time, but I dreamed she walked beside me. Come on. It's short but brings me peace."

"Lead on, Captain."

They walked the path, drank coffee Benjamin had prepared for them, and left for Idlewild. Abby was calm of spirit. Nirvana gave her peace.

This time, Abby didn't expect Samuel's automobile to blow up or run into a tree, so she enjoyed the ride. She filled her lungs with the earthy scent of leather, leaned her head against the seat back and watched the trees go by. Her contentment filtered over to him. The trip to her old home had done what she said it would.

Inside the auto, they were cocooned within its gleaming walls. It was a womb, and they were separated from the world and safe. If Samuel kept on driving, nothing would change or grow older. Time would stand still. It would always be today, summer, right now, and she'd never be anywhere but right here, heading home because she needed to, but never getting there.

She grew hypnotized by the motion, the rhythm of the tires on the road, even though it jarred and jiggled her body through the cushioned seat. A pleasantly numbing sensation stole over her, and she didn't want him to pull up to the hotel and expel her from the make-believe mechanical womb.

"Are you here?" he asked when they stopped, and she didn't move or make comment.

"I think so, but I'm not entirely sure. I was enjoying the experience. Thank you, Samuel."

She jumped when a fist knocked on the roof and groaned when she saw Joe. Foster's jeering eyes peered in the window at her. His wicked sneer showed only a few brown, broken teeth, and Abby wanted to take the rest of them out with her fist.

So much for a peaceful soul.

Samuel took his time unfolding himself from the auto and walking around it to open Abby's door. When he did, its corner accidently carved out a piece of Joe's shin. He hopped about, cussing, and Samuel apologized profusely.

"Damn door. Whyn't you look what yer doing?"

"Sit down on the step, Joe. I'll escort Mrs. Adams in and be back with a damp cloth for your leg." Samuel walked with her all the way to the bar and climbed on a stool.

"Could I have a whiskey, Shorty?" he said.

"Aren't you going back to see to Joe?" Abby asked.

"Sure."

"Have a good time, Abby?" Shorty poured amber liquid into a glass and slid it over to Samuel. "You working?" he asked her.

"I did and I am, and I thank you for taking over for a while." She stared at Samuel who had an elbow on the bar and his chin resting on the fisted hand. He looked in no rush to do anything but sit and sip his drink.

"Aren't you going out there like you said?" she asked. "He had blood on his trouser leg."

"What happened to Joe?" Patrick asked from the end of the bar.

"Ran into something. Got a little blood on him."

"Bad? What'd he run into?"

"A door."

"You told him you'd be back with a damp cloth, Samuel. I can't stand the man, but . . ."

"I can't either, and I didn't say when."

"Little blood doesn't hurt a body," Patrick said. "How are things at the old place?"

Abby told him everything – about the customers, how spit and polished it was, Benjamin promising to come once a week, and poor old Joe became a forgotten story.

"You sound a wee nostalgic. Are ye sorry we came to Idlewild, lass?" Patrick asked, patting the back of her hand.

She fingered the braid hanging over her shoulder as she considered her da's question and thought maybe she'd chop it off, cut it into a bob like Charity's. Shock her friends and father. She could see them staring at her, horrified and afraid to speak. But maybe not. She liked her thick auburn hair even if it did plump up into a riot of curls in wet weather . . . and she was avoiding the question.

He tugged at her arm. "Wool gathering?"

"Yup. I've got a wagon full. Want me to crochet you a sweater?"

"Well, lass?"

"I'm not sorry we moved to Idlewild, Da. I love it here. It's just . . . times are hard and peace stands inches out of reach. I miss peace."

"Got that," her da said, and Samuel stroked his mustache while he listened. He figured Abby's remaining serenity would soon suffer, some of it due to her prodigal husband.

"Oh, my God. We forgot Joe," she said, remembering the promise of help. She ran to the porch to check on him, but he'd left, and she was glad.

She sat with her father and friends watching the sun prepare to plunge into the lake. It never went gently. It sat on the edge of the world like it owned it and, in an instant, disappeared. You could see the splash it made if you watched for it.

Charles Chesnutt had joined them on the family side of the porch since his first night in town. He'd accepted the offered position with quiet gratitude. His toe moved the wooden rocker in time with the others like he'd been practicing for years to sit in the close-knit circle.

Fireflies lit the darkness with intermittent dots of magical color blinking in step with crickets' chirps and a loon's call, like it had all been choreographed for their pleasure. Night sat on bare skin in droplets of moisture and trickled at the edges of hairlines and into collars. It was a fragrant heat, mixed with the musk of earth from the lake's edge, the choke cherry and apple blossoms, and the animal scent of nearby boxwoods.

Charles thought he would write about it, capture Idlewild with sensory words and images, if he could get the hateful ones out of his brain and entomb them as he'd done in the past.

You could have had freedom. You could have been white. He heard the sudden offbeat tempo of his rocker on the wood planks of the porch and forced his breath to slow and his mind to calm. "Sorry," he said. After a few carefully constructed moments, he rejoined the pleasant rhythm practiced by his new friends.

When Patrick's chair stopped, all the others halted, and they waited for words they knew were coming. He wouldn't have ceased rocking for nothing. He lifted his small whisky glass toward Charles and held it motionless while he shaped the ideas in his brain into sensible communication.

"The Irish fairies would be proud to call ye their own, Mister Chesnutt. I'm sorry for the words of the ignorant lass in our house today."

"Wasn't your ignorance, Mister Riley. Was hers."

"Tis true. And I don't think she's an evil lass. Maybe a wee . . . thoughtless."

"Many are. In a bushel basket, it becomes an evil force."

"Stupid probably happened when she cut her hair," Shorty said.

"Likely," Bear said.

"Thought I might do mine that way," Abby added.

They knew better and ignored her.

"What is *your* freedom, Mister Chesnutt," Bear asked. "If you don't mind me asking."

Hiding in the darkness, like an opossum bumbling around in the night, their ideas bumped along on the warm air currents, and their notions were tainted by anxiety.

Was he offended by my question?

How do I answer without offending?

What does Bear want to know?

And I thought things were going so well.

Damn.

"I am a realist. A product of miscegenation." When he saw Shorty's head tilt and brows furrow, he added, "mixed-race sexual relations. I've seen the ghastly results of passing. I've written about it. It's all there in my novels and short stories."

They watched Cassandra move along the edge of the water, the clowder following. She raised her robed arms to the rising moon, and the dark purple fabric of her sleeves fell to her shoulders revealing even darker slender arms. She extended her fingers as if catching the moon and stood motionless. Communicating with the night? Calling to bats and owls and other creatures of the dark?

Charles smiled, and the others heard the slow release of his breath. "Cassandra is freedom personified. She lives as she chooses, goes where she chooses. She is who she wants to be and lives her freedom."

"But what if she tried to go into a restaurant and they told her she couldn't because she's colored?" Abby asked.

"But she doesn't want that," Charles said. "She wants exactly what she has."

"Well, not everyone has . . . kind of . . . simplistic needs and wants, I guess that's what I mean. Some want things they're not allowed to have . . . or do. I'm really struggling here, Charles," she said.

"I know, Abby. It's hard to talk about oppression, about disenfranchisement, about the harm owning others did to white souls, let alone the harm done to those who were owned. I've lived it for some sixty years and have tried to write about it for more than forty."

He smiled at her, a weak smile that told the tale of his sorrow. "I still don't know how to describe freedom, except I know Cassandra has it. She's free."

"So . . . is the key to freedom wanting only what is available to you? Wanting only what you have with no right to want more or make choices for yourself? No real rights at all except for those somebody else gives you?"

Abby's thoughts probed her marital relationship, as well as what Charles and all colored people had lived through. She looked for answers.

Bear, too. He sat forward in his chair, intent on Charles' words and wanting to pick the brain of this quiet, gentle man who looked as white as himself but had the heart and soul of a colored man.

"Can there be freedom while prejudice exists? I don't believe so. And how do you dismantle prejudice, get rid of it?" he asked.

"Stone by stone," Charles said. "And when it's understood we all have the same needs, the same ideals, the wall will fall, and we can rebuild on a new foundation of patriotism and esteem for all those who share it. It's about respect. Honor."

Silence fell, and no one noticed. Their eyes were on Cassandra as she caught the moon, and their hearts and minds were percolating Charles' words. Even his were.

An owl hooted, a loon lamented his lot in life, and a lone cricket whined an enquiring refrain. Night songs added to the beauty of his words, an apt serenade for the formless shape labor would assume, the labor that built the new world called freedom.

Shorty didn't know why his heart was heavy, but it was, and it matched every heart in the conversation circle. A long, bumpy road lay ahead, and he wished to be Cassandra, as did they all.

"So, ye paint a hard but pretty majestic picture, my friend," Patrick said, tiring of the cricket's chirp being the only sound.

"Yes. Sorry." He chuckled. "I'll move to the guest side of the porch tomorrow night."

"Nay. Stay with us, Passing. You're a good lad."

"Lad? I'm your age, Patrick."

"Not really. Leprechauns are ageless."

Chapter Fourteen

"You should see the place."

"I did. You two really spiffed it up," Abby said. "Did you bring the dust mop?"

"You left it outside the door. And I mean see the place *now*. It's even better than before. Shorty fixed the porch. Even put a whole new rail on it. The barn doesn't leak anymore, and we have a cow."

Abby's eyes grew wide.

"Honestly, a cow? Why?"

Betty smirked. "That's where milk comes from, boss."

Abby poured dirty wash-stand water into the bucket of clean and Betty pointed.

"Damn. Why did I do that?"

"I surely don't know."

"I'll be back," she said, and returned with fresh water.

Betty shook out the top sheet and let it float down in a perfect rectangle, tucked in the bottom end and squared the corners. Abby breathed hot air on the mirror she was cleaning, drew a smiling face next to a frown, and tapped it to draw Betty's attention.

"You trying to tell me something?"

"No. Let's move on. Come on cats," Abby said, wiping the mirror and picking up the buckets of water. Phantom and Cleo beat them to the next room and waited by the door, opposites like the faces she had drawn. She knew they'd hate it if Frank came back. Could he find it in his heart to treat them better? He said he could change, but . . .

"You out of sorts?" Betty asked.

"No, just thinking."

"Looks to me like you're not thinking much at all about making up the rooms. Want to spill it?"

"I don't think so. I don't know. Let's get this done."

"You're the boss."

By the fourth room, Betty closed the door and backed Abby up to the chair, making her sit while she perched on the edge of the messy bed.

"I could do these rooms quicker by myself, so why don't you just talk."

Abby's eyes teared in the corners, and Betty reached for her hand and squeezed. "Can't be all that bad. Come on."

"Frank wants to come back."

"Oh." She yanked back her hand like it had been burned.

Dead air filled the space. Neither woman met the other's eyes. Bird chirps and laughter came in through the open window, but a wall of betrayal prevented sound from infiltrating the room. Phantom rubbed Abby's leg, and she ran a hand down his back. Cleo leaped on the bed and used her claws to make a nest next to Betty.

"And you told him no, right?" Betty said in a voice laden with angst.

"I didn't say yes . . . and I didn't say no."

Betty's nostrils flared and her eyes glowered. Her hands were clenched by her hips.

"You wouldn't."

Abby stood and paced in front of her friend, remembering the words she'd said to convince Betty to speak out about what she'd endured at the hands of men. She'd told her about Frank, how he'd used her without regard for her dignity, comparing their marital bed to a kind of rape. She'd used her own condition to coerce her friend to speak out.

She'd meant every word, but . . . had she been wrong?

"I vowed to love, honor and obey, Betty."

"He raped you. Repeatedly. He should be in jail with the Tatums, not obeyed and honored, let alone loved."

Abby collapsed on the bed and gnawed at her thumb nail, a habit she had long ago broken.

"I let him. And he said he's changed."

"Men don't."

Betty marched to the window and stared out, looking but not seeing anything except the men who had raped her. The men who'd beaten her, broken her ribs, bloodied her face with their filthy, hard boots. Men who'd made her wish for a quick death. Thinking of Frank brought it all back. Abby *had* convinced her.

"I'll be going if he comes back."

She said it to the window pane, to the children playing in the lake and the half-built hotel on the island. Maybe she could get a job there. But that was a long time off.

Tears were running down Abby's face when Betty turned from the window, and her anger fled.

"I don't know what to do," Abby said. "I have to try. I have to work at our marriage. He can't do all the changing by himself. Don't you see that?"

"And if he just uses you again? Abuses you?"

"Then I have to make it stop. Letting it happen was my fault. Please don't quit, Betty."

It's about esteem, she thought. *Like Charles said. For their marriage to be rebuilt, it must be on a foundation of regard.*

Abby was tending bar when Frank visited again. He took the stairs two at a time, dropped a duffle bag in the corner of her room and came downstairs looking for supper. Patrick filled his bowl twice and welcomed him with a glass of Irish on the house. Shorty nodded a quiet hello, and Bear simply nodded. Samuel asked if he'd be here long.

"Most likely," Frank said. "That all right with you?" He didn't know why, but Samuel irked him. Acted superior.

Phantom strolled down the bar and paused to stare at him. He tried to avoid the cat's eyes, but Phantom insisted on being acknowledged by shoving his head into Frank's chin until he pushed him away – gently.

"Cat's haven't changed."

"They don't," Samuel said. "Much like people." The skin of his face glowed burnished bronze in the lamp light, and the tight muscles were fixed. He didn't even blink. The stillness bothered Frank, and he turned away so he didn't have to deal with it or respond.

Abby shoved a tray full of drinks Jackson's way and scooted down to talk with her husband. She hadn't been expecting him, and his appearance unsettled her. Was he moving in or visiting?

Frank grinned, the charming grin she'd fallen for, and grabbed her hand.

"Good to see you," she said, letting her hand lay in his, but not squeezing back. "Surprised, though. Have you been staying at the farm?"

"Yup. Back on the tractor just like I never left it. Can't imagine why I ever thought farming was a good thing to do."

"You're not enjoying it, even a little?" She took back her hand and picked up a bar towel to have something to do.

"Fishing in between field work. Now, that I enjoy."

"How are your parents? And Cecily and the boys?"

"The old man is crazy. Getting crazier by the day, and Ma is Ma. She never changes. Thank God there's something I can count on."

"Chunk and Bailey?"

"The boys are monsters. Cecily spoils 'em and Terry yells at 'em. It's a mad house."

She patted his arm and told him she'd be back, but it took a while before she could. The bar filled with regulars whose preferences they knew and strangers they needed to remind of prohibition. They danced this tango daily as they wiggled and jiggled around the words and the laws and the needs of the hotel.

Jackson ran back and forth trying to keep up with food and drink orders, and Abby filled them as fast as she could. Bear and Shorty filled in, helping Patrick in the kitchen and Jackson on the floor.

"I need to hire more help," she told Frank when she stood in front of him again.

"Do it. What are you waiting for?"

"The right person, I guess. I haven't seen the one."

"I don't think you want to find anyone." He looked hard into her eyes, wanting her to agree with him. "I think you want to be needed – by everyone."

He reached for her hand again, and she moved away. "Jackson has an order."

He was waving a scrap of paper in the air to get her attention, and his brows were drawn together distorting his handsome face.

"That table in the back corner. They insist on ordering whiskey. I explained our policy since prohibition, but they're adamant. What do you want me to do?" he asked, frustration showing in the wrinkled brow and hunched shoulders.

"We'll do this together, Jackson. Pay attention. Converse. Feel them out."

"Gentlemen," she said as she drew near the group. "Are you enjoying your visit to our town? Thinking of buying a lot here?"

"At a resort for colored people? I don't think so, young woman. But we are looking for a drink. We already ordered from your boy, here."

Abby bristled. Her jaw clenched, and the smile she gave them resembled the baring of teeth by an angry badger. One man edged his chair back from her.

"Jackson hasn't been a boy now for several years. Wouldn't you say so, Mister Parker?"

"I would. Been out of short pants for a while."

"I'm sure you meant *young man*, didn't you, Mister . . .?"

When he didn't respond, she put her hands on the table and leaned toward him. "You probably didn't realize I was asking your name, Mister . . ."

"I can't see as how that is any of your business, girl."

Abby glanced toward the bar to see if Shorty and Bear were still there and if they were watching. They were. She shoved her bottom lip into a pout and both men read it right. They left their stools and sauntered toward the corner table.

Eyes flickered from one man to the other when they saw the big men walking their way, and she could tell they wondered what hornet's nest they'd fallen into. They sunk back into their chairs as if they could grow smaller and the approaching men wouldn't notice them. The apparent spokesman of the group cleared his throat and tried to sit up straight as Shorty addressed him.

"Nice to meet new visitors to Idlewild," he said so softly the man had to lean in to hear him.

"Thank you.' He choked on his words but got them out.

"Anything we can do to help you?" Shorty asked.

Abby took his arm.

"He seemed to think Jackson was my son." She pulled Jackson next to her and kept an arm around his back, posing as if for a picture. "Do we look alike?"

"What?" Bear asked.

The stranger looked up at Irish Abby and colored Jackson and turned purple. He began several words and discarded them before finishing any.

"Did you, now?" Shorty said. "I find that odd, myself."

"I didn't say that."

"What *did* you say?"

"You did, Mister . . . Uh, I still don't know your name. Anyway, you did. You said you had already ordered from *my boy*. What else could you have possibly meant?"

"Apparently, misunderstandings abound," Bear said. "You probably didn't hear about prohibition. We don't sell alcohol, but if you head for Newaygo, you can find someone who will. If you leave right now, you'll make it about dusk. Good day, Gentlemen."

Bear lifted one man by an arm and Shorty another. The others followed, and Abby watched as she moved across the room, her arm still around Jackson.

"So, what should I have been paying attention to, Abby? What was I to learn from you at that table?"

She punched his arm. "Brat. I shouldn't have gotten mad, but I did. Don't do what I do. It wasn't supposed to go that way."

"As long as Shorty and Bear are here, I don't see a problem." He chuckled, rubbed at his neck and eyed the men as they left the bar.

"Unfortunately, they have real jobs." She pulled him to a stop. "I got furious when he called you *boy*. It's so disrespectful. You don't deserve that."

"None of us do, Abby. Unless we do something that earns it."

"What would you have done if he'd called you *boy* – if I hadn't been here? Would you have served him?"

He swallowed and pinched the bridge of his nose, giving himself time to think about it. He didn't know and didn't know what she would've wanted him to do. What would she expect?

"Why don't you tell me, Abby? What should I do?" His words had edge, but the anger didn't point at her. He was torn – stuck between the old rock and hard place. He couldn't turn away *her* customers . . . could he? They weren't his to refuse.

But they were *his* principles – he owned them.

"You shouldn't put yourself in harm's way. That comes first. But, my friend, you should never feel obligated to serve anyone who mistreats you – ever. But I repeat, don't put yourself in a situation where you could be harmed." She grabbed his chin and turned his face to hers. "Do you hear me? This hotel isn't worth it."

"I hear but refusing service could mean trouble. You know what I mean."

"Jackson, I think Charles missed something in his theory. I think prejudice can be broken by esteem. It's not only for after we dismantle prejudice. Demand respect now. That's what we have to do." She slapped a hand on her chest with each word like she was a political candidate on a soap box. "We have to demand it!"

"We?" he said, a glint in his eye. "Last time I looked, you couldn't really be my mother."

"Be your what?" Frank roared, turning around on his stool.

Samuel laughed out loud, his mouth open and pearly white teeth glinting in the lamp light.

"Were those men suggesting such a ridiculous thing? What went on at that table?" Frank tipped his glass, drained it, and tapped it with a finger to indicate he wanted more.

"A lesson in civility, I'm thinking," Samuel said.

"And why do *you* need to demand respect, Abby?" Frank said.

"Yeah, boss. Much as I appreciate your support, they weren't calling *you* boy. That was me."

Samuel swiveled his stool around and put a foot on the floor, ready to leave the bar and the conversation. He tilted his head toward Jackson and shook it as if in miserable awe over his words. He looked at Frank and finally moved his eyes to Abby's.

"You seem to believe coloreds have a corner on the oppression market, Jackson," he said. "Can you mix oil and water?" Samuel heard Jackson scoff but didn't look at him. His eyes bored into Abby's.

As nobody answered, he said, "Course not. Put domination and respect into a bucket and try to mix them. Doesn't work, and Abby's right. Demand respect, or you won't get it . . . even if it puts you in harm's way. Start by respecting yourself."

His eyes left Abby's as he left the bar.

"Well, that was interesting," Jackson said. "I'll get back to work." He grabbed his pencil and pad and walked off.

Frank continued to stare at Abby and fumed. Samuel hadn't been talking about coloreds. He'd talked directly to her. To Abby. And he sure enough was looking right at her.

"Can I get a refill?" he asked, clinking his glass again. "What's with him?"

Abby watched Samuel's back recede and pondered his strange words. Maybe he knew more than he should.

"Hey," Frank said, poking her on the arm. "Wife of mine. Can I get another drink?"

Abby grabbed his glass and tilted the bottle over it. When she turned, Charity Evans had slid onto the stool next to him, wrapped an arm around his neck, and surprised him with a kiss on the cheek.

"You don't mind, do you, Abby. I haven't seen this man since I went away to college."

"Kiss away, Charity. I'm sure Frank is in heaven."

Eventually, Frank had the decency to pull away from the embrace, but the light in his eyes was unmistakable.

"I wouldn't know you, Charity. You're all grown up."

"Yup. Lotta good it does me, stuck in Timbuktu with nothing to do."

"Girl as pretty as you? Doesn't sound right to me."

Bear and Shorty returned from their escort services, saw Charity, and took seats as far from her as they could. Memory of her words to Charles Chesnutt remained cutting and sharp as a steel blade. Neither wanted to hear it repeated.

Abby found ways to stay clear of Charity and Frank, leaving them to reminisce. It was good to see him smile and hear his laughter. It had been too long since he'd laughed with her. In fact, she couldn't remember when he had . . . if he had.

Certainly, they had laughed. Of course, they had. Hadn't they?

By the time the bar emptied and Abby could close, Frank had finished several glasses of whiskey and wasn't ready to retire to the small upstairs room. Hearing his fuzzy words, Abby wasn't ready either.

"Closing, Charity. Time to go home." She poured a small glass of sherry for herself, an Irish for her father, and called out. "I'm heading to the porch to find my rocking chair. Join me all who wish."

Her feet hurt. Her mind blurred. Her heart was . . . she didn't know, maybe a rock, a big chunk of black, shiny granite. She chuckled to herself.

Phantom and Cleo waited by her chair and took up positions on her lap and shoulder, abandoning Bear for the evening. Their purrs gave comfort, and she needed some. It had been a difficult day. Several bigots had treated Jackson disrespectfully. Frank showed up, had taken a bag upstairs and was still here. Charity Evans knew how to make Frank laugh . . . and she didn't.

Her husband and friends found the porch and their bottoms found the appropriate seats. Charity bounced through the door, tripped down the steps and giggled.

"Oops! Your steps are off kilter. Better fix 'em."

"Yup. It's the dang steps. That's what the problem is," Shorty said.

"You going to get home okay, Charity?" Abby called after her. "I can walk with you if you need help."

"You're not walking drunks home, now, are you?" Frank said. Charity whirled around, stuck her chest out and her fists on her hips.

"I heard that, Frank Adams, and I'm not drunk. I'm totally sober with a little bit of tipsy mixed in, is all."

"Sure, you are," Frank said, laughing at her.

Again, with the laugh. Hmmm.

Charity spun off, and Frank pointed after her.

"There's your help, Abby. She's smart, she's got nothing to do, and she's fun. People will love her behind the bar." Abby stared at him with saucer sized eyes.

"You're kidding, right?"

"Hell, no. She'd be great, wouldn't she boys," he said, looking at Bear, Shorty and Patrick for affirmation. "She's a looker, to boot."

The three men avoided the issue by gazing at the lake, and the air sizzled and cracked with their lack of comment. Everyone heard it.

"No," Abby said, a flat word left hanging without clarification.

"Patrick," Frank said, tilting his head to look him in the eyes. "You need help here, and Charity is available and perfect for the bar. Tell your daughter."

"Tis Abby's to hire or not," he said. "But if she asked me, I'd say nay."

"For crying out loud. Why?"

"Charity is unsuitable, Frank. She's not right for us," Abby said.

He leaned back in his chair and wiggled his tongue around inside his cheek. Abby saw and sighed. She had provoked him. Again.

"You know what I think?"

"What do you think, Frank? I want to know."

"I think you don't really want to hire more help. You like working constantly and being needed by everyone. It makes you the queen, and I think you like being the queen. You're never gonna hire help cuz everything would change. That's what I think."

"Is that what you think, Frank?" Shorty said, and Abby's eyes flicked sideways to see if he was annoying her husband or teasing him. With Shorty, she frequently couldn't tell.

"It is. You see it, don't you, Shorty?"

"What I see is a full moon lighting up the night. I also see my bedtime approaching. Good night, folks." He rose, dropped a huge hand on Abby's shoulder and squeezed. The warmth in his affection moved down her back and into her heart. He didn't need words with a hand holding love.

"Thanks, my friend," she said.

"Give it up, Frank. She'll hire the right person at the right time," Shorty said as he walked away.

"I can hire. I hired Betty and Jackson and Al." She snapped her fingers. "And I hired Benjamin. He's going to come and play for us."

Her words softened thinking of his music. She looked forward to hearing it again.

"You hired that . . . that colored man you went running around with but won't hire Charity? That makes no sense, Abby. When did you see him?"

Abby stiffened, squeezed her temples and ran a hand over her face. She felt a hot lump rise in her throat and tears at the back of her eyes. She hadn't meant it to be a secret. Didn't want it to be now, but what could she say? Frank was going to love this story.

This is the way it went. I went to Nirvana with Samuel in his new automobile. We had coffee with Benjamin, and I showed Samuel around the hotel. It looks great, by the way. Benjamin has done a wonderful job. Samuel and I took a walk on the path through the woods. I enjoyed the time with my friends. It was fun!

Between fingers of the hand covering her face, she saw her father scratch his curly head. Could the leprechaun hear all the unspoken words dancing a fandango in her brain?

"When's he coming, lass? I told you to ask him for Thursdays or Fridays. Did you tell me, and I forgot?" He was trying to help her.

Bless his Irish soul.

She pushed cool night air past the lump in her throat and sat upright.

"Friday, Da. He'll be here Friday." She looked at Frank. "I saw Benjamin in Nirvana. Samuel drove me out in his auto last week, and I showed him around. It was nice."

She stared into Frank's eyes. They seemed cold, or maybe she expected them to be. Maybe she felt guilty . . . and shouldn't . . . had no reason to.

"Going in," Patrick said. "You coming, Bear?"

"Soon." Bear settled back in his chair like he didn't exist. His breath quieted. He was still. Absent.

Frank broke the silence.

"So, you went to see the man we fought about. The same damn man. I hate that." He laced his fingers together and turned them inside out, knuckles popping and cracking. "What's the matter with you, Abby?"

"We didn't fight about Benjamin. We didn't fight at all, Frank."

"Well, I got mad."

"And I didn't even know . . . until it was done and too late. I invited you to go with us. Remember?"

Frank rose and planted himself in front of Abby's chair, feet spread, anger emanating in heat from his tense body. He leaned forward and put his hands on the arms of her chair, and his bicep muscles flexed and twitched beneath the cotton shirt sleeve.

Bear shifted. Frank noticed but decided to ignore it. "That kind of shit has to stop," he whispered.

"Don't do this, Frank."

"You need to listen to me, Abby. I mean it."

"It's not a good night to talk. You've had some drinks, and I've had a really long day."

"Always an excuse. Isn't that right, Abs." His face moved inches from hers, and she was afraid he would try to kiss her and afraid he wouldn't. She couldn't make herself kiss him. Not like this. She couldn't.

He saw the shutters go down over her eyes and his frustration got the best of him. He shoved hard against the arms of her chair, rocking it backwards with force. Cleo's nails found his arm, and Bear stood in front of him before he knew he'd been spun around.

"Time to leave," Bear said.

"I'm staying here." Frank threw his shoulders back and tried to stand as tall and imposing as the man who'd given him orders. The bravado didn't work. Abby saw it crumble in his eyes and moved to his side.

"It's all right, Bear. Really. You go on up."

His eyebrows rose and the scars in his black beard twitched white in the moonlight. She heard a sound that could have been *harrumph* or *hmmm* or *son-of-a-bitch* coming from the beard. She wasn't sure of the words.

Frank glared. "How many men do your bidding, Abby?" He bent to grab the whiskey glass beside his chair, drained it, and stomped over to the railing and perched there. With arms crossed like he hadn't a care in the world, he stared at the two of them, the hamster in his mouth working his cheek. Bear didn't move, but Frank watched Abby pat his arm like she needed to settle him.

"That isn't the way of it, Frank. You know it isn't."

"What I know is this town has been a mess since you moved here and started changing things. Such a damned mess, I had to leave and live in some rat hole in Newaygo because of it. You're running around stirring things up and creating problems for everybody. I don't know you anymore. Don't know if I ever did."

She tugged at the braid hanging over her shoulder, and the small discomfort of hair pulling on her scalp felt right.

"I understand, and I'm sorry, but Bear is right, Frank. You need to go home. Tonight isn't a good time for us to start our marriage again. Come back tomorrow. Please?"

He dropped his head as if it was made of concrete and let it hang on his chest. Abby's heart fell, too, and lay at the bottom of her stomach, too heavy to be lifted.

"Please?" she repeated.

He tilted his head to stare at her and saw Bear was no longer there. "He go in? Didn't even hear him move. He's a damn ghost. You have a ghost boyfriend."

"Bear isn't a boyfriend; you know that. You've known Bear and Shorty for years."

He shoved away from the railing and moved toward her. She tried not to back away and watched his eyes to see if she succeeded. Frank wrapped an arm around her shoulders and pulled her tight against him, her face pressed into his chest. "You win."

She sucked in the farm aroma of his shirt and tucked it away with the tears collecting in her throat. He smelled like old Frank, the one who raced to Nirvana to spend evenings with her whether she was working in the bar, digging in the garden, or sitting on the porch. His musky, male scent reminded her of wishing and longing, of marriage and family, of memories she'd forgotten or pushed away.

"Will I see you tomorrow?" she asked, her voice broken and raspy.

"We'll see."

He loped across the yard toward the back stable, and she waited, feet tucked up in her chair, arms curved around her legs and holding them hard against her chest.

She heard the clop of his horse's hooves like the only sound in the night and watched his shadow recede. He didn't turn to wave, and she might have called him back had he done so. She swallowed, again and again, trying not to sob. The night was dead.

Cassandra meandered by the water's edge, waved her walking stick, and the cats winked. Abby was certain they did. She put her feet on the floor of the porch and her hands on the arms of the chair. A toe tilted her backwards, and she let the chair swing forward. Soon, she rocked with calm rhythm, and a cricket chirped. An owl hooted, and a bat skittered by.

Chapter Fifteen

Dog struggled up the steps with a long, dirt-encrusted bone in his jaws. He flopped onto his stomach and held it between his front paws while he gnawed on it, the end with a round white knob protruding at an angle.

"That's disgusting," Betty said. "It has rotten meat hanging on it. You'll get sick, Dog."

"He's fine," Al said.

"Looks like a cow bone. Way too big to be a rabbit or possum. He couldn't catch one anyway. He's too old."

She poked Al who sat next to her on the bench Shorty had made for the porch. "Look at it. What do you think it is? Maybe a horse or a moose?"

Al snorted. "No moose here."

"Why didn't you give him a proper name? Dog is so . . . inconsiderate." She waved her hands in the air.

"Inconsiderate?"

"Yeah. Like you didn't care about him enough to think of a good name for him. It'd be like my Ma naming me Girl."

"Pa named him."

"Well, Dog is really liking the moose bone."

Al stroked the purring, orange fluff ball on her lap, who didn't have a name except Kitty because every name she came up with paled beside her value in the world. Kitty was all hers and special.

A shiny, black vehicle chugged down the lane making both women stand and crane their necks to see who it brought, like stretching might bring it into view quicker.

"Who do you know with an automobile, Al? You keeping secrets from me?"

Al shrugged and shook her head. She was still shaking it when two doors opened and Shorty and Benjamin climbed out. Betty flew down the step and ran to the auto. "Can I touch it?" she asked, her voice full of awe.

Benjamin smiled. "Sure. Touch away."

She ran her hand over the fender and down to the lights in front with a paper light touch. "What if it rains?" she asked, bouncing on her toes in excitement.

Benjamin patted the top lying collapsed behind the second seat. "It's a convertible. When it's nice outside, I want space, open air and wind in my face."

Shorty waved at Al who stood on the porch leaning against the new railing.

"Don't you want a ride?" he asked.

"Really?"

"Would I lie to you, Al?"

"Don't think so."

When Al left the porch, Dog followed, dragging his bone in the dirt.

"Holy shit," Benjamin said when Dog drew near. "Where'd he find that?"

"What? The bone?" Betty asked. "We thought probably on a Moose." She laughed at her own little joke.

Benjamin's brows came together. "You did?"

"I was joshing. It's probably a cow leg."

"No. He's chewing on a human leg. A femur. I saw enough of them in France to know the difference between animal and human. Do you have an old towel or a big rag we can wrap it in?"

Betty paled and backed up, her hand out in front of her like the bone might rise up and commit retribution.

"What for?" Al asked.

"It needs to go to the sheriff," Benjamin said.

Shorty's eyes roamed the clearing where the house and barn sat, looking for trails into the field on one side and woods on the other.

"What?" Al asked, watching him.

"Wondering where the dog wanders. Do you know?"

"The woods. He used to hunt."

Betty came back with a ragged towel and handed it to Benjamin who relieved Dog of his prize. He looked wounded, offended by the treachery and ambled off.

"A human leg? That can't be. Are you sure?" Betty cringed away from Benjamin's package.

"I'm sure."

Shorty watched Dog as he headed for the woods, his gait as determined as he could muster given his age and creaky joints.

"You might want to call him back, Al," he said.

"Yup. I figured." She whistled, and Dog spun, sat and glared. "Come on, Dog. You come back."

His head turned in the direction of the woods like he might go anyway, and Shorty was sure he heard the dog cuss. But he got up and ambled back - much slower than when he left, sat on Al's foot and gazed up at her, longing written in his sad, hound dog eyes.

"Good boy," she told him.

"We need to get the sheriff," Benjamin said. "Want to come along? We came here to take you ladies out for a ride."

"You'll have to leave Dog in the house for now, though," Shorty said, "less you want to bring him."

"No. I'm staying."

"Then I'll stay with you. You go on with Benjamin, Betty. Have a nice ride."

"You don't need to be here," Al said.

"I'm here cuz I wish to be."

"Kind of spoils the ride bringing a leg along," Betty said. "Don't suppose it comes with a ghost, do you? You good if I go, Al?"

"Yup. Fine."

They stood in the dirt drive until the sound of the engine faded into a consistent buzz no louder than a small swarm of bees

"I'll find us a drink," Al said.

"Come on, Dog," Shorty said, following. He lowered himself to the bench he'd made, knowing it would hold his weight but not sure at all about the chairs in the kitchen. Dog leaned against his leg hoping for a scratch or a pat, anything at all, given he'd been good enough to let go of the best bone he'd ever had . . . and he'd come when he'd been called. Exemplary behavior!

Minutes stretched with no Al, and Shorty wondered if she'd taken off for the woods. He wouldn't put it past her to investigate on her own. But she hadn't.

She stood at the back window staring at the forest, at the trees they'd hid behind when he thrashed around in a drunken rage looking for someone to hit. When he'd come close to finding them, her oldest brothers always gave in, let him find them, and took the beatings. They'd warn her and Marcus to stay hidden until night, until he passed out.

They did. And they survived.

Al heard the big man's footsteps but didn't turn. Shorty stopped behind her.

"It's him, isn't it?" she said.

"Who?"

"You know."

"Your Pa? Why do you think it's him, Al? Why would he be in the woods, dead?"

She shrugged. "Somebody besides me had to want him dead. He was Satan."

"Could be."

He spied the jug she'd been about to pour from before the distraction of the window and filled two small glasses. He waved it in front of her fixed eyes, and she took it, sipped and walked to the small kitchen table.

"The porch, Al. Your furniture isn't safe with me."

"Okay," she said, and Shorty saw her lips cease their grimace.

The smooth whiskey warmed from the inside where new fear lived. Shorty dreaded another ordeal for Al. She didn't deserve it.

They listened to daylight leaving.

Farm sounds at approaching dusk don't resemble any other. Near the lake, loons, ducks, frogs, and crickets own the evening and make their proprietorship well known. Sitting on Al's porch, Shorty couldn't spot a single one of those voices, except the crickets, of course.

What he heard, however, was strangely comforting. Chickens clucked, a cooing kind of sound as if they wanted to let you know how contented they were. The cow lowed, not an irritated – *milk me* – demand, but a breath, a song she sang to herself and the chickens. They communicated their comfort, and it surprised him. No wonder Al loved them.

She made breakfast for supper. No fried chicken for her, but she did use their eggs. He washed the dishes and she dried, murmuring silently about men in her kitchen. They'd put the last dish on its shelf when fowl squawking heralded the coming of the automobile before they heard it chugging.

Betty's voice competed with the birds. "I never ever, ever had so much fun. Al," she yelled, "you should've come. We flew down the road, and the wind in my face and hair was – well, you just can't imagine. You surely can't."

"The bone?" Al's eyebrows raised.

"Oh, I forgot. It's not moose. Definitely human femur like Benjamin said." Betty's silk skin flushed a deeper russet, and she turned away.

Al kicked at the dirt, and Shorty touched her arm, held it while he questioned Benjamin.

"Did you see Hicks?"

"I did. He'll be out tomorrow morning."

"What did he have to say about it?"

"You know Hicks. He stuttered, made a joke and clutched his chest. Man's gonna have an attack one of these days."

"Tomorrow? Do we need to be here? I have to work," Betty said. "Al, too."

"Do you want someone here? I could leave the construction site to Bear for the morning."

"You would?"

"I would. Nobody'll notice my absence."

Al's face turned toward the woods again, and her eyes clouded. Not with tears, but memory. Her nostrils widened as if attempting to get air into her lungs facing a downpour.

Shorty guessed at her thoughts because he didn't know for certain what lay in Al's mind. She rarely said.

"Come on. I'll pour. You've earned it, girl. Drink Benjamin? Betty?"

Al came in earlier than usual, hoping to see Shorty and make sure he had some breakfast before he left for the farm. She knew he couldn't function without his morning coffee. Sausages and potatoes were browning in their cast iron skillets when he swung through the doors and into the kitchen on cat's paws, silent and effortless, surprising Al. She made more noise walking than he did, and she took up less than half his space.

"Smells good," he said, as she moved the coffee to the back to keep warm.

"Where's Bear?" She handed him a large cup filled to the brim with Patrick's chicory blend coffee.

"On his way." He wrapped his hand around the cup and sniffed its steam. An involuntary moan of pleasure escaped.

"Does anyone else know?"

"Bear, but you know him. He wouldn't say feed me if he was starving and near death's door. You afraid of people knowing?"

Al yanked the faded blue ribbon from her hair and walked away. She came back from the pantry with her blonde hair retied into a neat pony tail and swinging behind her back.

"I didn't mean to insult you, Al. It's just a question."

"Sure. It's okay."

She poked the potatoes with a spatula and scooped a mound onto a plate, piled a bunch of sausages next to it and set it in front of him. "Want eggs?"

Shorty shook his head. They were a great pair. She never talked much, and, in the morning, before his coffee, he usually didn't talk at all. It's a wonder he hadn't put her up on the tall cupboard already. A black streak flew across the room and landed on his shoulder.

"Cleo," he said, and she tried to answer. Her mouth opened, but nothing came out. "Lot like Bear, aren't you?"

He left as Abby came in, timing it so he didn't have to answer questions. If Al wanted to, it was up to her. He tugged Al's pony tail, said thanks for breakfast, and waved on his way out.

Shorty waited on the porch, listening to the sounds of morning on the farm. "Not much different than evenings, Dog. Pretty peaceful."

Before she left, Al had tied Dog to his dilapidated dog house. He didn't like it much and bayed as only a hound dog can, until he figured she couldn't hear him anymore. He started in again as soon as Shorty rode in. To shut him up, Shorty let him wait on the porch with him.

"If you stay put, Dog, I'll fix your house. How'd you like a new roof?"

He was half asleep with the dog's head on his lap, when Sheriff Hicks stomped up the steps.

"Didn't hear you," Shorty said with a start. "Thought you'd bring that fancy new contraption the county got for you to ride around in."

"Woulda been nice, but might be riding through the woods a bit and thought old Maggie would do it better."

"That's a thought."

"That thing track?" Hicks asked, pointing to Dog.

"I wouldn't know, but he tried to head back into the woods after we took the bone from him. Al tied him up or kept him in the house after that."

"Smart move."

The sheriff sat on his horse like he wanted to leave. Even his mare wanted to be gone. She snorted puffs of air from her nostrils and pawed the ground, and Hicks patted her neck to calm her.

"Well . . . guess I better get at it."

"Want company?"

"Sure, and why not bring the dog? You never know."

"Name's Dog."

The sheriff gave him a quizzical look like he thought Shorty had been in the sun too long.

"I called him a dog," he said. "Did you think I thought he was a cat or a possum?"

"No. His *name* is Dog. Like Rover, only Dog."

Hicks snorted. "He'd do that."

"He?"

"Old man Tatum. Meanest son of a bitch I ever met."

"Think the femur could be his?"

"I hate to say I hope so, but I do, and I'll deny I ever did."

Shorty's big gelding stood in the shade of an old Ironwood, saddled and ready to go. He climbed on, tipped his hat to the Sheriff and said, "Come on, Dog."

His old bones creaked when he got up, but, once standing, Dog took the lead. Not looking right or left, long ears swinging back and forth, he trotted along the banks of a creek where a path had been made by feet other than theirs. The canopy of leaves shaded them and provided a place of serenity either man would enjoy under other circumstances and with a fish pole in their hands.

For half an hour, Dog's feet never strayed from the creek bank. He lifted his nose to sniff the air and moved on with purpose. He knew exactly where his paws needed to go.

The grave site was a feasting place for a forest full of animals. The digging talents of dogs and wolves had been employed, and bones lay scattered inside and outside of the shallow, ragged hole.

Shorty saw pieces of fabric, still attached to fragments of bone, and visualized the arm wearing a blue sleeve, a foot with a brown sock. Dog picked up a smallish bone, and Sheriff Hicks told him to drop it.

Dog looked at him and gripped harder. He didn't growl, but the look said he could and more.

"Dog," Shorty said, maintaining the soft whisper of his voice, and the animal rolled his eyes and put it back where he found it.

"How'd you do that?" Hicks asked.

"Don't know. Good Dog." He turned in the saddle. "What now?"

"I need to take a look around."

The grave hole held chewed pieces of unidentifiable bone, minus a head. Shorty recognized ribs, an ankle bone attached to a foot and a pelvic bone. A grime covered belt lay near the pelvic bone, coiled like a snake, and Shorty saw Al's bloody body and flinched. He knew whose bones were in the hole. He pointed to it.

"Is there a buckle attached?" Hicks asked. He got on his knees and shoved the bone aside. "Would be great identification." In the black dirt, still attached to the end of the leather belt, lay the buckle.

"What now?" Shorty asked again.

"This is going to tell us what we need to know." He held up the belt, buckle moving like a pendulum in the air. "Well, at least tell us who's dead, if not how he got that way."

Shorty nodded. "Pretty much sums it up."

"Yeah. I'm betting this buckle saw the backsides of all the Tatum kids. Bastard. Can't think of a better thing to steal from him for all eternity."

"What do you want to do with all this?"

"Fill in the hole with the rest of him and put some rocks on top. If I had my way, I'd give him to the wolves and coyotes, but . . . well, you know." He rubbed his chest and pounded a flat hand against his heart.

"You okay?"

"I will be." He grabbed a shovel hanging from his saddle and stuck it in the dirt. Shorty took it, gave him a *don't argue with me* look, and dirt and bones flew.

"Sit," Shorty said as he hauled rocks to the grave, but this time Hicks ignored him. They piled them a foot high and stood back to observe their work.

"We done?" Shorty asked.

Hicks picked up the buckle. "We are. Unless you want to say anything over the grave?"

"I do." He faced the grave. "The good Lord might forgive you, but I don't, Tatum. You're an evil son of a bitch, and you'll pay when the Lord turns you away. That's all."

When they neared the farm, he heard her calling for Dog long before they got to the clearing. He hadn't thought about leaving her a note. For all she knew, Dog had chewed through the rope and ran off to find another femur.

"My fault, Al. I untied him so he could show us where he got the bone," Shorty said.

"Did he?"

"Sure did. Dog is a good old tracker," Sheriff Hicks said. He threw a leg over the saddle and slid down.

"Coffee, Sheriff?"

"I could do with some."

She went through the open door to the kitchen and Hicks shoved his hand into the saddle bag for the belt.

"You showing it to her right off?" Shorty asked.

"Why wait?" he said, craning his neck. "Get on down here. You're a giant on the back of a damned elephant. Hurts my neck talking to you."

Shorty climbed down, but Hicks still had to lift his head.

"Why not show it to her and see if she recognizes it right now? We have to do it sometime," the sheriff said.

"Yeah. I know. It's just – shoot. She's been through a lot."

"And she's tough. To my way of thinking, she'll not want to ponder about those bones. And she'll want to know they're buried proper."

"I would," she said from the doorway. "What'd you find?" Al never wore the ribbon when she wasn't at work, and her hair fell over her shoulders, picking up the afternoon sunlight. It shimmered with gold streaks on a bed of snow. Both men stared at the picture she made, framed by the door opening as if she were a portrait.

"Go ahead and pour that coffee, Al," the sheriff said. "I'll bring it in.

She did, and he put the belt on the table by their cups. Al froze, sucked air into her lungs and let it out little by little like her chest had developed a slow leak. Shorty moved to her side and watched her face.

"You know this buckle?" Hicks asked.

"Yup. I know it."

"Is it your Pa's?"

"Yes."

She took her coffee and walked outside. They found her scattering feed to her hens. The doors to the barn stood open, and she had the strap to a feed bag over one shoulder. She sipped from the cup in one hand and tossed feed with the other. The hens pecked the ground around her feet, clucking pleasantries to her and each other, and she talked to them. She strung together more words than Shorty had ever heard her speak before. He took a seat on the bench to wait. Sheriff Hicks tucked the belt and buckle back into his saddle bag and mounted.

"She alright, do you think?" he asked Shorty.

"She will be. I'll wait here until Betty gets home."

Chapter Sixteen

"They burned crosses in Mancelona last week," he said and smacked the Reed City Herald with a disgusted flip of the hand. Jesse kept up with the news and filled them in. Abby poured the whiskey. It had become a weekly ritual the friends looked forward to.

Edna made a noise in the back of her throat that sounded like a Grandma chastising a four-year-old. "What're they doing that for? They think it scares us?"

"It's a hundred miles north," Samuel said.

"Might as well be next door the way it riles folks up," Jesse added.

"You mean coloreds," Samuel said. "It riles colored folks, but the crosses aren't for us. No, it's for all you white people."

Abby stopped rocking. "Want to explain yourself, Samuel?"

He sat next to her, not bothering to move when Frank showed up for the nightly porch sitting, and now he patted her arm just for amusement.

"Sure. The KKK doesn't like Catholics any better than they like negros. Probably doesn't say so in the paper, but Big Rapids, Remus and Morley have rising Klan numbers for a reason. White Cloud, too."

"Come on," Abby said. "In this day and age? Why?"

"Each one of those towns has a Catholic Church. The Klan believes only in Protestantism. Kind of takes the pressure off us, doesn't it Jesse?" Samuel didn't grin, but the light in his eyes said he was having fun.

Too much fun, Abby thought, but changed her mind. *Why shouldn't he?*

"As long as they leave folks alone," Edna said. "No blood. No killing."

"Speaking of killing, there's a story on the back page about old man Tatum," Jesse said. "You all hear about it?"

They had, but they needed to talk about it anyway, needed to scuff it up around the edges and make it old news. They needed to put it to rest.

"We all questioned it when he came up missing right after . . . well, after Al. His horse left," Edna said. "Thought he ran off, too."

"Didn't run far," Patrick said. "Or fast enough, apparently. Wonder who wonked him?"

"Why do you think somebody did?" Abby asked. "Wonk him, I mean." Patrick stared at her, a sweet gleam in his eye.

"That's one of the reasons I love ye, lass. Ye have the pure heart of a saint."

A snort came from Frank, but everyone ignored it and chuckled at Patrick's words. Abby widened her eyes and rolled them. "Really, Da. Why?"

"He didn't bury himself," Samuel said.

"Oh. Of course. I wasn't thinking. How stupid."

"Don't bother your pretty little head with thinking, Abby. It'll just tire you out. That's men's work." Samuel flinched when she backhanded his arm.

Their laughter took the edge off Jesse's news and memories of Al's struggle to live. Everyone nestled back, and the rocking chairs settled into a rhythm meant to respect the night.

Every chair but Frank's.

"How do they know it's him? Other than because it's his woods," he said.

"The buckle. It was in the hole with him," Shorty said, not wanting to relive the whole ordeal.

"How do you know that?"

"I found it."

"Why? Were you looking?" Frank's voice had an edge like sandpaper on metal, making heads turn and stare.

"Yes. Hicks and I were looking." Shorty put his hands on his knees and leaned forward. "Something wrong, Frank?"

Frank scratched his head. "Just trying to keep up with what's happening. I get left out of things being at the farm. That's all." His silence lasted a full minute.

"Why were you looking? Why now?"

"Jesus, Frank. Dog brought up a piece of him. Now, would you let it go?"

"Damned Dog." He rubbed his chin. "I mean, really, that's pretty damned horrible. Animals chewing on human bones. God. But that old man needed to die, doing what he did. Beating his kids and all. Especially Al. He was one mean son of a bitch."

No one had a comment. They, like Shorty, were hoping they'd heard the end of the story.

"It's getting late. I need to get home," Frank said.

He took the steps two at a time and didn't stop when Abby said she'd walk to the stable with him. She rose to follow, anyway, and called his name, but he waved a hand behind him without turning.

"Night, Abby. Maybe tomorrow."

Abby refilled glasses, sat again, and watched Cassandra and her clowder making their moonlight trek. She would worry if the night came when Cassandra didn't stroll by.

She was like fireflies, like the moon and stars, part of the night and as necessary and mysterious as they.

Breakfast sizzled when Abby came through the kitchen doors, smelling chicory coffee already percolated. Scrubbed potatoes were ready for slicing.

Al's ponytail hung down her back and her blue eyes shined clear and rested. She hadn't missed a day of work after finding out her father was dead and buried in her own woods, but Abby worried.

"You doing okay, Al?" She threw her apron over her head and peered into the girl's face.

Al backed up like Abby had invaded her space.

"Course. Why?"

"Just wondering. I mean, your pa and all."

"He was gone before."

"True. But now, well, he's gone in a different way."

"Yes, he is."

Abby scratched her head. Hard. She knew better than to offer condolences with a hug or even a pat on the shoulder. She knew what Al *wouldn't* want. But what would she *want*?

"Okay. But if you need time, you can take some days off. We'll get by."

Al walked away, went into the pantry and came back as empty handed as when she went in.

Abby flapped her hands. "Okay. I got it, Al. Finally. What you *want* is for me to shut up, so you leave me standing here and go into the pantry. Clever."

She rewarded her with a sort-of smile. "Thanks."

Al had two coffees poured before they came into the room. She set one in front of Shorty without a word. Bear grabbed his own and moved to the end of the table where Cleo waited. Abby's head swung back and forth between Al and Shorty, one eyebrow raised. What just happened?

She served Shorty. That's my job. Do I care? Hmmm.

Shorty finished his coffee and clinked his spoon on the saucer. The caffeine had done its work.

"I'll be out to work on Dog's house later today."

"I can do it," Al said.

"I know that. I'm bringing some leftover materials from the job site. It's free. We'll throw it away, otherwise."

"You sure?"

Shorty got up, tugged Al's ponytail and stood in the doorway, his face a picture of content.

"Good breakfast, ladies. Thanks. Coming Bear?"

Abby found it hard to move when they left the room. Her thoughts bounced around in her brain and came up against dead ends in a maze. What had happened? Before she could draw a logical conclusion, Betty swept through the doors with Patrick fast on her heels, and she had no time to ponder.

"Man named Longstreet is in the lobby and asking for you, Abby," Betty said.

"What does he want?"

"He didn't say. Just wants to see you."

She kissed her da on the cheek, and he wrapped his arms around her.

"You good today, sassy lassie?"

"I am, Da. I'm perfect."

"You are. You need me to meet with the Longstreet fella, just holler."

"Thanks. I'll meet you upstairs, Betty, soon as I'm finished with *the Longstreet fella*."

He leaned against the registration counter and gazed out the lobby window at the street. He was long and slender, light skinned with wispy blonde hair shadowing his upper lip. His mouth opened in a wide smile when Abby entered the room.

"Mrs. Adams," he said, extending his hand.

She took it, trying to settle the queasy feeling in her stomach. She knew this man from somewhere. Knew him and didn't like him, not at all. She pulled her hand from his, tried not to wipe it on her skirt, and asked what she could do for him.

"It's more like what I can do for you, Abigail." His gray eyes pinched shut like he believed it a handsome, congenial expression.

"And what is that, Mister Longstreet?"

"Is there a place we can talk privately?" His head rotated as he searched the lobby and eyed the upstairs rooms. "You have a private living space upstairs?"

Abby sucked in air, appalled at the man's gall.

"That's none of your concern, sir. What you have to say to me can be said right here. State your business."

He bristled, straightened his suit coat and pulled at the cuffs of the white shirt sticking out of his sleeves. He replaced the false, flirtatious squint with stiffened nostrils and pinched lips.

"I have friends," he said.

"I'm glad for you."

He made a disgusting noise in his throat, sounding like he might choke at any moment. It occurred to her she might have to save this arrogant man by pounding on his back – or maybe she'd do the world a favor and let him . . . But he wasn't dying; he was simply making a point.

"I am a member of an illustrious organization designed for the advancement and protection of humanity. Klan numbers are multiplying daily and include your father-in-law . . . as well as his sons."

Abby stepped back, unable to bear his proximity and fearful she might punch him. She didn't know why she would, other than she wanted him to shut up. She wanted to stop the hateful lies coming from his twisted lips.

"I don't believe you. What do you want with me, Mister Longstreet?"

He leaned forward, his gray eyes drilling into hers. "Prominent men in the four counties surrounding your little hotel have seen the light. They recognize Catholicism for the poison it is and realize the immigrant and negro blight our nation is suffering."

Abby turned white, and fury tied her tongue as he continued.

"Because I'm a generous man, I am giving you a chance to help us halt the forward movement of these evil . . ."

"Stop! I will *not* listen to another word."

"Yes, Mrs. Adams. You will listen. I know things."

"What things?" Her shoulders drew back. "What could you possibly know that would make me listen to your despicable drivel?"

He drew closer as if they were co-conspirators in some wicked plan. The sneer on his thin lips crawled over her skin, and she clutched her elbows with both hands.

"You sell liquor," he said.

She shook her head and shrugged a single shoulder. "Course not. Prohibition."

"Who gets your booze for you?" he asked.

"No one."

"You gallivant with prostitutes and allow them to solicit in your hotel."

"That's hogwash."

"You give jobs to negros when there are whites who need work."

"Get out," she hissed. "Get out! You are a hateful, ignorant, little man."

He ambled toward the door, determined to pay her words no heed as he walked, but he didn't make it in time. Patrick was a blur flying across the lobby. He came to a landing in front of Longstreet, drew himself up to his full, diminutive stature and put on his fiercest mask.

"If ye have a problem, ye need to be taking it up with me, mister, not me daughter. Do ye only fight the lasses?"

"Your daughter, Mister Riley, is looking for trouble – for you and for your hotel. The Klan wants what's best for America, and your activities prove you don't."

Patrick was staring up at Longstreet and didn't see Abby move behind him, didn't know she'd clenched her hand into a fist, and didn't see anything except her arm coming over his shoulder before Longstreet fell to the floor. When Patrick turned, she was rubbing her knuckles and smiling.

"God, that felt wonderful."

"Looked good, too, lass. You remembered not to tuck your thumb? Ye didn't put the rabbit in the hole?"

"I remembered. Good thing or I would have broken it."

Longstreet moaned and sat up. "I'll have the law out here. They'll shut you down."

"You do that, Mister Longstreet. I'll let the Clarion know a little girl knocked you out." Patrick hitched his pants by the suspenders. "Want I should do that?"

The man dragged himself upright, rubbed his jaw and glared at Abby. "You're crazy. You know that?"

Patrick opened the door, and the man went through. "What's the correct spelling of your name," he said with a chuckle. "The Clarion won't want to get it wrong."

Betty watched him leave from the upstairs landing.

"Pretty good right hook, Abby." She mimed the move and did a little two-step, dancing down the hallway.

Abby collapsed in the chair by the window, the starch in her spine leaving as the fury faded. She looked up at her friend miming a boxer.

And this is the woman Longstreet doesn't want working for me?

She chuckled and shook her head. "How much did you hear, Betty?"

"All the way back to 'Get out," and I'm surely glad I didn't miss that punch. Haven't had so much fun in a long time. You gotta teach me how to do that. Never know when I might . . ."

"You can stop talking, Betty. I know you heard a bunch, and I'm sorry. Longstreet's an evil man, and I can't even begin to know how his words make you feel." She stood to throw an arm around her da.

"Thanks for coming to my rescue."

"You were handling it all by yourself. I horned in on your party." He hugged her and headed back to the kitchen. Abby dragged herself upstairs. She had things to think about. Phantom and Cleo wrapped themselves around her legs and made sweet warbling sounds, trying to talk her out of the malaise Longstreet left as a parting gift.

"I can't work, cats, if I can't walk," she told them.

"Give Cleo some love, Abby. She wanted to fly off the landing at that man. Protecting you, she was, and I shoulda let her. She's got some long claws, too."

"Aw, my sweetie. Thank you." Abby stroked the black-haired beauty, and, for some strange reason, her eyes teared. She blinked it away and gave Cleo a kiss. "Love you both, now scoot."

They talked all around Longstreet's words as they swept, dusted, and changed linens. The mindless activities gave plenty of room for musing. In the last room, Betty confessed.

"I heard what he said about the Adams men."

Abby emptied the washbowl. "What about them?"

"You know. That they're in the Klan." She wiped the bowl dry and poured water into the pitcher, ran a cloth across the bureau and dusted the window sill. "You ignoring me, boss?"

"Just wondering what to say. I can't think of anything. I've got mush for brains."

Betty nodded. She understood. But she could think of lots to say about it, starting with calling them all kinds of names – none of them pretty.

"Maybe he was wrong. Maybe Frank didn't sign up," Abby said, but her words didn't hold conviction. In her heart, she figured the man knew, had seen the list. Frank would join. Bile rose in her throat, and she swallowed it back, trying to tamp down her sickening thoughts.

They finished the room in silence. Before she left, Betty patted her shoulder.

"I'm sorry, Abby. I surely am."

She went to her room, sat in the window seat and stared at the lake and the folks playing in and on it. They splashed in the water and laughed. Abby could hear their banter through the open window. In this moment, they were free . . . from worry, from harm.

She thought of Frank and went downstairs.

"I'm going for a walk, Jackson. Back in an hour."

Leafy limbs met in the center of Cassandra's path and made a lavender scented tunnel. An infinite variety of wildlife filled the nooks and crannies of the branches and it looked and sounded as if the vegetation, itself, rippled with life and movement.

A squirrel perched at the end of a branch, watching Abby who stopped, afraid the critter wanted to leap to her shoulder. She loved squirrels, but not their teeth.

"I don't think so, little one." It turned on the branch and flicked its tail with meaning.

Abby chuckled. "Feisty, aren't you."

He chattered back, and Abby pointed a finger at him. "Stay where you are. I mean it, bratty, fluffy tailed rodent."

Cassandra came around the bend, patted her shoulder, and the squirrel leaped on it.

"You hurt his feelings. Let's go in, Peri, and be nice to the nasty lady. She's had a hard day."

In the shade of the trees, Cassandra's weathered skin looked obsidian mixed with a little smoke, and her black eyes snapped with enjoyment. She wore a red and purple head-wrap tied on one side with the ends tucked under. It formed a perfect frame for her perfect face. She was regal. And beautiful. She could appear any way she chose at any given moment.

Abby wondered how she could have ever feared this woman.

Peri leaned against Cassandra's long neck as if relaxing in a hammock. He raised an arm when a finger stroked him, and Abby expected to hear the critter purr like Phantom or Cleo.

"Where's your clowder, Cassandra."

"Waiting for you. Tea, too."

"I'm not even going to ask how you knew I was coming."

Her home was a garden, today. Flowers painted every nook with color, either in vases or pots, and Abby's head spun in an effort to make sense of the visual and the mix of scents. "Where on earth did you find all these?" she asked. "They're . . . uh, stunning and . . . wow."

"You said it. On earth." Cassandra poured hot water into the tea pot and put it on the cloth covered table next to a blooming Christmas cactus. The plant apparently didn't realize it wasn't December.

"Both you and I believe a little color is a good thing, unlike Mister Longstreet. We think a lot might even be better. Look at the variety in this room; it's a rainbow."

Abby whirled, eyes wide.

"What do you know about him?"

Cassandra straightened, the teakettle still in her hand. "I know his essence," she said, her voice distant yet strong. "I know his heart is filled with sludge from the bottom of a swamp. Worse. He is a cancer."

She watched Cassandra's eyes smolder as if they would burst into flame and gripped the back of a chair, her fingers whitening as they tightened around the rail. Abby recognized a trickle of the fear she thought long gone.

"Cassandra?" she said, worried she'd fallen ill or something worse. The woman turned, smiled and put the teakettle back on the stove.

"Yes, Abby?"

"Uh, nothing. You okay?"

"Certainly."

Peri leaped from his shoulder perch to the table and lifted the top off the sugar bowl. Cassandra said, "squirrel," and he put it back, but gave her a pointed look of consternation.

Seated at the table with tea in their cups, the atmosphere returned to normal – as normal as could be in Cassandra's home. The cats took over furniture, shoulders and laps, and Cassandra told Abby what she needed to ponder in her bed at night.

"Trust your instincts, Abby. You know what you know. Partial evil doesn't exist. Only partial stupidity or blindness or half raw meat."

"Longstreet is evil. At least, I think he is."

"Did you not hear me?" Cassandra said. "You know what you know."

"No. I don't. I've made promises to people I love, and now I find they're at odds. Not the people, the promises. I can't keep both. It's impossible. One breaks the other."

"Yes," Cassandra said, like she hadn't heard a word Abby had uttered. "Some people live in a bubble. It's lonely there, but they don't know how to get out of it. And some people come out of their bubble to impact others by doing bad things for good reasons."

The words bounced around in her brain but never landed to make sense, and Abby shook her head.

She sipped her tea, breathed in its mint and jasmine scent, and sat back in her chair. She tracked its journey through her veins, from lips to legs to toes, and reveled in euphoria. She didn't know the cause of her serenity, either the tea or Cassandra or the house, but all was well.

And if not, she could handle it.

"Thank you, Cassandra. I feel so much better. You're wonderful."

"You're welcome, my friend. And a horse will come to town and speak your name. She isn't a foe. Have a conversation with her. You never know who she might know."

"I'll do that. I certainly will."

Chapter Seventeen

In the middle of their morning work, Abby heard boots pound up the stairs and Frank calling her name. She poked her head out the door of the room they were cleaning, thinking calamity had struck.

"What's wrong?"

He beamed. "Nothing. Why would something be wrong?"

"Well, you sounded like a herd of cattle on stampede. Everything all right?"

"Sure. Leave Betty to do this stuff and come for a ride with me."

"I can't just leave, Frank. This has to be done. People expect clean rooms."

"Go on, Abby," Betty said. "I'll finish up. I'll get Al to help when she's done in the kitchen if I need to."

"You sure?"

"Sure."

"You heard the girl. Let's go hitch up your buggy." Frank grabbed her hand and yanked her through the door.

"Hold on. I gotta tell Da I'm leaving for a bit."

"Right. I'll go hitch up."

Abby leaned against the seat back and wiped perspiration from her brow. The sun was high and hot, and Marie kicked up dust that swirled in the road like tiny tornados. Even the breeze from their movement made heat.

"Did you play hooky today, Frank?"

"No. Pa said it was too hot to be in the fields. We'll get back at it when the sun drops a little. Nice of your maid to let you have some time off. She the boss?"

Abby tilted her head to check his face, hoping he'd tried to be funny. If so, she couldn't see it reflected there.

"She isn't a maid, Frank, and, of course, I check with her, as I do all the employees when I leave the hotel. What I do impacts everyone. We're a family business."

"Whoa. Didn't mean anything. Sorry."

He turned down a two-track road that narrowed to a path and led to the Pere Marquette River. Its overhead branches cooled and refreshed.

"This is lovely, Frank. Do you fish here?"

"Sometimes. There's a good trout hole further up." He pulled the mare to a stop, leaped down and wrapped the reins around a limb.

Following the sound of flowing water, Abby picked her way toward the river, ducked under some low hanging branches, and found paradise with a rock to perch on. She had her shoes and socks off by the time Frank got there.

"I'm going to stick my feet in the water. Looks like heaven."

"I'm gonna stick all of me in it. In a bit."

"Sounds inviting, but . . . hmmm, I don't know."

Frank pitched an acorn in the middle of the river where the current flowed strongest and sat beside her. It bobbed once and disappeared. He flung a rock next. And another, even harder.

"This is nice, Frank. Thanks for thinking of it."

"I wanted to talk. Can't do it around the hotel, too damned many people. And you're always busy."

"That's true. I'm sorry."

He ducked his head as if he was trying to spit something out and swallowed. "When you letting me come home? I mean to the hotel?"

Abby found her own rock and tossed it in, terrified of the things she needed to reveal, afraid she didn't have it in her to talk about them.

She knew she didn't.

How do I tell my husband it seems like we've never made love, and I feel used? How do I say when you touch me, it feels as if I'm nothing more than the rock you threw in the river, and I cry? How do I say I need kisses and loving touches that don't mean you're going to pull up my nightgown?

The words were in her brain but wouldn't roll off her tongue. They were glued to the back of her throat and choking her. Tears formed and made her angry – at herself and at him.

"I don't know," she said. "You weren't very happy with me before you left. Can I ask why you even want to come back?"

"Why?" he barked and pitched another rock, but it splashed hard into the water a few feet from the bank. "We're married, Abby. Did you forget that?"

"I never forget it. Not for a minute."

"Well? I want my wife. With me, in my house. Or, at least, in my bed."

Abby stared at the current carrying long-legged bugs downstream. A heron stood on the opposite shore, watching them while keeping an eye on his prey. Without causing a ripple, he pulled a leg from the water, bunched it up into his chest, and put it down closer to shore. His head darted into the water, and he came up with dinner.

Abby understood the minnow and felt like prey between the jaws of a predator. But this was her husband, and she needed to speak. She owed him honesty, an explanation.

She started with the simpler issue and on an exhaled puff of air. "Have you joined the Klan, Frank?"

"Why?"

"I need to know. I need to know who I'm married to."

"It doesn't mean anything. It's like a business group. That's all."

Abby's eyes closed, shutting out his words and everything she knew about the Klan.

"Come on, Abs. You know it's not like you read in the papers."

"Isn't it, Frank? Isn't it the Klan men who are running around with hoods over their heads? Lynching negros? Burning crosses?"

"No. Not the men in this Klan. It's a bunch of small town professionals working for the good of the nation."

"Whose good? By whose rules?"

Abby grabbed her socks and pulled one over a foot, too angry to talk. Too disappointed. Frank pulled the other one from her hand and tossed her shoes behind them where she couldn't reach.

"Stop it! What are you doing?" She glared.

Who was this man?

"You're not running from me, Abby. We're gonna get this done."

She crossed her arms in front of her and grabbed her elbows, tried to still her pounding heart with slow breaths. But anger and confusion warred – and both won.

"Okay. Talk Frank. I'll listen."

He cocked one leg, put an elbow on it, and rested his head on his hand. He looked at her, at a loss for words. His mouth worked, but nothing came out.

A wound opened in Abby's heart, one she thought had been sutured and healed long ago. Her fingers ached to touch the corn colored curls lying over his collar and caress the harsh jaw line clenching in distress.

"We don't know each other, Frank. I don't even think we like each other. I don't feel liked by you. I know you don't like my friends. You don't like the things I do. I know you like to fish and hunt, and that's all I know about you. What do you know about me?"

His cheek bunched as he considered what she'd said, a sure sign he was frustrated.

"I know you have unreasonable ideas."

She scrunched her face trying to figure his meaning. "Okay, what ideas am I unreasonable about?"

"Thinking everyone wants this colored resort. And the Chautauqua things. Not everyone does."

"That's true. Not everyone does."

"Well, then," he said, as if all their problems were over, and they were in total agreement.

Abby smiled for the first time in minutes.

"But I do – and so do my friends."

"All your friends are colored, Abby!"

"Most of them, but far from all. What is your point, Frank?"

"Jesus." He threw the sock at her. "Listen. I just want to try our marriage again. Is that so hard to understand?"

"No. It isn't. I get that." She swallowed back the tears clogging her throat and threatening to make her mute. "The Klan isn't the only thing in the way. You need to know . . . I need to tell you . . . some other things. I find this hard to talk about."

"Spit it out, Abby. What is it? Some other man?"

"Good heavens, no. Nothing like that."

"What, then?"

"I . . . when we're . . ." She hissed and her lips fluttered. "I need to be kissed, Frank. Just kissed for the sake of kissing, and that's all. And when you touch me, I need you to remember I have arms and legs and shoulders and a face."

He wrinkled his forehead and scratched it.

"That's it? You want a kiss and for me to remember you have body parts?"

The sound of the words she *didn't* say echoed in her brain, bounced across the river, banged from tree to tree. She rubbed her face, felt it grow red and hated her inability to talk about making love.

"It's more than that, but I have trouble saying it." She turned away so she didn't have to look him in the eyes. "I'm more than a receptacle for your seed. It makes me feel used. Like our coupling is a rape without violence. But a rape, nevertheless. There. I've said it."

She gulped air like she'd been underwater and was about to drown. It felt like it. It felt like she *could* die. Perhaps even wanted to. Why was this so difficult?

Her words had hurt. She knew without even looking at him, without seeing the pain hiding in his eyes, he'd been crushed – by her.

Frank reached behind him for the shoes and tossed them at her. He stripped out of his clothes, made a shallow dive into the water, and came up for air in the middle amid a strong current that forced him to fight for shore. He paddled to the other side to a cove where deep water went calm, turned on his back and floated.

Abby watched through tears she let fall since he couldn't see them, and she couldn't stop them. Maybe she shouldn't have said anything. Maybe all women feel this way, and all men do just like Frank. Maybe Edna had fibbed or didn't know what she was talking about.

But she didn't think so.

Frank didn't speak on the way home, didn't even look at her, and Abby couldn't do either of those things. In the stable behind the hotel, he nodded at her like he would if dropping off a stranger and, without a word, unbuckled the traces to unhitch the mare.

She went to her room, washed her face and hands, and brushed her hair. She saw her mother's picture and thought about the number of times she'd found it on the floor after being knocked about by one of Frank's flying shirts. It had finally found a safe resting place in the window seat corner.

Abby sat next to it and stared at her mother. "I don't know what I'm doing, Mum. I'm ruining my marriage, and I don't know how not to."

Outside, she saw Bear and Shorty climb the steps to the porch and disappear from view. They'd be in the bar, and she needed them. She brushed her hair, thrust her shoulders back, and left the room. Music greeted her as she closed the door and walked downstairs. The soothing sound of Benjamin's hands on the piano keys brought a smile to her lips and part of the day's trauma floated away.

She wrapped an arm around his back and planted a kiss on the top of his head. His quick fingers danced two measures of a tango in the middle of his ballad and made her laugh. Heads turned, at the sudden change in music. Abby waved at them and raised her shoulders.

"What can I say? I bring out the tango in him. I have that effect on people."

Samuel grabbed a hand as she walked by and spun her around, pulled her against his chest and paraded her down the room cheek to cheek. Benjamin saw and made his music follow their tempo. Near the end of the long room, he spun her again and paraded her back.

"Now, that's how you tango." He kissed the back of her hand in mock formality and included a subservient bow.

"Why, thank you, kind sir," Abby said. "But are you on my dance card?"

"I filled it up, little lady." His eyes laughed as he sat.

Edna, sitting next to him, scowled and pulled Abby to her side. "You don't let any man fill up your dance card. It isn't appropriate, Abby. Didn't your mother teach you anything?" Her mock frown turned real.

"Oh. I didn't mean . . . I'm sorry, Abigail. I have a big mouth and no brain to run it."

Abby reassured her and went to pull her apron from its hook. She tied it around her waist and scooted behind the bar. "Looks like most of the town is here. What's going on?"

"My music," Benjamin shouted. "They missed me."

"And here comes the rest of Idlewild," Jesse said as Betty and Al came through the door.

Abby's eyebrows made big arcs on her forehead. Betty and Al *never* came back to the hotel after work. They found a table near the piano and sat with folded hands, expecting Jackson to wait on them. When he didn't, Betty called to him. "Sir, I'd like some service, please."

Jackson did a double take, and his mouth opened. "You what?"

"I believe you heard me."

He strolled to their table, eyes on Betty whose eyes didn't blink, not even once. "We'd each like a glass of Patrick's finest. Isn't that right, Al?"

Patrick, who sat at the end of the bar next to Shorty, nudged his arm. "I'm placing bets on the women. Who you taking?"

"Never bet against women," Bear said.

Phantom nudged his chin to regain lost attention, left white fur in his black beard, and Cleo purred on his shoulder. They watched Jackson's arms cross and his foot tap. He cocked his head and stared.

"You serious?"

"What do you think?" Betty crossed her own arms and furrowed her brows. "Do I have to get your boss and make a formal complaint about rotten service?"

Every eye in the room regarded the skirmish. The only sound came in through the open window, a stray cicada singing for a mate, his seventeen-year struggle for survival and the wait for reproduction nearing its end. His song was a musical picture of his life of anticipation.

Jackson glanced over to Abby who lifted her hands, palms out and shrugged her shoulders.

"A customer is a customer, Jackson. Be nice and treat them well. Maybe they'll leave you a tip."

Benjamin played *A Beautiful Woman is a Soft Summer's Eve*, and Betty smiled.

Abby handed the drinks to Jackson and heard her da say they were on the house, as Samuel, Shorty and Jesse all vied to see who would claim the honor of paying for them.

Bear tapped Abby's hand, and she peered up from pushing at her cuticles.

"Wet eyes?" he said, while everyone's attention was on Jackson. "Why?"

"Pretty sure Betty's here to see Benjamin. It's sweet."

"And that makes drippy eyes?"

She gulped and nodded.

Gus thundered through the door with Sally on one arm and Sue on the other. He bellowed his greetings, found stools for the ladies, picked Al up and swung her in a circle, threw Betty over his shoulder and set her on the piano, and looked around to see what other havoc he could wreak.

His smile stretched ear to ear and infected everyone's face. It couldn't be helped. Even if you didn't mentally commit to it, the grin made its own mark on your lips.

"Abigail, I've missed you. Your arms any darker than the last time I checked?"

"I don't think so, Gus. I'm still Irish, and my freckles and pasty face prove it. Whiskey?"

"Please. Gonna be a long night."

"Oh. For the three of you?"

He chewed on a lip and caught Shorty's eye, grabbed his drink and moved to a table where Bear and Gus joined him. Abby's eyes followed, and the tiny hairs rose on the back of her neck. After a few minutes, she wandered to their table.

"What's wrong?" Three pairs of eyes stared.

"What's wrong?" she repeated.

"Nothing, little girl. Why you ask?"

"You're lying, Gus." She put her fists at her waist and a glare on her face. "Is this about a booze run?"

"Not really," Gus said. "It's a couple of things. Sit down, Abby. Or should we get Patrick over here?" He looked at Bear for confirmation, and Bear went to get him.

"You're making me nervous," Abby said. "What's happening?"

Shorty didn't answer. He got up to get Patrick a chair.

"You boys got trouble?" Patrick said.

"We got some men trying to make us some trouble. They broke a couple of my windows. Bricks with notes attached."

"Saying?" Patrick said.

"Some cockamamie bull about not buying my booze from the right people anymore."

"What'd you do?" Patrick said.

"Fixed the windows. Didn't see anybody, so I couldn't *do* anything. But I'm watching. You had any trouble?"

Patrick rubbed his scruffy face and thought about Longstreet. He'd expected him back before this and was surprised he hadn't appeared.

"Abby had to punch a guy. That's all," he said.

A gust of laughter burst from Gus.

"You had to punch a guy?" He reached for her arm to test the bicep muscle. "You been my hero since the day I met you, coming into my bar like you owned it, sauntering up like you knew what you were doing. Now you punch a guy? I love you, Abigail."

Abby's face colored, and she looked at the bar to see if she needed to get to work. Samuel, sitting near their table, watched her, his eyes lit with a mix of enjoyment and concern. Abby knew he'd heard everything.

"Anything else?" Shorty asked. "Anything we should know."

Gus' eyes strayed to Sue and Sally.

"What?" Shorty's tone demanded information.

"Couple of the girls got knocked around a bit. Carrie Mae and Augusta. They're alright. A cut lip and a black eye is all. They laugh about it now."

Abby's eyes spit fury, thinking about Betty. Her chin raised in defiance, and her arm waved around in the air until Bear ducked.

"What about next time? Is that going to be *all* the next time?"

"I got a friend staying there, sweetheart. Right now, they're safe," Gus said. All eyes landed on Sue and Sally. "But I need help covering them."

Samuel left his stool and glided over to stand at Abby's shoulder. He listened to the suggestions and offers of help, picked a piece of lint from the sleeve of his jacket and touched her arm.

"May I?" he asked.

Abby hadn't noticed him standing behind her, didn't know how long he'd been there. She nodded, and he sat.

"It happens all over. Prostitutes are expendable trash," he said.

"That's ridiculous! You know . . ." Abby rose up half out of her chair until his hand on her shoulder pushed her back down.

"*I* don't think so, Abby. Others do. I'm suggesting our friends might need some sort of protection for a time. We may have to share that responsibility."

Abby sat back, chastised, and Samuel's eyes made a tour of the eyes at the table.

"I'm sure Jesse will agree to help – and Benjamin. Maybe even Benjamin's friends, if they visit this year. And I'd like to hear more about your right hook. Or is it a left?"

Samuel rested his back against the chair, knowing he'd stepped into another tangled nest of adders and didn't even know who the snakes were.

"Have you talked to the ladies about it, Gus?" Shorty asked. "Maybe they won't want somebody around."

"It'll just be a man sleeping there. That's all," he said.

Bear chuckled. "That could be a problem for them."

"Why?" Gus asked.

"Men don't sleep there."

Bear's words brought laughter, and tight neck muscles relaxed. Abby tried to halt the red creeping from her neckline to her eyebrows, but it didn't work.

Samuel said, "Give it up," and she punched him – not hard like the Longstreet right hook, but hard enough she heard an *oomph* that satisfied her need for revenge.

When the laughter died, Samuel asked if everyone would be comfortable with his taking charge of organizing protection for the ladies. He'd let the *sleeping* men know when they were needed. They all agreed.

"Are you three going out tonight?" Abby asked.

Gus, Shorty and Bear stood. So did Abby and tried to hug all three at once making an unusual picture – Abby, two giants and a bear.

"Be careful, please," she said, blinking and ready to round-house anyone who said it was because of tears.

Chapter Eighteen

"Why? That's what I want to know. He was as rotten as the Tatum men. Sorry, Al."

Betty flung herself away from Samuel's Model T and tugged at the collar of her blouse like she couldn't get air. He reached for her, but she slapped his hand away, not wanting consolation. She wanted to be mad.

"Get in, Betty. Benjamin and I are driving you two home."

"Why?"

"Because we want to. Now, get in, please."

Al found her spot in the small second seat. She nestled into the corner and ran a hand over the smooth leather, sniffed its musky scent. She refused to worry about George Adams or her four brothers sitting in jail. She couldn't do anything about them, and, until George got home, she couldn't do anything about him, either.

It was too dark to see, but she felt Betty squeeze into the seat next to her. The scent of anger and fear drifted to Al, and she wondered if she smelled like sorrow, if sadness leaked from her pores. She couldn't change what her brothers had done to her friend. The best she could do was understand. Be there.

Betty felt Al's tiny hand slide into hers, and tears tried hard to fall. She gulped night air to stop them.

At the farm, Samuel climbed the porch steps and peered through the window. He didn't expect intruders, but he wanted to be sure. He opened the door, slipped inside, and made a mental note to install locks on the front and back doors. The trick would be getting the women to use them. They were in the kitchen when he came down from checking the upstairs.

"You couldn't wait for an all clear?"

"Guess we didn't want you to have all the fun," Benjamin said. "The ladies were anxious."

"What's going on, Samuel?" Betty asked. "You think you're Sherlock?"

Samuel gave a lopsided, half grin. "As in Holmes?"

"I read. You'd need a pipe and a cape."

"Sit, please ladies," he said. "We need to talk."

"Jeez. More cloak and dagger." Betty sat after glancing at the looming annoyance on Samuel's face.

Benjamin sat next to her and draped an arm across the back of her chair. She felt the minute contact and didn't care what Samuel had to say. She was happy. Peaceful. Safe.

"I'm going to install locks on these doors, and you're going to use them when you leave – so, when you return, you won't have uninvited guests in the house waiting for you. And you're going to use them when you go to bed. Understand?" Samuel let his eyes drill into the blue and brown eyes of the ladies.

"That's fine," Al said.

"Why? What's going on that we need locks all of a sudden," Betty asked.

"A few incidences have occurred, and I want to be sure you and Al aren't on their party list."

"That's ridiculous," Betty said. "A party sounds nice. But why would we be on anybody's list?"

"A bunch of reasons," Samuel said. "Can't you simply take my word for it?"

"What happened?" Al asked.

Samuel cocked his head to look at her and decided to explain about the windows in Gus' bar and about the battering of the prostitutes.

Betty leaped from her chair at the word prostitute. It crashed to the floor, and Betty's lips whitened.

"You calling us prostitutes, Samuel? I knew it. You played all good guy with me, but you're no different than all the rest. Men do things to women, and women pay the price. Damn you, Samuel Moore."

Benjamin righted her chair and tried to wrap an arm around her, but she knocked it away.

"Sit down, Betty. I'm not saying anything like that. You know me better." When she remained standing, Samuel repeated it until she relented.

"We don't know who did these things, but we suspect it's the Klan being guided by bootleggers or vice versa."

"Why would they care about Al and me?"

"Not sure they would." Samuel tapped Betty's arm. "Don't know if you've noticed, but three of us in this room are black." He ducked his head and tried to get a smile. "You did notice that, right?"

"Quit it with the funny stuff. Just say it. Why would they care about us?"

"If it's Klan doing these things, they might care just because you're a negro, and you live with a white woman, and you work for Abby. If it's mob, because you both work for Abby. Either way, you could become targets. I don't know that'll happen and want to be careful."

"Oh. I thought this was all about George getting out of jail," Betty said, fiddling with her bottom lip.

Benjamin spoke for the first time. "Hope the man learned his lesson."

"How is it George gets off so easy?" Betty asked.

"Family hired a lawyer. The others didn't have one."

Samuel peered at Al. If hearing her brothers discussed this way bothered her, she didn't show it. But Al didn't show much of anything, even at the worst or best of times.

Her hands rested in her lap. Her eyes followed from Betty to Samuel and back again as they spoke. She filed the information, but it had nothing to do with her. She had perfected flawless stoicism in her body language, on her face and even in the movement of her eyes. Samuel wondered what flame burned beneath her cool exterior, or if the flame she was born with had been snuffed out by her family.

"We good?" Samuel asked.

"We good," Betty said, the sparkle back in her eyes.

"Al?" Samuel said.

She nodded and headed for the stairs to her bedroom.

"Guess we're invited to let ourselves out," Benjamin said. In the auto, he asked if Samuel really thought the women might have trouble.

Samuel shrugged. "I don't know. But those two have endured enough in their short lifetimes. I'd kill the man who gave them more." He turned his head to stare hard at Benjamin until he came close to driving off the road. "You included."

Benjamin's head jerked back against the seat, and he returned the stare.

"What the hell did *I* do?" he asked.

"Nothing, yet. Don't hurt that girl." His words were softer this time, and his lips quirked.

"Oh. I get it. By the way, if we need *friends*, I'm looking to have some company soon. Just so you know."

"How many?"

"Five. Same number."

"Thanks, my friend. I'll keep that in mind."

The bar was quiet in the hush before the evening rush, and Abby worried at a nail she'd broken, wondering if asking to talk with Edna had been a good idea. She'd thought so last night, but in the bright light of day she stewed over sharing her personal life. What did she want from her friend? Validation? To know Frank was just like Jesse and all other men – no better, no worse?

When Edna came through the door, she wanted it over with so they could move on to church matters, the real business of the day. She pulled out a chair for her friend, poured coffee for them both and blurted it out.

"Frank wants to come home."

Edna rocked back. Her skin flushed a gorgeous shade of mahogany, and she stuttered as she tried to respond.

"Y-you can't be serious?"

"I am, and I don't know what to tell him."

"You tell him, no. That's what you tell him. You surely know how to say that by now. I've been teaching you for a long time." She shook her head and tisked and hemmed, over and over, like somebody's granny.

"I can't just say no. He's my husband. I made vows before God."

"The good and all-knowing Lord would let you off the hook."

Abby sipped at her coffee and pondered how much her friend knew about their marriage. She figured Edna suspected things Abby hadn't had the courage to talk about. "Why don't you like Frank, Edna?"

"It isn't about liking. It's about how he treats you. And that isn't good, friend, and I know it."

"I talked with him about – some things. He's going to think about them. And that's good. That's the right thing to do, isn't it?"

Abby was aware of the fib and hoped it didn't show. He never said he'd consider what she'd said. He hadn't said a word after he dove into the water to get away from her. She stuck the end of the broken nail between her teeth to gnaw at something, and Edna slapped her hand and narrowed her eyes.

"You've heard about the leopard and his permanent spots, yes?"

"Sometimes you're a witch, Edna."

"I know." She smirked, and Abby put a hand on her friend's shoulder.

"Well, thanks for the insights, but Frank isn't the reason I wanted to see you today. I want to start having church services that include all of us. Whites and coloreds. Will you help?"

"Back to that, huh? I remember this same discussion when you first came here. Didn't work then, either."

"Did, too. I went. I still do, and I'm white."

"That's true, and you surely are white. I think they've all gotten used to your pasty face. You don't shock them anymore."

"I miss that." Abby chuckled, remembering some of the early expressions when she waded through the congregation to find an empty chair.

"So, what do you want to do? How do you want to go about this unification of our pious groups?"

"You're being irreverent."

"Yes. I am."

Abby hunched forward like she was plotting strategy for a battle, and Edna joined her. Patrick tapped them on their heads when he walked by, and they both jumped as if caught spying for the enemy.

"Darn, Da! You scared me."

"Are ye doing something you shouldn't be, then, lasses?"

"No. Planning church services. It's a virtuous thing."

Patrick left them to their plotting, and they did.

"We have two pastors. Why can't they alternate? Reverend Evans preaches one week, and Jenkins preaches the next. We hold all services under the pavilion."

"And if it rains?"

Abby pulled on her bottom lip with her teeth, and Edna laughed.

"God, you have big teeth. You're a beaver. Anybody ever tell you that?"

"I think you're trying to hurt my feelings, Edna."

"No, I'm trying to distract you from another crazy idea."

"It isn't crazy. We need to be together. It's being separate that's crazy."

Edna thought she'd hurt her, and it didn't feel good, but Abby wanted so much that couldn't happen overnight. And to her, it couldn't happen fast enough.

"Okay, Abby. What do we do?"

"I have a list of people who need to agree to the plan. I'll contact my in-laws, Reverend Jenkins, Reverend and Gertrude Evans, Charity, of course, Bunny Parker, Betty's folks, the Rumfords, and I'll even stop in and invite Joe Foster." She ran a hand over her mouth wiping away the vile taste of his name on her lips.

"And me? What do I do?"

Abby's face took on the cat and the canary look. "It's all written out for you. Thanks, Edna. I love you for helping. I have a glass of wine with your name on it."

"That's the first sensible thing you've said all day. Did the boys make it back without any trouble last night?" she asked over her shoulder as Abby went to the bar.

"They did. Bear and Shorty rode and Gus drove the wagon, just in case."

"And how would that help?"

"Bear and Shorty are tough. They've done it all, and they're smart. If necessary, they'd deal with enemies while Gus moved the wagon and supplies on down the road. Thank God, they didn't need to. I worry even though I have faith in them."

"I can see that."

"They're my brothers, Edna."

"I wouldn't mind a couple of brothers like the two of them."

"Oh, and Samuel put locks on Al's farm today. He's something."

Edna agreed, thinking she'd seen changes in Samuel she would never have believed possible.

"Once upon a time, I couldn't stand the man - and his arrogance and standoffishness. Is that a word?" she said.

"It is, now." Abby had thought the same. "Once, he told me he wasn't an Uncle Tom, in that uppity way of his, and I told him he didn't have a clue about Tom. And that insufferable man makes me use words I'd never use with anybody else."

She sipped her coffee and watched Abby's face.

"Like deem. I mean, really, Edna. Did you ever hear me say *deem*?" She put her pinky finger out and raised her chin.

"No, never did. But I'm gonna listen real good from now on."

"I have to get to work, but you are welcome to that glass of wine," Abby said as the evening's first customers came through the doors.

She flopped on her bed and the cats pounced – one on her stomach and one on her pillow. She could feel the rumbling of their purrs, and it satisfied in a way no other sound could.

"If I could purr, I would. Teach me how, you two. Teach me to make that glorious sound."

Phantom's round eyes stared at her. *You should know by now, Abby. What the heck?*

"Yeah, Bear probably knows how, doesn't he? He's a rat, stealing my cats."

The decibels increased, and Abby wished she hadn't committed to going. She wanted to close her eyes, snuggle with her cats, and learn purring.

"Gotta go, babies. Gotta see if Bunny Parker will let me invite a bunch of white people to her house."

Phantom had other ideas and met her at the buggy.

"You sure?" Abby asked the ghostly feline. He curled into the corner of the seat and closed his eyes.

She recalled the first time she attended church at Bunny's place. Everything was perfect . . . until she called Bunny's sister a witch.

She had yet to meet the strange, wild-haired woman, and, at the time, had only seen her. But when Abby uttered the *word*, Bunny's face went blank and stony in the flash of an instant. The beautiful, warm woman became granite, and Abby wanted to run, far and fast.

"It wasn't my fault," she said to the mare. "How could I know Cassandra was her sister? And she really is a seer . . . a prophetess, cat-woman kind of witch."

Marie didn't respond.

"I'm talking to you, Marie."

The mare nickered and bobbed her head.

"Thanks. I like to know I'm not being ignored. I think Bunny and I are alright, now. I hope so, but she's hard to know and so intense."

She pulled into the yard, and her skin grew clammy as she leaped down, drew the mare into the shade and threw the reins over a branch.

"I won't be long. Don't run off, Marie. Phantom, stay put. I don't want to have to go searching for you."

Mrow.

When she turned, she saw Bunny on the porch. Her arms were crossed, and the look on her face was indecipherable, but Abby was determined to think it placid – peaceful.

"Cassandra said you talk to animals."

Abby's feet stuck to the ground. "Um, why do you say that?"

"Because Cassandra said it, as I believe I made clear."

"Oh. Of course."

"Of course, you *do* talk to animals? Or, of course, I'd made myself clear?"

"I'm confused, Bunny. I can still call you Bunny, can't I?"

"Yes. Come in."

Abby unglued her feet, and they moved of their own accord up to the porch where Bunny took her arm and gave her a look. It didn't come off as a real smile. The lips moved, but not so much you'd notice, and the eyes slanted, but you wouldn't notice that, either. On her, though, it looked like she could be smiling.

"I was teasing you, Abby."

"About talking to animals?"

"No. Cassandra did say that, and she never fibs. I was playing with you with words. I like to do that sometimes just for the fun of it."

Bunny opened the door and waved Abby in.

"Okay. I feel better now, and I do talk with animals. Cassandra does, too."

"Yes. They respond much better than people, occasionally. Have a seat, dear. What can I do for you? This isn't about Jackson, is it?"

"No, Jackson is fine. This is about church – and about something we discussed a long time ago." Abby looked for courage. "You said whites and coloreds need to worship separately. That we weren't kin. That we didn't understand each other. Do you remember that?"

Bunny's regal head moved back and forth on a long, slender neck. Abby wanted to be behind those black eyes, to crawl around in her mind and know what she knew.

"But when Al was fighting for life, you invited me to a family gathering. Your family."

"I recall."

"I want . . . I want us to worship together. One family. Because that's what we are in His eyes."

Bunny's head swung as if she heard music Abby couldn't. Back and forth it went while Abby waited for her music to end and her words to begin. She got up from her chair and squatted beside Bunny, took her hand and looked up.

"Please, Bunny. If you hate it, we'll stop. Just try it for a while. See how it goes. Maybe you'll love it."

She explained how they'd rotate preachers and places, always trying to be at the pavilion when weather permitted. Bunny grunted, an unusual sound to come from this imperial woman. She shoved a nonchalant hand at Abby who landed on her bottom on the floor.

"Get up, girl. You look silly."

Abby scrambled and stood at Bunny's side, a wayward school child, waiting and hoping.

"It's at my house on Sunday, so I'll invite who I want. Who do *you* want, Abby?"

Abby told her and she frowned.

"Then I'm inviting them. You tell them to come."

Tears came to Abby's eyes. She didn't know how to control her excitement and joy.

"Thank you. Thank you so much, Bunny." She wrapped her arms around the seated woman who pushed her away.

"Stop this nonsense. What are you doing?"

"Sorry."

Abby stepped backwards toward the door and said goodbye, wanting to be gone since her goal had been met. On the porch, she spread her arms to embrace the day. It was glorious. Though there were others to talk to and miles to go, she walked on a cloud.

"Did it rain on the way here, Marie?" She untied the reins and climbed into the buggy. "I have no idea. Could have been snowing."

She nickered and Marie moseyed off.

Abby didn't relish the visit to Reverend Evans' home, but he was necessary to the completion of her plan. He opened the screen door and stood in the doorway without inviting her in. She smiled, talked about the beautiful day and how well he looked. Phantom leaped from the buggy seat and landed at the Reverend's feet. He lurched sideways, hit his head on the door frame and collapsed in a soft mound in the opening. The cat walked over him and went inside.

"Phantom! Get back here! Reverend, are you okay. Can I get you a glass of water?"

He tried to sit, put a hand on the back of his head and scowled harder than usual.

"What was that animal? Why did it attack me?"

"He didn't attack you. He leaped from the buggy. That was him leaping."

"Are you arguing with me, young woman? That animal attacked me, and I have a huge knot on my head to prove it. Probably bleeding."

Abby reached a hand to help him up, but he wouldn't take it, and she couldn't help disagreeing with him.

"Phantom didn't put a knot on your head. You fell, Reverend. And now he's in your house . . ."

A screech from inside interrupted her words, and a loud clatter followed.

"Reverend! There's a wild animal in the house!"

"Oh, for Pete's sake," Abby said, walking over the top of the pastor to look for her cat.

Gertrude Evans stood on a dining room chair, her hands pulling at the sparse, gray hair in disarray on her head. Pieces of something broken lay scattered on the floor, and Phantom, with a 'who me?' look in his eyes, sat in the middle of the room, washing his face.

"Guess they aren't animal lovers," Charity said from her seated position on the stairs. "Come here, kitty." He strolled her way, slowly because indolence was his charisma.

"It's Phantom," Abby said.

"Did you scare Daddy, Phantom?"

"He attacked me, Charity," the reverend said as he stumbled into the room, one hand on his cat-created knot, and the other holding the wall like he couldn't walk without support.

"Can I help you down, Mrs. Evans?" Abby asked.

"No. Get that rabid animal out of here."

"He isn't rabid."

"I'll take him," Charity said. She lifted Phantom into her arms and strolled to the door.

"I guess this wouldn't be a good time to talk with you about integrating our church services, huh? Sharing the pulpit with Reverend Jenkins?"

She put on a hopeful, innocent face that did nothing to develop their charitable feelings.

"Get out," he said, a shaky finger pointing the direction like she might have forgotten the way.

"I'll come back when you're feeling better, Reverend. Hope your . . . uh, knot feels better soon."

Charity sat in the buggy stroking Phantom who lay sprawled half on her lap and half on the seat. He was a big cat. "I think he likes me."

"He's a bad boy. And I have places to go. What am I to do with him?"

"Bad boys and I get along." She gave Abby a wicked grin. "I'll go with you. Take care of him while you do – whatever you need to do. I'm not busy."

They pulled up to Reverend Jenkins' home, and he met her at the door. A smile welcomed her, and Abby made a justified comparison to Reverend Evans' sour greeting.

"Welcome, Miss Abby. Miss Charity. Come on in the house. Want some lemonade?"

"I'm taking care of Abby's bad Phantom, or I would, Reverend."

"All apparitions are welcome here, Charity. Even rogues. Never know what interesting things they might have to say." He turned to Abby, still holding her hand.

"What'd you do to warrant a bad spirit, Miss Abigail? I can't imagine you doing anything too terrible. And how did you manage to hand it off to Charity?"

Abby tried not to laugh, but the thought of Charity hanging onto a rogue spirit jiggled her funny bone, and the giggle escaped. Reverend Jenkins looked wounded, his big brown eyes went sad and his smile upside-down.

"Oh, I'm so sorry. I didn't mean to laugh, but Phantom is my cat – my bad cat who made Reverend Evans fall and knock his head, walked on top of him to get in the house, and made Mrs. Evans climb on a chair and smash something."

"What did he do?"

"Washed his face."

"The reverend washed his face?"

"What? No." Abby scrunched her forehead, trying to interpret the reverend's words. "Phantom did. His own."

He slapped his leg and let out a bellow loud enough to wake the dead.

"Oh, Abby. This is delightful. Almost as good as baptizing Sue in Lake Idlewild with the whole congregation looking on in amazement and some horror."

"It is?"

"Yes. We're speaking different languages.

"I think so. I've been speaking twaddle most of the day."

"Bring your bad apparition, Charity, and come on in for lemonade."

Abby stood at the door leading to the kitchen to soak it in. The table was covered in yellow oilcloth, and four chairs held yellow, checked cushions that begged you to sit a while. The cheerful atmosphere made her sad, and she cocked her head in an effort to understand the contradiction.

Phantom *mrowed* behind her, and she turned.

"You're not going to knock me down too, are you Phantom?" the reverend said.

He poured a bowl of milk and three glasses of lemonade and set them all on the table. Three people and a cat took seats around the yellow circle.

"Here we are, then. To what do I owe this great honor?" Abby explained. The reverend laughed, and Charity's eyes got big.

"I love it," she said. "I'll bet Papa had a fit."

"I didn't get to describe it completely what with Phantom and the fall and all."

Reverend Jenkins took a long swig of the sweet drink and wiped condensation from the glass. His eyes took on a playful quality.

"Wish I'd been there," he said. "And I like your ideas, Abby, but I don't know that we're ready for it."

"Can't we try to be ready?"

"How?"

She drummed fingernails on the side of the glass, bit her bottom lip, thought of beaver teeth and quit.

"I want to just make people do it, damn it," she said. "Oops."

"Yeah," he agreed, and the devil pranced in his eyes. "I want to force folks to come to Jesus, too, but it doesn't work that way. Maybe if we withheld food? Took away their children?"

"What are you trying to do, Abby?" Charity asked, and Abby saw depth she hadn't known the woman possessed.

Abby drained her glass and took a hard look at the reverend, hoping to find words that would convince him her plan could work.

"Charles Chesnutt says we need to dismantle prejudice stone by stone and build something new, build it on esteem – something like that. I'm not sure of his exact words, but I believe him. He is a beautiful person, and he's smart."

"Yes," he said. "And how does his beauty impact your plans?"

She tapped his arm. "I think he's right, but its upside down. We need to dismantle prejudice *with* esteem. We can't *esteem* one another if we're strangers. And worship is fundamental to who we are, so if we want to know each other . . . we need to know our churches."

He steepled his fingers and bounced them off the end of his nose.

"I see, sort of. Through some strange deductive reasoning process, you've come to see the integration of our churches as the slayer of prejudice."

Abby stood up and danced in a circle, waving her arms. "Yes! So, you'll do it?"

"No! Not so fast. I have a flock to think of. And we've held pavilion services in the past."

"But not advertised as willingly integrated."

They stared at each other without words, thoughts waddling around in their brains, both wanting the same end without knowing the workable means.

"What about once a month?" Charity said. Two heads swung around, mouths open.

"Out of the mouths of babes," he said, as Abby reached across the table.

"Then you'll agree?" she asked, holding both his large hands in hers. He liked Abby, liked her soul and her wayward spirit – and her Phantom. He nodded, happy they'd found some compromise.

"Don't schedule the new *integrated* service until you've spoken with Reverend Evans and his flock. Understood?"

"Gotcha. Thank you."

She threw her arms around his neck and squeezed. Abby wouldn't dream of hugging Reverend Evans, but this felt right. She stepped back, and her face flushed with the half fib forming on her lips.

"But . . . I have to invite folks to Bunny Parker's on Sunday. Um, she asked me to."

"She asked you to?" His eyes rolled to the corner of the ceiling, looking for truth. It couldn't be found. "You sure?"

"Sort of."

Charity eyed them and shook her head. She picked up Phantom who'd made a ball of himself on the yellow cushion like he owned it.

"Let's go bad boy. Let's see what other trouble we can cook up."

Chapter Nineteen

Besides Joe Foster, she had to persuade one more family to attend church at Bunny's house. Her stomach turned crooked summersaults all the way there. She didn't know if her in-laws would invite her in or shoot her full of buckshot. Abby wagered on the latter.

She'd been to the Rumford's, whose eyes tried to burn holes in Abby's face. She didn't even make it inside their home, not even all the way onto the porch. Darnell walked off immediately, and Mrs. Rumford poked a stubby finger into Abby's chest and backed her down the steps.

"But don't you see, Ma'am, this will help our community. It will . . . ouch! That doesn't feel good, Mrs. Rumford."

"Cuz you're skinny. Stop running around all over the place with God knows who and settle down with your husband. You might put on a little womanly weight, and you wouldn't feel my bony finger on your scrawny chest." She added "Jezebel" from the other side of the screen door after it slammed behind her.

Abby's lips fluttered when she let out the air she'd been holding. Her lungs were full since she'd been sucking it in, in preparation for letting it out on a string of words directed at the woman. But she never got the chance.

Marie picked up on the state of Abby's mind and pranced sideways down the road.

"It's alright, Marie. Everything's good. We're going to have a nice ride. That's what we're going to do."

She whistled a deliberate tune as she guided the mare into the woods, taking the shortcut to the Adams' farm. The heat had let up since the blistering day Frank took her to the river. It was cool under the canopy of leaves, and the critters didn't bother to interrupt their work to notice them. They were undisturbed by Marie's movement over the soft ground. A doe looked up, glanced at her two spotted fawns, and went back to nibbling the grass, but kept her eyes on Marie until they were past.

Near a stand of oak trees, three full grown turkeys foraged on fallen acorns. Abby drew Marie to a halt to watch them scratch the damp ground with one foot and peck at the tasty treat they'd unearthed, wattles wobbling. Hearing a noise overhead, she looked up to see several more turkeys resting on branches.

"Feeling fat and comfy?"

One gobbled back at her, and Abby didn't know if she'd been berated for disturbing them or told to have a nice day. She went with the pleasantry and told herself to bone up on turkey talk.

Marie looked back at her in agreement, long dark, eyelashes fluttering. *You're just finding reasons to put it off. Get on with it.*

"You're right. Let's go, Marie."

She squinted when they came from the shadowy woods into the bright sunlight, and it took a moment for her eyes to adjust.

"Abby," Cecily said. "I haven't seen you in so long. What are you doing here?"

Abby slid from her mare and wrapped her arms around the shorter woman. She'd forgotten how much she missed her sister-in-law's company. "Where is everyone?"

"Men are in the fields, Ma's in the kitchen, boys are fishing." Cecily looked at Abby as if she could glean her thoughts by staring hard, like they might be written on her cheeks and forehead.

"Do I have something on my face?"

Cecily laughed. "No. I was just wondering."

"What, Ceci?" She put an arm through hers and moved toward the house. "What are you wondering?"

"Are you and Frank . . . you know . . . getting together again?"

"I don't know. I hope . . . I don't know."

Frank's mother was tall, broad shouldered and wide hipped, but without excess fat. She came from sturdy farm stock and moved and talked like it – no wasted steps, no wasted words, do what needs to be done, take care of family. That personified Emily Adams.

Her hands were in dishwater when they walked in, and her lips went white when she turned and saw Abby.

"Hello, Mrs. Adams."

Emily went back to scrubbing the large kettle.

"What do you want, Abigail? Why are you here?"

"Can we sit a minute, please? I want to talk with you about something."

"You can talk standing, can't you? I have things to do. Working men to feed."

Abby moved across the kitchen, so she could see her mother-in-law's face. It wore more lines than when she'd last seen her, or so it seemed, around the eyes and by the sides of her mouth. She wondered if she'd put them there – or maybe George had, but that would still mean she'd done it. He wouldn't be in jail if not for her, but jail was where he belonged, and she couldn't regret it.

"Alright. I'll stand here then."

She stepped from one foot to another and back again, laced her fingers together and steepled the pointers. A nervous sound came from her throat and startled her. She cleared it to make room for speech.

"Something wrong?" Emily said, glancing her way.

Abby loosened her fingers and dropped her arms. "No. I just don't know what to do with my hands. You know, they're just hanging there, kind of at the end of my arms, and . . . God, I'm rambling."

"You are. What do you want?"

Abby eyed the door, wanting more than anything to run through it.

"What I want is . . ." she stuttered, and the dam broke. "I want you to come to church this Sunday at Bunny Parker's house. I've invited several other families and hope you and Ceci and the boys will come. It's important. It's the beginning of what Charles Chesnutt says builds esteem, and I really hope you'll come."

"Does Frank know what you're doing?"

Abby chewed her lip and shook her head, knowing she should have found a way to say something to him first.

"Didn't think so."

"I *will* talk with him about it. As soon as I see him. I'd love for him to go, too."

"Reverend Evans preaching at the Parker house?"

Abby shook her head again. "No. Reverend Jenkins is."

"Why, Abigail?"

"I just said."

"No. You said garbage. Something about that Chesnutt man and somebody's esteem. That's all. And I don't care to know any more."

Cecily's head moved back and forth from Abby to her mother-in-law, fear in her unblinking eyes. She put a hand over her mouth like it might help her speak no evil. She certainly felt like she was *hearing* evil. Church at a coloreds' house? Her sister-in-law had gone off the deep end, for sure.

Abby moved closer to Emily and peered into her face. "To dismantle prejudice, Mrs. Adams. That's why. To learn about our folks, our community, so we can respect one another through knowledge of *all* of us. Faith is part of us."

"No. They have theirs. We have ours. Quit interfering, Abigail. Quit sticking your nose into places you don't belong. I'm sick and tired of you messing with this family. My family!"

Emily pulled her hands from the dishwater, dried them on her apron and took it off. She headed out the back door, but turned before she stepped through it.

"You aren't part of it anymore, and you need to leave."

Abby's face went white, her eyes wide with unshed tears. She turned to her sister-in-law. "You understand, don't you, Ceci? Say you understand."

"No. I don't, Abby. Why can't you just be happy with things the way they are? Why do you have to mess with everything?"

Abby pulled herself up straight and pushed her shoulders back. She nodded once.

"If you wouldn't mind, I'd rather tell Frank about all this myself."

"I'm sure Emily will tell everything at supper tonight."

Abby's next words were a whisper. "He's going to be mad at me."

"Sorry, Abby."

"Me too."

The ride back wasn't as pleasant without the hoped-for acceptance of her invitation. No acceptance and no family. She'd been disowned.

"You knew that before, Abby. You were fooling yourself. Dolt."

Marie stepped quicker going home, the idea of oats and her stable freshening her pace, but she didn't know they had one more stop to make. Abby pulled up in front of Foster's store and went inside.

Joe gave her his normal smirk, like he knew something she didn't. God, she wanted to wipe it off by planting her fist on his face, but that wasn't Christian, now, was it?

"I included His name in the fist-planting. So maybe it is," she said.

"What?" Joe said, hearing her mumbling. "Speak up."

"I will when I'm talking to you, Joe. And now I am. You're invited to church services out at the Parker home this Sunday. I hope you can make it."

She turned to leave without further explanation while his mouth still gaped, but she didn't get out the door before he'd gained control of it.

"You're crazy, woman, if you think I'm going to a colored's house for anything."

"Your immortal soul would benefit, Joe, but it's entirely up to you. Have a good day."

Joe grabbed the doorknob before she could open it and shoved himself in her face.

"Somebody's gonna hurt you someday Abby. And you'll deserve it."

Abby choked from the stench of his breath and his unwashed body. She'd never been this close to him before, by design, and tried to control a gag reflex, but it came out as a kind of grunt.

Why had it seemed necessary to invite him? In retrospect, it was stupid. Another stupid move by Abigail Riley Adams. She hung her head, as much in distress as to bring her nose close to her own body instead of his.

He gave a satanic chuckle that turned into a yelp as the door knob jerked from his hand.

Bear had Joe backed up to the counter before Abby finished saying, "Hello. Sure is good to see you."

"Thought that was Marie at the rail," Bear said. "What you doing, Joe? Keeping customers from leaving the store till they buy something?"

"She's no customer. She's a witch."

"Not nice, Joe." The scars nestled in Bear's beard grew red in his annoyance.

"But true."

Spittle gathered at the corners of Joe's mouth and flew out when he spoke. Abby sidestepped to avoid contact.

"She's got some cockamamie idea about church at a colored's house. She's doing Satan's work. Oughta be flogged. We used ta do that to witches like her."

Abby stepped forward in spite of spittle-fear and lifted her chin.

"Which am I, Joe? One of Satan's helpers or a witch? Make up your mind."

"You and that other cat woman. You're just alike. You're a menace to white men."

Bear tried to move Abby to the door, but she wasn't ready. "If you're talking about Cassandra, don't. She's my friend."

"Yeah, her," he sneered.

Her elbow raised, and a perfectly formed fist aimed at Joe's few teeth . . . but it didn't move. She twisted around to see Bear holding her arm.

"Why'd you do that? I was going to give him what he's been asking for." Her nostrils flared in anger at both of them, now.

"Let's go, Abby," Bear said, and he guided her out the door to the music of Joe's laughter biting her in the back.

"You shouldn't have done that," she said.

"You would be saying something similar if I had let you punch him."

"He needed it."

"I know." Bear's grin took the sting out of her fury, and she found herself laughing.

"You invited him to church?"

She laughed harder. "I did."

"Why?"

"I don't know. I thought I did, but it's gone." She tugged at her hair, and he took Marie's reins and ambled home.

"It hasn't been a good day, Bear. Mrs. Adams kicked me out of the house – and the family. Cecily hates me. And the Rumfords drilled me with bolts of eye lightening."

He chuckled. "Eye lightening? What in hell is that?"

"You know. When someone opens their eyes so wide you can see the whites all around the colored circles, and they glare at you without blinking. It looks strange and scary, and you feel it stinging your skin."

"Hmmm. Never had anyone give me eye lightening before. I'd kinda like to see it sometime."

Abby took his arm and pulled him close as they walked. "That's because you're sweet. They wouldn't do that to you."

He chuckled again. "Don't think so."

It was cool in the stable. They talked about nothing and took care of a grateful Marie.

"I'll brush her out, Abs. You go on in."

Abby kissed his cheek, left the stable, and went to her room. She heard voices in the bar on her way through the lobby, so she quick-stepped washing her hands and face. She kissed her cats, brushed her tangled hair and was out the door in minutes, Phantom and Cleo at her heels.

In the dim bar, she saw Samuel sitting next to Charles Chesnutt and her heart lifted. She patted his back and greeted him on the way by.

"No pat for me, Abigail? No greeting for me?" Samuel said, a hand over his broken heart.

"I'm just really happy to see Charles. I mean . . . you, too, Samuel. You know, I am." She spun in a circle behind the bar. "I'm happy to see everyone: Sue, Sally, Jesse, Edna, everyone. Thank you for coming."

A cacophony of thanks and laughter bounced back at her. It refreshed her spirit, and the breath she took came easy. "What are you all doing here so early?"

Several eyebrows raised, and a mouse tiptoed down her spine. "What?"

Her father came through the doors from the kitchen, a big wooden spoon in his hand. "Thought I heard your voice, lass. Having a good day?"

She tied her apron behind her and scrunched her face. "Could have been better, I guess."

Sue slapped the bar and hawed, and Sally slapped Sue. "Be nice. Abby means well. She has a big heart."

"I can see it. It's on her sleeve," Sue said.

"What's going on?" Abby asked, eyebrows raised. "You all know something I don't?"

"We know you've been all over town kicking up a rumpus. But in a nice way." Edna added the last part when Sally poked her.

Abby put both hands in her hair and scratched at her scalp, ruffling the recently brushed curls.

"You gonna use that spoon on her derriere, Patrick?" Jesse said.

"Nae. She beats herself up more than anyone else could. I'll stand behind me lass." He tossed an arm around her shoulder and squeezed.

"Glad I am to have your name, Da," she said, watching him head back to the kitchen.

"I hear mine has been thrown around a bit," Charles said, his eyes twinkling. Fun poured from them, and Abby envied his good humor.

"I've been using it. In a good way, like Edna said. Trying to tear down the stones of prejudice."

She stood with hands on her hips, a proud warrior with an apron for a shield.

Bear and Shorty took their favorite stools at the end of the bar; like sentinels, they watched the patrons. They didn't need to, hadn't been asked, but it was automatic, an intrinsic part of their personalities and an offshoot of affection for the Rileys – father and daughter. Phantom and Cleo appeared and strung themselves over a shoulder and arm.

Sue pointed to the stool next to her and shouted, "Saved this one for you, Bear. Knew you'd be here soon."

"You come down here, sweetheart. I don't like my back to the door."

Sue kicked her legs back and forth to get her bottom near the edge of the stool and slid off in a breath-holding moment for everyone who watched. Sometimes, she landed on the floor on her bottom when the jiggles and wobbles got the best of her legs and feet. She grinned when she was sure of her success, waddled over to the stool by Bear, and climbed on.

"Good to see you, Ursus."

"You, too, sweet Sue. Looking busy in here tonight."

"Everyone wants to hear about Abby's day. She's a pip."

Minutes later, Daniel Longstreet strolled in, dipped his head to Abby and found an empty table at the back corner.

"Now there's one I'll bet you haven't invited to Bunny's church service," Sue said with a smile so big it closed her eyes.

"Does he not recall our little conference?" she said to Sue and Bear.

"Probably knocked it right outta him," Sue said.

Jackson came with Longstreet's order, and Abby scooted down the bar, glad for an excuse to flee questions, if not to see Longstreet. She stayed too busy during the next couple of hours to get questioned by her friends or to worry.

The screen door opened hard, slammed against the wall, and Frank strode in. Her heart went cold, filled by a spring runoff. She knew Frank's mother had sunk the blade into her back, likely with a smile while she plunged it over and over, the blood of her resentment flying.

Frank's eyes were hard and narrow, his lips pulled back in an angry grimace he tried to make into a smile. He walked up to the bar and stood with his foot on the rail of Samuel's stool.

"My regular," he said.

"Hello, Frank." She didn't say 'good to see you.' She wasn't, and she couldn't make it be.

"A double."

Abby poured a hefty shot and put it in front of him. He stared at her, picked up the glass and drained it. The sound of the empty glass hitting the bar turned heads his way.

"Another, a double this time, Abby."

She didn't fill this one as much, fearing Frank had no aim to remain sober. He took a gulp but didn't empty the glass, and she swallowed her fear, turned to Jackson and filled his drink order.

Samuel swiveled to stare at the man crowding his space and put his hands on his knees, elbows out, taking up significant space of his own, forcing Frank to give way.

"Do you mind?" he said without change of expression.

"What?" Frank said.

"If you want this seat, simply ask."

"Why would I want your seat?"

Samuel pulled his watch from a pocket in the black, satin vest and flipped it open and shut without looking at the time. He put his back toward Frank, and his jaw muscles twitched.

Abby saw it all and caught her lips between her teeth until she realized it and stopped.

She should have closed the bar for the evening. She should have taken Frank outside to talk with him about her efforts in the community. She should have refused to admit Longstreet into the bar. She should have . . . done anything except what she did – let things happen.

Longstreet left his table in the back corner to stand near Frank. He eyed Samuel with contempt, looked down the bar at Sue, Jesse, Edna, Sally . . . and shook his head.

"Hear your wife is unifying Idlewild, maybe even the whole damn state," he said. His lips spread in a snide sneer, and he emphasized *unifying* like it was a dirty word.

"I guess," Frank replied, and Abby saw anger flare. She'd hoped his ire had been doused by the drinks, but whiskey didn't dampen a fire. It added fuel to irrational flames of fury.

"You need to put a stop to her meddling, mister." Longstreet glared at Charles Chesnutt with intent. "There is no esteem to build on, *Sir*, never will be. Yes, I've read your . . . literature."

He turned away from Charles, an insignificant insect, and put a hand on Frank's shoulder like an old friend. Abby wondered if he was.

"Women need a strong hand. Take control, mister," he said, "before she turns this town into a haven for sin, a bed of mixed races where nobody knows what they are, and America is lost to ignorance, degradation and sloth. Do you want your child to marry a mulatto? Put your back into it, Adams. Be a man."

Frank glared at her. "Oh, she'd like that, wouldn't you, Abigail? To have a colored son or daughter-in-law? Or one of your own? Maybe you just want to bed down with a damn colored . . ."

Samuel shook his head and turned to face Frank, nostrils flaring. Sue and Sally gave identical, horrified gasps, Edna poked Jesse to do something, and Shorty got off his stool, followed by Bear a half-second later.

But Jackson got there first and, before anyone could stop him, planted a fast fist on Frank's jaw.

Frank went down and got up swinging and swearing. Shorty grabbed him from behind and held on while Bear seized Longstreet and dragged him to the door.

"Don't think about coming back. I've tangled with a bear you can't hold a candle to." He shoved, and Longstreet double-stepped and slunk away with a quick glance to see if Bear followed.

Inside, Frank flailed, still trying to free himself from Shorty's grasp, but not having any luck, and the object of his cursing switched from Jackson to the big man squeezing his arm.

"Let me go, you son-of-a-bitch. You've been in my way since the day I met these people. I should've let you have her." Frank glared at Abby, not Shorty, his barb well placed and piercing. His words filtered into her brain and stayed, but she couldn't deal with him now. She was talking with Jackson.

"You can't punch people. You know that. I can't have you doing that here."

"*You* did," he said, his chin raised in defiance.

She had tears in her eyes, and when she spoke again, they streamed down her cheeks. "I know, and I'm sorry. You can't punch Frank, Jackson. He's . . . it's . . ."

He untied his apron, threw it on a table and walked out without another word. Abby watched him go, her heart broken too many times this day. She didn't bother trying to hide it. When she returned to the bar, silence thundered in her ears like she'd dived too deep into the icy lake.

"Let him go, Shorty." The muscles of her jaws ached as if she'd guzzled a quart of pickle juice, and she swallowed back the saliva threatening to choke her. "Go home, Frank."

Her voice rumbled low and soft, but not sweet. It had the tenor of someone who had just buried a friend, and the mound of dirt over the grave was still fresh.

"Go home," she repeated. He left, and Abby hoped he wasn't chasing Jackson.

She saw empty glasses on the bar and filled them, glanced at the faces of staring people at the tables and refreshed their drinks as they dipped their heads in thanks.

Abby sighed when the bar emptied, and she poured a drink for herself, shut down the lamps, and went to the porch. Shorty, Bear, Patrick, Charles and Samuel followed – her family.

The loon called, and she told it to shut up.

Abby put her head against the wooden slats of the chair and watched the water ripple in concentric circles where a night bug gave its life to sustain a fish. For some reason, she wanted to weep for that insect and thought *but not for him, the trout would die* and wept for it, too. She rubbed her head, frustrated with the reverberating impact one thing had on another. It reflected her life.

If I did nothing at all, I wouldn't harm others. The thought ricocheted off the walls of her mind.

Cassandra and her clowder glided to a stop in front of them and raised her walking stick. She and her cats appeared not to use feet for travel. Did they simply visualize themselves wherever they wanted to be?

Charles hummed a greeting. It wasn't a real word. Nor was it *not* one. Abby's half-smile said she understood. The rest nodded or waved their greetings.

"Nothing is harmful," Cassandra said to the group on the porch. "And that can be misconstrued, but this is a truth. Nothing creates a vacuum which causes implosion. Be aware of the power of nothing."

"How do you know what I'm thinking, Cassandra?" Abby said, her voice an unintentional, sorrowful plea.

She waved her stick and walked on, stopped to pick something from the mud and stuck it in her sack. Abby envisioned a mud toad, but what would Cassandra want with a mud toad? And why did she even think that?

The crunch of rockers on wood rolled deathly slow, a rocking dirge, and matched the hibernation breath. Eyes lowered to half mast, and hands lay limp on laps.

Patrick left them and returned with a tray of small drinks, his best Irish. He passed them around and held his toward his daughter. The rest followed.

"Here's to you, lass."

Chapter Twenty

She couldn't sleep, hadn't most of the night, so she got out of bed, washed her face and dressed. It took a while to untangle her hair, and she regretted not braiding it before bed. She'd tossed around, squashing cats and cussing out the full moon.

Al was messing with her own hair when Abby pushed through the swinging doors to the kitchen.

Both were startled.

"Thought I'd beat you, Al."

"Please don't," she said, the twinkle in her eye almost visible.

"What?" Abby was fuzzy-minded with sleeplessness and didn't recognize Al's seldom seen humor.

She stoked the fire, filled the coffee pot with grounds and water, and set it on the hottest corner of the big, black stove, while Al brought bacon from the larder and worked at sawing thick slices from the slab.

"Hurry."

"With the bacon?" Al asked.

"No. Sorry. Talking to the pot. I need coffee, fast. Lots of it."

Al didn't respond, but the look in her eyes said she understood, and, for some reason, Abby felt humbled. They worked with nods and raised eyebrows instead of words, and it suited both. It had been an agreeable kitchen all week.

Al preferred stillness. It suited her. But Abby liked the hum of conversation, until lately, and Al understood the reasons for her sleepless nights and morning silences. Betty had filled her in.

Breakfast aromas filled the kitchen and oozed into the bar and lobby, bringing Bear and Shorty with the cats. Al poured coffee, having taken over Abby's chore of her own volition, and the men sat and continued the silence, cats coiled around their selection of the moment.

Shorty sipped the last of his coffee and gave the okay-to-talk signal, a marginally louder clink of cup on saucer. Al filled plates and put them in front of both men.

Abby couldn't contain a grin. If she stepped back for a single moment, Al might take over the entire kitchen – maybe the whole hotel. She'd be out of a job, and what would she do then? The grin faded in a flash of insight.

What Frank always wanted her to do, be a farmer's wife. Maybe everything wrong with her marriage *was* her fault. She'd been selfish and stubborn, thought her da needed her. Could it be he didn't? She sucked in a harsh, hitched breath.

Bear heard, tilted his head toward her, and, for a flickering moment, he saw a crushed woman, and his eyes questioned.

"I did my stint sleeping at the cousins last night. Kinda noisy there until pretty late," he said.

"Have to get some ear plugs," Shorty said, and his words were for Bear, but his eyes were on Abby. She'd been troubled all week but wouldn't talk about it.

"Going out to the Parker's for church Sunday?" Bear asked. "If you are, I might want to go."

Abby's head swung sideways so fast her neck cracked, and everyone looked at her like she'd broken herself.

"You want to go to church?"

"Me, too." Shorty stood, put his empty plate in the dry sink and headed to the door. "Coming, Bear?"

"On my way."

"Wait," Abby said. "Hey, what's going on?"

The doors swung back and forth, in and out, and Al and Abby were left to stare at them until momentum gave way to inertia.

Abby held up her empty coffee cup, queried Al, and poured for both of them. She sipped, retrieved the large bowls from an overhead shelf, too tall for Al, and scooped fried potatoes into one.

"I'll go," Al said. The potato pan clattered as Abby put it back on the stove.

"To church? What the heck? What's going on? Why?"

Al shrugged, embarrassed. She yanked on the drab, pink ribbon holding long, white hair back from her face, and it came loose. When she tried to corral it, Abby took the ribbon from her hand and stepped behind to retie it.

"Why, Al? Why would you go to church?"

She wasn't miffed, even though it might sound that way. She was confused and had been all week, ever since the fiasco of trying to convince people they were one community even if they were different. They were pebbles in a stream, stars in a galaxy.

"Because I'm Strange Al."

She knows what we call her.

Tears seeped into the back of Abby's throat, but she swallowed them, stuck her chin on Al's head, and held it there. Al let her . . . for a moment, before she dipped her head and moved to turn the potatoes.

As Abby watched her work, she thought about Jackson. He hadn't been back since he'd punched Frank, and she'd been questioning all her ideas. She was a mess, couldn't even tie a pink ribbon without tearing up. She'd shed far too many tears this week, and she wanted, needed to be done.

"I'd love to have you attend, Al. Want to go with me?"

"With Betty."

"Oh, okay. Speaking of the devil."

Betty pushed through the doors like fresh air through an open window in a dusty parlor.

"Coffee . . . need coffee," she moaned.

"You look perky. Why the desperation?"

"I was up late. Didn't get much sleep."

Abby walked close, peered into Betty's face and went back to the stove. "You look pretty good. That's just wrong. *I* didn't sleep and look like an old lady. Not fair."

"You should have my skin, boss. Wanna be colored for a week?"

"Maybe I would, Betty. Just maybe." She stopped flipping pancakes and turned. "Wait. Why were you up so late? What were you doing?"

"Nosy, aren't you."

"Do you know, Al?"

"Don't tell her. Let her wonder a little."

Al went to the larder and came back when she heard Betty tell Abby about the company Benjamin brought with him last night.

"With him where?"

"Our place. I mean, Al's house."

"All five soldiers are here?" Abby asked.

Betty's eyes sparkled. "Do you remember them? Handsome. Strong. Made my head spin trying to look at all of them at once. Fun, wasn't it, Al?"

"Are they staying with Benjamin?"

Betty nodded.

"Sounds like fun. Worth a late night, right?" She poked Betty with an elbow, grinned, and wondered if she had ever looked like her – eager, full of youthful spirit.

Patrick came in, grabbed an apron and pulled the strings on Al's. He'd untied her apron from day one, trying to get her to talk, thinking she was shy. He finally figured out shy didn't have a place in her body. She was simply Strange Al, but he still plucked her apron strings because he liked to.

She left her da in the kitchen with Al, grabbed Betty and went up to clean the never-ending dirty guest rooms. Halfway through the morning, Phantom took Abby's feather duster between his teeth and tore down the hallway. Abby followed on hands and knees, grabbing for Phantom who stayed just out of reach.

When she stood, duster in hand, she saw a stranger standing inside the door to the lobby. He wore a scraggly, straw hat and tattered work clothes.

Abby brushed the dust from her skirt and patted her disheveled hair. "I'm sorry. I didn't know we had a guest. Can I help you?"

He removed his hat, waiting for her. "Edwin Emerson."

"What can I do for you, Mister Emerson? I'm Abby. Are you looking for a room?"

Edwin shook his head, and long dirty brown hair flew into his eyes. He swatted at the hair and showed her his missing teeth.

"I'm looking for work, Missus. Yard work, wood choppin' or anything you got needin' to be done."

Abby rubbed at her chin and glanced out the window. "You know, we may be able to use you. If you'll have a seat, I'll check with my father." She pointed to chairs lined against the wall and grimaced when he chose the yellow, cushioned seat.

Lunch preparations were about complete, and Abby left to drag her da from the kitchen to meet the would-be handyman. She hoped he'd hire him, save himself some of the backbreaking outside work he didn't have time to do.

"Push the kettle to the back, Al, and you're done. See you tomorrow," Patrick said, before walking through the swinging doors. After introductions were made, he asked Edwin where he lived. "I don't think I've seen you before."

"All around," he said. "Over by Newaygo, recent like."

"Are you living in Idlewild now?"

"A ways off, but not so far I can't go back and forth."

They moved out of Al's way when she left, but the screen door no sooner slapped shut when she was back inside, her face the color of a cloud in a clear, blue sky.

"That's Pa's horse," she said, pointing to an old mare hitched to the porch rail. Dead silence filled the lobby until Mister Emerson's voice fractured it.

"You saying I stole that horse?" His voice rose in anger and disbelief. "I ain't never stole a horse in my life. Ain't stole nothing."

"That's Pa's horse." She looked at Patrick when she repeated the words.

"You know for sure, Al?" Abby asked.

"The three whip marks."

Patrick tried to put a good face on a bad situation, and his mind raced. Tatum's horse had never been found. Maybe it ran off after the old man was killed, and maybe this man found it. Or maybe he bought it from somebody. Or maybe he killed him.

"Are ye hungry, Mister Emerson?"

People began coming in for lunch, and he asked Edwin into the bar, so he could keep him there while he got ready.

"Will ye stay and help a minute, Al?" Patrick asked.

She nodded, and, with one eye on the stranger, he prepared the buffet while they brought out the food.

"Give Mister Emerson some lunch, Al. Keep him here," he whispered. "Abby, go find somebody to get the sheriff."

Abby ran upstairs.

"Sorry I abandoned you, Betty. I got waylaid. A man's downstairs with Mister Tatum's horse," she said.

"He has a horse downstairs? In the lobby?" Abby smirked at her smart-mouthed helper.

"I gotta go. I'll be back as soon as I can."

"Wait." She grabbed Abby's arm. "Mister Tatum's horse? How can that be?"

"Gotta go." She flew down the steps and out the door, heading for Jesse's office.

"You realize this man could be a killer," Jesse said after she explained. "Who's at the hotel right now?"

"Some guests. Us."

"Damn. I'll go for the sheriff. You head to the island and get Bear or Shorty to go back with you. The man could be dangerous."

"You think so? Seemed to me he just bought the horse off somebody. Dangerous?"

Jesse took her by the shoulders and turned her in the direction of the construction crew on the island.

"Get somebody, Abby. I mean it." He gave her a shove, and she ran.

Edwin shoveled in Patrick's cabbage soup and mopped the bowl with several pieces of Irish soda bread. He belched, rubbed his stomach, and sat back in the chair.

Patrick sprinted to the table, afraid the man would leave now he had a full belly. He pulled out a chair and sat. Al watched.

"Where'd you say you got that horse, Mister Emerson?"

"I don't believe I said." Edwin cleaned between his remaining teeth with the point of a jackknife and eyed Patrick. "But I will. You seem like a nice enough man."

A full belly made him garrulous.

"I bought her off a young buck down near Newago. He was selling her cheap cuz he was in a bad way. Wife was running around with another man, and he was leaving. Getting as far away from her as he could. Right mad, he was. Took my money and skedaddled."

"This young man give you a bill of sale for the old girl?"

"Sure. I ain't stupid."

"Care to show it to me?" Patrick saw a slight irritation cross the man's face as he stood up.

"The horse is mine. I done paid fer it."

When he started to leave, Patrick put a hand on his arm. "Sorry, Edwin. Tis none of my business. Abby said you were looking for work. I could use some help around here, at that. Ye want to start today?"

"I could do some. What is it you want done?"

"First off, you can clean out the stable. You can put your horse in there, too, if you want." Patrick made sure to point out the mare was *his* horse. He didn't want him running off.

Edwin wiped his mouth on a part of his shirt sleeve that had been used for that purpose before and groaned as he bent to stand.

"Where might this stable be, Mister Riley?"

"I'll walk ye there. Just give me a moment."

"Irish, huh?" Edwin said, brows wiggling like he knew some things about Patrick nobody else did.

"I am."

Patrick went over to Al and asked her to stick around until he got back.

When they walked out front, Edwin ran a hand over the mare's neck. "Come on, old girl. We'll get you fit up in the stable." She nickered, and Patrick's eyebrows rose in unexpected interest. The man didn't seem to be a bad sort. He gave affection to the animal, and it wasn't a trick because the animal returned it.

"Out back," Patrick said, and led the way. He threw the large doors open to let in some light, and dust motes danced in the sudden rush of air. He patted Marie on the way to a narrow stall at the end of the walkway, well beyond horses belonging to hotel guests.

"Ye can put her here. Give her a rest from the saddle and some oats and water."

"She'll appreciate it." He removed the saddle and used the blanket to wipe the sweat from her back.

"When you're done there, the pitchfork and shovels are on the wall behind you. Wheelbarrow's back of the building. Spread the manure in the field behind and lay fresh straw in here. Hay's in the racks. Come on in for your pay when ye finish."

Patrick's spine prickled as he left the stranger with all the horses, and he muttered to himself on the way back to the bar.

Could be a horse thief, and ye put him in the stable, just to make him happy til the law arrives. What kind of a fool thing was that to do? Hope they don't send that useless deputy.

His bow-legged waddle became more pronounced as he stewed, and it took a while for him to get there. He slumped on a bar stool.

"You can go, Al. Thanks for helping out."

"I'm staying."

"Ye don't need to do that, girl. The sheriff is coming, and we'll see what's what."

"Abby's gone. Jackson, too. I'll stay."

She went around the bar and put Abby's apron on. It hung down to her ankles, but it made the point. She could tend bar, and she would. In fact, she started by pouring whiskey for her boss.

"Aw, ye be a good lass," he said with grateful affection.

He was sipping and Al was waiting on guests when Abby ran in, red faced and panting. Shorty and Bear followed.

"Where is he?" Bear said, looking around the bar. "And where's the mare?" Patrick told him they would find the fox in the chicken coop, and his ears turned red as they stared at him in disbelief.

"You put a horse thief, maybe a killer, to work with our horses?" Shorty asked. He spun to head for the stable, but Patrick stopped him.

"The mare likes him."

"So, maybe he's a killer who likes animals but not people?" Abby said.

"Could be," Bear added. "I'd be that kind of killer."

"I needed to keep him here. Couldn't think of anything else." Patrick rubbed a hand over his gray stubble.

"You need a shave, Da. I can hear your beard." Patrick tilted his head to look up at her.

"Now? You're concerned about my need of a shave, now?" He shook his head and groaned. "Lass."

"I'm just nervous. I don't know what I'm saying – or thinking. I wish the sheriff would get here."

She heard a glass clink, saw Al mixing a drink, her own apron hanging long and limp on the small woman, and her eyes widened. "I didn't know you were back there. Can you see over the bar?"

Al smirked and didn't respond. She handed the drink to a guest and turned to make another, a *southside*.

"What's in it, please," she said, and the man told her.

"Gin, lime, mint, simple syrup. Got it all?" he asked.

"I don't see mint."

"It'll be fine, sweetie. Whatever you've got to cover the taste of bad gin."

"It's good gin."

Sheriff Hicks' heartburn was acting up, and he held one hand over the left side of his chest. He knew it didn't make it any better, but he couldn't help himself. Jesse kept glancing his way, worried he might fall off his mount and die at any moment.

"You okay, Sheriff?" he asked.

"I am, and you need to quit asking me. I'm not gonna croak. I just got an acid stomach. That's what the doc says." The hand did circles, and Jesse forced himself to look away.

"You said the man showed up out of the blue. Didn't have any idea the mare came from this area?"

"That's right. If Al hadn't started for home just then, no one would be the wiser."

"And she's sure?"

"You ask her. Al isn't prone to shooting off her mouth."

"True."

They tied their mounts at the hitching rail and took the steps two at a time. Several pairs of wide eyes greeted them.

"Gentlemen. Ladies." He pointed his hat at Patrick. "Where's this suspicious character and the mare?"

"In the stable, I hope. That's where I left him."

The sheriff raised an eyebrow. "With all the horses?"

Patrick lifted a hand high in the air to halt the words. "I know. Believe me. I said it to myself. As did a few others."

"I'll follow you."

The wheelbarrow moved down a grassy path made by feet, and the single wheel pointed at them. Behind it, Edwin whistled a jaunty tune. Patrick and the sheriff walked into the stable to wait. They were met by the sound of molars grinding hay and hooves sashaying a contented shuffle. It was a pleasant serenade, especially side-by-side with the fear of Edwin running off with a dozen horses.

He saw the shiny star when he stepped inside, hung the pitch fork back on its hook, and upended the wheelbarrow in the corner.

"Guess you'll be wantin' to talk, and then I'll mosey on."

"No need for that, Edwin. The sheriff just needs you to answer a few questions."

He propped a foot on the underside of the overturned wheelbarrow, stuck a fresh piece of straw in one of the holes between his teeth, and said, "Shoot. Mebbe I got answers."

"Our friend, Al, says this was her pa's mare."

"Well, coulda been. She's mine, now."

"Do you have proof you own her, Edwin?"

"Why would I come to town on a horse I didn't own, Sheriff?" His head moved back and forth in aggrieved wonder. "Course I do."

Edwin went to his saddle, flipped the saddlebag open and pulled out a ratty looking slip of paper. Irritation pulled at the muscles of his jaws as he handed it to Hicks.

"There ya go, Mister. All legal like."

The sheriff's hand crept back up to his chest as he read the short note. "Do you know the name of the man who sold this horse to you, Edwin?"

"Naw."

"Jesse James. This says you bought that mare from Jesse James for ten dollars. Is that right?"

"Never asked his name."

"Can you read, Edwin?" Sheriff Hicks asked, his voice apologizing for the question.

"I can sign my name," he said, thrusting his shoulders back and standing taller than before.

"I'm sure you can," Hicks said. "That I can get behind, but that's about all."

Patrick scratched his head, curious about where the sheriff would go next.

"Did you know when you bought this mare that the man who owned her was dead? Dead and buried in a shallow grave in the woods. Did Jesse James tell you that?" Hicks watched Edwin's eyes for a flicker of guilt and didn't see any, but he did see regret.

Edwin shook his head in a slow dirge. "Sorry about the man. Mister James' pa?"

Patrick slapped his leg and dust flew. "Don't you know who Jesse James is? He's an outlaw. A famous outlaw. You didn't buy the mare from Jesse James. He's dead."

"I'm sorry. Lots of dead men here. I should probably think about moving on."

Sheriff Hicks snorted in exasperation and stepped outside into the bright sunlight.

"You can finish the work Mister Riley gave you, Edwin, and then come on in the hotel. I need to think about things. Don't *you* think about wandering off."

The chuckle coming from the stable was soft and unnerving. They stopped, stared at each other and, without a word, moved on.

They paused to let their eyes adjust to the dim lighting and saw Betty in an apron moving from table to table with a pad of paper and a pencil in her hands. Al was missing, and Abby stood behind the bar.

"I can't keep up," Patrick said. "Minute by minute life whirls in a circle. Where's Al, Abby?"

"In the kitchen, Da. Starting on the stew. Don't worry. She knows how to make it by now. Where's Edwin?"

"Finishing up the stable."

"You're leaving him there?" Shorty moved to toward the kitchen to head out the back door.

Hicks stopped him. "Does a window in the kitchen look out at the stable?"

"Two." Shorty understood. "I'll help Al out and watch him from there. Make sure he stays put."

Folks were gathering in the bar for supper by the time Edwin finished work and came in. He'd washed up at the outside pump first. His shirt was wet, and his hair slicked back, but his scent said stable, nonetheless.

Patrick led him toward the back– to what he now called the *Longstreet* table. *Renegade Corner*, he thought, and chuckled.

Sheriff Hicks strolled over and took a seat.

"Can I eat?" Edwin asked.

"Sure. Can't keep a working man from his food."

Patrick brought stew and left the sheriff to do his job.

"I'm laying it on the line, Mister Emerson. You got a hokey bill of sale for a mare I'm sure used to belong to a man who was murdered. It sets me to thinking you might be somehow connected to the killing, but I can't prove it right now."

Edwin scooped stew into his mouth and took his time chewing, perhaps because the number of teeth caused prolonged mastication. Or perhaps he pondered a way out of his predicament.

"I didn't kill nobody and take his horse. You can't prove I did."

"Well, you know you didn't buy her from Jesse James. That was somebody's little joke on you. So why don't you describe the man who sold her to you?"

"He looked like any normal man, ya know?"

"No, I don't. How tall? What color hair? How old? Help me out here, Edwin."

"He was sorta your height, and maybe around thirty. Not old like us."

"Thanks, Edwin. Appreciate that. Hair?"

"Yeah. He had hair."

Hicks glared. "More information, please."

"Light brown or mebbe dark blonde like. Came down over his collar, and he was kinda scruffy like he hadn't had a bath in a while. And he was sure mad at his woman. Cussing a streak."

"Did he call her by name?"

Edwin pondered and chewed. "Nope. Don't think he did. Just said she was running around and into everything."

Sheriff Hicks sat back and stared at his suspect. He didn't think of Edwin as a pillar of the community, but he couldn't see him killing a man for his horse, either. He stood to leave.

"Stick around, Edwin. Until I say you can go."

At the bar, he talked to Patrick about keeping the man doing odd jobs for a while. Patrick agreed and said he could sleep in the stable but shook his head and chortled at the incongruity of the whole thing.

"For a while, Patrick. If he takes off with somebody's horse, I'll track him down. And thanks."

Chapter Twenty-one

Bear hitched the buggy early Sunday morning wearing his best blue shirt under a brown leather vest. He pulled at the collar and stretched his neck as if the starched cotton hindered swallowing.

"Didn't plan on having to wear these clothes, Marie. Don't believe God cares one whit about a starched shirt, no matter what Shorty says."

Marie blew air through her nostrils in response, and he led her around to the front porch.

Edwin stood in the stable doorway and watched them go. He had come to the conclusion he'd be better off gone, but that could only happen if the old man went to church, too. If Patrick stayed, so would he. He was getting antsy, though, and it didn't feel good. He didn't want to hang for somebody else's killing, and, from what he heard, the man needed killing.

Abby and Bear got in, and the big one climbed on the horse he'd already saddled, but no Patrick. He was stuck and decided stuck on a full belly beat an empty one. Patrick was in the kitchen cleaning up breakfast, and Edwin looked around for leftovers.

"Got yours right here, Edwin. Wouldn't let ye go hungry. Sit right here while I finish up."

They found a spot in the shade for the horses and secured them. When they walked in, Abby did a double take and stepped back. Bear put a hand on her shoulder to keep her from treading on his toes.

The small house overflowed with church goers. Abby had kicked up religious fervor when she went around inviting people to Bunny's house. Either she'd reminded them of their need to be blessed by the Lord, or they didn't want to miss any fireworks that might occur.

As Bunny's son, Jackson welcomed people at the door. When he saw Abby, he pretended a nonchalant pose, leaned back against the door frame and crossed his arms. He still felt the sting of her words and held the door, waiting, eyes wearing a sullen squint.

"Coming in, Abby?" he said. "If not, I have other things to do."

"Oh. Sorry. Just . . . there's so many people."

"Yes. You stirred the pot. But they're all my relatives, not yours."

"You're mad, Jackson. Can we talk?"

"No. I'm busy. Go on in and find a seat."

Abby obeyed and found space at the back of the room. Bear and Shorty followed.

"I know you hoped for a better turn out, Abby," Bear said. "We three are the only white faces in the room. Sorry."

"Four," Shorty said as Al and Betty walked in.

Samuel watched from across the room and raised four fingers when their eyes met. Abby couldn't tell if his expression mocked or empathized. He was more than hard to read. She raised her chin, rejecting his sympathy and lifting a shield against his scorn. She was covered either way.

He grinned and went off to speak with Sue and Sally who came from the kitchen. Seeing them, Abby couldn't resist her own smile.

Reverend Jenkins called for the parishioners to take seats, if they could find them, and admonished the men to be gentlemen and leave the chairs for the ladies.

"Bow your heads," he said, and began the longest prayer Abby had ever heard. He blessed every person, animal, vegetable and insect in the world, calling them by all the names he could remember and making up ones he couldn't. Abby glanced at him during what she thought must be nearly the end, and he caught her dead on. He looked right at her, eyes lit in pure evil pleasure over her discomfort.

"And bless Abigail Riley Adams for this wonderful turnout today. Amen."

Feet shuffled, butts moved on seats seeking relief, and heads craned to stare at her reddening face.

Reverend Jenkins continued. "If you think that was an unnecessarily long prayer, too bad. I took advantage of having all of you in one place, as it might not happen again soon. None of you are strangers here, but some of you are strangers to one another. I hope that comes to an end."

Heads turned from side to side to ogle the outsiders. Their eyes were curious, though not disapproving, and Abby applauded the newcomers, her own friends.

Bear, Shorty and Al looked around the room as if they were searching for strangers, too, not *being* them. Abby snorted in a caught laugh and tried to cover it with a cough.

"You alright?" Shorty asked.

"Yes. Remind me to tell you later."

"Open your Bibles," Reverend Jenkins said, "Matthew 25:35. *For I was hungry and you gave me food, I was thirsty and you gave me drink, I was a stranger, and you welcomed me."* His eyes roamed the room. He didn't speak about what he had read, but let the silence speak for him.

After a few minutes, he said "Galatians 3:28. *There is neither Jew nor Greek, there is neither slave nor free, there is no male and female, for you are all one in Christ Jesus."*

Again, the silent treatment. On and on Reverend Jenkins read brief verses from his Bible and stared at his congregation. They no longer bothered to open their own when he named a verse. They watched, listened and waited.

When over an hour had passed in this manner, he closed the *Good Book* and said, "So apparently, Abby is on the right track. Let's eat."

It took a while for those last two words to penetrate. No one moved. They peered from face to face, questioning the strange sermon from their familiar pastor. They felt chastised but didn't know what they'd done to deserve it, and burdened by guilt without knowing the deed that had caused it.

The flood gates opened when someone spoke, and mass movement created an exodus to the kitchen where potluck waited. Abby headed straight for Jackson standing near the door. She intended to speak with him whether he wanted it or not. She caught his arm and dragged him outside. He did little to prevent it.

"Are you ever coming back to work, Jackson?"

"You fired me," he said, kicking a stone across the yard like a little boy.

"I didn't, Jackson. I said you couldn't punch people, you couldn't punch Frank."

"Sounded like firing to me."

Abby chewed her bottom lip as she recalled her words. It probably sounded that way, and she regretted it and told him so. "Will you come back, please? I miss you."

"Can I punch people?" He grinned, and Abby's heart split open and poured out all over the ground.

"No. No punching."

Jackson held onto the smile for a while before it disappeared with his boyhood, and he turned into a man.

"But I will, Abby. If anyone says something bad about you – like I heard that day – I will punch them. You have to know that going in."

Abby put her arm through his and squeezed it. He'd grown inches since the day she hired him, and his shoulders had broadened. When had that happened, and why she hadn't noticed it?

"You're a good friend, Jackson. Thank you."

"Okay, boss. Can I have a raise?"

"Yes. You can. Let's eat. I'm starved."

"And you're a hero. A whole sermon just about Abby. Wow."

"That wasn't about me."

"Yes, it was," said a voice behind her.

She turned to see Samuel holding a full plate and a fork on its way to his mouth. She salivated at the scent of his food.

"It was about all of us. You, too, Jackson," she told him, as he ran off to the kitchen.

"Hear you have a new worker. Tell me about him," Samuel said.

Abby didn't know what she should say, what the sheriff would want known, so she waffled. "He's kind of a drifter. Sleeps in the stable with the horses."

"Old guy? Young?"

"Kind of old, I guess."

"Uh-huh. And what about the horse he rode in on? Why are you not telling me about that?

"I'm not, not telling you."

Samuel stabbed a big bite of ham with his fork, and Abby nearly snatched it from his hand.

"I have to get some food. I'm famished."

He shoved it in her face, and she groaned and opened her mouth. Samuel grinned as she chewed.

"What will folks say? I'm feeding a lily-white stranger." He stabbed again and held it out to her.

"Stop. People *will* talk. I'm going in for food."

"Ride home with me. I have some questions."

"No. Maybe. We'll see."

While she filled her plate with a little bit of every woman's special dish, Bunny came to her side. Regal in her caftan and head wrap, she looked like a princess straight out of Mali, and Abby felt a tiny prick of envy.

The flawless russet skin. The high cheekbones and long elegant neck. The poise that must have been purchased at a price Abby would never know and couldn't pay. She looked at the freckles on her own arm and frowned.

"You look chastised, Abby. What did you do?"

"Nothing," she said, but guilt laced her voice, and she wondered if Bunny was a bit of a soothsayer like her sister Cassandra.

"I was teasing, but now I don't know. You look sheepish."

Bunny's inscrutable half smile left Abby feeling like her hands were all thumbs, both feet were lefts, and she had a wart on her nose. She looked at the pile of food on her plate and knew she'd never resemble the willowy Bunny.

"Thank you for letting me invite folks to your house."

"You filled it, although not the way you intended, I'm sure."

"I'm finding resistance, Bunny, from every corner. I don't know how to combat it."

"Don't. Woo, instead."

"Woo?" Abby's face scrunched in thought.

"Like a beau woos his sweetheart, with gentle persuasion." Bunny removed an empty dish from the table and replaced it with a full one. Pushed another dish a few inches for the sake of symmetry and brushed some crumbs into her hand. "Don't use a stick."

"You think I brow beat people into doing what I want?"

Bunny didn't need to answer. The words were written on her face. "I'll say this – we have different ways, and what you desire may never happen, but I've come to like you, Abigail."

Abby's hands were full, or she would have used one to cover the mouth full of teeth suddenly in full view. For some reason, Bunny's approval was – had always been – desperately sought.

She took her food outside and sat on the grass to eat. Jackson plopped next to her with a plate piled high with a variety of pie slices.

"Don't know why you're not fat, Jackson."

He ignored her and shoveled.

"Have you seen Al or Betty?" she asked. "I wanted to thank Al for coming."

"Bear drove them back to the farm."

Abby's head swung to where the buggy had been tethered and saw the space empty. Shorty's horse was gone, too.

"They left me. The skunks."

"Samuel told 'em to."

"What? Why?"

"Don't know. You'll have to ask him. Here he is now."

She stood, gripping her plate and glaring.

"Why do you think you can run my life, Samuel? What makes you . . . How can you just . . . God, you make me mad."

"Settle down, Abby," Samuel said.

"Quit telling me what to do." She spun away. "Damn."

His eyebrows rose and a hint of a grin moved his cheeks. "Swearing? And one could say we're still in church."

She refused to look at him and finished her plate standing.

"I wanted a chance to talk, Abby. That's all. It seemed the easiest way for a private conversation."

"About what?"

"Finish your meal, tell Bunny goodbye, and let's go. I'll tell you on the way."

Abby did as he said, though she didn't know why and didn't want to. She *was* curious about what he had to say.

When she melted into the leather seat of his beautiful Model T, anger trickled away, and she let the scent of luxury seep in. Exquisite didn't begin to describe it. He started the engine, and she waved to the many eyes watching them roll down the drive to the road. Abby's thoughts turned to Frank, and she must have made a labored sound because Samuel turned to her, a question in his eyes.

"What?" she said. He shook his head and turned back to watch the road.

"What did you want to tell me, Samuel?"

"Nothing. I had some questions."

"So, you lied."

"Sort of. How long has Edwin Emerson been working for you?"

"Not long. A few days. Why?"

"Does he eat meals in the hotel bar?"

"Sometimes. Sometimes the kitchen. He has to eat."

"Has he met all the regulars?"

"Samuel, what are you getting at? Why all the questions?"

"Well, rumor has it he rode in on Tatum's mare. That he bought it off a man with a fake name."

"You seem to know a lot. What do you need me for?"

"Maybe the company?"

"Hmmm."

He didn't ask what he really wanted to know and had changed his mind about wanting to know it. He'd let things lie for now. If Edwin shook the town at some point, that would be his doing and the end of it.

Samuel determined to enjoy the ride, the sunshine, and the lady beside him.

Abby went still but watched him from the corner of her eye and wondered why he'd given up on his questions so easily. It wasn't like him. She gave another "Hmmm."

He noticed and didn't comment. That made her want to ask *him* questions, but she didn't.

"There's a lot of not talking happening." Abby shifted in her seat.

"How can not doing something be happening? That's an oxymoron."

"Could be."

"It is. I deem it so."

Abby laughed, and Samuel couldn't help but join her. She was glad he remembered her *deeming* tirade and thought it funny. It was, but only in retrospect.

He drove through town to show off his shiny automobile, scowled at Joe Foster, turned around and stopped in front of the hotel. Abby let herself out, thanked him, and waved as she opened the screen door.

"George is due home shortly, Abby."

She whipped around, and the screen door slammed shut. She ran back down the steps and leaned over the auto door.

"You throw that information out like it's what you want for breakfast? Like it's a fried egg?" She stomped a foot. "When?"

"Soon. The next month or so. He's being paroled – good behavior."

"George Adams doesn't know the meaning of good behavior. Is this what you were *not* saying all the way home?"

Samuel let his eyes roam Abby's freckled face and knew he didn't want to be the one to put tears in those green eyes. He told a partial truth.

"Yes. That was it. I'm sorry I had to tell you." Abby's head jerked his way.

"Al's brothers aren't paroled, are they? Tell me they're not going to show up at the farm some night and find Betty conveniently asleep in their old house. God, what a horrifying thought."

Samuel shook his head and reached across the seat to put his hand on hers before she turned and walked into the hotel. He knew what she envisioned. He'd been there, had seen Betty after they raped and beat her.

He'd kill them himself, first.

Abby shouted hello to her da and ran up the stairs to her room. She flung herself on the bed in between Cleo and Phantom who rose, turned in circles a couple of times and flopped down next to her.

Mrow, Phantom said, not happy she'd been gone.

"I know. It was a pretty long sermon. My fault, they tell me." His round, blue eyes accused her of multiple crimes, and she had to work to get a decent purr out of him.

"There's so much going on, Phantom. George is getting out of jail. How can that be? He beat her. Raped her. He should rot in prison, not be released because they think he behaved. It's bull! Sorry," she added when he complained her caress had gotten heavy.

He rose, circled and flopped again.

Sun streamed through the window. Its gold rays warmed her and made shadows and patterns on her mother's embroidered quilt. Abby traced a yellow rose with her finger, as she always did, bringing her mother closer, and she dozed in the Sunday early afternoon quiet.

She woke to voices below and got up to peer out the window. Benjamin, Shorty and Bear were in an animated discussion, but she couldn't tell what it concerned.

Don't eavesdrop, Abby. You'll hear bad things about yourself. That's a rule, Phantom told her with a blue-eyed glare.

"I know you don't actually speak," Abby said, "but it sure sounded like it. I'm going downstairs."

Nosy.

Abby whirled, frowned and left. Phantom and Cleo followed. The men were in the bar when she got there, and they were still bandying words. The cats took up their posts on either end of the bar.

She heard the names Al and Betty and little warning hairs stood on end. "What's wrong?" she said.

Benjamin took a seat on one of the stools, and Shorty leaned against the bar. Bear stood close enough she could feel the comforting heat of his body.

"Nothing. Just thinking and talking," Shorty said.

"So, can I ask why you're talking about Al and Betty?"

"Gus got another brick through a window, and so did the cousins," Bear said.

"A brick through Sue and Sally's window?" Abby was stunned anyone would try to frighten those sweet ladies. "Did their night sleeper recognize anyone?"

Bear shook his head. "The coward was horseback and didn't even stop, from the sounds of it. He came fast, pitched the brick and rode off."

"That's terrible. I could learn to hate, but what does that have to do with Al and Betty?"

None of the three men wanted to offer an answer. It seemed ridiculous, but, at the same time, they all knew the reality of their world. Al and Betty didn't kowtow to the Klan's social rules. They thumbed their noses at conformity by living together some of the time – a white woman and a colored woman. It wasn't allowed. It had consequences.

Bear put an arm on Abby's shoulder. "They're different, and some folks don't like different. You know that. We just want them safe."

"It gets worse," Abby said. "George Adams is getting out of jail."

"Damn," came out of all three men at once.

Patrick came through the kitchen doors carrying the kettle that would begin his lunch buffet. "Heard what ye said, lass. Maybe he's learned his lesson."

Abby glanced away. She didn't want to meet her father's eyes because she knew better. She knew deep inside that any man who had so little regard for a woman, for any person, wouldn't change because the law said he had to. She didn't understand how she knew it, but she believed it true, totally, emphatically.

"Maybe I'll drive out and get them in the morning and take them back when they're done working. You know – provide a buggy service."

She smiled when she laid out the plan and watched their eyes. Brows raised like she wore horns on her head or was a child they wanted to encourage but not placate.

"Stop it. I know what you're doing," she told them.

"We'll figure out something, Abby. Before George gets home, I promise," Shorty said. "We're all kinda fond of those two."

"And you're not going to put yourself in harm's way," Bear said. "Do you hear me, Abby?"

"Hear him, lass?" Patrick said.

"I did, Da."

Chapter Twenty-two

The day covered her in a mantle of freedom. She left Jackson in charge of the bar, stopped for Sue and Sally, and headed for Baldwin. She hadn't been able to get away while Jackson was gone, and she cherished his presence and tried not to tell him so every minute of the day.

She pulled up to the multicolored house and giggled. It was so much like the cousins, she'd know who it belonged to without being told. Purple and pink and yellow and green splashed over the wood siding like an artist had gone crazy with a giant brush.

Sue and Sally sashayed toward the buggy in bright red dresses and matching hats. They knew they looked good, and it showed in their strut and the wiggle of their hips. Abby got down to help.

They went through the usual gymnastics pushing and pulling Sue up and onto the seat of the buggy. Once there, she straightened her hat and dimpled her face in a broad smile. Sally wore regal like a satin gown.

Abby breathed in the sunshine. "Where to today, ladies?"

Sally turned her way and winked. "Your boyfriend's club, Abby. Don't even need to tell you where it is anymore."

"Gotcha. Not even going to argue with you about the boyfriend thing. It's too beautiful a day, and I do like Gus."

"Most folks do. He's a real man."

Gus leaned against the doorjamb, soaking in the sunshine. He left his post to give Sally a hand down and put his massive arms around Sue to lift her from the buggy. He'd seen the difficulties she had getting in and out of the buggy seat. She threw her arms around him and squealed like a little girl.

"You're the only man in the whole wide world who can lift this hefty hunk of loving, Gus. The only one."

She kissed his cheek, and he patted her bottom.

"Glad to see you, ladies. Anything special going on, Abigail?"

"No. A little shopping and checking on you. You good?"

"I am, sweetheart. But I can be bad just for you if you like that better." His lips split in a wide, toothy grin.

"Good is good, Gus." She tipped her head, indicating a window boarded up with old wood and making the bar look abandoned. "Did you give up replacing the glass?"

"Think I'll save all the bricks they toss in and use them. Make a nice, fancy design with them instead of glass." Gus scratched his head, and swore under his breath, but he didn't look angry or even upset over the damage. Abby wondered what would ruffle the big man's feathers. If anything.

"I'll be back in a couple hours," she said and nickered to Marie. "Have fun ladies. Win the shirts off their backs. I mean, maybe not. Don't do that."

Abby spent time catching up with people she'd known all her life at the dry goods store, bought the needed linens, soaps for the washstands, and new curtains for the kitchen windows. She spotted a large framed landscape picture with bright sun glancing off a river and chuckled all the way back to the bar. Eyes that used to stare at the out-of-place white woman, now ignored her as she walked in, and Abby felt right at home.

"Whiskey, please, bartender, with ice."

"You're looking like somebody fed you a canary while you were out and about. You still have feathers sticking outta your mouth." He made as if to pick one off. "Yep, yeller."

"I have a present for you."

"What?"

"I want to put it up. You can't look. Go away."

"I have a business to run, Abigail."

"Okay. Don't watch. Got a hammer and a nail?"

"You gonna do some repair work? I admit it could use some, but . . . I'm not paying you."

He dug in a drawer, came up with what she wanted, and tried not to watch. She dragged a chair over to the place where there used to be a window, hammered the nail, and hung the bright picture.

"There. You can look."

"Not bad," somebody yelled from the back corner. "Almost like you got a window, Gus."

"Better. The old one just showed a dirty old street," another voice offered.

Gus lit up. "You're a pip, Abby. I like it. That old . . . son of a gun can take out all my windows. Who needs 'em?" He came around the bar, picked her up, and swung her around. A shoe went flying. A man named Dugan caught it and held it in the air for ransom.

"A kiss. You can have it back for a kiss," Dugan said.

Sally came through the back door in time to see Gus carrying her across the room, her shoeless foot sticking out. "What in God's name is going on out here?" she asked. Abby wrapped an arm around Gus' neck and relaxed in his arms.

"Nothing. Why?" She widened her eyes, working for innocence. "Is something wrong, Sally?"

"I guess I wouldn't know, but that shoe doesn't belong to Dugan. Never saw him wearing ones like it, anyway."

The man stuck it back on Abby's foot, but Gus didn't put her down until he got back to her glass of whiskey. He set her on the stool like she might break if he dropped her. Sally sat next to her.

"That was a sweet thing to do, Abigail. Thank you."

"Welcome, Gus."

In the buggy, Sue pulled bills out of her dress and stuffed them in her handbag, talking all the while about the benefits of bluffing.

"You gotta watch me sometime, Sally. I'll show you. You just think of how boring some of the men are. You know, the ones we entertain at our establishment. Your eyes go kinda flat-like and nobody knows what you're thinking." She snorted and topped it with a giggle. "If they knew . . . we'd be outta business."

"I do alright for myself, Sue. I won some."

"Sure, you do, cousin. You're a real good . . ."

The tree crashed across the road smack in front of Marie who bolted to the right, screaming with fear and scrambling to keep her feet. She dragged the tilting buggy along the ditch for as long as she could and came to a stop when the axle broke, and the buggy jolted to the ground on its side. Abby hung onto the reins with one hand and the strap with the other to keep herself from falling on Sue.

"Are you alright Sue? Sally?" She looked sideways and panicked. "Sally! Where are you? Answer me."

"She left a second ago. Just kind of stepped out. She always was quick on her feet."

"You okay, Sue? I need to find Sally."

"Sure. Easy to get out, now. Ground is right here."

When Abby saw Marie had stopped trying to drag them, she let go of the reins and climbed out of the sideways buggy to look for Sally who ambled out of the ditch only a little worse for wear. Her red dress had dust streaks, and she'd lost her beautiful hat, but she moved down the road with grit and style.

"Thank God, you're alright," Abby said, putting an arm around her. "Help me get Sue up, please."

They helped Sue stand and checked her for injuries. She slapped their hands away, dusted herself off and looked for her handbag.

"Don't want to lose that. I cleaned up back there. What happened anyway?"

"A tree fell in the road," Sally said. "Didn't you see it?"

"No. I was counting. A tree, you say?"

"Yes. I find it odd," Sally said and went off to look at it.

Abby unhitched Marie and led her toward the woods at the side of the road. She ran her hands over the mare's legs and back, searching for injuries that might not be obvious and grateful not to find any.

"Thank you, Marie," she whispered. "I would be devastated if you were hurt. Thanks for taking care of us." The mare nickered, and Abby knew she'd been understood.

"Well," Sue said. "We can't just tip the buggy back up and get on the road. This thingy's broken." She pointed to the axle and frowned. "What now?"

Sally, coming back from her tree inspection said, "We walk or Abby goes for help, and you and I wait. By the way, that tree was cut."

Abby's head spun. "Somebody felled that tree on us? Who? Why?"

"I can guess why, but I have no idea who."

"That is unacceptable," Abby said.

Sally cocked a leg and tilted her head, looking oddly elegant in her dusty, red dress. "Unacceptable? I'll be sure to tell them that when I figure out who did it."

Her lips wore a grin, but it didn't hold joy, and Abby felt stupid and angry and frustrated.

"Damn. I'm so . . . Don't be mad at me, Sally. Please?"

Sally snuffled and showed her teeth in a good way. "Friend, I don't know what you're talking about. Why would I be mad at you?"

"I don't know."

She shook her head and walked over to Sue who sat on the ground next to the buggy. She'd taken off her hat and was fanning herself with it.

"I'm going to ride Marie into town and get someone to come back for you," Abby said. "Will you be okay here for a bit?"

"Do I have a choice?" Sue said. "I could use a drink. I surely could."

"I'll bring one."

"You don't have a saddle, you know."

"Yeah. It's just Marie and me. We've done it before." She climbed on Marie's back and told them to stay put.

"Where we gonna go?" Sue yelled. "Bring drinks when you come back."

Abby went straight to Jesse's office. She knew he owned a good-sized buggy; she'd been in it plenty of times when they drove her to church. She explained the situation, leaving out the suspicion about the deliberately cut tree, and asked for his help getting the ladies back to town.

"I'll bet that was a sight to see." He chuckled after hearing no bones were broken, but sobered hearing about Sally. "God, she could have been seriously hurt climbing out while it was moving."

"I know. It was terrifying but happened so fast we didn't realize the full danger. I have to go back to the hotel and get some liquid refreshment for Sue. I have my orders. Can you help?"

"Wouldn't miss it." He held a hand in the air. "Not that I enjoy catastrophe, but those two are entertaining."

She put a hand on his arm and squeezed. "Thanks. I knew you'd help. Pick me up at the hotel?"

"Soon as I hitch the buggy."

She dropped Marie in the stable, thanked her with a double dose of oats, gave her father the news, and poured a large container of gin and tonic, Sue's favorite. She waited on the porch for Jesse, climbed in, and he clicked to the double team.

"You're nice to take the ladies into Baldwin once in a while. It means a lot to them, I know."

"I love doing it," Abby said. "They're fun and funny. Gus, too. I gave him a picture today to cover a boarded-up window. He thinks it's a hoot."

"You're special, Abby." Jesse gave her a look that said more than his words, and she turned a delicate shade of pink. "Now see what you did?" she said, fanning her face.

"So how did you not see the tree in the road on the way to Baldwin?"

"It wasn't there."

Jesse tipped his head to check Abby's face, eyebrows raised.

"Seriously. I guess I didn't make it clear. The tree came down right in front of us. Sally says someone cut it."

Jesse was skeptical but kept that information to himself. He'd not ponder it until he knew for sure. It should be clear if the tree fell from old age or an axe.

Sue sat where she'd been left, fanning her red, sweat beaded face. Abby climbed down, reached behind the seat for her container of drinks and looked around for Sue's tall partner.

"Where's Sally?"

Sue pointed down the road where the tree lay, and Abby spotted her at the edge of the woods near the stump that once supported a tree.

"What's she doing?"

Sue pretended to choke and indicated the jug in Abby's hand.

"Sorry." Abby pulled several tin cups from a sack and handed them to Sue. She filled one, and Sue upended it and held the empty cup out for more.

Jesse wandered off to inspect the tree and stump. Abby watched him bend to study the cut ends, rub his chin in thought, and take Sally's hand. They talked and nodded back and forth, scowls marring their foreheads.

"Jesse agrees. Somebody cut that tree. Somebody meant it to fall when and where it did," Sally said when they got back to the buggy.

"Sure looks that way. Anybody know you were heading down this road today?" Jesse asked.

"I could name about ten I told in the bar last night," Abby said. "Why? You think this tree was meant for us?"

"Well, unless where it fell was accidental, and they took off instead of stepping forward, or this was someone's terrible idea of fun, then, yes. It could be for you, specifically or as a group. The question is did they meant it as malice, and were they warning or trying to harm?"

"I told a few last night, too. You know – pillow talk," Sue said. "Gotta have something to say; otherwise, I get those flat kinda eyes I told you about earlier, Abby."

"So, anybody could know," Jesse said. "Sheriff Hicks needs to see this. After I drop you girls off, I'll run get him."

"No harm was done," Abby said, wanting to make light of the whole thing or make it go away. "Except for my poor buggy. What can I do about it?"

"I'm sure Bear or Shorty can get it fixed for you."

"Is it safe here?"

Sue let out a guffaw. "About as safe as we were, I guess."

Abby's face fell. She felt responsible. Her friends could have been hurt, even killed.

"Sue. Stop it," Sally said, one fist on a hip, and the other holding her tin cup, her chin in the air. Abby thought she looked like a movie star.

"You didn't do this, Abby. Some son of a gun with an axe did, maybe an axe to grind. Let's get our things out of your poor broken buggy and go home."

Bear and Shorty showed up at the hotel about the same time as Sheriff Hicks. Jesse had, of course, told him about the tree coming down in front of the mare, and he'd verified their findings. The tree had been cut, but why?

"Did you hear anything or see anyone in the vicinity of the stump? Any movement at all?"

Abby shook her head. "Sue was counting her money and I was paying attention to them talk about bluffing and how their eyes go blank when . . ." Abby stopped talking, and her face grew hot and red as she remembered Sue's words.

"And what, Abby?" Hicks said.

"Nothing. None of us saw anything. We were busy talking."

"Jesse said a lot of folks knew you three were heading to Baldwin today. That right?"

"I didn't think it needed to be a secret. Why would I?"

"You might consider a little silence for a while. This might not have been meant for you, Abby. But it could've."

"That's ridiculous." Her hands fidgeted in front of her; her jaws clenched. "Who'd want to hurt me? Or the cousins?"

Hicks sighed. "I'll make a report. That's about all I can do. Keep your eyes open."

"That's it, Sheriff? You're just going to write something down?" Shorty asked. Hicks leaned in to hear the big man and whispered back. He didn't know why.

"That's it. For now. If something else happens, let me know." He eyed Shorty. The man fumed, and he didn't blame him. "You going out to get the buggy?"

Shorty nodded.

"Take a look around. See if you can spot something I missed, would you?"

"Bear's the woodsman. He'll track the bastard."

"Don't do anything stupid. You hear me?"

"Like?" Bear asked.

"Like taking the law into your own hands. You know damn well what I meant."

"Sheriff, if I find out somebody tried to hurt Abby and the cousins, I *will* have a little wall-to-wall counseling with them. But I'll be sure of who and what first. You can depend on that. Are we clear?"

"That's a lot of words out of your mouth, Bear. Most I ever heard. Stay in touch."

The bar filled while Hicks looked for answers no one had, and he noted the familiar faces watching him. Eyes were wary, voices quiet. Many of them had seen too much of him during the fires on the island a while back.

The fires ended when the Tatum boys went to jail, and the people who owned cabins, or wanted to, breathed a symphony of relieved sighs. Today their eyes reflected anxiety answering questions again.

Sheriff Hicks rubbed his chest, walked behind Abby and ruffled her hair on his way out. "You stay out of trouble. Why are you always in the thick of things?"

"They're not really thick."

"If you'll go out to where the buggy sits and take a look around, I'll go get Abraham's farm wagon," Shorty said to Bear. "You won't want to wait til dark."

"On my way," Bear said, and headed for the door. He'd saddled his mare by the time Shorty got to the stable.

"Look for boots," Shorty said as Bear rode out. "Might not have had a horse."

Bear lowered his head, and his brow wrinkled. "You giving me tracking lessons?"

"Guess not." Shorty grinned, but barely.

Abraham had a deceptively scrawny frame. Underneath his work shirt was sinew and lean muscle from his work on the farm. His weathered skin and sharp eyes told the story of his life. He didn't get many visitors. Didn't trust any. When he saw Shorty, he stepped out from behind a tree.

"Must want something. You don't come calling," he said.

"I do. Abby left a broken buggy on the road, and I'd borrow your farm wagon if I could. Maybe bring it back here to see if you could fix it."

"What's broken?"

"She says axle."

Without a word, Abraham ambled off toward the whitewashed barn and threw open the doors. A rooster flew out over his head, and Shorty heard him sputtering at the fowl, arms flying to keep it away.

"Damned bird. Gonna make stew outta you."

Shorty dismounted and led his gelding to the barn. "Feisty bird," he said.

"Yeh. Take a look at the scars on my head. Only keep him cuz he's good with the hens. And cuz I can't catch him."

Shorty chuckled at the admission. "We can use my horse if you want, Abraham. He's strong."

He looked closely at the animal and back at Shorty, assessing the strength it would need to carry the big man around.

"If he'll take a collar, bring him in. Be faster."

Abraham had one speed, a notch past standing still, and Shorty tried to help in order to hurry him along. But the man's old, he reminded himself.

His parents had fled southern slavery with the help of the underground railroad. Abraham, the only surviving child of his parents, had farmed their small holding his entire life, happy to live in peace, happy not to have lived the life his parents described in colorful, haunting detail. Their stories had one moral – stay away from white folks.

On the way to the buggy, the old man asked questions about the accident until he knew as much as Shorty did. He scowled when he heard about the felled tree.

Shorty whistled when he didn't see Bear near the buggy. They'd need him to help lift the thing onto the wagon. Abraham poked at the axel and spun the wheel, looked at the spokes on both wheels and grunted.

"I'll have it fixed by tomorrow if we get it back there today. Where's Bear?"

"Likely found some tracks, and he's following them. Sit a spell."

"I'll just get started taking it apart now. No use wasting time." Abraham had the wheel off and the axle pulled by the time Bear returned, leading his mare.

"What'd you find," Shorty asked.

"Tracks all the way across the section to the road."

"Straight across?" Abraham asked. "Or kinda kiddy-cornered to the north?"

Bear's eyes squinted. "Why?"

Abraham rubbed the bristles on his chin. "Back side of the Adams property."

"All the way out there?" Bear asked.

Abraham's eyes were annoyed. "Back of Tatum's buts up to it. Well?"

"Off to the north."

He grabbed the wheel that lay on the ground and nodded to Shorty to heft from the front. Abraham took the rear, and together, the three of them loaded it onto the wagon. Shorty threw a rope over the whole thing and tied it down.

"Doesn't mean anything," Bear said. "Lots of tracks on the road. Could be anyone."

Abraham's eyes narrowed. He had an opinion, but they hadn't asked for one. "Let's get it home."

He climbed on the seat and grabbed the reins. Shorty knew he'd get left if he didn't get on.

"I'll need you at Abe's farm, Bear."

It was dark when they got back to the hotel, and they were hungry. Abby laid plates in front of them, drew two beers, and stared into their eyes, looking for answers.

"Well?" she said, prodding for news.

"It's at Abraham's getting fixed," Bear said. "Should have it back tomorrow."

She rolled her eyes. "I knew the buggy was broken. I wanted to know about tracks. Did you find any?"

"Yup. To the road. Could be anybody."

Patrick, sitting next to them, sipped his drink and stared at his daughter. "I don't think ye should be going off by your wee self for a while."

"Wee? Nothing wee about me, Da. And I wasn't alone. I had the cousins with me."

"Ye know what I mean, without a man by yer side."

Abby's hands went to her hips, and her face took on *the look*, the one he never liked to see. She was her mother when she was irked, and it brought back both good and bad memories. "Ah, lass. You know what I mean."

"He's right," Bear said. "I agree."

"And how about you, Shorty? It's so nice when the men in my life try to run it. I'm not hiding. Not from anyone, much less a wanna-be lumberjack."

"Got something against lumberjacks?" Shorty said.

"Oops. Not you and Bear. I love you two. But I'm still not hiding." She pulled her apron off and hung it on a nail. "I'm closing. Finish your dinners and meet me on the porch."

She collapsed in the rocker, and they joined her soon after. Night wrapped her in warm and gentle arms. By tacit agreement learned through years of caring about one another, they left the day behind and enjoyed the silence. In this peace, it was hard to believe someone may have tried to cause her harm.

It would have continued if Samuel had not come by. "What in the hell have you been up to, Abby?"

"Not much. How bout you?" she said, determined to leave the day behind – in the forgotten past.

"Abigail, what happened?"

She exhaled a huge amount of exasperated air. "A tree fell. The buggy broke, but we didn't. That's pretty much it. Would you like a nightcap?"

He followed her inside, took her arm, and turned her to face him. "Are you unscathed? Sue said the mare dragged your buggy sideways down the ditch. You could've been killed." Samuel's eyes ran over her face and arms as if searching her for hidden bruises or wounds.

"Samuel, I am fine. Really."

He took his hand from her arm, realizing he'd been holding it with a too-tight grip. "Sorry. About that drink?"

She poured, handed it to him, and they headed back to the porch in time to see Edwin Emerson limp up the steps. He passed a piece of paper to Patrick and stood eyeing it, arms hanging like wet wash by his side.

"What's this?" Patrick asked, looking at Edwin instead of the paper.

"Don't know. I can write my name, and that's all."

"Right. I knew that. You want me to read this to you?"

"Please."

"Your time in Idlewild is done. Leave."

Edwin looked dumfounded. The lines between his brows deepened and his eyes squinted.

"You want me to go?" he asked. "Why didn't you just say you didn't need me anymore? First, you make me stay. Now, you make me go. Damn." Hurt, he turned to go back down the steps, and Patrick's voice stopped him.

"Wait. I didn't write this, Edwin. Where'd you get it?"

He scratched his scruffy head and blinked several times. "On my bedroll in the stable. Found it after I ate dinner. Thought you musta left me a note."

"No. I didn't."

Samuel reached for the piece of paper. "May I?"

"Maybe Sheriff Hicks is okay with me not staying here anymore. Maybe he left it."

Samuel shook his head. "No. He wouldn't have left a note. Someone wants you gone, as much as the sheriff wanted you here. Probably the horse."

"That's my horse. Bought it from Jesse James. I keep on saying it and saying it."

It was Samuel's turn to scratch his head. He sat in an available rocking chair and lay the paper on his leg. A finger tapped it. "Sue said you two went out to get Abby's buggy. See anything?"

"Tracked a ways," Bear said.

"Direction?"

"Northwest."

Samuel nodded, listened to an owl ask who.

"Think they're related?" Bear asked.

"Who?" Abby asked.

"It's what," Samuel said. "And I do. It's a thin thread, but a strong one."

"What on earth are you talking about, Samuel?"

His black eyes bored into her, hoping she'd accept what he said and not question deeper. He didn't want to tell her what he thought he knew. Not now.

"Your tree and the note. Someone is making a point. Someone wants Edwin out of town. Wants you and Patrick to let him go."

"That's crazy."

"Is it?" He looked at Bear, Shorty and Patrick. "Can you convince her to be safe? Not take chances?"

"Oh, my God. You, too? Take a man with me when I go somewhere. Is that it?"

He pulled his watch, opened it, and flipped it shut. He still didn't know the time. A delicate thing, time. An important determining factor.

"Yes."

He leaned his head against the slats of the chair, held onto the note and put his other hand on her arm. He clasped it – lightly this time – and watched Cassandra as she came into view in the slanted rays of moonlight and shadows. Maybe she'd know. Maybe he'd visit the seer.

Chapter Twenty-three

"Betty walked with you this morning, right?"

Al nodded as she put the heavy coffee pot on the hot spot. Her face was a map of minor irritation at Abby's insistence she and Betty come in to work together.

"No trouble?"

"None."

"Maybe because there's two of you. Maybe not if you walked alone. You never know."

"I've been walking alone my whole life."

"Placate me for a while, please. I couldn't live with you getting hurt again."

Al shrugged, and a half-smile replaced annoyance. Betty bopped in and out over the next hour, looking for work to keep her occupied until the guests left their rooms.

"Want me to polish the lamps? I could do that or mop the bar floor."

"You pick . . ."

Her words were cut off as Frank shoved the doors open. They bounced off the walls as he strode through.

"Are you alright?" he asked.

"I was until you scared us to death. My heart's still pounding. What are you doing here, Frank?"

"Seeing if you're okay."

"Of course, I'm okay." She paused and remembered. "Oh. The tree. We're all fine. Thanks for asking."

"Got some coffee?" Frank looked out the window while he sipped from the cup she handed him.

Abby flipped pancakes and stirred a dozen eggs for scrambling. "Need you to move over a bit, Frank. Was there something else you needed?"

"I need a reason to visit my wife?"

Frank tried for a wounded expression, but it didn't look real to Abby. He looked like he wanted answers to questions he hadn't asked. He shuffled his feet and wiped a palm down the side of his work pants.

"No, you don't. But shouldn't you be in the field?" she asked.

"Sure. Just wanted to see for myself."

"That's really sweet, Frank. Thank you." She patted his arm, trying to make up for hurting him.

"Your handyman still around?"

"Edwin? Sure. Why do you ask?"

"No reason. Can we talk sometime, Abby?"

Al took off for the larder. Abby watched her go, and her bottom lip slid between her teeth. She didn't understand the undercurrents in the room, but they were there.

"Sure. I'd like that. What do you want with Edwin, Frank?"

He scratched at his neck. "I don't want anything with him. Curious is all. I was checking on you, and I did. Gotta go."

He wrapped an arm around her, planted a hard kiss and ran out the way he came, doors making a racket against the walls again. Al came back into the kitchen when she heard the doors swinging.

"Why'd you leave, Al?"

"No reason."

Abby flung the towel in her hand across the room. "Nobody has a reason for anything. What's going on?"

"Getting out of the way."

Al turned the sausage patties, and Shorty walked in followed by Bear draped in cats.

"Did I just see Frank leaving?" Bear asked.

"You did. He was worried about me. Wanted to make sure I'm okay. Nice, huh?"

Shorty chewed his lip. Al put coffee in front of them, and they reached for their cups, not looking at Abby or responding.

"Well, it was."

Bear moved Phantom's tail so he could drink his coffee. "Sure."

"Should I go out to Abraham's today for the buggy?" she asked.

"He'll bring it."

Abby flung her hands in the air. "Everybody's so terse today. It's like you're all mad or something. What's wrong? This doesn't feel good at all."

Shorty stood, put his hands around Abby's waist, picked her up and put her on the tallest cupboard. He went back to the table and finished his coffee. Abby sat with her chin on her fists, her legs swinging sideways. When he put her feet back on the floor, she hugged him and apologized.

"You're forgiven," he said. "I still love you."

Patrick came in, pulled Al's apron strings, and sent Abby off to work with Betty.

"Guests are up and about. I'll get the buffet on."

"Sometimes I feel like a wind-up toy," she muttered to herself as she climbed the stairs.

Before saddling up, Shorty and Bear pulled Edwin from his bedroll, looking for the note.

"We'll drop it at the sheriff's office. See what he thinks about it," Shorty said.

"I got it here somewhere, but you really think you need to?"

"Don't know, but it can't hurt."

Edwin pulled the crinkled note from his pants pocket and handed it over.

"Sticking around?" Bear asked him.

"Guess so. Got nowhere else to be right now."

They saddled up and said *so long* to Edwin. After dropping off the note at Hicks' office, they headed south toward White Cloud and Longstreet. They didn't talk. It had all been said the night before. If Longstreet had played lumberjack, he wouldn't be cutting any more trees. If he had thrown the bricks through their friends' windows, he wouldn't throw any more.

They stopped at the real estate office first, the one the Branch brothers owned, figuring they could get an honest answer out of them about where to find Longstreet. Ratty told them, and they found him at a small hardware store behind the counter.

"Gentlemen," he said, not identifying them. "What can I . . ." He backed up a couple of steps when recognition hit, before he regained his composure and finished his sentence. "What can I do for you?"

Shorty's fist pounded the counter, and he leaned over to grab the man's shirt collar.

"You can tell us who dropped a tree in the road right in front of our friend's mare. That's what you can do. Now."

Longstreet gurgled as he tried to swallow and suck in air at the same time, not having success at either. Shorty released a bit of fabric.

"Speak. Now," he said.

"I . . . I don't know."

"That's not good enough. Try again."

"I don't know anything about it. Truly. I don't." Longstreet whined. He cajoled. He begged. "Please. I wouldn't hurt Abigail."

Shorty lifted him off the floor and dragged him across the counter. With one hand holding the back of his shirt collar and the other gripping his belt, he held him in the air. He pumped him up and down like he was washing clothes on a washboard. Up to his own chest and down to the floor, he lifted and dropped the terrified man but stopped in time to keep him from smashing into the wooden planks.

Longstreet's legs bicycled faster and faster, and tears dripped into the dust at their feet. Bear smiled when Shorty set him on the counter and handed him his own handkerchief.

"Now, let's talk." Bear leaned in. "Who said anything about Abigail? Did you, Shorty?"

"Nope."

"I . . . I just figured, knowing you, and her and all."

Bear pointed to the scars crisscrossing his beard. "See these? I killed the bear that made them. With a knife. Understand my point?"

Longstreet's head jerked up and down, chin meeting his chest each time, being obliging and supportive.

"I understand. Please. Let me get down."

"If you didn't do it, you know who did."

This time his head went from side to side, eyes rolling around with each swing of his head. "No. I don't know. Nobody from here. I know that much."

"How do you know that?" Shorty whispered.

"Because . . . Because at the club we all have to approve, uh, events. This wasn't approved."

"That's what you call it? *The club*? Was it discussed, this non-event?" Bear asked.

More shaking of the head. "No! Not discussed." He stared at Bear trying to convince him of his innocence.

"Bricks in the windows of our friends?"

"What? Who?"

"Gus and the cousins."

He rubbed his nose, and snot came away in a string. Bear turned and Shorty swore. "Use your damned handkerchief."

Longstreet blew his nose, widened his red rimmed eyes and stared at the door. He didn't want to answer. God, he didn't want to answer. He wanted someone, anyone, to walk into the store to buy a nail, to save him.

Shorty went to the open door and pulled the key sticking out of a hole in the lock. He closed the door, put the key back in and turned it. The click it made deafened the room. The window shades rolled down without a whisper. Not even Shorty's boots interfered with the silence as he walked back and stood in front of the man.

He picked up Longstreet's hand and turned it over and back again, looking at the long, slender fingers. He patted the back of it.

"Nice hands. Bet your mama said you should play piano, didn't she?"

His head bobbed. Eyes widened.

"I'd hate to see 'em all broken up," Shorty said. "Tell the *Club* to leave our friends alone."

"I will. I'll do that right away, but sometimes they don't listen to me, you gotta know that. It's not my fault if they don't listen."

Shorty squeezed the slender hand until he felt the grind of knuckles, and Longstreet began to sob.

"Sometimes they don't tell me things either, so I can't stop things from happening."

"What kind of things, Mister Longstreet?" Bear asked.

"Like when they're making a point about where people buy booze. Or . . ."

"Or throwing bricks in the windows of nice colored women?" Bear asked.

His head went up and down. "They didn't tell me. Honest."

"Sure. Just make sure it doesn't happen again the next time they *don't tell you*. And Mister Longstreet?" Shorty said, his voice so low it couldn't be called a whisper.

"What?"

"Make it your business to know what's gonna happen and ride your ass to Idlewild to tell me. Do I make myself clear?"

Longstreet obliged throughout his blubbering, and, when Shorty released his hand, he cradled it to his chest with the other and watched them leave.

They led the horses to a water trough and let them drink while they took a long look at the town. Rumor had it one in five men in White Cloud had signed his name to the Klan rolls, and they spoke of it with pride.

A man stood in the doorway of the general store and watched them. Another sat in front of the barbershop. A third took his time with a broom on the sidewalk in front of a small hotel.

"Are we that pretty to look at?" Shorty asked.

"Seems like."

"I don't think he knew anything about Abby's accident."

"Agreed. But he sure as hell knew about Gus and the ladies."

Shorty mounted and walked his gelding close to the sidewalk, so he could get a good look at the men who were eyeballing them. He nodded to each one and commanded them to have a good day. Bear followed and repeated the pleasant warning.

Abby was cleaning the last room when she heard Edna's demanding voice calling her downstairs. She went into the hallway and peered over the railing. Bunny, Mildred and Edna milled around the lobby, waiting.

"Come on down, Abby. We want to talk with you," Bunny said.

"Give me a minute."

"Go on, boss. I'll finish up. Looks like a posse," Betty said with a grin.

Abby scrunched her face, concerned the term might be true. They did look that way, and they'd never come to visit her all together before.

"What's going on, ladies? Betty thinks you're a posse. Are you?" She skipped down the stairs. "Want some tea? Coffee? Cognac?"

"Coffee would be nice," Mildred said, but her words were undermined by Bunny's request for cognac and Edna's for tea.

"All three it is, then. Come on into the dining room."

"You mean bar, don't you, Abby?"

"No. It's prohibition, so it's a dining room."

Abby filled the order, brought it to their table and sat.

"This looks serious," she said.

"It is, and I feel responsible," Bunny said. "I believe your . . . accident could be related to the work you're doing in the community. I allowed it, and you must stop."

Abby's jaw set and her lips pressed together. "You can't possibly mean that."

"I do. We do." Bunny's regal chin raised a fraction of an inch, enough to tell Abby she meant what she said and expected to be obeyed. She sipped her cognac and let unblinking eyes lay on the recipient of her words.

How did she do it? Abby wondered. Did *the look* come with practice, or did one have to be born royal? Regardless, she didn't plan to obey the queen on this day.

"You can't believe that tree had anything to do with my involvement in the town." Her eyes roamed from face to face and went back to Bunny. "You do?"

"We do," Mildred said.

Abby shoved her sleeves up to her elbows, planted them on the table and leaned in.

"Well, I don't. And even if I did, I still wouldn't stop doing what I'm doing. They, whoever it is, can't make me."

"The next time, someone could get hurt, Abby. Think about that," Edna said.

"Who says there will be a next time? And if they wanted to hurt me, I'd be hurt. I've given them lots of opportunities. They just wanted to scare somebody. Don't even know for sure who."

She steepled her fingers and bounced them off her chin. "Besides, this is too important. One stone at a time, ladies. We're dismantling prejudice one stone at a time and building on love."

"That's all true," Edna said, swayed by Abby's determination and fervor. Bunny sat back in her chair and thought about Abby's words. She steepled her own hands and held the tips to her lips.

"Am I missing a prayer meeting?" a deep voice asked.

Abby turned toward the voice. "I'm sure you could use one, Samuel, but no."

"I can leave if I'm interrupting," he said.

Bunny pushed a chair out for him. "Sit."

"Yes, ma'am."

"Abby seems to think having a tree almost fall on her is unimportant, just meant to frighten. Do you agree?" Bunny said.

"I assume I need to steeple my hands to be part of this group?" he asked, intertwining his fingers. Bunny slapped the back of his head. He tried to duck but didn't make it in time.

Abby gasped. Nobody smacked Samuel. It wasn't done. She expected to see anger in his eyes, but he gave Bunny a sheepish grin and un-steepled his fingers.

"I don't believe what I just saw," she said. "Do it again, Bunny."

The queen sighed and peered through thick lashes at all of them. "Can we move on?"

"I agree with Abby. I don't think real harm was intended. But it could have turned out that way." Samuel pulled at his cuffs and straightened his shoulders.

"Think it's connected to her activities?" Edna asked.

"Like?" Samuel asked.

"Desegregating church? Hauling the cousins around? She's basically an activist, like Charles Chesnutt and Harrison Bradford and Garvey," Edna said, throwing her hands in the air. "I never saw her that way before, but that's what she is. Look at her."

Samuel leaned sideways to peer at Abby. "Could be. She could be an unwitting activist. Are you fighting racial bias, Abby?"

"I'm fighting stupidity. That's all. I dislike stupid. Racial bias is . . . stupid, so . . . I guess I am."

"You could get hurt," he said.

"I already hurt watching us be forcibly separated."

"Maybe we're supposed to be apart." He stared, forcing her to look at him, and held her gaze.

"No. We aren't."

"You're certain?"

"I am."

For a moment, they were alone in the room – until Edna cleared her throat. Abby didn't know what had just happened, but it was uncomfortable. She got up, refilled drinks, smoothed the front of her skirt, yanked at her sleeves and sat back down.

"So, we're all agreed. I'm an activist, and I can continue my incorrigible, unwitting, activities, and you'll all forgive me. And . . . I can smack Samuel in the back of the head like Bunny does. Right?"

He smoothed his mustache with a thumb and forefinger and acknowledged her with the raise of an eyebrow.

"The first three."

"I didn't think I would like you," Bunny said with a nod toward Abby.

She preened and grinned. "But you do, don't you?"

Bunny stood and gazed at Samuel. "We'll see. I'll ask Cassandra. She'll know."

Samuel wondered if Cassandra suddenly had friends and family pounding on her door looking for answers. He'd been one just this morning. When the three ladies rose to leave, Abby started to rise, too. Samuel tugged on her arm.

"I need to talk with you. Can we go to the porch?"

She told Jackson where she'd be and followed him out.

He waited for Abby to sit and settled in the chair next to her. Except for children's laughter coming from the sandy beach where they built castles and swam in the warm, summer water, quiet fell around them. He watched and wished.

She hadn't seen Samuel unsure of himself, and it concerned her. In fact, it scared her.

"I'm not sure how to say this, and it's my hope you'll simply do what I ask and not question it." He raised his brows and tilted his head at her. "I realize that's totally out of character and asks a lot."

"Sounds pretty serious.".

"It could be. Here it is. I want you to let Edwin Emerson move on. Give him his pay and ask him to go."

"But I like him, and he's helping us, and . . ."

Samuel rubbed his eyes and groaned.

"I knew this wouldn't be easy. You wouldn't do that for a friend?"

"Maybe if I knew why."

"I can't say."

"Then I can't do it."

Samuel banged his head against the back of his chair and tapped his fingers on the arm. He pulled his watch out, flipped it open and shut, and put it back. He stretched his neck, and Abby heard it crack.

"Ouch. Sounds painful," she said.

"You've got that right. It's a real big pain in the neck."

"You going to tell me?"

Samuel rose and put his hands on the arms of her chair, his face a foot from hers. He noted the green of her eyes, the determined set of her chin, and her lips.

"I'll have to think about it. I'll be back."

Chapter Twenty-four

Samuel heard their voices as soon as the engine shut off, long before stepping inside the barn.

"Hello," he called out to make them stop shouting at each other. He didn't want to be a party to this angry conversation. The yelling stopped, and they turned to him.

"Samuel," the brothers said together. It didn't sound like an invitation. He considered uttering a few cordial words, for the sake of civility, but the identical furrows between their brows scattered that idea to the wind.

"I'd like a word with you, Frank. Alone, please."

"Why?"

"I have something to say you might want kept private."

Frank stuck a piece of straw between his lips and rocked back on one foot. The other he left forward in a pose designed to appear relaxed. The twitch in his jaw muscle proved otherwise. Terry moved toward Samuel and stopped a few feet from him, trying to intimidate.

"You can say whatever you came to say right here in front of me," Terry said, defiantly.

"You're probably right. Frank?"

"Go ahead."

"I'm sure you're aware that old man Tatum's horse is in the stable at the hotel, as well as the man who bought it from Jesse James. He's already spoken to Sherriff Hicks, and fortunately for . . . *Jesse*, Edwin hasn't seen him around town – yet. You'd agree, I think, it would be in Mister James' best interest to stop coming by the hotel."

"What's that to Frank?" Terry asked. "Why should he care about that old coot and his horse?"

"Mister James shouldn't have written a note. That was stupid. Handwriting analysis is in its infancy, but still..."

Samuel walked to the barn door and turned around with iron resolve in his eyes. He looked first at Terry and settled on Frank.

"If another tree happens to fall near Abby or her friends, Mister James, and his . . . *gang*, are going to regret it."

Samuel didn't hang around to see their reactions but heard nervous mumbling all the way to his automobile. He stopped before cranking it and looked around.

The place was immaculate, from the freshly painted porch to the kitchen garden at the side of the house. Oat fields waved deep golden heads, nearly ready for the cutter. Heifers grazed in fenced pastures, and faces pressed into windows, their noses squashed flat for a better view.

"Not many negro visitors, I guess." Samuel's lips curved in a pained grimace. "I did what I needed to do."

He took his time on the circle drive in front of the house to let them have full view of his shiny Model T. Near the end of the circuit he opened his mouth in a full-bodied laugh.

The spicy scent of cabbage rolls and sound of clinking cutlery greeted him when he got to the hotel. He took a seat next to Charles Chesnutt and clapped him on the shoulder.

"Good to see you back in town. You might as well buy a lot and build a house."

"Maybe someday. I like hotel living. Someone else has to clean up after me."

"You the keynote at Abby's Chautauqua?"

"It's not mine, Samuel," she hollered from the other end of the bar.

"You have ears like a bat," he said.

She pulled her hair from her face and ran her fingers around her ear. "I do not. Bats have little, tiny, baby ears."

"I meant . . . Never mind. Could I have a small cognac, please, Madame barkeep?"

"Yes, I'm keynoting," Charles said, answering his earlier question. "Buddy Black is here. Florence Mills is going to sing and dance. And that girl can dance." His eyes filmed over, wanting to be left in his daydream.

Benjamin and his five soldier friends walked in and the place exploded with chatter. People remembered them with affection, and everyone enjoyed Benjamin's fingers on the piano.

"I wasn't expecting you, but I'm sure happy you're here. All of you," Abby said.

Benjamin headed for the piano, and Abby brought his drink to him. She wrapped an arm around his back and kissed the top of his head.

"Did you close down the town of Nirvana?"

His fingers ran over the keys in a cascading melody that sounded like a water fall.

"Heard you had some trouble and could be more. Thought a few folks might need a reminder what your friends look like." No humor touched his eyes.

"It was nothing. Don't get yourself hurt, Benjamin. I would hate that."

"Then it wasn't nothing, was it?"

"I don't know."

"Well," he said, nodding toward his buddies. "They're pussycats, but they look enough like trouble to scare most folks."

"You need rooms? I only have two left."

"A few of us will take them. A couple are keeping watch on the cousins. Andrew and David are sleepers for the ladies tonight."

She kissed his head again. "You're all sweet men. Don't tell them I know how kind they are."

Sheriff Hicks leaned against the door frame and watched people laughing and talking, and one man sitting alone doing just what he appeared to be doing – assessing. He wore a pin stripe suit with a white triangle sticking out of the breast pocket, and his eyes scanned the room as if he documented each individual.

Hicks knew faces, if not names, but he hadn't seen this one around. Before he could wander over and cordially welcome him to town, the man tossed back his drink and left.

"What are you doing here tonight, Sheriff?" Abby asked. "Are you drinking or working?"

"Not working tonight, Abby. I'm just looking around. Make a short one for your favorite sheriff, please. Pretty quiet around here?"

"Sure," she said, pushing his drink toward him. "Friends and family having food and company."

"Know the man at the back table?"

"Said he was heading west to the big lake. That's all I know."

"Seen him before?"

She shook her head and looked for him. "I didn't realize he left."

"Pretty soon after I got here." Hicks twirled the glass on the bar and made it sing when he rubbed a finger over the rim. He wished he'd put civilian clothes on – didn't even remember if he had any. He'd been sheriff too long.

"Okay if I take this to the porch?" he asked.

"Sure. Looking for something?"

"Just looking."

He pulled a chair into the shadows and sat. Before long, he spotted the man coming out of Foster's store. He could have made a purchase for the road. Or he could have been having a conversation with Joe. Asking would get him nothing, unless he accompanied the question with his gun, and he didn't want to do that. Sometimes a gun didn't work, either.

More and more he hated his job. Time to quit. Maybe run a small hotel in some warm southern state. He rubbed his chest, walked around the building to the stable, and talked with Edwin.

"I can't hold you here, Emerson. Guess you can leave whenever you feel like it."

Edwin squinted at the shadow that was Hicks.

"Now, you say. Thinking I'll stay a while – til the snow flies, anyway. These folks treat me good, and I've got a bed at night."

"Your call. Wanted to let you know. You look a sight better than the first night we met. Must be feeding you alright."

"The leprechaun can cook. For sure."

Hicks stopped at the door and turned back as if he'd forgotten something. "You haven't recognized your Jesse James around town, have you?"

"Nope. Thought I did once, but he was a long ways off, and then he was gone. Get old and your eyes start playing tricks on you."

"That they do. Get old and life is one big bad trick. You see him again, you let me know, Edwin," Hicks said, but he didn't believe the man really saw Jesse. Didn't know what to believe except Edwin didn't kill anybody and steal a horse.

Mister James did.

Besides hotel guests, Benjamin and his five buddies, Samuel, Charles, Shorty, Bear, Patrick, and Abby packed the porch. It was definitely a man's world, Abby thought as she carried the heavy tray of drinks to the porch. Bear carried a second tray. In fact, he fought Samuel for the right.

Hicks hung around long enough to sip a cup of coffee before he strolled off like he had the weight of the world on his shoulders.

The pavilion glowed in the light of the moon and cast a monster shadow on one side. They had decorated it with crepe paper and lanterns in preparation for the next day's Chautauqua events. In the dark of the night, it looked somehow eerie, like a ballroom with all the dancers gone or dead, the structure abandoned for eternity. Abby shivered, ridding herself of the macabre ideas.

"Spirits tapping on your spine?" Samuel said.

"Must be. It's a strange night."

Cassandra ambled by, cats following, but her clowder seemed to have doubled in number. Some were tiny fuzz balls who stopped to bat at the water, tumble with another fuzz ball, and roll around before getting back into line. She ignored their antics and continued plucking unknown things from the mud. Abby wondered if the *things* became part of the tea she drank when she visited her.

Cassandra raised her stick. "Yehudi walks tonight."

Phantom climbed down from Shorty's shoulder and glided to the edge of the porch. With a leap that should have been impossible, he landed on the railing post and posed for the clowder. Cleo took the other one, black and white effigies, bookends with glowing eyes, awaiting Yehudi.

She rinsed her hands and face at the wash stand and slipped into the nightgown Frank thought too virginal, picked up her brush and turned out the light. Long auburn tresses seized the moon's light as she brushed out the day's tangles, one hundred times as her da had told her so long ago. Had her mum brushed her hair a hundred times? Had her da watched?

Abby sat in front of the open window, listening, brushing, watching shapes appear and disintegrate into imagination. The quarter-moon moved across the sky, leaving enough light for shadows to skitter over the ground behind it. An unnatural quiet claimed the dark.

Sleep eluded her. It eluded Bear and Shorty, too, but the first to reach the hushed, but far from silent, commotion in the stable was Benjamin and his friends.

Two men, hearing the slap of footsteps heading their way, slipped out the door and disappeared into the dark before they got there. Moses, Mick and Chuck saw the shadows and raced after them, going on sound alone.

Shorty and Bear got to the stable and found Edwin lying bloodied on the floor. Benjamin, trying to raise him, told them the little he knew, and, after a quick survey of the situation, Bear found the lantern and lit it. He held it over the silent Edwin, and Shorty kneeled to assess his injuries.

"He's alive. Need to get him into better light to see the damage." Shorty picked him up like he was a baby and headed out the door as Abby rushed in.

"What's going on? Is that Edwin?"

"Inside, Abby," Shorty said. "Get some light in the kitchen. We'll see what's what."

"Thanks for being so quick on the mark," Bear said to Benjamin. "You coming inside?"

"Think I'll wait here for the boys. Maybe look around for something the intruders might have dropped."

Shorty put Edwin on the kitchen table and opened the bloodied shirt. His torso was already beginning to bruise where muscle had met fists. His face was raw, and one eye had swollen shut – or would be soon. He came to and swung his fist when Abby put a wet cloth on the bloodied lip, but Bear saved her by grabbing Edwin's arm.

"Stop, man," Shorty whispered. "You're safe. You're in the hotel kitchen, and Abby's trying to clean you up."

His eyes rolled around in bloodied sockets, looking for validation of Shorty's words. He saw Abby with the wet cloth, waiting his permission to clean the blood from his face. His eyes shut briefly and his chest expanded in a relieved breath of air. He grabbed for his side where painful ribs screamed in criticism.

Shorty ran a tender hand over them, located broken bones and asked Abby for a sheet he could tear up.

"Doesn't have to be a good one, just clean," he said.

Together, they washed and wrapped his chest, got the worst of the blood from his face, and found a knot the size of a walnut on the back of his head.

"I don't know much," Bear said, "but I think he's supposed to stay awake for a few hours, or he might never wake up again. Cuz of the bump on his noggin."

"Can you sit, Edwin?" Abby asked. "You want a cup of coffee? Water?"

He squinted in pain at the movement of his head.

"Can you make a pot, Abby?" Bear asked. "Think we all might want some."

Like magic, when the coffee had perked, Benjamin and the friends came in the back door.

"Catch them?" Bear asked. The solemn shake of their heads told the story.

"Too fast, too dark," Moses said.

"We could track 'em," Mick offered, his youth making light of the darkness that had shrouded their quarry.

"Too dark, Mick. Might find some tracks come dawn."

"Have a seat, boys," Shorty said, sliding Edwin off the table and onto the nearest chair. "Did you catch a face on either of them?"

"Got conked on the head first. Then fists flew so fast I was just trying to keep from dying. Don't know who it was." Edwin's chin dropped to his chest.

Abby set out the cups and poured coffee. She pulled the leftover soda bread, strawberry jam and butter from the pantry, and none of the men had a problem digging in.

"Saw their backs," Moses said. "We should've sneaked up on them instead of rushing in like a bunch of kids. We heard somebody getting hit and yelling and ran toward the sound."

"They say anything?" Shorty asked, looking at Edwin.

"Kept asking where the booze was hid, where I was gettin' it from. I didn't know anything about no booze. Told 'em that."

"That doesn't make any sense," Benjamin said. "I understand them wanting whiskey if it was youngsters out on a lark, but why look for it in the stable?"

"Think a bunch of kids were looking for a drink?" Abby asked. "Why beat him?"

"Weren't shaped like no kids. Didn't hit like 'em, either. Maybe had something to do with the note?" Edwin asked.

Moses ran a hand over close-cropped, black hair and rubbed at the back of his neck. "What note?"

Abby had a hard time seeing the slender man as part of Benjamin's 369th regiment. His elegance suited a salon more than a battlefield, but his intellect was sharp and his resolve intimidating. The ice in his voice chilled her, and she felt like she'd made a mistake in not telling him earlier about the note left for Edwin. But she didn't know why she *should* have or why she *would* have.

"Sorry," she said, wincing. "Edwin got a note saying he should leave town. We gave it to the sheriff who told Edwin to stay in town."

Moses clenched his hands. "Is there anything else I should know?"

"The short and sweet is that Edwin came to town on a horse that belonged to a man who'd been killed and buried in a shallow grave that a dog dug up. Said he bought the mare. Has a bill of sale from a *Jesse James*," Shorty said.

Edwin sipped his coffee and turned to Abby. "Think you could find a little of that whiskey they were looking for to put in this cup?"

"Would that be good for him?" she asked Bear.

"For all of us," he said.

Abby brought the bottle to the table as Patrick wandered in, rubbing his scruffy face with one hand and his curly head with the other.

"Feel like I'm missing out," he said. His eyes looked sad, like they'd forgotten to send his party invitation.

"Coffee?" Abby got a cup, and he used it for whiskey.

"Too late for coffee. I won't sleep. Fill me in?"

They did, and at the end of it, Patrick had some insights.

"Sounds like Klan and Newaygo thugs getting together. We're getting our own booze, and the thugs don't like it. We're selling booze, and The Klan doesn't like that. And we're entertaining people of all colors and women of . . . all sorts. The upstanding members of the Klan are selective and um . . . discriminatory. Is that a word?"

Chapter Twenty-five

"I can sleep better in the stable. I'm used to it."

Edwin stood, ready to head for his bed after a long night of being babysat by the men he called *the colored boys.*

Mick shook his head. "You're the stubbornest old coot I ever did see. Bet you had a yard full of mules when you were a kid, didn't you?"

"I did. And pigeons. Homing pigeons. Fan tails. I kept selling 'em and they kept coming home and I'd sell 'em again." Edwin's grin was self-satisfied, and Mick liked that about him. They'd spent what was left of the night in the rocking chairs on the porch and Mick kept him awake by telling war stories – some were even true.

Edwin shuffled down the porch steps, waved goodnight and grimaced. It hurt.

"Get some sleep, old man," Mick said.

In the kitchen, coffee percolated, and Al kept looking at the door. Abby smiled knowing she anticipated Shorty and Bear coming through.

"They'll be a little late this morning. We were up most of the night taking care of Edwin."

Al's head swung to stare at Abby.

"Somebody beat him up last night."

"He got in a fight?" Al's eyes widened.

"No. I wouldn't say that. Somebody, a couple somebodies, deliberately beat him."

"Why?"

"Da thinks it might be crooks and Klan trying to shut us down, but I think it has to do with the note." Abby told a puzzled Al about the note and what it said.

"I lay awake last night wondering about it, and I think it has something to do with his mare – your pa's mare. Maybe whoever killed your pa sold that horse to Edwin, and they don't want to be recognized as Edwin's Jesse James? Which would mean the man who did it probably lives here and isn't a drifter like we all thought. Do you see?"

"Yup." Al turned back to shaping the sausage into patties, and Abby shrugged.

"But Edwin said he bought it in Newaygo, not here," she said, not really to Al, more puzzling to herself. "Hmmm."

Abby's face went white, and her hands came up to cover her mouth. She hadn't said anything, but words and pictures banged against the walls of her brain, trying to get out.

"No!"

"What?" Al said.

"Nothing. I need to check on Edwin. Be right back." Abby strode through the kitchen doors into the bar.

"Wrong . . . way," Al said, finishing when the doors had made their backward swing.

Abby raced up the stairs to find their single wedding photo, stuck it in the pocket of her apron, and went out the front door to the stable. She tiptoed inside, though she didn't know why because she intended to wake him anyway. She had to know.

"Edwin, are you asleep?" she whispered.

He groaned, his foggy brain crying out for numbness.

"Please wake up, Edwin. I have a question to ask you."

His good eye popped open, and he grabbed a tattered blanket to pull it up over his chest to his chin.

"It's okay, Edwin. Can you see alright?"

His brow wrinkled and the open eye squinted.

"You feeling okay this morning?"

"Tired. I need some sleep."

"I know, and you can go back to sleep in a minute."

She pulled the picture from her pocket and covered half of it with her palm, leaving only Frank showing.

"Do you know this man, Edwin?"

"Humph. I'll be damned. It's Jesse."

"Are you sure? It could just look a little like him."

"No. I'm pretty damned sure. That's Jesse James. How'd you get a picture of him?"

"Um, I can't say right now, Edwin. Please don't say anything about this. To anybody. Not yet."

He eyed her, the good eye squinting again, his face lined with years of living and a long night of pain.

"Please?" She waited, holding her breath until she saw his head begin a slow, cautious nod.

"Thank you, Edwin. Thank you. Do you want breakfast now?"

"No. Sleep."

Shorty and Bear were at the kitchen table, drinking their coffee, when she got back. She peered into Shorty's cup to find it half full, whispered good morning and went back to cooking. She dropped the metal bowl she'd lifted from the overhead shelf, spun to put her hands over her ears and winced at him as it bounced on the floor, making noise like an army with metal shoes.

"Sorry."

The spatula clattered into the bacon pan and sent grease flying over her arm. She winced again, held the painful burns, and tears rolled in waves down her cheeks.

Bear was there in an instant. He pulled her hand away from the reddening arm, drenched a towel in cold water and laid it over the burns.

"Don't cry, Abby. You'll be okay," he said, and glared at Shorty. "Ass. If she hadn't been catering to your stupid need for morning quiet, she wouldn't have done this."

"No! It isn't Shorty's fault. It's mine. Just me." The tears rolled faster, made rivers and dripped off her chin.

"What's wrong, Abby?" Shorty said. "This isn't because you burned yourself. I've seen you do that twenty times or more." He rose and tipped her head up. "Want me to set you on the cupboard?"

"Leave her alone," Bear said.

Shorty pulled her to his chest and then to his chair and pushed her into it.

"Want to tell us?" he said.

She shook her head. "No. Not now."

"Want to go lay down for a spell?"

"No, Shorty. Thank you. I'll be okay."

She sniffled, and Bear held out a clean, white handkerchief he'd magically pulled from the air. Her friends had what she needed most – they always did.

When she went back to work, her hands moved in a mechanical fashion, and her brain traveled back through time, reviewed conversations, pictured expressions. The breakfast buffet went out on time, and she went upstairs to make beds and clean rooms.

"What room we doing, boss?" Betty asked as she flipped the bottom sheet, landing the white cotton rectangle squarely where she wanted it.

"Huh?"

"Where are we right now?"

"You okay, Betty? That's a dumb question."

Betty flipped a top sheet and made hospital corners. "I'm more than okay, but you been gone all morning. Where are you?"

"Sorry. It was a long night. And then I burned my arm because I wasn't paying attention, and . . ."

"And you still aren't. You poured dirty water into the clean washbowl. Saving that water for a reason?"

"Damn."

She dumped it back into the dirty bucket, wiped the bowl out again, and poured in water from the right one. Phantom crawled out of the bottom drawer, and Cleo raced out from under the bed to attack him.

"God, white hair on somebody's clothes," Abby said. "Bad cat."

Phantom strolled to the doorway and sat, raised a cat eyebrow and turned away.

"Just Charles Chesnutt's. He won't care," Betty said.

"I forgot the Chautauqua in all the commotion. Have they started?"

They stood at the window side-by-side and watched folks setting out chairs, putting up the small stage where the podium would stand. In the middle of the group, Jesse pointed and his mouth moved as he gave directions. Abby opened the window so words could match the movement of the mouths. Charles hauled chairs and opened them up. Even Samuel had his immaculate shirt sleeves turned up.

In a moment, Shorty and Bear leaped down the porch steps. One headed in the direction of the pavilion. The other went around the side of the house toward the stable.

"Going for the sheriff," she whispered, and a shiver shook her.

"What in God's name is the matter, Abigail?"

"Nothing. I don't . . . I can't talk about it."

She saw Bear speak to Samuel and the latter spin around and head to the hotel. His shoes tapped on the stairs as he ran up them and into the room they were cleaning.

"Can we speak privately, Abby?" he asked.

Betty's eyes narrowed, and her fists went to her hips.

"What? In one of these bedrooms? That is in-ap-pro-pri-ate, Samuel Moore, and you know it. You surely do." Her dark skin flushed rosy, and her eyes flashed.

"I realize you're protective of her, Betty, but I'm not about to ravish her in broad daylight."

"You only ravish in the dark, then?" Abby said. Her hands flew to cover her mouth to contain the wicked thoughts. "Sorry. We can go to my room at the end of the hallway, Samuel – if you deem it important."

Jeez, Abby. Again with the deem?

"Come on," she said to him. "We'll leave the door open, Betty, in case you're worried or want to eavesdrop."

"Tell me what happened," he said, as soon as his foot stepped across the threshold.

Abby remembered the last time Samuel had been in her room, when they'd brought a bruised and broken Al here after her father had whipped her nearly to death – the night he disappeared and, *most likely*, ended up in the shallow grave Dog found.

The same night his mare went missing and was later sold, *most likely*, in Newago where Jesse James, *most likely*, sold him to Edwin who thinks Mr. James looks a lot like Frank – who lived in Newago at the time.

"Stop!" she groaned, a loud noise that, even to her, sounded like a crazy woman's howl. Abby's hand squeezed her forehead.

"What?"

"Not you. God, my mind is doing bad things. I'm a mess. I'm not even sure . . ."

Betty's head poked into the room. "You okay, boss?"

"I'm fine, Betty. Please go back to doing what you were doing, unless it was eavesdropping."

Samuel pulled her by the arm over to the single chair next to the table. He pushed her into it and stepped back.

"You hurt yourself," he said, looking at the red blisters below the pushed-up sleeve. "How'd you do that?"

Abby ignored the question with a shake of her head. She wasn't going there.

"Okay, talk," he said, crossing his arms.

"I think Bear already told you everything." She crossed her own arms and looked toward the window. He sat on the edge of the bed – her bed.

Betty wouldn't like that.

"Bear said a couple of men beat Edwin and asked where he kept the booze," he told her.

Abby watched clouds skitter across the white-blue sky. It was going to be a beautiful day. Sunshine. Nice breeze.

"Abby!"

Her head jerked to him. "What?"

"Tell me what's going on."

"I don't know any more than you do right now," she said, and the lawyer in Samuel recognized the lie.

When he defended people, he knew when they were economical with the truth and when their stories were built on facts as solid as concrete. The tilt of their heads and the jawline muscles, the lips and the hands all told the tale. Along with the eyes which remained windows, not to the soul, but to the mind. Open windows.

"What aren't you saying, Abby? What has you so afraid?"

"I'm not afraid of anything. You're imagining things."

He stood and moved to the window, pulled his jacket back and shoved his hands in the back pockets of his trousers. She joined him, and they watched folks working like she and Betty had done.

Joe Foster stood a few feet away from the activity, fists on his hips, looking around like he owned the pavilion and the workers. Terry Adams joined him, and Abby watched their mouths move, pictured words coming out and hovering above their heads like cartoon balloons in the Sunday papers.

Joe's arm raised, and a finger pointed at the hotel. It moved up until it aimed directly at the window framing Abby and Samuel. She wanted to duck as if bullets would fire from his finger's end. Bullet holes riddled her chest.

Terry's head nodded, and he tilted it back so she would know he'd seen her in the window. Was seeing them now. Her and Samuel Moore. Together. In her bedroom.

Terry spun on his heels and went in the direction of the store. Joe followed.

When they were out of sight, she backed away from the window until her numb legs bumped into the bed. She sat and put her face in her hands. For the second time today, tears streamed down her face. She shook with sobs, but couldn't have said for whom or what. She didn't know and couldn't control it.

Samuel sat and put his arm around her shoulders. He drew her to his chest and held her until she quieted.

"You don't have to talk to me if you don't want to, Abby. But when you can, you may. I'm here. Well, not right here. That would be inappropriate, as our Betty would say."

He rambled on and on and felt Abby's face nestle into the crook of his neck, the sweet space between shoulder and jaw. Samuel continued mumbling inane words and let his lips rest like two butterflies on her head – on the top of her beautiful, auburn haired head, where the part divided the mass of her thick hair.

When he left, Abby felt the lack of his warmth by her side where he'd been moments ago. She rinsed her face with cold water, yanked her hair back and tied it with a ribbon. Sheriff Hicks entered the hotel the moment she stepped out of her room.

"Abby," he said, seeing her and removing his hat. "Let's chat."

It took days for her to walk down the hallway, stop to tell Betty where she would be, descend the stairs and shake his hand.

"You okay, Abby?"

"Sure. This day keeps getting better and better. I'm loving it."

She led him into the bar and poured coffee. He stirred the spoon around and around in his cup even though he'd added no sugar or cream.

Abby decided to get on with it. Her arm burned. Her brain throbbed. Her heart ached. She wanted to go outside and listen to Charles Chesnutt, Buddy Black, and Florence Mills. She wanted to sway with the music and be part of the people who had normal problems like, what to eat for dinner, what ribbon to weave through your hair, what to bring to the potluck. She wondered if those were Edna's problems.

"You're in the thick of things, again, Abby. You keep apples in your pocket to attract trouble? What's your secret?"

She flinched. "I don't have any secrets. What do you mean?"

"It's an idiom, Abigail. Just learned that word in the Reader's Digest *Word of the Week*. Idiom." He savored the word like a sweet treat. "A new magazine I think you'd like."

"Idiom is?"

"A saying. An expression."

"But it's a magazine, too?"

"No. Reader's Digest is. You're a bit caflooied today, aren't you?"

"Guess so. Is that a *word of the week*, too?"

Hicks stretched in his chair and threw the hat he'd been holding onto another. He scrubbed his face with a calloused hand and made a rasping noise with the shadow that came close to being a beard.

"So, you've been taking care of Edwin after the thugs beat on him."

"Trying to. Poor man."

"Somebody sure wants him out of town. Mighty suspicious."

"Of what? Who?"

"I don't know. Have any ideas?"

"No. I don't."

"I didn't think so, but Edwin said to ask you. You might could know something."

Abby couldn't look at the sheriff. She knew the knowledge she had would be written in her eyes. She should have listened to Sue, learned from her about making dead eyes.

"Don't know why he would say that. Did he say why?"

"Nope."

"Have you talked with Benjamin, or Mick and Moses? They were the first ones there, but they didn't see faces."

"Not yet, but I will."

"If there's nothing else, Sheriff?" She stood and tried to look at him straight on but saw her shoes instead and felt beads of sweat form on her upper lip.

"I need to get back to work."

"One more thing," he said, and drained the coffee in his cup. "The cousins and Gus have had some problems with bricks flying into their windows like they had wings. Any ideas about that? Think they're connected?"

"It's confusing, Sheriff. Da thinks it sounds like Klan members and bootleggers working together, but those people have totally opposite ideals. Why would they cooperate with each other? It makes no sense. The men did ask where we kept the booze. I just don't know. Sorry."

She chafed her arms, wanting to be gone, when she saw Jackson stroll through the door ready for work.

"Will you bartend for me today, Jackson. I have an errand to run."

"Sure. It'll be slow til the Chautauqua is over."

"Need a lift?" the sheriff asked.

Abby shook her head and ran to find her da.

The sheriff scratched his.

She threw a saddle on Marie, climbed on, waved at the crew setting up the pavilion, and regretted not being there for Charles' address. It couldn't be helped.

Samuel, back at work setting up the stage, straightened and watched as she rode by. He tipped his hand in a salute but made no comment.

Joe Foster and Terry Adams stood outside the store, and their heads followed her.

It felt as if every eye in the world saw her, stared through her, like every person watching knew the terror in her heart. She turned her face from them, ran a hand over Marie's neck and finger-combed her mane. It was damp with sweat, and she soothed the mare with gentling words.

"We'll go slow, Marie, and enjoy the fresh air."

Marie nickered and said *I'm tougher than I look.*

"I know you are. Thank you, girl. I don't want to do this, and I don't know what else to do. He's going to hate me."

Maybe. Marie was a horse of few words and kept plodding on toward the Adam's farm. She knew the way.

Frank pulled his team to a stop when he saw her and sauntered across the field. He looked like the man she married, sandy hair curling over his collar, sweat stained shirt pulling against his muscular back and shoulders, skin bronzed and hands strong and calloused.

Could this man, her husband, really be Jesse James? A murderer?

"What brings you here, Abby? Miss your husband, finally?"

She dismounted and walked under a tree at the corner of the field. Abby held the picture so Frank could see it. "Why does Edwin think this is his Jesse James?"

He stared at her, his eyes blank, unreadable. He removed his hat and beat it against his leg. Dust curled around it like a cloud had been harbored in the brim. He slapped it back on.

"Because he's a crazy old coot?" He poked the toe of his boot at the tree trunk. "How'd he get a hold of our wedding picture?"

"I showed it to him."

"Why?"

Her words came fast, but they were addled, pieces of ideas strung together.

"I added two and two and came up with you, Frank. It wasn't a stranger passing through. It was you who sold Tatum's horse to Edwin. You were in Newaygo at the time. You said so, and that's where he bought it. You've been checking on Edwin's whereabouts. I think you wrote that note telling him to leave town. You wanted him gone so he didn't see you – Jesse James."

Abby put the picture in her pocket and looked across the field. Her next words were whispered. "You killed Al's father and buried him in the woods."

He slapped the tree, and Abby backed away.

"So, you think I'm a killer. And a horse thief. My, we've come a long way from our wedding."

"Tell me no, Frank. Tell me I'm wrong."

"An old man claims I look like the man who sold him a horse. So what? His thinking so doesn't make it true. You might be willing to jump to conclusions, but, when push comes to shove, who do you think the law is gonna believe – a stranger with a muddled memory or a man who's lived here his entire life? And why would I kill him?" Frank moved closer and put a hand on her arm.

"Why do you even care? You know what kind of man Tatum was, Abby. You saw what he did to Al. He beat his sons, too. He was a drunk, a mean drunk who never did a lick of work in his life and used his kids like slaves. Worse than most slaves. He made monsters out of his sons."

Frank wrapped her in his arms. She didn't object, but she didn't lean into the embrace, either.

"He needed to die, Abby," he whispered, "and you know it. Al is better off. The world is."

Her body stiffened, and she pulled back and tried to see him objectively, tried to know him, but truthfully, she didn't. Tears formed at the outer corners of her eyes when it occurred to her she hadn't really tried. He was a stranger.

And guilty.

She was sure of it.

Abby moved toward Marie in a trance, her head lowered, her shoulders bent. Frank followed.

"What are you going to do? You gonna run to your buddy Hicks with your ridiculous suspicions? You'll stir up the whole town and try to put your husband in prison? Is that what it's come to?" He spun and walked off, back toward the team left standing in the hot sun in the field a few rows away.

Abby watched and lifted a foot to the stirrup. It weighed a hundred pounds, and her body, when she hefted it into the saddle, weighed at least a ton.

Marie said *hello*, and she patted her neck, a contact that comforted them both.

"Abby," he called out. "You going for Hicks?"

Two rivers ran down her cheeks. He saw them glistening in the sun, and part of his heart melted. Regret was a funny thing. It came at the strangest times for the strangest things.

"I don't know, Frank. I just don't know."

The words were choked between sobs. She put her heels into Marie's sides and didn't look back.

Chapter Twenty-six

It was noon. Charles Chesnutt's keynote address neared its conclusion, and Abby halted Marie in the shade of an old oak at the back end of the pavilion and listened.

"Dubois says justice and common sense must sit in the same hand as right. Is he ignoring legal precedence or counting on it? Garvey wants segregation, a separate black nation dedicated to, among other things, a social, humanitarian and educational institution. Is he calling on us to embrace each other? All others in the creation of it? The NAACP shouts that separate is *not* equal. They march in the thousands to decry the increasing horror of the practice of lynching."

Charles paused and eyed the audience from front to back and left to right, taking time to rest on each face and set of eyes. Feet shuffled in disquiet, and throats cleared in unrest.

"I'm not telling you who you should endorse. That would go against everything I believe. I *am* saying you should know their ideals, learn their ethical standards, recognize parts of yourself in their words. Think. I beg you."

He smiled, a twinkle that quirked his lips, spread to his eyes, and turned into the flickering gleam that made him beautiful.

"Patrick Riley called me *Passing Through* when I first came to town, a prophetic name given my books about the pitfalls of passing. All of us are simply passing through – unless we leave a legacy of thoughtful work. Then we're here for eternity. That's all."

He left the stage. Hands slammed together and feet thundered on the concrete. Shouts in praise of him rang out.

Abby sat entranced by his insights and fell a little in love with the older man. His words began to heal the wounds of minutes ago. They still hurt, but she could live with pain and deal with tomorrow because people like Charles lived – here in Idlewild.

She slid from the saddle and found Samuel next to her, taking Marie's reins and searching her face.

"What?" she said.

"Where have you been?"

"Kinda nosy, aren't you?"

"Yes."

"I was taking in a little air. My best girl and me."

They ambled to the stable and met Edwin coming out. He reached for the reins, ready to unsaddle Marie and brush her down, but caring for her mare was therapeutic. She wouldn't give it up and said so. His eyebrows lifted.

"I always do it, Edwin. I like it."

She unbuckled the cinch, and Samuel lifted the saddle.

"Where you been?" Edwin asked.

Abby's head swung back and forth between the two.

"What's with the inquisition, today? Am I not allowed to take a ride?"

"Never do," Edwin said.

"Well, today, I did. Leave me alone."

"Just wondered. Did the sheriff come see you this morning?"

Abby's hands stilled, and she rested her forehead against Marie's damp body. Moments passed before she could answer.

"He did, Edwin." She turned an inquiring eye his way, knew the answer but wanted to hear it from him. "Did he talk with you, too?"

Edwin shifted and dipped a cup into the oat mixture reserved for Marie. He dumped it into her feed bucket and backed away.

"Guess I gotta clean stalls. Getting smelly in this heat."

Samuel stood off to the side, listening to what hadn't been said. He'd perfected the art and waited to speak until Edwin left the building with his wheel barrow piled high.

"Did you go out to the Adams' farm today?"

The brush in her hand stalled mid-air.

"Why do you ask, Samuel? Why are you pushing me?"

"Am I pushing, Abby?" He took the brush from her and stroked Marie's back. It gave him something to do rather than watch her face. He didn't like the story written there, a tale of sadness and confusion.

"Yes. Yes, you are. I . . . I don't like it."

"I'm sorry. I want to help you, Abby. At the risk of being repetitive," he turned to her and grinned, "you can talk to me. I care. I'll listen."

"Thank you."

"You going to the music tonight?"

"I don't know. I'm not feeling like kicking up my heels."

"It'll be good for you." He handed her the brush and walked to the door. "I'll see you there."

The bar emptied, and Abby told Jackson to get out and listen to the music before it ended.

"Buddy Black is starting. Heard him tuning up. You coming out, Abby?"

"I believe I will."

She found Patrick, Shorty and Bear on the porch and was trying to talk them into moving down to the pavilion when Samuel bounced up the steps.

"Come on, folks. Music is down there, and Florence is dancing soon."

"You go on, lass. These feet are tired."

Bear and Shorty waved them away, too.

"Be down in a bit," Shorty said.

"Surprised you let that happen," Bear said after the two of them were out of hearing.

"Why?"

"Didn't think you cared much for Samuel."

"He's alright. He'll take care of Abby. I know that now. Didn't then."

They found a place at the back of the crowd behind the chairs. Abby could see Florence and the musicians but not feel pressed in the middle of the people. When Florence finished her song, Buddy kept playing, and she took over the small dance floor, skirt flying, feet moving, hips swaying. She held them mesmerized.

"How does she do that?" Abby asked. "She bounces and glides at the same time."

"You kind of do that, too, when you're working behind the bar and you're not troubled." He tapped her shoulder until she turned to him.

"You're a good dancer. I have proof."

"You do not. What proof are you talking about, Samuel?"

"You don't remember the one-step we danced awhile back? You wanted to learn, and I," he pointed to his chest, "am a magnificent teacher. You learned fast and well."

She shrugged her shoulders like she didn't remember.

"You do too. You got in trouble for it, if recollection serves. Dancing with the enemy."

"Maybe. Sort of. Enemy?"

"White woman frolicking with a colored man. One of us is the foe. Maybe both." The contempt flickering over his face made her take a step back, away from him.

She was never sure of his thoughts and wondered if the scorn she saw in his eyes had grown with the idea of *frolicking* with a white woman.

He followed her backward move.

"Did I scare you away with the truth?" he asked.

She crossed her arms, creating a barrier, something between herself and Samuel. One foot bounced.

"You're impossible. Why must you do your best to antagonize me? At every turn?" His lips curved, and she knew he'd baited her once again. And she'd let him – once again.

"Damn you, Samuel. I don't like you."

"Yes, you do, Abigail."

"I think she likes you too damned much," Frank said, coming up behind them in the dark. He stepped in front of Samuel and glared. "Wouldn't you say so, Mister Moore? A married woman, too."

"I don't think it's too much. Just right, in fact. Hello, Frank." Samuel refused to give in to Frank's encroachment on his personal space. His eyes glazed with the infamous blank expression, the poker eyes that won the biggest pot on the table.

Frank ignored Samuel's greeting and asked Abby if he could speak to her. "Alone. Unless, of course, you're too busy with your friend."

Her gaze darted to the hotel, and she gnawed the inside of her cheek. She hadn't decided what to do with her suspicions about Frank and didn't want it forced on her by a chance encounter with Edwin. At any moment, he could walk up to them in the crowd . . .

"Let's go for a walk, Frank," she said. "Excuse me, Samuel."

Abby took his arm and moved into the darkness surrounding the pavilion. It was a deeper dark, a cavernous and unknowable space outside the yellow glow of lanterns hung from posts around the stage. So dark, she couldn't see Frank's face, look into his eyes and search for the meaning of his presence tonight.

She sensed tenseness in the periodic nudge of his arm against her side, the squeeze of his fingers twined with hers. His body felt coiled, ready to strike.

"What's going on, Frank?" she said, continuing to walk into the black of night. He filled his chest with air and spit it out.

"I killed Tatum. Didn't mean to do it until I did. I wanted to beat him like he did little Al. Like he did his boys.

Abby couldn't breathe. The knife twisted, and she bled. "What happened?"

"He was drunk. I yelled, and he came at me, arms flailing, bellowing. I was glad he did, because I didn't know if I could just start beating on him. But after he swung at me, it was easy. I couldn't stop. And then, I didn't want to. I kept slamming him against the ground until he was dead.

Abby stepped back, needing space to think, to contemplate the fullness of his confession.

"Why didn't you tell me, Frank?"

"How could I? *Why* would I? You already hated me, thought of me as a rapist. I didn't want you to think of me as a murderer, too. He was a bastard, Abby, and I killed him. But I'm not sorry he's dead."

"I didn't hate you, Frank. I don't hate you now, and you weren't a rapist. I felt used, like a convenient receptacle, and that's what I told you. I need you to understand that. Please say you do. Part of that problem was me. But that's a different issue. What will you do? Go to the sheriff? Tell him what happened?"

"Don't you understand? Don't you get why?" He pleaded in the murky night, his voice the only connection, the only path to her.

"Why what? Why you killed him?"

Frank's hand covered his face and pressed against his eyes. His fingers squeezed at the throbbing temples.

"That man would never have gone to prison for what he did to his family. He would have lived out his life beating the shit out of them, and no one would have done a damned thing about it. Someone had to stop him."

"I understand that." Her voice was soft, a whisper from the heart, wanting him to know she'd heard. "But you're not the one who gets to decide that. You played God. You think that's a good thing?"

"Some people would say so. Some would say I did the world a service taking him out of it because God wasn't paying attention." He reached for her hand, and she let him.

"I don't believe we have the right to take a life, Frank. That's His business." Her words trembled but were firm.

Silence crawled around them. It lay on their skin like a damp shroud and screamed questions for which neither had answers. A loon called for his mate, and she answered. A sliver of moon crept over Frank's face, and Abby pulled it to her, put her cheek next to his and stayed there, still and quiet, one heart thrumming between them, angst swirling from one's thoughts to the other's.

Days crept by, a lifetime, while they stood cheek to cheek, breathing each other's warm air. Both knew there was no good answer to Frank's dilemma. There were only solutions that didn't solve much, ones that would take him away from Idlewild no matter which path he chose.

"What will you do?" she asked.

"Depends kind of on you. You talking to Sheriff Hicks?"

Abby squeezed him hard and dropped her arms to her sides. Her words were shallow containers filled with pain.

"I don't know, Frank. I just don't know. But I will tell you first when I figure it out."

"For sure?"

"Yes. For sure."

"Abby?"

She turned to him.

"Why'd you show Edwin the picture? Why'd you do that?"

"I had to know. I'm sorry."

Samuel faced away from the pavilion watching for her. He didn't plan to. It simply happened, and when her pale skin picked up the moon's growing light, he turned back to the dancing Florence and waited.

"I'm back." Abby stood close, his nearness a strange but strong comfort.

"I'm glad."

"Thank you."

"For?"

"Being here."

"Want to dance?"

"No. I want to go sit on the porch. Join me?"

Words weren't needed. They ambled toward the hotel, and she wondered when Samuel Moore had become kind. When had he become a friend?

They joined Patrick who sat snoring in his rocking chair, Bear and Shorty drifting off next to him. They awoke with the sound of footfalls on wood, and Patrick stirred enough to ask Abby to get a glass or five of his cherished Irish whiskey.

"To celebrate the Chautauqua," Patrick said, and added, "You look like a man with something on his mind," when Abby went inside.

Samuel nodded.

"What is it?" Shorty's voice was sweet, a papery sound in the night.

"George is getting out. Tomorrow or the next day."

"Jesus." Shorty's rocker stalled. "Couldn't they keep him for a bit longer? Between the bootlegger thugs and the Klan, we can't get a minute's peace."

"Al and Betty need to know," Bear said.

"Ye don't think he'd take it out on the wee lasses?" Patrick asked, his brogue deepening as concern grew.

"He hurt Betty before. Didn't have a qualm about it," Shorty said.

"But maybe the lad learned his lesson in prison."

"What lesson? Who?" Abby pushed through the screen door with a tray of small glasses and the decanter of Irish. Samuel wiped a hand over his face and ran a thumb and forefinger over the black mustache.

"What lesson?" she repeated. "Or I keep the whiskey to myself."

"George is due out in the next day or so," Patrick said, unwilling to give up his glass of whiskey.

"Damn." Fear wiggled at the base of her neck in the little hairs growing there. She passed out the glasses and poured generous amounts of the brown liquid. They waited for her to fill her own and take her favorite chair, tilted their drinks to her, and sipped.

"George was always the sweetest boy," she said, pondering the man who'd gone to jail for assault – not for the rape she knew he'd committed. "Of all the Adams men, he seemed the one who would do kindnesses. I don't understand at all."

Samuel watched Abby's face. He sure didn't want to hurt her, but he didn't know how not to. "Frank Sr. has strong opinions and a big ego. He likes power."

"What does that have to do with George?" she said.

"He raised his sons as reflections of himself – to take control." He put a hand on Abby's arm, trying to soften his words. "I think the Adams men were responsible for your accident. In whole or in part."

"No! Why would they do that?"

"Because they're telling you something."

"What?"

"Possibly making a comment on the nature of your friendships – the cousins, for example. Maybe others."

Shorty, Bear and Patrick had leaned forward in their chairs, listening intently, whiskey glasses in their hands. Samuel lifted his shoulders, indicating he didn't know.

Buddy Black's guitar strings rang, and Florence Mills' sweet voice played with the stars blinking on one by one.

"I hope you have good reason for saying such a slanderous thing, Samuel." Her words were shot with quick anger. Samuel continued as if she hadn't spoken, trying to help her draw conclusions on her own so he didn't have to spell it out.

"The egomaniac can be charming, can make you feel safe, even loved, but if he is slighted – even a little bit – he can be dangerous. He doesn't have the same conscience that controls the rest of us. He believes he is right, always, and has a perfect right to think so."

"Where did you learn all this?" Abby pulled her arm from under his hand.

"Lots of psychology in law school. Have to be able to read people."

"I'm not buying it." She turned from him to stare out at the water, at the stars reflected in the inky ripples.

"Tracks from the tree that almost fell on your buggy led to the back of the Adams' property." Samuel replaced his hand on her arm.

When she tried to move it again, he gripped it harder. Not enough to hurt. He wouldn't, but with enough force to keep her there, looking at him. At some point, she would understand.

"I don't like this conversation. Not at all."

"But hear it, lass. Ye need to be safe." Patrick tipped back in his chair. He was done, too.

Shorty and Bear followed, and three chairs rocked rhythmically. Two others were motionless and connected by the hand on Abby's arm. It had relaxed and lay warm and gentle; friendship passed through the fingertips.

Abby sighed. Samuel heard and returned it.

Chapter Twenty-seven

"What are you doing here, Al? You don't work on Sundays," Abby said as the slip of a woman pushed through the swinging doors to the kitchen.

"Chautauqua church."

Abby's face scrunched in confusion.

"Didn't know you were interested? That's at nine."

"I know."

"So why . . . Never mind. You confuse me, Al."

Abby turned back to the sizzling skillets and pushed sausages around in one, frying potatoes in another. Al dumped flour into a bowl, added baking powder, and poured in the buttermilk.

"Ready for pancakes?" she said.

"Griddle isn't hot. Be just a minute." She threw a few drops of water on the cast iron and waited. When the bubbles jumped, she nodded to Al.

"I'm glad you're here. I was going to ride out to your house today."

Al ladled perfect white circles onto the flat pan and watched bubbles form around the edges. "Why?"

"George may be home today."

Abby might have prefaced the harsh words, softened the blow with consideration for her feelings, but this was *Strange Al*, not a simpering little girl. Al met misfortune head on, like a tiny bull with big horns, and Abby wouldn't demean her by dancing around the information.

"Betty know?" Al asked.

"That he's coming, but not that it could be today."

"She'll be at church. You going to say something?"

"Yes. Thanks for coming in this morning, Al. When Da gets here, I'll leave you two to finish breakfast – if that's alright."

"I'm here. Go on now."

She tugged Al's long hair tied back in its blue ribbon as Abby had long ago requested. She wanted to hug her, but respected Al's reserve and distance. She ran up the stairs and smack into her da who stood in the doorway to his room, pulling suspenders over a faded shirt.

"Al's in the kitchen. I'm going to church," she said as she passed him in the hall.

She threw water on her face and toweled dry, pulled off her work clothes and drew a pale-yellow dress over her head. It showed off her auburn hair, even if it did pop the freckles across her nose and cheeks. She tried not to care about them, brushed her curls and left them flowing down her back.

Abby made it in time to shake Reverend Jenkins' hand before he took the pulpit. He pulled her into an embrace, instead of shaking the offered hand, and she slammed against his chest. The reverend was a big man, and she disappeared when his arms went around her slender back.

"You need to eat, girl," he said.

"I'm a pig."

"You wouldn't bring much at market. Maybe it's all the running around you do."

"So I'm told. You want to chastise me, too?"

He pushed her away from him, held her there by the shoulders, and ducked his head to look into her face.

"What's this? You'll get no reprimand from me young lady. You're my little white activist. I need you."

Abby melted and snuggled back into his chest. Tongues would wag, she knew, but she didn't care. He served her soul and could hug away her sins in front of the whole world.

"Have you seen Betty?" she mumbled into his robe.

"She's here. Why?"

"George Adams might be home today. She needs to know."

"Heard that. Hope he chooses another path or a different town."

She pulled back from him. "How'd you hear?"

"Samuel. Every once in a while, despite his seemingly arrogant manner, he seeks advice from a man of God. You look surprised."

"I am. Stunned, in fact. Wouldn't believe he'd think your advice necessary." A hand flew to cover her mouth. "Sorry. I didn't mean your advice wasn't good. Just that, you know . . ."

He pulled on her arm to slow her down.

"Yes. I do. Samuel is more than meets the eye. He worries about people he cares for."

She remembered his concern for her the night before. "He does."

"Betty's in the back with her mother. Benjamin is next to her."

Abby's eyes lit. "Good. That's really good. Thanks for your time, Reverend."

He moved toward the elevated stand where he would welcome, chastise and feed the souls of all sinners, and Abby ambled to where Betty sat waving her hand in the air, motioning to her to join their small group.

The pavilion overflowed with parishioners, and Abby scanned their faces, noting the sad fact that only two were white, her own and Charity Evans.

What will it take to bring us together? Maybe I'm an unrealistic dreamer.

"Good to see you, Benjamin. Didn't know you were a church goer."

"Sometimes I am. Especially when I can sit next to a pretty girl." He stood and moved to let Abby take his chair.

Betty beamed, and Abby watched Mildred Gerard's eyes flicker over the young man. She liked Benjamin but didn't want him playing with her daughter's affections. She'd been through enough, and Mildred wondered how much he knew about Betty's past and if he'd care enough about her for it not to matter.

"Can we speak after the service, Betty?"

"Sounds serious. You firing me again?"

"Never fired you, and no. Nothing like that."

Reverend Jenkins' voice boomed loud enough to reach the heavens as he belted out words to the first song, *God grant me strength to fight for right every day in your light.*

Abby's eyes widened and she smiled. Had he switched songs? She let go of the wayward thoughts and let her voice ring out, joining him and the rest as they caught up with the pastor.

Heads turned toward another white face, George Adams, strolling across the grass toward the pavilion. He stopped a short distance from them, spread his legs wide in a battle stance and crossed his arms over his chest. He'd lost the tanned skin earned from hours in the field, and his face was immobile, a marble bust, as he watched the large group of worshipers. He didn't participate, but his eyes moved from face to face, searching, until he saw them.

A shiver crawled down Abby's spine, and she reached for Betty's hand, heard her deep intake of breath and felt her stiffen.

"It'll be alright," she whispered. "That's what I wanted to tell you."

Betty's black eyes glared at him.

His lips curled in a seductive, mock smile, and Betty's resolve grew. She threw her head up, chin in the air, and defied him. Benjamin stood, ready to rid the service of George Adams, and Betty reached across Abby to pull him back to his seat. He chose, instead, to stand behind them, sentry.

"No. Do nothing," she told him.

Abby couldn't concentrate on the reverend's words. She tried to focus, to leave George's face and watch Reverend Jenkins, to hear the holy words, to bow her head. But, before she knew it had happened, her eyes were back on the man who watched them, the man who had raped Betty, the man she'd helped send to prison.

Her husband's brother.

The service ended, and she raised her forcefully bowed head to see him strolling toward the hotel.

"You alright, Betty?" Abby asked.

She nodded, her face grim, and Benjamin put a hand on her shoulder, felt the rumble of her insides trembling, the hidden consequences of her horror.

Mildred saw the hand, her daughter leaning back and into him, and her heart warmed. He knew. It was alright.

"You staying for the Chautauqua?" she asked Benjamin.

"Think I will," he said, his words a quiet drawl. "Would you have a spare room for an old soldier?"

"We'll make one. Maybe stack up Shorty and Bear for a few days. Come to the hotel, Betty, before you leave, please."

She heard Charles Chesnutt's soothing voice as she strolled back to the hotel and watched for George, or any Adams, as she walked. She found him in the empty bar. Patrick was behind it with elbows on the wooden top, listening to George talk about prison.

"I'm here, now, Da. You can go back to your kitchen."

"Maybe we were having a conversation, Abby. You always make people do exactly what you want them to?" George said with a smirk.

Abby didn't answer but marched around the bar, grabbed her white apron and thought about a response as she tied the strings. A blur of words tangled with each other. Some she wanted to hurl at him with hurtful force, and some she struggled to keep from darting out.

She decided on "Hello, George."

"Cordial, as always, sister-in-law."

"Have you been home or did you come straight here to say how much you hate me?" He smirked and Abby wanted to slap him, wipe the satisfied leer from his face.

"What makes you think I hate you? Maybe I'm even grateful."

Abby wiped at water spots on the wooden bar and tried not to look his way. He annoyed her. His arrogant expression, his voice, even the way he held his body ignited anger in her.

"Why would you be grateful to me for turning you in? That's ridiculous."

"Frank said you wouldn't understand." He pushed his empty beer glass her way. "Fill it up, sister-in-law."

"I wish you'd quit calling me that."

"Why? Cuz you really aren't?"

"Stop it, George." She filled his glass and pushed it back to him, marking the bar with more spots she could busy herself cleaning.

"I'm happy for your family that you're home. I'm sure they missed you, but I have to tell you, I'm not glad to see you. I'm still furious and disgusted about what you did, and I don't think I'll ever *not* be."

He thrummed his fingers on the wood like he hummed a song in his head, as if the conversation couldn't keep his full attention.

"Frank told me you don't comprehend men. I can see that now."

Astounded, Abby's head whipped around.

"What does that mean? And what does my comprehension of anything have to do with what you did?"

He laughed, his mouth wide open and white teeth gleaming. The harsh sound grated on her jangled nerves. She wanted him to leave so she could spend a few quiet minutes in her room, contemplate the number of ways she could kill him and not get caught – or at least mangle him to the point of satisfaction. The thought gave a brief respite to her mounting anger.

"Well?" she said. "Make the connection, George. I have things to do."

"What you don't get is that men, real men anyway, take what they want – eventually. They may prance around it for a while, but, in the end, they take it or they're not men. You showed this town that I'm a man. You showed my big brothers that little Georgie is something to be reckoned with. All the rousting they did on me . . . all the pushing around. They'll think twice and take me seriously now. I did it, but *you* told them I did. We're a team."

He eyed Abby and raised a brow. "Think you and me might have a go around since you're not so happy with Frankie boy?"

Abby flew at him, fingers grabbing hair, shirt, ears, whatever she could grasp. She screamed obscenities, enraged and out of control and lay half-way across the bar top with her arms flying and hands punching when Patrick tore out of the kitchen.

"What in the name of blessed wee Ireland is going on?"

Al followed, eyes wide, a heavy skillet in her hand ready to whack the loud ruffian – who turned out to be her boss.

Patrick pulled on his daughter's arm until she slid all the way across the bar. When she landed on the floor, thankfully feet first, her arms continued to fly, trying to connect with George. But her da put both his arms around her middle, and his extra weight leveraged her away from the scratched and disheveled man.

"What's going on, Abby? George?" he gasped.

George let his eyes roam Abby from top to bottom and back. Deliberate insolence and lewd suggestion poured from his eyes.

"George is leaving," she growled. "He has someplace he needs to be. Give your family my regards and condolences, you filthy piece of . . . filth."

George picked up his glass, drained it, saluted Abby with it, and slapped some coins down on the bar. He turned his back to them and left without a word, the screen door banging shut behind him. Patrick chuckled.

"You really got him with your cursing, lass. Bet his ears are still stinging with the verbal tongue lashing. Want to tell your da?"

She shook her head. "Later. Tonight."

The Chautauqua wrapped up following Buddy Black's music. Abby stood at her window and watched the tents come down and the musician's instruments get packed in their protective cases. She felt the familiar let down the soon to be barren sight caused. The Chautauqua and its magic were dismantled piece by beautiful piece and chunks of Abby's heart packed up and went with them.

The late day sun hovered in the water, rippling and waving with the movement of row boats gliding across the lake. Children splashed or huddled in towels, shivering when mothers called them to shore. Their lips were purple with cold and their eyes bright with the joy of their freedom, their innocent play.

Cleo nudged Abby's hand, forcing attention. She picked up the black cat and let her nuzzle into her neck, the loud purr soothing exposed nerve endings and calming the turbulence in her soul.

"Help me not to hate, Cleo," she said. "Help me to scratch his eyes out and let it go. That's what you'd do, right? Scratch, run, and love with a clean heart?"

Phantom leaped onto the window seat in front of her and plowed his massive white head into her leg. He continued until she sat and let him curl on her lap.

"Thanks, babies. You get it."

"You don't need to drive us around like we're a couple of old ladies, Benjamin. We've been walking to work forever. And it makes me feel like a baby. It surely does."

"Well, which is it?" he said, grinning at Betty's sputtering.

"Which is what?" Betty asked.

"Old ladies or babies?"

"Neither. And I'm not afraid of him anymore. I have my walking stick, and, if he tries anything ever again, I'm swinging for his head. I'm not stopping till he's down."

"I believe you, girl. Let's do this for a few days. Just until he gets settled in."

"I don't like it."

"You don't like riding round with me?" He raised a brow to lure her and ran a hand over hers.

"That's not . . . you know . . . Dang it, Benjamin."

"It's either Abby or me. You know her. She isn't about to take no for an answer. She made that pretty clear. We'll take turns for a bit. Shorty and Bear both offered. Samuel, too." He glanced her way. "Don't be angry."

She glared at him, but couldn't stay mad at Benjamin. Betty had fallen for the piano man. Hard.

In the back seat, Al snuggled into the corner and ran her hand over the fine leather of Benjamin's automobile. It was cozy and floated over the road like a magic carpet. She'd never ridden in one so fine, not even Samuel's.

"What about you, Al?" he asked. "You'll let us drive you around for a bit?"

"I don't know."

"And when will you know?"

"When I leave for work."

"Damn it, Al. Don't."

"It was Betty he hurt. Drive her."

"You're two of the stubbornest women I've ever come across. I'm serious."

His head tilted as he stretched his neck to work out the knots, and looked at Betty's profile. She turned, and what he saw pierced his heart - bold determination, resolve made of pure grit and covered in anxiety. He closed his mouth on the words he'd been about to say. She deserved that regard and much more.

After Al unlocked the front door, he walked through the house, found it empty of intruders and cautioned them to lock it behind him when he left.

"Can I feed my chickens?" Al asked.

The cat wound around her legs, his purr at odds with the fear in Benjamin's mind.

"Of course. Just, you know, be safe."

Neither women earned what they'd received at the hands of men. He cursed George Adams and the Tatum boys and wished he'd been the one to beat them when his soldier buddies had done the job. He should've been with them. But he might have killed them, probably would've, and he'd be the one in prison or in the electric chair.

Colored men can't kill white men.

He released a breath tainted with sour anger and jumped off the porch. Dog followed him to the auto and sniffed at the front tire.

"Get on back to the porch, Dog, and you set up a howl if you hear anything at all. Use your sniffer, old boy. Need to get you a pup to help out."

When Benjamin returned to the hotel, he took the steps two at a time and headed to the rocking circle gathered at one end of the porch. Charles and Samuel had their own chairs now, and Benjamin hoped he'd rate one, someday.

"How'd it go? Shorty asked. "They agree to being carted around for a few days?"

"Not sure," Benjamin said, and shrugged his shoulders. They're . . ."

"Women," Bear said.

"Excuse me? What does that mean?"

"Nothing, Abby. You're all lovely ladies."

"Can't get out of it that easily." She turned away from Bear. "Thanks for taking them home, Benjamin. Can I offer you a nightcap?"

She came back with his drink and heard her da talking about their hotel in Nirvana, the one Benjamin took care of and lived in now.

"Peaceful place. Maybe we shouldn't have abandoned it, but nobody was left, just about. Lumber goes – so do the people. But it was restful."

"It is that, Patrick," Benjamin said. "Calming."

"Too bad we can't think of a way to have Betty work there for a while. She'd be out of harm's way," Abby said, her voice wishful and far away, not part of the world.

"That would never be allowed. Young woman off alone with a man." Shorty leaned toward Benjamin. "Not that you're a bad sort, but I'm pretty sure Mister Gerard wouldn't take to Betty living with you."

Benjamin slapped Shorty's shoulder. "Thanks, but even I can see it would be inappropriate."

"I've been hearing that word way too much lately," Samuel said. "Coming at me from the oddest places. Betty said it last."

"Then maybe you should be a little more circumspect," Charles said.

"Big damn words flying around here tonight. I simply meant appropriateness is relative. Right, Abby?"

"Huh? I don't know what you're all talking about." Abby stared at the night sky as she talked, and watched the moon melt into the lake, spreading a velvety white glow on the water. The sight of it had become part of her, like an arm or a leg, and she couldn't be sad they'd moved to Idlewild. The loons, the geese and ducks, friends sharing the porch.

"You want to answer that loon?" Samuel said. "Seems to be you went there for a minute."

"Maybe. I love his voice."

"Looking for a loony mate?"

She snorted, a sound suggesting disgust with herself.

"I have one, Samuel."

"That was tactless of me. Sorry."

"No. You were just being funny, and I'm no fun anymore."

She waved at Cassandra who appeared out of the shadows, the clowder circling her like a wagon train moving in a protective ring. The old woman responded by flapping her walking stick in a circle over her head as if she was casting a spell. She could have been.

Cleo and Phantom moved to the bottom step to keep an eye on the other felines. They'd never tangled with Cassandra's clowder cats, but Abby sensed their unease. They weren't sure about them, and that was understandable. They weren't real, didn't act like other cats, but Cassandra didn't act like other people. They were perfect for one another.

"I wonder - were the cats strange before living with Cassandra, or did they become strange from proximity to her?" she said to no one in particular.

"Good question," Samuel said.

"Do you think people can change one another by living together?"

Samuel watched as she fidgeted with the plain gold band on her finger, turning it round and round. She twisted a long strand of hair over and over and bit the inside of her cheek. A war waged inside her.

"You didn't change Frank, Abby. He is who he's always been. You're not responsible for anything he does or did." His words were whispered, for her ears alone.

"You can't know that."

"Yes. I can. And I do."

"Who's picking up our girls in the morning?" Shorty said. "I'll take them home, but Bear and I have a trip planned with Gus the day after. So, we're out."

Between the five men, excluding Patrick, they scheduled the week and said goodnight.

Chapter Twenty-eight

Benjamin was early and only Dog greeted him from the small porch. He stretched and took his time getting to his feet. The chickens squawked and flapped their useless wings as they pecked the ground for kernels of corn lying in the dust. The sight gave him peace.

But he knew it hadn't always been serene, and, if it had seemed so, it had been a façade. A painful lie. He raised a hand to knock on the door when he saw Al coming from the barn and toting a milk pail filled with frothy white.

"Hey," she called.

"Hey, yourself. You're pretty busy, aren't you?"

"Yup. Go on in."

Betty had her hands in the sink, and she dried them on a towel before acknowledging him.

"I'm early," he said.

"I know. Afraid we'll run off by ourselves?"

His smile won them over. It spread from his lips to his eyes where it danced and crinkled the corners. "You two about ready?"

In the auto, he thanked them for agreeing to be escorted. "Abby worries about you."

"Well I'm worried about her," Betty said. "Something's going on that's troubling her. A lot. She forgets what she's doing, talks to herself, gets ornery. It's not like her. You see it, Al?"

Al nodded, thinking back. Abby had been flighty lately, and depressed. She'd wondered, but would never ask.

Dawn broke at the end of the road with a red sun heralding the coming autumn, a beacon drawing them onward, promising a day of glory. Betty let herself lean against Benjamin's arm, just a little, enjoying the ride and the promise she saw in his eyes. Life was good.

Shorty took them home, and it was a different kind of ride. Al's one-word responses and his whispered words made for a quiet trip. Betty tried to spark conversation, but gave it up and decided to sit back and relax.

"Maybe next time, you sit in front, Al, and I'll take a nap in the rumble seat."

"What?" Al said.

"Nothing. You are two of the most silent people I know. Except for Bear. He doesn't say anything at all. Shorty talks, but so softly I can't hear him, and you . . . well, you know about you. I'll sing a song, I guess. What do you want to hear?"

Shorty grinned. "Silence. Know that one?"

Al put plates in front of three men the next morning, and Gus picked her up in a bear hug that earned a scowl from Shorty.

"You're always hugging on our women. Don't you have any of your own to maul?"

Gus' head snapped back, and his face darkened in a scowl.

"You mean colored ones?" His entire body stiffened thinking Shorty could be plagued by bias. He hadn't thought so before. "And I don't maul. I embrace."

He stabbed his fork into a crispy potato slice and shoved it in his mouth. "Hell no, I don't mean colored. Nothing to do with your skin."

"Well, what exactly does it *have* to do with then?"

"I mean . . . Al is . . . Damn. I don't know what I mean. If Al wants your *embrace*," he grimaced as he said the word, "I guess she's free to do it and so are you."

Gus turned to the diminutive woman. "Well?" he said, bending to stare into her eyes.

"I just cook." She tugged the blue ribbon from her hair and went to the pantry to retie it.

"Now see what you did," Shorty said.

"This is all your doing, you fussy old woman. I didn't do a darn thing." Gus pulled out a chair and sat to dig into his breakfast.

Abby came through the swinging doors with an empty bowl and filled it with fried potatoes.

"Why don't you pick *him* up and put him on the cupboard?" Bear said. "I'd like to see that."

Shorty snorted, and gnawed on a piece of bacon.

"Like to see him try," Gus said.

"What's going on?" Abby faced them with the steaming potato bowl in her hands.

"Boys are fighting over Al," Bear said.

"That's plainly not true," Shorty stood and put his dish in the sink.

"Is too."

"Nuts. I'm done. Let's go, Shorty." Gus walked out with the big man following, leaving Bear to finish his food alone.

Abby eyes were wide as she watched them go.

"That was strange."

"They're a couple of . . ."

Bear's words were cut off as both men crashed back through the doors.

"White hoods in the road," Gus said. "About thirty of 'em."

"That can't be." Abby 's voice crackled with fear. "What are they doing?"

"Recruiting, most likely. They're carrying a cross like they're some sacred holy group." Shorty rubbed his eyes.

"I'm going out there," Abby said, and pushed between them, shoes slapping the wooden floor with purpose.

On the porch, their small group grew as people who had been eating breakfast joined them, or folks rising and hearing the commotion threw on some mismatched clothes and came down to see for themselves. They crossed their arms in front of them and stood motionless, side by side, shoulders and arms touching. They whispered to one another, eyes wide in awe and not a little fear. Nostrils flared in anger at the insolence of the display marching down the street.

White robes flowed and flared around their legs. Pointed hoods where, like cowards, the wearers hid their faces and identities and peered through black eye holes. Through them, they could see the folks they deliberately tried to instill with the horror of Klan deeds past and promise of actions present and future.

The white robed group stopped in front of the hotel and turned to face it. One robe moved to the front of the assembly.

"We are here to save America!" his voice shouted.

Abby shivered, and Bear put an arm around her shoulder.

"We are here to redeem your church from the encroaching insolence of Catholicism. We are here to save your women from brutal abuse and negro molestation."

Faces looked up when Betty's voice cried out from a second-floor window.

"White men rape! White men beat women! You white racist cowards. Show your faces if you want to talk and you want people to listen."

Her voice was raw with rage, and her eyes bulged, making her look deranged. Abby flew through the door and up the stairs to stand beside her, an arm around her screaming friend, both of them leaning out the window and looking down at the hooded men.

The Klan leader lifted a flaming torch into the air.

"We are here to save you from ignorance, from diluting racial purity!"

Patrick hobbled forward to put himself in front of the crowd. "You mean from the people who settled this land? Like the Irish Catholics?"

Shorty didn't need to move forward. He could be seen above the heads of the rest.

"How about the Swedes?" he shouted, his voice miles above its usual whisper. "We spoiling the melting pot?"

"And the Germans?" Bear said. He took the steps two at a time and confronted the Klan leader. "It's time to move on. We've seen enough of your spectacle. I'm inviting you to leave. Now."

"Wait!" Abby shouted. "Wait a minute."

She sprinted down the stairs and across the porch, weaving in and out of the people in her way. She leaped, soaring over the steps entirely, and planted herself at the head of the column of Klan members. One by one, she inspected shoes and boots and into the eyeholes of each mask. When she found what she hunted, she pulled herself erect and stared into his eyes.

"Hello, Frank. Terry. George. Frank Sr. Nice of you to visit." She greeted them all, but kept her eyes on her husband. "I'm ashamed of you. All of you."

She reached for Frank's hood, but Samuel grasped her wrist and stopped her. He pulled her hand and wrapped his other around her back, trying to turn her from the Adams men, from the devastation of disclosure. Not of who belonged to the Klan, as she'd already succeeded in doing that, but the revelation that would come with Edwin standing with the crowd on the porch.

She resisted, but it was half-hearted and fleeting. As she turned away from her in-laws, Abby's certainty became concrete.

Her shoulders drooped, and she went where Samuel led, arms hanging. In moments, Betty stood by her side.

"They don't matter, Abby. He doesn't matter. Put it away, now. You hear me?"

"Sure," Abby said.

"You say *sure* like you don't mean it, girl. *Mean* it." Abby gave her a half smile and let her pull her through the crowd.

"Why'd you stop her," Shorty asked Samuel.

"She didn't want to do that in anger. She'd not feel good about it later."

"So what if everybody sees Frank and his brothers are Klan?" Shorty said, perturbed with Samuel. "Half the white folks in the county are."

The big man glared, not liking his unsolicited interference and wanting the truth.

"There's more to it. Ask Abby," Samuel said. "It's hers to tell."

"Stop being so damned mysterious, Samuel. I was starting to like you."

Samuel stepped back and pulled his watch from its special pocket in the satin vest. He flipped it open, glanced without seeing, and closed it. He knew it irritated folks when he did it, and that was the purpose this time. He wanted Shorty to walk away, which he did.

Straight to Abby.

"What's going on, Abigail?"

"Nothing. What do you mean?"

"Why did Samuel prevent you from showing Frank's face?"

Abby rubbed her neck, twisted her head sideways, back, forth, up and down until her eyes landed on her shoes. She saw his, too, and love for the man in those worn boots warmed her.

"I don't know for certain, but I have an idea. I'll explain, my friend. Later, okay?"

Bear walked up in time to shove Shorty aside. "Leave her alone. How many times do I have to tell you?"

"I didn't do anything, you crochety old man. Tell him, Abby."

"He didn't, Bear. Honestly."

"We're putting off the run for a couple of days. Letting tempers settle a bit," Bear said as Gus ambled up.

"Staying the night or going?" Shorty asked him.

"Think I'll hang out. Never know what might happen. Maybe invite the cousins here for the evening and walk 'em home after."

"Good idea."

People came in and out of the bar all day, eager to speculate about the robed parade. She left Bear behind the bar so she could do a quick job of cleaning upstairs. Shorty helped until Jackson showed up for work.

She heard patrons' voices as they shifted from awed to angry and back again. Abby watched Betty's face. How supposedly intelligent people could imagine skin color made one inferior or tainted was impossible to understand, especially when she viewed her friend – her friend since the day she came to the hotel looking for work. Honest, intelligent, loyal, funny, hardworking, loving Betty.

"You're something," Abby said.

"I surely am."

"You confronted that mob like nobody's business. You told them the blatant truth."

"Yeah, but they didn't hear it. Never will because they don't care about truth. They care about being on top of the heap. That's all."

Betty flipped the bottom sheet and tucked in the corners while Abby ran the dust mop. She pondered Frank. Did that explain why he'd joined? To make sure he was on top? To make sure Betty and her relatives were on the bottom?

"They're afraid," Betty said. "That's all."

"Of what?"

"Of us not being ignorant. Us taking their jobs, maybe even being their boss. Wouldn't be easy on them. Maybe what scares them most is the lash – getting back some of what they gave. That's what I think, anyway."

Abby scooted Phantom out the door, and he stopped in the hall to glare at her.

"You're a wise and tolerant woman. I hate all this." The silent wail in her voice said it all.

"I'm sorry, boss, about Frank. I truly am."

"I should be saying that to you."

"Don't need to. I know what it makes you feel. It hurts me for you."

"I'm going to the next room. See you there." She put an arm around Betty for a quick hug. "Thanks."

Samuel waited in the bar and called her over when she entered. Abby paused. She was glad he'd stopped her from pulling the hood off Frank's face but . . .

"What can I do for you, Samuel? Did you get some lunch? Da made colcannon today."

"I had some. It's tasty, but I came to talk with you. Is this a good time? Figured you be done upstairs and not swamped here, yet."

"You been following me around, checking my schedule and work habits?"

He smoothed the fingers of both hands over his mouth and Abby saw a brief, rare smile – with teeth. It looked good on him.

"I guess I'm guilty as charged. Can we talk?"

"Here?"

"Best not. How about a ride in my shiny automobile? I promise not to keep you long."

Abby backed away thinking she didn't want to hear what he had to say, and, if she went with him, she'd have to listen or walk back.

"I'm safe, Abby. I won't hurt you."

"Hmmm. Not sure about that. Let me tell Da."

He remained silent until he stopped the Model T at the end of a two track, its nose edged up to the river and away from prying eyes. All she could see were trees and swift current filled with dancing diamonds as the water traveled over rocks and branches jutting from the banks.

"What, Samuel? Why this clandestine meeting? You're making me nervous."

He turned, leaned his back against the door and looked at her, trying to gauge how prepared she might be for what he had to say.

"Do you know why I kept you from pulling off Frank's hood?"

"I . . ." Abby stopped. She could see knowledge in his eyes. "How did you know?"

Samuel tilted his head and watched the current ripple.

"I noticed something in the way he looked at Al when he came back to town. His regard for her was – different – protective. I can't explain how, but I knew what he'd done. And Abby, I understand his actions."

He hesitated at the sudden jerk of her head and put a hand over hers. "Old man Tatum was a monster, and . . ."

"Yes, but . . ."

"Let me finish, please, Abby."

He watched the conflict battle on her face, and when she looked away from the window and back to him, he continued.

"Vigilante justice is complex, and I'm not advocating it, but there are times when it serves a purpose. *I* called for those men who beat up George and the Tatum boys. I did it because Betty wouldn't press charges, and they would have continued to abuse her if something wasn't done."

"*You* didn't beat them." Her words were more question than statement, her eyes bright with unshed tears.

"No. I didn't. But I was responsible."

"How could you? Wait . . . I know how." She covered her face, hiding her remembered guilt and talked between her fingers. "I was glad they were beaten. I felt joy as I considered each punch of my fist in their faces. I'm as guilty as you are."

Samuel pulled the hand from her face and tilted it up with a finger under her chin.

"Not true, Abby. You wouldn't have followed through with it. I know that. And feeling good about it is different than doing it. Or making it happen."

"Why are you telling me all this, Samuel?"

"What your husband did may be the one honorable act he's ever performed. He risked his own freedom for Al's."

"You think I should forget it? Let it go?"

"I'm not saying that or telling you what you should do. I'm just giving you a perspective."

"Beating someone is different than murder."

Her voice was a whisper of despair, a wish that she could go back and be ignorant of it all. He patted her hand again and ran the palm in circles over it and down her tanned fingers, connecting with her in ways he would never admit to.

"Pretty sure you'll tell him that when you decide what to do."

Silent tears fell, streaming down her cheeks in two glistening paths. She widened her eyes, trying to stem the flow and swallowed back a sob. Samuel pulled her to him and held her against his chest, ran a hand down the back of her head and caressed the silk of her auburn curls. He breathed in lavender scent and let his lips linger against her hair.

Minutes passed. The river moved by, and a heron darted for his dinner. The sun shone, leaves fell and swirled in the current, dragon flies played tag in the air. The world was the same today as yesterday, except it wasn't because *everything* was different.

He loved.

Chapter Twenty-nine

The bar filled early all week. People needed to talk about the Klan, speculate about what they were doing. Charity Evans knew because she'd been home when they stopped by her father's house at the end of their march.

"We'll build you a church," Longstreet said to Reverend Evans as he pulled the hood from his face. "We have the backing and need to establish a white protestant stronghold before anyone else builds in the area."

Evans puffed his chest and his eyes gleamed. He'd had visions of the church they would build, tall and with a steeple, a grand church with his name in the concrete cornerstone. When the Methodist Council of Bishops sent him to the area, he knew it had been done as a slap on the hand for his indiscretions. He'd hated them for it. Now they'd see. They'd know his power. His smile widened.

Gertrude Evans bustled into the parlor holding a tea tray and dipping into a small bow in front of each of the men. Her dream blossomed. If she'd been the man in the family, they would never have been stuck in this backwater, hick town – colored hick town.

She set the tray on a polished table and poured weak tea from the pot. She'd been too anxious to hear what was happening to let it steep to its full flavor.

"Gentlemen."

She stood back with her hands folded in false submission, and Longstreet stared, waiting for her to leave, but Charity bounced in, her bob bouncing with her.

"What's going on? Why are you men out in costume? Think it's Halloween?" She flopped into a chair and dangled her booted foot, flirting with the males in the room and watching them watch her.

Charity knew her effect on men and used it. She enjoyed it, but her power turned to dislike of them for being fools, easily captured by fluttering lashes.

She thought of Charles and her pulse quickened. Now, there was a man who couldn't be swayed, a man who knew exactly who and what he was. Samuel, too.

Gertrude moved to stand in front of her daughter.

"The men have things to discuss, Charity. You should leave them to do it."

"What about you, Mother? Shouldn't you leave?"

Gertrude puffed her chest and huffed out some hot air. "That's different."

"Is it? Oh, yes. You've said you're the real reverend in the family. Haven't you? More than once. Perhaps you've taken over Papa's job." She rose from her chair before her mother recovered enough to respond.

Gertrude's daughter flustered her, defeated her. She'd been glad the girl left on her own because she couldn't have forced her from the room. She didn't know how.

Charity swayed her hips as she walked away, and a smile played on her lips. "I'll be at the hotel."

The cousins were flanked by Gus and Bear who listened with grins to tales the women told. Behind the bar, Abby poured Jackson's drink orders fast so she could hear Sue tell about the twins who'd shown up at their *salon* the night before.

"I think their daddy sent them. Wouldn't you say, Sally?" She waited for confirmation and attention.

"Where they from?" Gus asked.

"A long way away, I think," Sally said. "He didn't want them coming of age in their own town. Happens a lot. Twins are a good time."

"That's not why, Sally. He sent 'em to us because we're the best in the whole state, and everybody knows it." She looked around for agreement and continued when she didn't hear any.

"Look, just say maybe if you're not sure or agree," she said, and gave a satisfied look when she heard the many *maybes* offered.

Sue swiveled around and kicked her stubby legs to get some blood pumping back into them and spun back to continue her story.

When Charity entered, she sidled up to Samuel, who was still chuckling over Sue's tale, and ordered a whiskey, straight up.

"Tough cookie, aren't you, girl?"

"Is whiskey reserved for men only?

"Not reserved, maybe preferred. What are you doing out and about tonight?"

"Thought I'd share what I know."

"Everything?"

Charity nudged his shoulder, and Samuel backed sideways to give her more space. The last thing he needed was Charity's kind of problem.

"Where's Charles tonight?" she asked, peering into the crowd of people at the tables.

He ignored the question. "And what do you know that I would want to know?"

"Our hooded friends were at Daddy's house." She watched for a reaction from under her lashes and didn't get one.

"Our friends?"

"Okay, maybe the reverend's friends."

"And?"

"They're wanting to build him a church. They have money."

"Of course, they do." His voice dripped with sarcasm.

"Daddy is ecstatic. He thinks all the sinners will flock to him and bow down and kiss his hand. He'll be the king of Idlewild sitting on his pulpit throne, dispensing pardons and ecclesiastical wisdom."

Samuel showed his teeth in what could have been a smile but didn't stretch to his eyes. "It won't change anything. People will go to church where they want," he said.

"We know that. Mother doesn't."

Samuel noted the look that crossed Charity's face but couldn't define a grin or a frown. He saw a look that a mother might give a child who had scratched a place on his body after being told not to scratch there in public. It was an eye-roll filled with half amusement, half contempt, half humor, and half wonder. Too many halves by half, he told himself and put on a look similar to Charity's.

Abby pushed a tray full of drinks his way. "Be a friend and take this to the table in the far corner, would you, please?"

"I'll be glad to," she said, and grabbed it before Samuel. And that is how Charity Evans got the job she'd wanted. She covered several tables for Jackson and treated folks to a generous smile and bob of her shiny blond head. They enjoyed her flirting and gave it right back. She was in her element.

Charity stayed when the bar cleared and made herself at home on the porch with the *family*, dragged a chair from the other side and shoved it right next to Shorty's.

"It's late. Won't the reverend worry?" he asked when she plunked down and made herself at home with one of the nightcaps Abby carried out.

"Maybe," she said.

"I don't want you to get in trouble, Charity," Abby said.

"I'm always in trouble. It's my middle name. Want to hear about Longstreet?"

They didn't. They didn't want to think about the Klan and the destruction it embodied, even though they all did. They couldn't stop or change the visions that came in the night and plagued their dreams.

She told them, anyway, and they listened. It sounded like she wanted them to interfere in the building of her father's church, but they didn't acknowledge it. They were surprised by some of the names they heard, but not very. Deep down, they knew. They had always known.

Abby didn't hear Charity's tale, even though she sat nearby. She'd flown somewhere else where rightness and morality and ethics lived. Where it might be clear what she had the strength to do. Or not do.

Across the lake, her loon wailed, and she wailed back, inside where no one could hear. She tipped her head against the back of the chair and let her body sink, fade into absence and slide into the water. She felt it pull her down, and her body went into a neutrally buoyant state. She was at one with the snapping turtle gaping at her, and the trout and bass gliding by. She felt their scales rasp against her skin and called to them.

Wait. Don't leave me. I need your help.

Cassandra chose that moment to appear. She stared at the porch family and her head moved from side to side, indicating her disagreement with something or someone. Sorrow hung about her like a dark, damp cloud.

"Tea tomorrow," she said.

"We all gonna fit in your tiny house?" Charity's flip words drew a scowl from Samuel.

"Behave or go home," he said.

"The fish," Cassandra said. "But not the piranha," and pointed her walking stick at Charity.

Abby smiled. "I'll be there, friend. Thank you."

"Fish?" Bear said.

Abby's look was inscrutable. "I took a swim in the lake. How did she know?"

What looked like small daisies filled the kitchen and living space of Cassandra's home, and the strong, pungent odor of citrus made her gasp when she entered. She held her hand over her nose.

"It will abate," Cassandra said.

"What is it?"

"Feverfew. Good insect repellent."

Abby smiled. "Looking for an influx of flies or mosquitoes?"

"Gets rid of unwanted pests." Her eyes lit with intent and humor. "Also good for headaches, fever, other ailments. Clears your head for thought."

"How did you know I need to think, Cassandra? How do you know the things you do?"

Cassandra moved to the whistling teakettle, her purple and green robe flowing around her feet like waves on the ocean.

"Some things come to me. Not all. I know you need help understanding, Minnow."

She poured steaming water into a bright yellow teapot in the middle of a table covered in a flowered cloth. In between the flowers and vines, fat cherubs frolicked, and, as Abby studied them, she saw they weren't mindlessly frolicking as she'd assumed. Some carried small clubs and were using them on strange looking creatures.

She pointed to one. "What's this?"

Cassandra looked surprised and amused.

"Fairies, kelpies who lure unsuspecting travelers into the woods for nefarious purposes."

"And the cherub-looking creatures?"

"Just that. People types."

"They're clubbing the kelpies. Strange."

"Kelpies aren't good sorts."

"Where on earth did you find this tablecloth, Cassandra? It's so . . . It's strange, even bizarre."

"It appeared."

She poured the steeped, fragrant tea into cherub covered cups, and Abby wrapped her fingers around its warmth, letting the aroma overwhelm her.

"People shouldn't play God," she blurted out after the first sip. "We don't have that right."

"Laws allow us to."

Abby chewed her lip. "I guess. But then it's within the law."

"It used to be lawful to hang a man for stealing a horse."

"Yes, as ridiculous as it seems now to kill a man over a horse."

"A horse could have meant life or death. Not so much anymore."

"But it was still a lawful thing, Cassandra."

"Help me understand. Laws dictate right and wrong, when and who we kill, when it is *right* to take a life. Laws are God-like. Or do they simply reflect what men say is *right*?"

"I guess." Abby thrummed her fingers against the cup, uncomfortable with the conversation and its direction. She wanted to know Cassandra's thoughts. She respected her, was in awe of her.

"Laws are made by men to preserve right, yet laws change. Men change them. So, when that happens, does *right* change?" Cassandra asked.

Abby ran trembling hands through her hair and ruffled it until she looked like a mad woman.

"You're confusing me!"

Cassandra relaxed in her chair, let the feverfew and tea do its work. The clowder materialized. From where, Abby had no idea. One moment they weren't there, and, the next, they were rubbing her ankles and climbing in her lap.

"*I* told the boys they weren't finished with the lessons in the woods," Cassandra said sucking the steam from her tea into elegant nostrils.

Abby couldn't respond. She didn't know what her friend meant. It was a big leap from laws and questions of right and wrong to woodland lessons.

"I watched those beautiful boys teach the Tatums and George what it means to hurt, what it means to be a victim, what it means to curl into a fetal position and cry out for your mama. They didn't want to teach the lesson. Reluctance varnished their hard eyes."

Now she understood. "You saw it?"

"I did, and after the first one, I told them they had more to do. All the boys who hurt Betty had yet to learn the lesson. *I* am responsible as much as those who did it, as much as those who organized it. I didn't stop them."

Abby stared at her friend and tried to comprehend Cassandra watching one man beat another, but the idea was incomprehensible. She remembered her reaction when she'd heard about it. She'd been joyful, or a close likeness, felt the punch in her own hand and satisfaction deep in her stomach.

She drained her cup and put it back in the flowered saucer, looked at the club wielding cherubs and wondered again where the tablecloth and tea set had come from. Did Cassandra wave her walking stick and produce thought provoking tableware to match the situation?

"What do I do, my friend? Turn him in? Leave him be?"

"You're the one who believes man should not play God. But you did when you saved Al. She surely would have died if you hadn't gone there."

"That's different."

"Maybe. This is the question. What can you live with? Can you be imperfect?"

Her head snapped to face Cassandra.

"What does that mean? This isn't about me."

"Isn't it?"

Abby stood and moved toward the open door, disappointment slowing her pace. She'd gotten used to coming to Cassandra's house for peace, for answers, but left today with more questions . . . and frustrations.

She shook her head in exasperation seeing Cassandra beside her on the long trek down the path to town and snorted at her foolishness.

"Why should I be surprised?" she said, not really speaking to Cassandra. "Likely a squirrel will respond to me – or maybe a toad."

"Toads don't speak, Abby. They mostly grunt or at the most make some guttural words that are hard to decipher."

Abby stopped dead and stared at Cassandra.

"Are you serious? Grunts and guttural sounds?"

Cassandra's smile spoke centuries but didn't make her seem old. The opposite, in fact.

"Maybe."

When they resumed walking, Cassandra said, "You can't wear another's deeds or shortcomings or turn them into nightgowns, Abby."

Abby's chin met her chest. She was tired inside and out. "I think I actually know what you mean with that one." She hugged her, and this time Cassandra let her go on alone.

Jesse met her at the door to his office and held it open.

"How'd you know I was coming to see you?"

"Saw you in the window. Where's Phantom?"

"Home I guess. Why?"

"He takes the chair next to you."

She smiled, remembering her first visit to his office, but her lips only curved with the effort.

"I need help." She couldn't look him in the eyes when she said it, so she went to the window and stared anywhere else, everywhere else.

"What can I do for you, Abby?"

"I need a divorce. Can you do it for me? I don't know how it goes or what I have to do or what Frank has to do. I don't know . . ."

The words drowned in sobs coming from deep in her gut, and she quit talking. She felt a hand on her shoulder turn her around and two arms around her back pulling her close. She let his shirt soak up the tears streaming down her face. When she was done, he led her to the chair.

"Let's try this again. You want a divorce?"

"Yes."

"Does Frank know and agree?"

"He will."

"Is he still at the farm?"

She nodded.

"We can file based on desertion. I have to ask this Abby, so please don't be upset. Is there no other way to make your marriage work?"

"No. It's done." Her voice dropped to a whisper. "It never began. It's not his fault. It isn't, Jesse. Whatever you hear or think, Frank Adams isn't a bad man."

Jesse held up a hand, palm out, stopping her from further explanation.

"I don't know Frank well, but I'm fairly certain I know you. You're good, too, Abigail. Don't forget it."

"Don't send him any paperwork, please. His family doesn't need to see. I'll speak to him about coming here for it. Is that alright?"

"Yes, Abby. Yes, it is."

In her room, she splashed water on her face, changed her dress and brushed her hair. The long braid she plaited was tight and tugged the skin of her cheeks.

Good. Feels right.

She went downstairs, tied the apron and picked up the wet dishrag to wipe down the bar.

"How many times have I done this?" she said. The room was empty, so it should have been a one-sided conversation, but a voice answered.

"Since ye started as a wee lass, and since ye do it every day and night, I'm guessing thousands, my Abigail."

He hiked his suspenders and cocked his head at her.

"You're right about that. Right about most things, Da."

Her sigh drove an ice pick into his heart. He knew she'd been struggling, more so lately than before, but it had been going on for a long time. As always, he asked why, but didn't expect an answer.

"Ye need a shoulder, lass? I see sad eyes." He tugged her braid, and her head tilted back to look him in the eyes.

"I'm leaving Frank, Da," she said before she could think about it, before she had time to change her mind. Saying it made it real. No going back, now. Words layered it in concrete.

Patrick scuffed his boot on the floor and wanted to kick something. He knew how she hurt – his little girl. In his mind, Frank was responsible for her pain and didn't deserve her.

Never had.

"I'm thinking he left a long time ago, sweetheart. Haven't seen a husband around here lately."

She agreed with a nod because more words wouldn't happen. They were lodged in her throat with Cassandra's toad. The toad spoke in guttural words and grunted. That's what she heard and understood, but she couldn't explain it to her da, her loving da whose arm went around her shoulder and squeezed. He knew better than to go for a full-blown, tear-inducing hug. A punch on the arm worked best for Abby.

A moment later, Jackson walked in with Charity by his side. She needed to get rid of the toad and speak to them both about work schedules. Jackson needed to approve.

He came first.

Chapter Thirty

She left Charity to make beds and clean rooms with Betty. She'd like to have stayed to see the dynamics, but had another place to be. She'd have to be satisfied with the look on Betty's face when she told her she'd be in charge, Charity's supervisor.

"I get to tell that girl what to do?" She did a little jig, dancing with the broom she'd been using on the bar floor. "This could be the best day of my life. Or the worst. What if Charity doesn't want to be bossed around by a colored girl?"

Abby laughed at the wide-eyed dismay on Betty's face.

"Then she won't work here. Understand?" When the eyes didn't go back to normal, Abby tried again.

"Be yourself, Betty. Be sweet and helpful like you always are, and it'll be fine."

"What Betty do *you* know?"

The sun warmed her back as she headed to the Adams farm. Abby would enjoy the morning ride if she'd been going someplace else. But Marie didn't know that. She picked up her feet like a circus horse and tossed her head, pitching the long mane into the air, happy to be out of the stable and into the fresh air.

"Want to run a bit, girl? Let's go. For a minute or two. You're not a spring chicken, you know."

I'm not a chicken at all, Abby.

"Sorry. I know. You're a beautiful talking mare, I think, cuz I'm answering you."

Hang on.

The breeze splashed her face and whipped her hair, pulling it from the ribbon binding it. She bent low in the saddle and stood in the stirrups, letting her knees take the jolts as Marie's feet thudded on the road.

Marie knew her rider well. She'd been carrying her around for years, and her gait was effortless because Abby moved with her, became part of the wind. She lowered her head to stretch her neck, working for more speed. When she'd had her fun, Marie took her time slowing down to an amble, snorting her pleasure and tossing her head.

"You're welcome, girl. Anytime."

Abby flung the reins over a low branch, leaving the mare to graze in the shade, and went to look for Frank. She hoped to find him alone, but didn't think she would be that lucky. She was right.

"Looking for me?" George said, a smirk on his handsome face. "Did you reconsider my offer and come to make plans?"

She thought about wiping the smirk from his face and ignored his question. "I'm looking for Frank. Do you know where he is?"

"Sure, I do." He stuck the shovel into the soil and perched a boot on it.

"Would you mind sharing that information?" He left the shovel and moved nearer.

"How bout a trade?"

"You're an ass, George Adams. I'll find him myself." She spun and walked toward the house, mumbling. "Insufferable, foul man."

Her mother-in-law stood in the open door waiting for Abby to climb the porch steps, her arms crossed, her face a marble mask.

"Hello, Emily," Abby said, wishing she could have had a better relationship with her. She'd never had a mother. Emily might have stepped into that role, but it hadn't happened. She didn't know why.

"What do you want, Abigail?"

"I need to speak with Frank. Do you know where he is?"

"Why?"

Abby ran a hand through her tousled hair and tried not to be frustrated. "It's important, Emily. Please tell me where I can find him."

"Fixing fences. North corner. I don't need to see you here again, Abigail."

"I understand, Mrs. Adams. I'm sorry."

Instead of cutting cross country, she went around the section, past the place where she and the cousins took the ditch when the tree fell across the road. She shivered with the memory.

Around the corner, she spotted Frank and Terry replacing rotten posts in the barbed wire fence. Terry looked up from digging around the old post, saw her, and said something to Frank who let the wire go and spun around. The wire snapped back at Terry, making a deep welt on his cheek.

"Damn it, Frank. Pay attention. Abby, you spread devastation wherever you go, don't you? You're a regular little tornado."

"Hello, Terry. Frank, can we talk for a bit?"

"I'm a little busy, Abby, as you can see."

"So am I. It's important."

She dismounted and walked to the fence line, thinking again about the felled tree. It would have been an easy walk from here. Could Frank have done it? Terry? Why would they?

"Did you drop a tree on the cousins and me, Terry?" She stared at his eyes, as if looking into them would give her the truth. They didn't even flicker or blink.

"Nope. Heard that happened. Scary, huh?"

"Yes, it was, and tracks led here - to the back end of your property."

"Now just how do you know that?"

"Bear followed them. They led here."

He opened his mouth and laughed, slapped his thigh like he'd heard a great punch line, and Abby wanted to punch him. She'd been wanting to punch a lot lately, and that made her want to punch somebody, too. Anybody.

"The great lumberjack-tracker bear fighter! Guess if Bear the wonderful said so, it must be true."

"Stop it, Terry. Bear is my friend."

"Yeah. I know all about your *friends*. Seen it firsthand."

"Frank? Can we talk? If not, I'm leaving. You'll want to hear what I have to say."

He kicked at the post and watched it wobble.

"Say it."

Abby looked hard at Terry, anger igniting a fire in her eyes.

"Fine. Here it is. I'm filing for divorce. You can pick up the papers at Jesse Falmouth's office anytime next week. I'm not going to talk with Sheriff Hicks about you and Tatum, but you probably need to leave town before Edwin spots you. Finally, if anything happens to Edwin – anything – I will go to the sheriff with all the details. If anything happens to me, the information is written down."

She paused like she'd run out of air, but she hadn't. She was fighting tears clogging the words at the back of her throat.

Is this how you kill a relationship? Is this how you end a marriage God had created? You say, I'm done. It's over. You and I are not in love now. See you later. Bye, bye.

"You got what you wanted, Frank. You're free. Of me and from the law."

He grabbed her hand and tugged her to him. "It isn't like that, Abby. This is all just wrong."

"Yes. It is, and I'm sorry."

She put a hand on his face and caressed the stubble, memorized the eyes and lips, the curl of sandy hair over his ears, and told herself to leave before she said something stupid.

"Why should Frank have to leave town? Send that old man away," Terry said. "That's the stupidest thing ever."

"Shut up, Terry," Frank said. He squeezed her hand and pulled her with him as he walked down the road. She let him lead her, trailing Marie on her other side.

"Have you said anything to anyone else?"

"I told Da about the divorce, and Jesse, of course."

"I meant Tatum."

"I haven't, Frank, but I think Samuel knows."

He rubbed his head and fingered his day-old beard.

"That damned weasel gets his nose into everything, especially anything concerning you. Better watch out, Abs. He's got his eye on you."

"Nonsense. Samuel is a friend, like Bear and Shorty."

"I know. Friends. The list goes on and on."

"I'm sorry I couldn't be what you wanted, Frank. I truly am."

"Me, too. You could've. You didn't want to."

She swished air at a dragonfly that had attached itself to her arm. It lifted and found a seat on her hand. She watched it test her skin and flicker its two intricate, transparent wings.

"I hear you have ferocious mandibles. You won't bite, will you? You're beautiful, my big blue friend."

"Another friend? A blue one, this time." Frank's harsh laugh twisted the blade in her heart.

The dragonfly tiptoed to the plain gold band, reminding her. She dislodged the insect and drew off the band, put it in his hand, and closed the fingers over it.

"Maybe you'll find the one you need, Frank."

She mounted Marie, and he watched her leave.

Abby heard laughter coming from upstairs when she walked into the lobby. She recognized Betty's voice, but she hadn't heard Charity guffawing and snorting before. And she was certainly cracking up at the moment.

She headed for her room to wash the dust from her skin, and heard Betty say, "You're the damnedest woman in the world. How can you not know how to do anything? You're a useless fool."

"Don't be calling me a fool, itty bitty Betty. You're a skinny runt, and I can whip your butt."

"Flip it out. Like this so it lands on the bed, not the floor. Good Lord, Charity. How hard can it be?"

Abby stood at the door to the room they were supposed to be cleaning and watched the antics. It was entertainment at its best.

"Like this?" Charity said.

She flipped the sheet in the air and it fell on her. She waved her arms under it and managed to tangle herself in it until she fell on the floor, enshrouded like an Egyptian mummy, and giggled like a school girl.

Betty laughed and cussed, dragged the sheet from her and flipped it in the air. It landed in a perfect rectangle on the bed as intended. She folded hospital corners and stood back. Charity sat watching with a big got-your-feathered bird grin.

"Like that."

"Hello, ladies," Abby said. "Having fun?"

Betty didn't miss a beat.

"What's she supposed to do around here? She doesn't know anything. Who made your bed at home, girl?"

"Mother. She said I didn't do it right."

"I don't know your mama very well, but she was right about that."

"So how has the morning been going?" Abby asked, although she had it pretty well figured out.

"Didn't you see, boss? She's entertaining, and that's about all she's good for."

"Didn't want to take all your fun away, Betty. You had a good time. Admit it."

Betty's eyes sparkled.

"Didn't think I would, but . . . You're okay, Charity Evans, preacher's daughter, college girl, goofy blonde-bob-haired woman. Did I forget anything?"

"Think you got it all." Charity said. "Want me to wash out this bowl thingy?"

Betty rolled her eyes. "Yes. Wash the bowl thingy."

Abby left shaking her head. It was going to work. Against her better judgement, she had hired Charity. She liked the girl, and even more important, Betty liked her.

She removed her dress, splashed water on her face and arms, and felt a little bit clean. The day had been muddy in so many ways. It clung to her like campfire smoke filled with Frank's opinion of her. His disdain.

His blame.

She stared at the white ring on her finger, a stark reminder of the absent wedding band.

Divorce.

An ugly word, a failure. She slid a clean dress over her head, brushed her hair and went to work.

Al was cleaning the kitchen after Patrick's cooking frenzy. Tendrils of long blonde hair hung around her flushed face, and her cheeks were rosy with the heat of the kitchen. She looked like an angel, or a cherub from one of Cassandra's teacups, but she wasn't. She was a strong, young woman who knew her own mind, had been using it to stay alive since childhood.

"Betty is finishing up," Abby told her. "She's had quite a day breaking in Charity."

"Imagine so," Al said. "Be done here soon."

Abby left to prepare the bar for the dinner hour, and sat at the corner table to rest and wait after she'd finished. Her three employees came in at the same time. She waved them over and asked them to sit. She had some things to say.

"Coffee?" she asked.

They looked at one another and each one wondered what they had done or didn't do or would be asked to do.

"I'll get it. Sit, Abigail," Charity said, and sashayed to the kitchen. She brought them on a tray held high in the air and distributed the cups with a flourish and a smile.

"Nicely done, Charity," Abby said. Betty rolled her eyes heavenward, and Al sat in stillness.

"See. I'm not a totally useless person."

"Sit. Wish Jackson was here. He's part of this hand-picked posse."

"We going after some outlaws, boss?" Betty asked, eyes reflecting her curiosity.

"No. I wanted to say how pleased I am to have you as part of this family. You are special to me."

"You including me in this posse thing?" Charity asked. She reeled back in her chair and pointed a finger at her chest, surprise on her face.

"I am. I'm hoping you will stay working with us. That is, if Betty approves. She is your upstairs supervisor as Jackson is your bar supervisor."

Abby glanced at Strange Al who watched and listened. "If you work in the kitchen, Al will supervise."

"Wow. A white one," Charity said, eyes wide but without malice.

"Problem?" Abby asked. "While the others have fairly specific jobs, yours will fluctuate as need arises.

"Nope. No problem. Kinda neat, actually." She nudged Betty's elbow off the table and giggled as Betty's chin dropped. "Does it work for you?" she said, staring into Betty's dancing eyes.

"How come you never grew up?" Betty asked.

"Never needed to . . . or wanted to. Someday, I might." Charity glanced at the table where Abby's hand lay. "Any reason for the missing ring?"

Betty gave a harsh gasp, and the hand she put on top of Abby's said it all.

"Don't be asking stupid questions. That's my first supervisory order." She turned to Abby.

"Can I fire her, too?"

Abby retrieved her hand and swiped it over her face.

"Not today, Betty. It's a legitimate question, although a mite insensitive." Abby paused to think about how to phrase her response. She didn't want to say bad things about Frank, but she didn't want to take on the entire burden of the divorce, either.

"Frank's an ass," Betty said, "so don't ask Abby questions about him."

"No . . . It's just . . . We have come to an agreement that our marriage was . . . is . . . should be dissolved. That's all. Let's move on to work."

"Sorry," Charity said, and Abby saw what could have been the start of tears in her eyes.

Who was this girl?

"Tomorrow, you'll work upstairs with Betty, Charity. Learn from her. She's the best. When you're certain of the routine, you'll work with Jackson in the bar. Following that, you'll be in the kitchen with Al. Questions anyone?"

"Yes. Why?" Betty asked.

"The Oakmere hotel will be done in the spring. Da will want to run it. If he does, we'll need you all to run this or the Oakmere. Without me."

Abby glanced at three sets of eyes, from light blue to deep brown, and knew she'd made the right choice. They were good workers – and loyal to her and her da. Her heart sang a little for the first time since Marie took her flying down the road that morning. She felt for the missing ring, and guilt crowded her heart, nudging out the song.

"We'll be back by morning, Abby," Bear said. "Gus thinks it's safer in the dark."

"I still don't know why we can't have it delivered. That's normal, isn't it?"

"They don't need to know where it's going, my fair friend. That's why," Gus said. "Can't put bricks through windows they don't know anything about."

Samuel watched from his perch at the end of the bar next to Patrick. Jesse and Edna watched her, too. It seemed like all the eyes in the bar were looking at her. For what reason, she didn't know.

"I don't like it. Let's just serve lemonade."

Bear ran a hand over hers and fingered the white ring.

"Sorry," he whispered.

She couldn't answer and knew, now, why so many eyes were watching her. She hadn't forgotten, but she had pushed it way to the back of her brain where it could be buried by work and people and the words from those who loved her.

"Thanks," she croaked, sounding a lot like Cassandra's toad.

"Want to talk?"

She shook her head, swallowed, and was grateful her friends wouldn't be on the porch tonight in the family circle. She didn't want conversation.

Gus picked her up in a massive goodbye hug, and Shorty put an arm around her shoulder and made her walk him outside. When he moved down the steps, Bear brushed his scarred beard across her cheek. "We'll talk tomorrow."

She stood on the porch and watched them leave – Gus and Bear in the buckboard and Shorty on his big Belgian draft horse. He could have used a smaller, lighter horse, but his own size and weight made him sensitive to the animal's comfort. He ran a hand over the gelding's blonde mane and whispered words of love.

Three of the men in her life made her eyes water and her smile grow in defiance of sorrow as they waved and shouted goodbyes to her. Life was a paradox.

When she went back to the bar, a fourth watched, his eyes dark and dangerous. She didn't know why that word came to mind, but it did. He tapped his glass for a refill and, when she brought it to him, he touched her ring finger. Edna left Jesse and moved to sit by Samuel.

"Leave her alone, Samuel. You hear me? Leave her alone."

"So, I guess lawyer-client confidentiality doesn't exist?" Abby said.

Edna drew back like Abby had slapped her. "You would guess wrong."

"How does everyone know almost before I did?"

"You're waving your ring-less finger around like a flag, Abigail." She drew herself up tall, and her words cut like a sharp blade, proud and haughty. "Jesse, if he is the lawyer to whom you refer, said nothing. But you just did. You have only yourself to blame if you didn't want to share the information with your friends."

Edna fumed. No one attacked her husband. Not even her friend, Abby. She spun off and rejoined Jesse, fire flying from her dark eyes.

"I'm sorry, Edna." Abby chased her down and threw an arm around her. "I don't know what I'm saying or doing. I'm a mess. Please forgive me. You, too, Jesse."

He shrugged his shoulders, unaware he'd been insulted.

"Please forgive me and don't be mad," Abby said.

"Would clemency buy me a glass of your finest cognac on the house? And one for my obviously offended wife?" he said, milking the moment and whatever it was she needed to be sorry for.

"Two each, and I'm really sorry."

Jesse winked. "This could work out pretty well. How can we do it again?"

Jackson had drink orders piled up, and Abby spent the rest of the evening filling glasses with no time to think about Frank or the day. She filled the last three and took them to the porch, one for her da, one for her, and one for Samuel. The three made a much smaller group than they were used to, and this night Abby sighed in contentment.

Her loon wailed, and the haunting sound lit the sky with twinkling stars. Moonlight split the lake in two, a separation like the one Moses had helped God make in the Red Sea.

Abby closed her eyes to savor the song of her loon, and when she opened them, the lake was one again.

"I'm going crazy."

A bat darted into the nearby trees, and an opossum waddled to the edge of the water, its white fur picking up the moon's light. Samuel's laugh startled the rodent-like critter who flipped onto his back and lay still, his feet in the air. "Playing possum," Patrick said.

"I don't think he's playing. It's a sort of involuntary catatonic state he goes into when everything else in his arsenal hasn't worked. People do that, too. Something scared him. Maybe Cassandra?"

Abby started. "I didn't see Cassandra. Did you?"

"Sure. You didn't?"

"No. I saw the lake split in two and . . . Never mind. I don't care for the way you're looking at me. Either one of you."

"You're not crazy, lass. Only a bit addled."

Patrick patted her arm on one side, and Samuel wrapped his fingers around the other. He let his thumb roam the ring-less finger.

"It will get better, Abby. I promise."

Chapter Thirty-one

Gus pulled the buckboard into the dark, narrow backstreet and waited with Bear while Shorty rode on down to find Hank. It smelled like rotting vegetables, and laughter bounced off the walls of the structures hiding the wagon and two men.

"Coulda found a better place to sit," Gus said. "Thirsty, too. Maybe we slip into the bar a have a quick one."

"We wait here like we said, Gus."

Bear thought he saw him nod, but it was so dark he couldn't be sure. Rustling in the scrub brush on the other side of the wagon made his head swing to spy the culprit, but the moonlight glanced off the buildings and fled, leaving black night and even blacker shadows.

Down the alley, a door opened and light from inside showed a man step out, hold the door and relieve himself.

"Ass," Gus said. "Somebody's gonna step in his piss and track it inside. Coulda gone across the alley and peed on the critter making a ruckus and trying to scare us."

"A bit nervous, Gus?"

"Hell, no. I just got a jumpy thing about night critters. That's all. Don't like 'em creeping up on me in the dark. Don't like snakes either. Day or night. Don't you hate bears now?"

"No. Just don't want to meet up with another momma protecting her cubs. Mommas do that."

Bear looked in all directions, trying to manufacture Shorty and his horse out of the night gloom. He cocked his head to listen and knew it wouldn't help him materialize.

"What the hell's keeping him?" Gus shifted on the hard seat. "We gonna wait here all night or go find him?"

"Give it a couple more minutes. If he doesn't show, we'll go." Bear regretted the wait.

They found Shorty's gelding tied in front of the real estate office and found him behind it, beaten and unconscious.

"Get a light, Gus."

In the lantern light, the damage staggered them. Eyes were closed and bloodied. His nose lay off to the side and an arm in a position not natural for unbroken bones. A bloody lump on the back of his head made the story clear.

Someone with a heavy club had to have come up behind the big man. No other way could this have happened because Shorty would have won the battle if they'd been straight about it. He likely fought back when he should have just gone down and stayed there, but that wasn't his way.

Bear's rage was tempered only by the need to get Shorty home.

"Lift his feet, Gus."

Bear put his arms under Shorty's shoulders, and with strength born of friendship, lifted the giant onto the straw in the back of the buckboard. They covered him with the blanket meant to hide booze, collected his horse, and made the slow ride back to Idlewild.

"Who did this?" Gus said. "Klan? Chicago?"

Bear shook his head. "I got a feeling otherwise."

"Well? Wanna share?"

"I don't know for sure, but somebody's mad and making a point. The tree falling on Abby and the cousins. Bricks in their windows and yours. Edwin's note and getting beat up.

Gus pondered. All those things didn't seem to be connected in any way, and he said so.

"What's the one single common piece?" Bear said.

Lantern light swayed and cast moving yellow shapes on the road and the backs of the horses. It didn't do much to ensure their safety. In fact, it worked otherwise. The ditches and trees on either side of them were in pitch dark, made more so by the artificial light of the lantern. The foliage could have harbored an army of cutthroats, and they wouldn't know it. But in the lantern light, Bear could keep an eye on Shorty, and that mattered more than all else.

He groaned a couple of times, but didn't wake up. When he tried to move, Bear handed the reins to Gus and got in the back to sit with him. He put a hand on Shorty's right shoulder and pressed him down, spoke to him to let him know he was with friends, not back in Custer with . . . whoever had done the work. It must have been many.

"Abby," Bear said. "Abby is the link. Don't know why I know it, but I do. Don't know how to prove it, either, but I will."

Bear climbed the stairs and tapped at Patrick's door, and then Abby's. Four men carried Shorty up to his room, and Abby went to work.

"Get Cassandra," she said to anyone listening. "She'll know what to do and have stuff."

"I'll go," Gus said.

"You know where?" Bear asked.

"Sure. She's the witchy woman. I know her."

"Put some water on to heat, Da. She'll want it."

With Bear's help, she cut off Shorty's clothes and bathed the blood from his head and face. The wounds on his swollen face scared her, but the bruises on his chest and midriff concerned her the most – and the fact he hadn't awakened.

Tears formed at the corners of her eyes, but she couldn't, wouldn't let them fall. They had work to do, and he needed her. When he was as clean as she could make him, she pulled a chair over to his bed and sat. Bear took the other side, and they waited.

In a moment, Patrick entered with a tray of glasses and decanter of whiskey. He poured three.

"Drink, lass," he said. "I wonder if a wee drop would bring our friend around?"

"Wait for Cassandra, Da. Please. Thank you for the drink."

"How'd this happen? Didn't think anyone could ever whip Shorty."

"We separated. Shouldn't have done that."

"Any clues about who?"

Bear's head moved from side to side, but Patrick didn't buy it. His face wore more than sorrow and guilt for leaving him by himself. Patrick saw resolve, not uncertainty. He saw deep seated, smoldering fury, and a prickle of fear crawled up his spine.

Gus brought Cassandra in through the kitchen where she spotted the tea kettle steaming. She grabbed a cup, pointed out the whistling kettle to Gus, and, holding a heavy satchel in her other hand, climbed the stairs.

"More light, please, Abigail." She pulled the sheet from his body, and Gus flinched.

"Modesty, Cassandra?" he said.

The glare she gave sent him to the whiskey decanter. He poured a healthy tot, swigged it down and poured another. "First one was medicinal," he said.

Cassandra pulled a brown packet of dried herbs from her satchel and mixed it with a clear salve. She dipped two fingers into the jar, scooped out a big glob and dropped it onto Shorty's chest.

"St. John's Wort. For internal contusions. It'll help the bruising."

She handed Abby a second brown packet and instructed her to mix a strong tea.

"What is it?"

"No toad's eyes or bat's feet. It's burdock, to purify blood of toxins . . . and maybe ward off the evil eye."

Cassandra's own eye looked sideways toward Abby and around to the men in the room. She saw Abby's hand still, spoon hovering in the air, and after a moment of hesitation, it stirred the liquid in the cup.

"If you believe in such things," Cassandra said. "I certainly don't."

"You're a bad witch, Cassandra." The twinkle tried to come back in her eyes but didn't succeed. "How are we to get this brew inside him."

"I'll show you . . . after we set his arm."

With Bear on one side and Gus on the other, Cassandra put a foot on the mattress, grabbed Shorty's arm, and pulled and pulled. The snap ricocheted off the walls when it went back into place, and Abby's eyes leaked tears she'd been holding back all night.

"Oh, God, Shorty, I'm so sorry."

Cassandra took the chair by the window. "Spoon in the tea, Abby." She could look out of it and see the lake and watch events inside by the reflection in the glass. She propped her feet on the window seat, let her chin drop to her chest, and went into a reflective state.

No one spoke above a whisper. Out of respect for the woman's sleep? Out of fear? They didn't want to speculate.

Gus went to a vacant room and tried to sleep, but the night kept interfering. Abby moved a chair closer to Shorty's bed with no thought of sleep. Bear dragged in another. He'd not be leaving or sleeping. Patrick went to his own bed. Sleep came easily to the leprechaun.

Cassandra was spooning tea between Shorty's lips when Abby lifted her chin off the mattress. Bear had left the room.

"St. John's Wort?" Abby asked, wanting to learn some of the woman's skills.

"Dandelion. There may be inflammation in his head. We need the swelling gone."

"How often should I give it to him? How much?"

"Every couple of hours until he wakes up. I'll leave packets."

Abby rubbed her wrinkled forehead. She didn't know how to keep the hotel running and care for him, too. He was more important, but she needed help.

"Can you stay until I talk with Da?"

"Sure. Gotta get a cat."

Abby was out the door and down the hall before it occurred to her to wonder what a cat had to do with anything.

Al had coffee going and bacon in the pan when Abby got there.

"Have you seen Bear this morning?" she asked.

Al shook her head and continued pushing the bacon around.

"Shorty was hurt last night." She watched Al's complexion turn whiter than its usual cream, and it occurred to her the girl might faint.

Then what? Abby asked herself.

"Can you handle breakfast until I get Da down here to help?"

"Course," she said, poured coffee for Abby who looked like she could use a cup, and fled to the pantry. She came out tying her hair in the pink ribbon. "What happened?"

"Shorty was beaten up by some bootleg thugs. I don't know why."

"No, couldn't happen."

Abby studied her face. Al's certainty always surprised her. Her attitude on any day, this one included, left no room for doubt.

"Why do you say that, Al?"

"He would know to be aware. He wouldn't let strangers get that close."

"Seems like, doesn't it?" Abby sipped her coffee. "When Da gets here, come on up to see him, if you want."

Al nodded and poked at the bacon sizzling in the pan, her face turned away, her shoulders set. Abby pushed the door open, about to leave, when it occurred to her Betty wasn't bustling around.

"Where's your sidekick? You didn't walk here alone, did you?"

"No. She and Benjamin went for a ride."

Abby closed her eyes in relief. She didn't need to worry about another friend. She couldn't.

Al waited until Betty and Abby were cleaning a room down the hall before tiptoeing in to Shorty's. She stood just inside the door, eyes wide with fear and heart pounding. It pained her to see the big man so immobile, so pale and dependent. He was the one others relied on, the strong one.

"Won't bite you, girl. You sit here until I get back. Gotta run home for a cat." Cassandra rose from the chair.

"Orange," Al said as if she knew exactly what Shorty needed. Not black or white or tiger or calico. Orange, as if it was the missing ingredient in his recovery.

She pulled Cassandra's chair closer to him and kneeled on it, her tiny body poised like a hovering hummingbird that could fly off should his eyes flutter open. She grew comfortable with his proximity and, as time passed, straightened the white sheet, folded it neatly over his chest and smoothed the wrinkles. She moved his good arm to lay beside him and let her hand rest a moment on his.

Al found a cloth to dampen in cool water from the pitcher, ran it over his brow and watched the twitching at the corners of his eyes where faint lines were etched. He needed a shave, and she thought about running the back of her hand over the bristles just to feel them.

She jumped back when Abby entered feeling like she'd done something she shouldn't have.

"Would you mind giving him this tea, Al? He should take it every two hours, according to Cassandra."

"How?"

"Spoon it in."

"I could do that."

Abby left with a half-smile on her face. The girl was smitten. She knew it and wondered if Shorty did.

The orange kitten sauntered in like he lived in Shorty's room and always had. He leaped on the bed, kneaded the pillow next to the man's head and curled into his neck. His purr rumbled loud enough to wake the dead, but not Shorty.

Like black and white statues, Phantom and Cleo posed at the door and watched the interloper make himself at home.

Cheeky, Cleo said.

Phantom rolled his eyes. *Orange. They all are.*

"Be nice," Cassandra told them.

"I can take over, Al. I'm done cleaning," Abby said as she came into the room and stopped when she spotted the orange kitten, her worry about Shorty overtaken by sight of the kitten. "Aw. Cute."

"Healer cat," Cassandra said. "Al knows about orange."

Abby scrunched her brow. She loved her cats . . . but healers?

"Only orange ones?"

"Of course," Cassandra said. "Making tea. Do you want some?"

"Regular tea?"

Cassandra tugged on an earlobe and squinted at Abby as if she'd lost her faculties.

"Of course," she repeated. "My superior regular."

"Sounds wonderful. I'd love some. Betty, too. She'll be here in a minute."

Abby brought in another chair and pulled a small table away from the wall so the four women could sit and sip their tea and still watch for movement from Shorty. The room warmed with afternoon sun shining in through the open window, making a deceptively serene space.

Abby couldn't take her eyes from the man in the bed. She was responsible and knew it. He'd been doing them a favor, getting the whiskey. He wouldn't have had it any other way, but . . . She pushed a fisted hand to her bottom lip to stop it from trembling. She was the cause.

"Fall soon," Betty said. "Lots of acorns. Big winter."

"Listen to the walking almanac," Abby teased, her effort to grin a dismal failure, but she tapped her friend's shoulder with affection. "Distract us with some other handed-down goodies, will you, Betty? We need some good news."

"Wooly worms are mostly black. Know what that means?" Betty said.

"They're going to a formal dance?"

They laughed, but softly, and passed guilty glances over at Shorty to see if they were disturbing him. How could they even smile when he lay hurting? His hand lay where Al had left it. The sheet hadn't been disturbed. His face was immobile, if not tranquil.

"Bad winter. Heavy snow."

Phantom and Cleo strolled in and took up positions at the foot of Shorty's bed, on either side of his feet. Orange kitty stood, stretched, opened his mouth in a silent meow, and lay back down, apparently undisturbed by the intruders.

"His face looks like a bobcat," Betty said.

"You see them around here?" Abby asked.

"No."

"Good, I guess. Until Shorty names him, that's who he'll be. Bob Cat. Does that work, Cassandra?"

"You ever going to talk about your ring-less finger?" Betty asked.

Abby's right hand flew over the other as if hiding the offending finger could make it go away.

She chewed her bottom lip, her chin lowered, and her voice thickened when she finally opened her mouth to speak. She cleared her throat and tried again.

"I've told you all there is to say. I . . . Frank and I . . . Our marriage hasn't worked. We are dissolving it. We think it's best to. . ."

She couldn't continue because the dam broke and Charity entered to find Betty, Al, Abby, and even Cassandra, with arms stretched across the table and hands wrapped around the nearest neck, all eyes leaking tears. All except Cassandra's. Hers were dry and annoyed, but not toward anyone at the table. These she hugged.

Charity huffed. "I was going to ask if you missed me, but I guess not. Shorty's the one on the bed, Dr. Dan. I'm sure they won't mind if you take a look. Maybe not even notice."

The foursome broke apart, surprised and self-conscious, especially in the presence of the famous Chicago heart surgeon. They leaped to their feet with a clatter of tea cups and tried to recover.

"Dr. Williams," Abby said, extending her hand. "I didn't realize you were in town. How fortunate. Would you mind taking a look at our friend?"

"It's what I'm here for, but since Miss Cassandra has already processed his injuries, I'm unnecessary – like another appendage."

"Do it anyway," Cassandra said, waving a purple, wide sleeved arm at the doctor. "You know you want to."

He pulled back the sheet exposing the massive bruised chest and abdomen and *uh-huhed*. He felt the knot at the back of Shorty's head and *hemmmmed*. He ran fingers over all the ribs and sighed.

"He's been beaten."

Every head in the room cocked to look at him as if he really did have an extra appendage – maybe an extra head.

"Yes," Abby said. "That was fairly clear."

"He needs to wake up," Dr. Dan said. "Wake him up."

"How do you suggest we do that?" Abby asked.

"Spirit of hartshorn." Cassandra moved toward her medicine bag. "I have some."

Dr. Dan grinned. "Did you trim the hooves yourself and leave stags running around the forest hoof-less?"

Cassandra gave him a look that might have melted a lesser man, one not so sure of himself. But he was having a bit of fun at her expense, and she didn't mind answering.

"They drop it off."

He tilted his head and the rest followed the conversation with head swivels, watching and listening.

"I simply have the red deer come to my back door, scrape their hooves on my mat, and take off. I collect the hoof shavings, and we're all happy." She lifted a small bottle from her bag that said *Smelling Salts*.

"Smelling Salts? You're talking about smelling salts?" Abby said, her voice coming close to a soft screech.

Dr. Dan knew he'd been bested by Cassandra. "Originally, natives made it from the hooves of the red deer which contain ammonia. Cassandra is too smart for me. I knew it before, but thought I could get her. I'll keep trying."

Cassandra waved the bottle under Shorty's nose, and the big man jerked back from it. An arm flew into the air, knocking Al to the floor.

"I'm okay," she said as everyone race to her side. "See to Shorty."

His eyes had closed again, but this time in pain instead of unconsciousness. One hand covered his head and the other lay over the ribs on his left side.

"God, what happened?" he whispered. "I'm so sorry, Al. You okay? Come here."

His eyes were slits when he opened them to see Al slipping into his view, and his lips formed a pained smile.

"Sorry."

She patted his hand.

"I'm fine."

"Where's Bear?" he asked, his voice less than a whisper.

"We're not sure," Abby said. "He stayed in this room most of the night. I fell asleep, and he was gone when I woke up.

Shorty started to nod, slammed his eyes shut and squinted in pain.

"Need to see him," he said, trying to rise.

"What you need is rest and recuperation. You're not getting up." Abby pushed him back and got little resistance.

"Things . . . to do," Shorty gasped.

Dan gave him the doctor glare. "Who knows what's going on inside your body? Those bruises are deep and organs could be bruised, even bleeding." Dr. Dan waited for his words to settle. "Can you make a fist with your left hand?" He did.

"Sling it for a couple weeks," Dan said. "Let the joints rest. Tie him down if you have to." He drizzled laudanum between battered lips and watched as Shorty fell into a restless sleep.

A long line of folks came bearing soup, pie, home brewed healing potions, and curious eyes. No one could believe Shorty had been felled by mere mortals; they had to see it for themselves. And they cared about him. Shorty was as sweet as he was big, as caring as he was quiet. People who knew him, loved him.

Edna brought his favorite muffins and Daisy, who wanted to climb on Shorty and make him swing her around in the air like he always did. Edna had to hang on to her young daughter to keep her away from him. They talked in whispers at the door, eyes scrutinizing his chest as it moved in shallow, painful breaths.

They hadn't reached the bottom stair step when Sue and Sally filled the doorway to his room, tears rolling down their cheeks.

"How could this happen? Who would do this terrible thing?" Sally said.

"We don't know, ladies. But we'll be talking to Sheriff Hicks as soon as possible."

"Does he ever wake up?" Sue asked.

"Laudanum makes him sleepy. Doctor Williams prescribed it."

"I'd rock that big boy to sleep any day. I surely would. Give him this when he wakes up." She handed Abby a crystal decanter half full of brown liquid.

"What is it?"

"Glenlivet. Best scotch you can buy. Isn't full because I drank some, but it'll perk him up."

"Thanks, Sue. I'll tell him you brought it, but Da might be a bit put out having whiskey from Scotland in the house."

"He'll sure take a finger, though." Sally said with a grin.

"That's true." Abby said. "Maybe I'll hide it."

They vacated the doorway when Bunny got there with a steaming kettle in her hands, chicken noodle soup, prepared by her from the bones of her own barnyard stock.

"Not my favorite rooster, anyway. He was getting a might too feisty with the hens – and me," she said in a whisper.

Her dark eyes sparkled when she handed the pot to Abby, but they softened when they landed on Shorty. He slept, but his brow creased in pain. Bunny smoothed the furrowed brow with her cool hand, and Abby could see his face relax and grow younger.

Maybe Bunny had powers like her sister? Maybe she healed with her hands instead of ancient herbal concoctions. She wrapped an arm around Abby before she left and nuzzled her cheek with her own.

"You've had your sickroom problems, young woman, and a host of others, too. I'll be around town asking folks to pray for Shorty. White folks, too." She grinned with the last words. "Maybe especially the white ones."

"Ask all of them, Bunny. Mix it up."

"Just can't give it up, can you, girl?"

Abby's head moved back and forth, and her eyes filled with determination and sorrow. "We can worship together, Bunny. I know we can. Some things are simply right. This is one."

Chapter Thirty-two

Bear strode up the porch steps as the sun rose orange at the horizon. He didn't want them heading off to the fields before they had a chat. They *all* needed to hear what he had to say.

He saw Emily Adams shuffle into the kitchen, light the lantern, and fire up the cook stove. She filled the coffee pot, added grounds and pulled a cast iron pan from an overhead hook.

Her moves were automatic, having moved to the same choreography year after year with no change in her dance card. But there had been change in *her*.

Her gray hair was tied in a messy bun at the back of her head, and she wore a shapeless faded day dress. It hung from her shoulders and gaped where a button was missing. That surprised Bear. He recollected Mrs. Adams as a picture of meticulousness. Strong and robust. He knocked softly, not wanting to startle her, but she jerked anyway.

Emily glanced toward the stairs, wondering if she should get her husband or one of the boys but, instead, answered the door herself.

"What can I do for you Mister . . . What do I call you?"

"Bear. I'm Patrick and Abby's friend. We've met."

"Yes. I know. It's just hard to call you an animal."

"I would like to speak with you and your husband, ma'am, and your sons."

Emily's eyes narrowed, and she glanced again at the stairs hoping to hear feet coming to the kitchen. Her arms tightened against her sides, and she went motionless and stared toward the bacon beginning to sizzle in the pan.

"Why?"

"I'd prefer to wait for the rest. Would you get them, please?"

Bear's voice was respectful, almost peaceful. He'd thought about how best to deal with the Adams men, how to do it without harm to innocents. He didn't know if this would work, but he wanted to give it a try.

Frank Sr. came in first, still tucking his shirt into his trousers. His hair stuck up at odd angles like thick, coarse hair will, and he hadn't bothered to put on his socks. They stuck out of one pocket. He stopped when his head came up and he saw Bear in the room.

"What the hell. What are you doing here? It's damn near dawn."

"Hello, Frank."

He didn't return the greeting and sat and tugged on his socks, still staring at Bear. "What do you want?"

"To talk with your family. And you."

"I'm here. Talk," Frank growled.

"I'll wait for the rest."

"You'll do what I damn well say in my house, mister. You can get out if you think otherwise."

"Frank," Emily said. It was a soft word but punctuated with years of knowledge and life. She poured three cups of coffee and slid the bacon to the back of the wood stove where it wouldn't burn. She didn't take a seat, but stood at her husband's shoulder with one hand on it while she sipped. "Get the boys," Frank told her.

"Cecily?" she asked.

Bear nodded. "But not the youngsters.

She left, and the two men glared at each other without speaking. Bear's jaw clenched when he pictured Shorty beaten and bloody. Frank's did when he felt the shackles of feeling a prisoner in his own kitchen. For some reason, he did, and they pinched.

"I don't have time to sit around talking to Abby's friends," her husband said, coming down the hallway. Fact is, I don't want to talk to him at all."

"Well, I'll be doing most of the talking," Bear said when Frank came into the room, followed by Terry, Cecily, and

George who rubbed his eyes with one hand and ran the other over his head. He looked like he'd had a rough night, and his eyes were shot with red.

Terry didn't look much better, but at least his eyes were clear. Cecily grabbed at the ties of her robe and pulled them tight, her startled eyes, moving from one face to the next, lit with questions.

"Have a seat," Bear said.

"Can we at least get coffee?" Frank growled.

Bear waved a hand, and Emily moved to the pot, pulled out four more cups and poured. She distributed the hot liquid and reclaimed her stand at her husband's side.

The lines in Bear's beard were red, but no one at the table knew what that meant. They only saw the eyes, the direct gaze, the rigid stare. They were opened wide, showing white all around the dark irises, pupils large and somehow frightening. But Frank Sr. wasn't afraid of Bear – because he didn't fear anyone.

Bear lowered his head like a bull about to charge, his chest filled, and he lifted his hard eyes to them.

"I've been considering the events going on, in and around Idlewild, for some time. Bricks thrown through windows. Trees falling in front of buggies. Stable men getting thrashed. Last night I put it together. I figured it out. It's the Adams boys."

"Look here, you ass. You can't come barging into my home and say . . ."

"Yes. I can. I am. Shut up and listen." He turned to Emily. "Your sons have been up to no good, Mrs. Adams. Or do you think they're just boys being boys?"

As Bear watched, a bit of his resolve melted at the pain in her face. It was scrunched up like a piece of old steel wool, her lips were grimaced and pulled in between her teeth so she wouldn't cry out. She shook her head.

He turned back to old Frank. "I believe your . . . boys, dropped a large tree on Abby and her friends. Could have killed them. Most likely they meant to."

"I'm not listening to this crap," the old man bellowed, and rose from his chair.

Emily pushed him down.

"You need to leave, Mister Bear. It's time we get to work."

"No, Mrs. Adams. I'm not done." Bear took a sip of coffee and a breath.

"My best friend in the world is lying in a bed at the hotel in a coma. Last night he was beaten. Not by one man. *One* didn't do it the honorable way because *one* couldn't. They probably clubbed him from behind while he was talking with people he knew. Otherwise, he would've been on guard for trouble." He inspected each set of eyes before continuing. "Boys will be boys?"

"Probably bootleggers," Terry said with a sneer.

"You're crazy, mister," Frank Sr. said, his face purple with rage.

Bear held his hand up for silence and stood, his eyes black and menacing.

"I promise you this. If Shorty doesn't recover, if Abby or Edwin or anyone else is harmed, those responsible, one by one, I will see dead. Look behind you. I'll be there."

Al sat at the small table watching Shorty in repose, at peace and warm in the sunlight. Her quiet hands rested on her lap, and her face wore content. She didn't mind the hours spent with Shorty, even though he slept and wasn't much company. It seemed as if they were communicating without words – something she was used to and good at. Shorty, too.

Once in a while, she dampened the cloth and ran it over his face. She didn't know if it helped or not, but she saw the muscles of his jawline relax when she did and figured it felt good even if no one had told her to do it.

She put a hand over his and was only mildly surprised when he covered it with a warm palm. A smile lit her eyes and reached her lips, and she felt a faint spark of hope. When he opened his eyes again, she'd know.

Cassandra flitted in and out of the room all day, pulled up his eyelids and peered in. She grumbled a few words, mixed more tea and handed it to whoever stood watch.

If it happened to be Al, she took direction and didn't question her. If Abby stood guard, she wanted to know what it contained, what it would do for Shorty, and if it came from a bat or a toad. Sometimes Cassandra raised an eyebrow and answered her. Other times, she made gurgling sounds in the back of her throat, and Abby backed away and let her do her work.

"Why won't he wake up?" Abby asked. "Shouldn't he be awake by now?" Darkness had fallen, and Shorty had been asleep for most of twenty-four hours. "This can't be good for him."

"Why?" Cassandra asked.

"Because . . . well, he's not eating anything . . . and he needs nourishment to get well, and . . . I don't know, Cassandra. Because I want him to wake up and for everything be normal again."

The healer almost smiled.

"If we could run the universe by your desires, Abigail, what a strange place it would be."

Abby tilted her chin and snorted, wanting to be miffed, but couldn't find it in her.

"Why? Why do you think so? I'm not so strange."

"Maybe not strange, as in bizarre. That's me," she said with some satisfaction in the knowledge. "Your kind of strange is more like unusual and sometimes inexplicable. That's not so bad."

"And sweet," Bear said from the doorway. "Our Abby is sweet."

"That's not a word that comes to mind when I visualize Abby," Cassandra said. "Doesn't show up in the tea leaves either."

"Then you don't know her like I do." Bear kissed her cheek. "How's our boy?"

"Still asleep. Did you get some?

"I did, and I know you need to get downstairs, so I'll take over here."

Phantom climbed his leg and curled around his shoulders. He shoved his white face into Bear's neck, cat-talk for *I love you.* Cleo waited for him to sit. She behaved slightly better when it suited her, and orange Bob increased the decibels of his purr to remind them who Shorty belonged to. It was a feline festival – their favorite humans held captive.

Abby kissed the top of Bear's head and lingered there.

"I know," he said.

She went to her room to splash water on her face, brush her hair, and slip into a clean dress. She didn't check the mirror because she knew what would be there – puffy eyes, drawn face. Sleep deprivation did that. She pinched her cheeks, hoping for some color, and gave a ragged laugh at herself.

Sure, and that will make you beautiful, Abby.

"I can work the bar, lass," Patrick said, his tired eyes taking in Abby's drawn face. "It's quiet tonight. Maybe close early."

"Thanks, Da, but this is where I need to be right now. Bear's sitting with Shorty, and Cassandra will be checking on him in a while. This will be good for me."

"If you're sure, I'm gonna retire. Would ye pour a wee Irish for your favorite man?"

"I'd prefer ale, Abigail," Samuel said, taking the stool beside Patrick.

"So, you think you're my favorite, Samuel? Since when?"

"Sure, I am. Always was."

"Somebody's been lying to you, probably your mama since the day you were born." She slid a glass to her da, said goodnight and went to pour Samuel's amber colored ale.

"Thank you, Abby. How's our boy?"

"Sleeping all the time. How'd you find out about it?"

"Everyone's talking."

"I never thought to see my Shorty this way. He is . . . has always been a rock. My rock. And Bear, too"

"*Your* Shorty?"

She felt tears at the back of her eyes and turned away, grabbed a towel and dragged it across the wooden bar, rubbing where there was nothing to clean.

"Yes. Mine." When Samuel lowered his head to peer at her, she squinted her eyes and tossed her hair in defiance. "He is, Samuel."

"I saw Frank today."

Abby stepped back, looked around the bar for some reason to not have to listen to Samuel, but only three people sat at a table, and they were nursing drinks that didn't need tending. Two others sat at the bar, Joe Foster at one end and a man she didn't know at the other.

She asked the stranger if he wanted a refill. He declined, gulped the last of his coffee and left. She couldn't make herself ask Joe and strolled back to Samuel.

"You're stuck with me, Abigail."

"Where'd you see him?"

"Coming out of Jesse's office."

She chewed her lip and lowered her head. So, he'd gone to get the papers like she'd asked him to do. It hurt. She didn't know what to do with her feelings, with this entire day of sorrow, and it felt like it had been with her for a lifetime.

"Did you send him there?" He touched the newly empty finger.

She raised her head and looked into his black eyes. They were empty of everything but empathy. What she saw reflected her wretchedness, her worry and guilt, her doubt, and she wondered how that could be. Did he see inside her, or was she an open book and he a looking glass?

"I'll leave you two love birds alone." Joe slid off his stool, pasted a nasty smirk on his face and watched for a reaction. They disappointed him.

When the three at the table left, Abby took the glasses to the kitchen, wiped the table and was done – in so many ways.

"Want some company on the porch?" Samuel asked.

She didn't think twice. "Yes. I would. Let me check on Shorty first." She poured three short whiskeys and took one upstairs with her.

Bear sat relaxed with his feet on the table, his eyes on his friend. An open book rested in his lap. She put the glass in front of him and her hand on his.

"Thanks."

"I can take over in about an hour, Bear."

"No need."

"You can't stay up all night again."

"Cassandra will be back at three. I'm picking up Al, and she'll take over till she has to work."

"God, you are something. All of you."

He stood and wrapped his arms around her. His chin rested on her head, and his heart beat with hers. They were siblings without seed, loved without lust. She, Bear and Shorty shared one heart, and she'd always known it.

"You are, too, Abs. Get some sleep."

"Soon. I want to talk with Samuel for a bit - some family porch sitting. Then I will."

Bear pushed her away and peered into her eyes.

"You need me?"

"Course not. Samuel's a friend. I'm convinced of that - sometimes. Other times - well, he knows how to incite my wrath." She chuckled with the thought, and Bear relaxed.

"Shorty thinks he's a good man. That says something. Go have porch time." He walked her to the door and reclaimed the chair and book.

Samuel had their drinks and two chairs pulled into the far corner of the porch. They were the only ones enjoying the night, a rare occurrence. It took Abby a moment to locate him and thought he might have changed his mind and gone home.

"Over here, Abby."

She took the glass he offered, sat and sipped. The breath leaving her lungs took too long, held too much angst, and Samuel took care with his own breathing not to repeat it.

He put his head against the seat back and made careful, meditative fills, watched her hand on the arm of the chair and waited for the fingers to still. He didn't comment on the day or the moon or Cassandra who prowled the water's edge. He let the owl speak without an aside, the croaking frog make his thunder and her loon wail, waiting for her to give life to his song with her own words.

"Yes. I sent him to Jesse's."

"Good for you."

Samuel retrieved his watch, flipped it open and stared at it. He didn't care what time it was. Never did. What he cared about was her voice. It resonated pain, and he didn't want to cause her any more.

"You have somewhere else to be?" she asked.

More hurt. It reached across the brief space between their chairs, and its fingers wrapped around his throat. He struggled to speak without revealing how much he saw.

"I don't have much good to say about your husband . . ."

"I know that," she interrupted, with snapped intensity.

"I'm sorry, Abby."

"No, I am, for barking at you." She pinched the bridge of her nose and closed her eyes. "You didn't know Frank very well. He didn't understand me . . . at all, but he wasn't a bad man. He cared about a lot of things. The farm, the land, animals, and about Al. But. . . He killed. And I let it go. I told him to go." She bit her knuckles and her eyes filled with tears. "I'm going to have to live with that.

Samuel pulled his chair around in front of her. He tilted her face up and took her hands in his.

"Listen to me. I believe you did the right thing." He smoothed a hand over her fidgeting fingers.

She pulled them from him and covered her face. In time, she took them away, and her back was straight and stiff, but to Samuel, it looked breakable. Like a brittle limb, she could snap in a gentle breeze.

"It was right. I know it," she said.

"Why don't you sound like you mean it?"

Her shoulders gave a tired shrug.

"Frank took matters into his own hands," Samuel said, "like my friends and I did – just one step further. Maybe he shouldn't have taken it that extra step, but a lesser one wouldn't have saved Al from more abuse."

"I know. But death is so . . ."

He let it go. He couldn't make it right for her. Some principles didn't leave room for what her husband had done, and she'd sacrificed ethics to let him go free. What had it taken to get her to this point? A storybook belief in love? Desire for a marriage like her mother and father's?

He looked at her hand without the ring, wanted to put his over it, but didn't.

"Do you love him, Abby? Maybe you could go with him? Some place where no one knows him and start over again."

She snorted, a laugh without mirth.

"If I'd gone where he wanted in the first place, this might not be happening. I didn't. We didn't love each other enough." The next words came from the back of her throat. "Maybe not at all."

Samuel's resolve gave way, and he put his hand on hers. He didn't respond to her admission, didn't caress her hand, didn't do anything but breathe and let the skin of his palm sense the back of her slender hand.

The moon crawled across the sky, and the loon was silent.

Chapter Thirty-three

Emily twisted the flowered apron in unsteady hands and watched her oldest son pack clothes into an old army duffle bag. He didn't bother to fold them. He never did because he wouldn't be bothered. He stuffed them into corners and pockets, any place they landed that had an inch of space. The bag bulged, and he swore and yanked on the straps to get it to close.

"Please don't leave, Frank. Why do you have to?"

She'd been talking, nonstop and following him since he'd come back from Jesse's office. She'd followed as he took the stairs two at a time to the room he'd lived in since boyhood and out of the bassinette.

It hadn't changed much. A few small shooting trophies stood on a shelf, aligned by year. A baseball mitt crouched like an animal on the dresser, waiting for a hand to slide into it and punch it into shape again. His first pellet gun leaned in a corner, covered in dust and cobwebs.

Cleaning was off limits.

They were remnants of his boyhood. Nothing decorated a wall or a surface commemorating his adult life, his marriage, his service. Either Frank quit making memories at some point in time after a specified number of years called him grown, or he didn't care enough to be reminded. No wedding picture hung on the wall. No mention of life as a married man.

She followed him when he sprinted down the stairs and went to the back porch where they kept the fishing gear. He wouldn't leave his rods and reels – nor the twelve-gauge hanging on the wall. His eyes ignited, and he shed some of the long-harbored anger as he thought about all the hunting and fishing he'd do in Montana. He didn't need Abby. He didn't need anyone. He was free.

"Will you be back? When will you come home again? We're your family, Frank." Tears flowed down the deep creases in her face, and her lips trembled. She shriveled in front of his eyes, and her death occurred to him. He didn't know if he'd ever see her again. He lied.

"Course I'll be back. I just can't say when."

Terry came in twirling a revolver, pointed it at a flower pot and pretended to shoot it.

"Nice, huh? It's yours. You might need it up in the mountains fending off the wolves and women. Damn. Wish I was going."

"Come on. Room for two on this trip," Frank said.

"Stop it. Both of you. You've got a farm and a family to take care of, Terry. And quit shooting the plant. I don't like it when you do that."

Terry's eyes narrowed, and his lips painted a white slash across his face. "Don't I know all that." He tossed the gun at Frank and spun to leave. "Anything you want me to tell your dearly beloved about your little vacation?"

"I think you've done enough. Leave things the hell alone."

"Somebody'll pay for breaking up this family, Frank, and you know it. George is mad as a hornet. Spitting mad. No telling about him. Dad, too."

"I said leave it be."

"You can tell George yourself. He's right here."

The sneer on Terry's face ate at Frank. He was his little brother, but he didn't trust his common sense. George either. They lived in a bubble and thought rules were only for other people. Never them. He recognized that trait in himself, too, but . . .

"Lunch is ready, boys," Emily said. "Be good, now, and come on in and eat."

"You hear me, George? Let it go. I mean it, damn it."

Cecily was putting food on the table and Chunk and Bailey were tousling on the floor, one crying and the other laughing. Frank Sr. booted one in the back.

"Quit bawling like a girl. Punch him back."

"Stop. Be good boys and go wash up. Now," Cecily said.

She tugged at Bailey's shirt to pull him from his brother. Bailey swung and connected with Chunk who wailed louder. She sent Bailey off to wash his hands and snuggled the crying boy to her, patting and making soothing sounds to stop his tears.

Frank Sr. glared at her. "You're making babies out of your sons. Boys fight. That's what they do, so let 'em do it." He shoved his chair out with the toe of his boot and sat, his heavy body punctuating the words and making the chair creak.

"That idiot friend of Frank's wife got one thing right; boys are gonna damn well be boys, and they ain't worth a damn if they ain't."

Shorty woke to see her silhouetted in the window of his room. Warm early morning sun bathed her in a yellow glow and made her look like an angel or a daffodil with a white center. Long blonde hair fell past her shoulders and across her face. She held a book in her lap but wasn't reading. She'd been staring at the silent man in the bed.

When his eyelids fluttered, so did her heart, and she worked at stilling it so she could disguise her happiness, shove it back into the crevasse where it wouldn't be seen and recognized and taken from her.

He blinked quickly, thinking the angel would disappear if he closed his eyes and opened them again. Once. Twice he did it. She was still there – the angel.

"You're awake. I'll go get Abby."

"Wait."

She waited, watched his mind work. He looked around, stretched the fingers on both hands, flinched when the left one gave pain, and flinched again when he turned his head.

"You have a knot on your head," she said. "And your arm was sort of . . . distorted."

He moved his toes and legs, and she saw relief pass over his face. When perspiration beaded on his forehead, she dipped a cloth in cool water and passed it over his brow.

"How long have I been out?"

"Long enough I worried."

"Have you been here awhile?"

"Not too."

He stopped her hand and held it, looked at the pale translucence of her skin, almost transparent in its whiteness, her clear blue eyes, the half-smile that was wholly Strange Al, and knew she had been with him during his recovery. He'd felt her there through the fog of pain, through the comatose, laudanum confusion. He grasped a thread of knowledge; she'd been beside him, tending him.

"I thought I was dead, and you were an angel."

"Hardly that."

Shorty cleared his throat. It hurt to move. A hand went to his chest and touched the wrappings meant to brace his broken ribs.

"Get these off, please. I can't breathe."

"You need them."

"No. Help me take them off."

Al pulled down the sheet covering his chest, looked away from his eye, and began unwrapping the bindings. She had to stretch across the bed and over his massive chest since the tight wraps encased his torso in one long, slender strip of fabric.

"Just kneel over me," he said

She did and unwrapped several layers, her hands sliding under his back and dragging the wrap from under him, when she felt his hands on her arms. He groaned, a soft sound that whispered like his words.

"Sorry. Trying not to hurt you."

"You're not. Look at me, Al."

She did, hair framing her pixie face, eyes wide.

"Could you love an old man like me?"

"You're not old."

"Older than you."

"I'm older than anyone my age."

"I know. I'm sorry."

There were no words to describe the joy coursing through her. Heart exploding, beating. Blood pounding. But she couldn't say those things.

She said, "Yes. I could. I do."

He placed a soft kiss on her forehead and a slow, even more tender one on her lips. She stretched beside him and fell asleep, exhausted from the vigils she'd undertaken and the worry. When Abby walked in, Shorty's eyes were on Al's face as she slept. He put a finger to his lips for quiet, and Abby closed the door to let them sleep. What she saw was the best medicine. For both of them.

Hundreds of Canadian geese crashed into Lake Idlewild, wings flapping in panic as they tilted and wobbled over the water's surface before settling on it. Their honks filled the sky and competed with several green-headed mallards and a pair of trumpeter swans trying to stay out of the way.

Fall had arrived. Red and orange leaves played in the crisp breeze and piled at the edge of the woods.

Abby and Edwin brought in the last of the garden vegetables: large beets with wilted tops, acorn and butternut squash that would winter in the cool root cellar, and the last of the curly kale that would make its way into Patrick's potato soup.

"Thanks for your help, Edwin. I love the garden, but it is a lot of work."

"I'm here to do what I'm told."

"We're glad to have you, Edwin. However, . . ."

"Uh oh. Here it comes." He peered over his glasses at her. "Time for me to move on?"

Abby lifted a basket of beets and balanced it on a hip.

"No. Not at all. I'm worried about winter coming and you still sleeping out in the stable. It's going to get cold."

"Nah. I'll be fine. Animals keep it warm in there. If it gets too cold, I'll slip in the back door and sleep in the pantry. Won't be nothing to do that." He peered at her again, taking note of her acceptance of his words. "Less you want me to skedaddle, that is. Is that it?"

Abby headed for the kitchen door, basket on one hip, a bag of kale in the other hand.

Is that it? Do I want Edwin gone?

"No. That isn't it, Edwin. I'm sorry if it sounded so. Will you bring the bushel of squash, please?"

"Look, Missus. Can you stop a minute?"

When Abby stopped walking and turned, he continued. "I'm sorry if my coming here caused you a problem. And I'm sorry if I thought I recognized Jesse James in that picture you showed me. I was probably wrong, you know. I get addled, and I don't even know my own name sometimes."

He tried out a smile to see how she'd taken his words. He didn't want to leave Idlewild and the hotel. He knew a good thing when he had it. Three meals a day – tasty ones – a place to sleep and nice people to spend a few minutes with.

Abby's lips fluttered when she blew out a breath. She dropped the bag of kale and kicked at it.

"You don't need to lie, Edwin. It's over. We're just living each day the best we can. All of us. But . . . if you wouldn't mind not saying anything about the picture, I'd really appreciate it."

Edwin's grin broadened. "What picture? You got a picture?" He led the way to the kitchen with his load of squash. Abby picked up the abused kale and followed.

"Oh. Forgot to tell you. I'm gonna give my horse to Al. She can ride it back and forth to work."

"You don't need to do that."

"Kinda do."

"You're a good man, Edwin."

"Maybe."

Al had taken over breakfast preparations, Charity the room cleaning with Betty, and Abby was free. She dumped the garden bounty in the pantry and asked Edwin to saddle Marie. She didn't want to, but she had to go.

When she knocked on the door, her mother-in-law didn't turn. Abby heard a tired voice say, "Come on in," and opened the door.

"Saw you riding down the drive. What do you want, Abigail?"

"Can we have a cup of coffee and talk? Will you sit a bit?"

"I don't want to see you, Abigail. I don't want to look at your face."

"Please?"

Emily swallowed hard, dried her hands on her apron and grabbed the coffee pot sitting at the back of the stove keeping warm. She poured a cup and put it in front of Abby.

"I don't even know how my daughter-in-law drinks her coffee. Isn't that something?" She warmed her own cup and sat. "I should know how you drink coffee. A thing like that family knows."

"I like it black." Abby wrapped her hands around the cup, warming them.

"Of course."

"What does that mean, Mrs. Adams?"

"Nothing. It doesn't mean anything. Why are you here?"

"I wanted to explain, to try to help you understand why Frank and I, why . . . We didn't know each other. Not at all. We wanted different things. I know divorce is an ugly thing, and I know you hate it that your son moved away. It was best for him." She looked at the coffee in her cup through shimmering eyes and blinked. "I care about Frank, Mrs. Adams. I don't even know where he went."

"Montana. Frank went to Montana where he could hunt and fish all he wants. That what you wanted to know?"

"I hope Montana makes him happy. And that you'll be contented knowing he's happy." Abby fumbled for words. She wasn't sure why she needed this talk with Emily, but she wanted her to understand as much as she could. Maybe it would be easier when she missed her oldest son. She couldn't tell her the real reason Frank had to go.

"And I wanted to invite you to church with me. I know how hard this is for you, but you might find some peace there, Mrs. Adams. I'll come out and get you in the buggy and bring you home afterwards. Please say you'll think about it."

Emily's eyes hardened. Her hands shook, and coffee sloshed into the saucer.

"You and your colored church! You just don't get it, Abigail. You're the reason Frank is gone. You!"

"That's not true. It isn't, Mrs. Adams."

"You and your colored friends. And you want me to sit with them? You want me to sing with them? Pray with them? The only praying I'll do is for my family. Not you. You're not family. And not at your church. I'll pray here in my own kitchen."

"Mrs. Adams . . . Please believe I want the best for Frank, for all of us." Abby begged with her eyes, with her heart.

Emily shoved back her chair and stumbled. Abby reached to steady her, and Emily slapped her hand away. She straightened her back and strode to the door. Autumn air gusted in as she threw it open, and Emily glared.

"You want the best? Your friend is spreading lies about all my sons. Ask him. And now you want to make nice and take me to your heathen church? This is not the first time I've told you to stay away from me and my family. You're poison. And I'm saying it again, you're no kin. You're not welcome here, Abigail Riley."

Abby gave up. She shouldn't have come. It was a stupid idea. She wanted to ask what Emily meant about her friend spreading lies but couldn't. It was time to go.

"I'm sorry. I truly am."

She fled through the door, grabbed Marie's reins, and, without a backward look, rode hard for town. She slowed her mare halfway home and let her amble.

"Sorry, Marie. Saying that a lot lately, aren't I. How do I manage to mess things up so badly?"

Marie snorted, and Abby took it as assent.

"Thanks a lot. A simple shake of your head would be better. I could use a friend."

Bear eased Shorty down the stairs late in the afternoon after a brief discussion concerning Bear's visit to the Adams' farm. He'd waited for his friend to recover a bit before sharing what he'd done.

"They seem to believe you?" Shorty asked.

"They might want to. If they need reminding, I'll do it."

Shorty ran a hand over his head and grimaced, spiking Bear's anger once again.

"You didn't tell me I had it wrong about the men who attacked you, so I'm assuming my two and two addition did add up to three?"

"I only saw two. Never saw the one behind me. Damn coward."

"They say why?"

"I remember so many words being tossed out in between boots and fists. Mostly about ruining Frank's marriage and sending George to jail, but about Sue and Sally and Gus and Betty, too. All mixed up together. They're crazy, those Adams men."

Bear's beard map grew red thinking about what they had done.

"You talking to the sheriff," he asked.

Shorty shook his head. "If need be, I'll take care of them myself."

"Not without me."

"Thanks. How's Abs?"

"Better off without Frank."

"She know about your visit?" Shorty asked.

"Nope. Or about who attacked you. Guess she doesn't need to unless one of them spills it."

"Then what?"

"Then I'll explain the best I can." He sat back in his chair. "You got anything you want to explain to *me*?"

Shorty's bare head grew pink. "Don't know what you mean."

"I think you do."

"Al said yes."

"Course she did. Knew that was going to happen a long time before you did."

Shorty swatted his best friend in the world, the brother he never had, the man he trusted with his life and more – with his respect, and he only needed an arm over Bear's shoulder to navigate the stairs.

The goal was the bar. He collapsed on a stool and tried to relax his shoulders. The ribs caused most of his pain, and shallow breaths were all he could manage.

"Praise the Lord," Sue said. "The big man is back, Halleluiah."

"Thanks, Sue," he whispered.

"Big guy. You're gonna have to do better than that, or I'm gonna stick my ear in your mouth."

"I'll try. No air."

She put an arm around his back and scooted closer.

"That's just fine. I kinda like the idea of my ear right up next to those pretty pink lips."

"Leave the man alone, Sue. He can hardly breathe with those broken ribs. He doesn't need you hanging all over him." Sally pulled her cousin off Shorty.

"Good to see you downstairs, my friend. Whiskey?" Abby asked. Her eyes were red rimmed but dry, and the sparkle hid somewhere down in her boots or she'd left it in her room when she dressed for work.

"Please. A hefty one. Upstairs seems to have taken the prohibition laws to heart."

He smiled. Shorty couldn't keep contentment from spreading all over his face. It shimmered in his eyes. He loved that slip of a woman and couldn't believe she gave it right back to him, bigger, harder, more. And she was beautiful and strong and didn't chatter on like a magpie. She was his very own Strange Al.

Seeing the light in his eyes brought a little to Abby's. She knew what kindled it and waited for either him or Al to spread the news. She slid the glass to him and reached out to brush a hand over his cheek. He held it there with his for a moment, warm hand on warm hand, and watched her eyes cloud. "I'm sorry, Abby."

"Don't be. You should be happy. When you going to say something?"

"That's up to Al."

"I'm happy for you, Shorty. I really am."

"Those are awful sad eyes for a happy woman."

"Don't look."

Samuel sauntered in and sat next to Bear. For some irrational reason, his flawless elegance annoyed her. She wanted to mess something up, wrinkle his satin vest, spill ink on the white cuffs sticking out a perfect half inch from his suit coat sleeves. She wanted to muddle up his meticulousness.

He must have picked up on her attitude because he reverted to a discussion they'd had long ago, one that had broken the constraints of their earlier cantankerous relationship.

"Mrs. Uncle Tom," he said, raising both eyebrows and smoothing his mustache. "Might I have an ale?"

"Certainly, Samuel. I would *deem* it a pleasure to serve you."

"Touchy, tonight, aren't you? And I told myself I'd be nice. Be ready for church by eight. I'll be picking you up."

"Don't tell me what to do." She whirled around to get his ale, filled the glass and plunked it in front of him. Foam spilled over the rim and pooled around the bottom of the glass. He picked it up, ran a finger under the glass, and looked for something to wipe it on.

"Use your sleeve like everybody else," she said, and walked away.

Samuel grinned at her retreating back. She made him smile. Patrick shuffled in from the kitchen and took the stool next to him. Abby brought his Irish and set it down.

"Thanks, lass."

The look she gave her da wasn't a smile, but something more, something undefinable, a passing of affection without words, and Samuel pondered the bond between this father and daughter.

It seemed they had perfect accord, and maybe their unity had defeated her marriage. He scoffed at his musing but reconsidered. Maybe their relationship hadn't caused the crack, but he figured it had allowed a fissure to turn into a canyon.

He didn't think Frank was a bad man, but he hadn't merited Abby. He couldn't think of anyone who did, and if *he* was smart, he'd stay away from the hotel and everyone in it.

Her.

Samuel sipped until the guests were gone from the bar and helped her tidy the room and make a tray for the porch.

"It'll soon be too cold to enjoy this," he said by way of excuse. "You'll have to wear your woolies."

"My woolies aren't appropriate conversational pieces, Samuel." She sat next to her da with Bear on her other side.

Samuel furrowed his brow, but only slightly. "Intentional?" he said in an aside to Abby as she handed him his nightcap.

"I don't know what you mean."

"Yes, you do."

"Be quiet, Samuel." Her sass wiggled his mustache into a grin and lit his patrician features.

She sometimes wondered what it would take on any given day to loosen his attitude of indifference. She never knew in advance what his response would be and was glad to see a grin tonight.

"Ye good, lass?" Patrick asked. "Ye seem a mite perturbed. Yehudi living under your petticoats?"

"What's going on with the attention to my undergarments tonight?" she asked and followed it with a huff. "I'm okay, Da. Just tired."

"Me too, lass. I'll sip a bit of Irish and slip into the fairy forest early. Will you check on Shorty, Bear?"

"Edwin gave his mare to Al. Did you know that?" Abby said. Two heads nodded, and Samuel turned to stare.

"An appropriate move. She'll use it well."

The loon wailed, twisting Abby's heart. She missed him when he left for winter and looked forward to his return in the spring because his moan heralded the coming warm weather, crocus blossoms and green buds making a haze on the maple trees.

But this night's song blew shivers down her spine. Winter was on its way.

"Beaver moon tonight," Samuel said, and added a goodnight to Patrick when he rose to leave.

"A few years ago, I'd be setting traps," Bear said.

"Why is it a beaver moon?" Abby asked.

"Algonquin name for November's full moon," Bear said. "They set traps by its light minutes before the swamps freeze. But some say it's because beavers build their winter homes under its light. Others call it a frost moon, instead." He studied the moon's face and its path on the rippled water.

Abby studied him.

"Lots of words for you. Were you happiest in the woods, Bear? Are you happy here?"

He drained his glass and stood. "I'm needed and loved. What more can a man ask?"

He waved to Cassandra who appeared in the shaft of moonlight streaking across the lake. She returned his greeting and spread her arms, the long sleeves of her gown draping downward. Her shadowy image looked like a seraph, and her sleeves were its wings.

Abby expected her to fly off into the dark heavens at any moment and closed her eyes to rid herself of the sight and the impression. When they opened, Cassandra had blended into the dark shadows and Bear had gone inside.

"How does she do that?" she said.

"What?"

"Appear and disappear. Turn herself into things she isn't. It's . . . uncanny and . . . disturbing."

"What things?"

"Seraphs, witches, you name it. Maybe cats and squirrels." She watched the smile grow on his face and blessed the moon for giving her the view. "I was the witch tonight. Thanks for putting up with me, Samuel."

He moved to Bear's chair and put his hand on hers. "Like Bear, I'm needed. Probably loved, too."

The last two words danced on his lips. He was playing with her, and she needed to play. He could leave and save himself, or he could stay.

"I'm happy," he said.

Chapter Thirty-four

Betty climbed on the mare behind Al early Sunday morning to ride to Bunny Parker's house. Al promised Abby she'd attend church, and she knew Abby had spent long hours trying to encourage white residents to help her desegregate services. Al didn't care where she attended or if she went at all. This was for her boss – because she cared about her.

"Hold on," she told Betty as she kicked the horse in the side to get her moving. "Let's go, Nag."

"Nag? What kind of a name is that for a horse?"

"Pa's idea of a good name, like Dog. Like Al."

"We could change it," Betty said, sounding girly and giggly. Her mood had always been sunny, but lately it had gotten downright giddy. Al knew the change in her friend had something to do with Benjamin. "Let's do it," Betty said, "and we could change yours, too."

"Al suits me."

"Shorty coming?"

"Didn't say."

He was standing outside the door when Nag ambled into the yard. He moved toward them, tied the reins Al handed him to a low branch, and lifted Betty from the mare. He took a little longer letting Al's feet touch the ground, and the color on his cheeks told a perfect story, a fairytale, complete with damsel and knight and a rescue in an enchanted forest.

"Is Mama here yet?" Betty asked, and tried not to watch. "Or Abby?"

"Your mama," Shorty said. "She's organizing food."

"Darn. I didn't think to bring any." Shame flooded Betty's face. She was an adult, living away from home, taking on all the responsibilities of adulthood, and she had committed the first in community sins – no dish to pass.

Al pulled two loaves of bread from the saddlebag and squinted her eyes, let them play for a moment on Betty's face before handing one to her. "Gotcha covered."

"You're something, girl. How'd you get so smart?"

Shorty held out his arms to escort both women into the house, one on either side. He couldn't remember feeling so good about the world.

Jesse met them at the door and held it open with a wide, toothy grin.

"Do my eyes deceive me? Mister Shorty in church?" While Daisy climbed up Shorty's leg and into his arms, Jesse stuck his head out the door and looked in all directions.

"What you looking for?" Betty asked.

"The posse chasing Shorty. Can't see why else he'd be here less it's feminine persuasion."

He glanced at Al, but not too long. He didn't want to embarrass the girl – his word for her – tiny, fair faced, fragile, even though she wasn't. She just looked that way. He was happy to see her in church. Shorty, too.

A shiny automobile pulled up to the door, and Samuel hopped out, ran around to the other side and opened the door. After some pushing and pulling, Sue rolled out, and Sally spewed from the tiny back seat, followed by Abby.

An audience had gathered, eyes wide and lips tilted in surprised delight, as they watched them maneuver out of the vehicle.

"Any more in there?" Jesse asked. "You packed them in like sardines in a can, Samuel. How long did *that* take?"

Samuel couldn't help the grin dancing around his lips when he remembered getting them all in. Abby thought she'd outsmarted him by inviting the cousins to go to church with her, and the light of amusement had played in her eyes and on her lips.

He'd like a picture of her and Sally stuffed into the second seat that wasn't meant to be a seat. He'd witnessed some inappropriate visions while they settled and knew Abby would blush if she realized. He'd long remember the tangle of their arms and legs.

"Need to stretch a bit, ladies?" he asked, and Sue answered.

"I'm peachy, Samuel. That leather seat is perfect for my round bottom. I might have to buy myself one of these . . . What is it, Samuel?"

"Model T. And I think you should. We can paint it shiny red."

Bunny's elegant form greeted them at the door and calmed the hilarity. Not intentionally, or maybe so, but, when she put her satiny cheek to the newcomers' as she welcomed them, one by one, they calmed and set aside the jokes and improper thoughts. They were in church, in Bunny's house.

Pastor Jenkins bowed his head and raised his hands, the signal for everyone to be seated, and like good little sheep, his flock found chairs or a space to stand at the back. He lifted his hymnal, told them the song they were to sing, and the door opened. Charity Evans walked in to a sustained gasp and barely muted whispers from the congregation.

"That's the white preacher's daughter."

"She's been to college."

"Trying to show she's open minded, now, showing up here."

"Shush and be nice. You're in church.

Charity's bob swung as she acknowledged wide eyes and moved across the room to stand with the men at the back. A calf length dress hung from her shoulders in the new shapeless, shift style and shocked the matrons by exposing calves and ankles.

Benjamin, sitting next to Betty, rose and pointed to Charity and back at his now empty chair. She shook her head.

"I'm in good company," she said and indicated Shorty and Samuel who she'd come between.

"She's gonna get herself in trouble," Betty said, and pulled Benjamin back down in his chair.

"I think she likes trouble," Abby said, remembering the first time she'd attended what many called the *colored* church. Edna and Jesse had called for her at the hotel, and she'd leaped at the opportunity to go. She'd met Samuel that day, and he'd been obnoxious. At least, she'd thought so at the time.

She looked at the people sitting on the chairs, children on the floor in the corner, and mostly men standing against the back wall. There were no strangers now. Even if she couldn't call them all friends, many were, and she knew them all by name. And they knew hers. She was acknowledged, if not accepted, and it felt right and good.

But the absence of white faces didn't feel good. No matter what she did to bring them all together, she could count them on the fingers of one hand. It was perplexing and frustrating.

"Maybe I'm wrong to want it," she whispered.

"Let's try this again," Pastor Jenkins said, adding, "Welcome, Charity."

Following the service, Al rode Nag back to the hotel. She'd promised to help Patrick with the evening meal and planned to spend some time with Shorty who rode next to her on his gelding. Samuel loaded the cousins and Abby back into his automobile, and Benjamin gave Betty a lift back to the farm.

It was a crisp fall day, and Dog met them on the porch. He'd been stretched out in a warm patch of sunlight and didn't hear them ride up, but felt their footsteps on the wooden slats of the porch. Benjamin scratched the old dog's head and sat on the swing.

"Catch some sun here for a bit?" he asked.

"I'd like that. Want some lemonade or coffee?"

"Nope." He patted the swing beside him. "Just yourself, Betty."

He put his arm around her shoulders when she sat and toed the porch to move them in a lazy, contented, soothing motion. She rested her head against the indent between his arm and chest, and her smile spoke to the trees and birds and sky. The world grew lilacs and butterflies. She'd been through the nightmare, and it had ended.

He knew about it and still loved her. The Lord was good, and Benjamin was perfect. What had she done to be so blessed?

A short distance away, eyes watched, hidden by the bushes at the side of the yard. He'd been there before. A matted patch of grass and weeds in the middle of the undergrowth showed where he knelt to observe. He'd been worried about the damned dog hearing the brush rustle, but it didn't care.

He'd seen Al as she fed the chickens, her slippered feet moving dust, fowl clucking their love, and heard the lowing of her heifer when she milked and brought the pail from the barn. Morning and night. But Al didn't bother him.

Betty did.

George had watched her stoke the stove and put breakfast on the table. Sometimes she still wore her nightclothes, and he created a tale. A passionate story of the two of them together. She set the table for him, too. He imagined the small breasts and brown legs he'd seen before and would again.

He took another swig of the whiskey in his nearly empty flask and choked back a cough. He'd sipped on it all the way through the connecting woods. He thought about Bear destroying his family. Making Frank leave. Threatening him. Threatening them all, and his anger burned deep. A fire in his belly grew as if someone deliberately threw tinder on it, stoking the flame. Over and over.

And he thought about Betty, remembered her under him like he did every night.

She belonged to him and always had. Betty was his. He'd claimed her with his body. Nobody had the right to take what belonged to him, and, when Benjamin brushed his hand over her hair, he jerked backwards, almost fell, and had to stop himself from bellowing.

Benjamin stood and strolled to his automobile, with Betty alongside. He had an arm around her waist as they walked, in no hurry to separate.

"What's the rest of your day like?" he asked, just to prolong his visit.

"Making a nice meal for Al. She'll be home soon."

"You like it here? Living with Al?"

"I do. We've become more than friends."

She laughed, and her smile reached Benjamin's eyes, too. His Betty was extraordinary, a beautiful woman inside and out.

"Explain," he asked.

Betty wrapped her arms around his waist and leaned back to look in Benjamin's face. George burned. His face grew purple, and he leaned forward to see better.

"When Abby asked me to be a friend to Al, I thought she was crazy. That could never happen." She tilted her head sideways. "You know we call her *Strange Al*? And she knows that's her name."

He nodded.

"She hardly talks at all, so you might think she isn't smart. But she is." Betty punctuated the point with a small fist on his chest. "She is smart and loving and loyal. I know that about her, and I love her. Is that weird?"

"No, but it's rare. You're lucky. Both of you are."

"But she's white. You noticed I'm not, right?"

"Guess I did." He dipped his head and touched his lips to hers, and she lifted her arms to wrap them around his neck and stood on her toes. A low groan came from Benjamin's throat as he tightened his hold on her.

A silent growl came from George. It took his total concentration to stay hidden. That man would be leaving soon. And she'd be his.

"I have to go, Betty. See you on Tuesday at the hotel?"

"Nothing could stop me." She turned to walk back to the porch. "You're something, Benjamin."

"And you. Lock your doors."

She sat in the swing before going in, watching him drive away, remembering how his hand had felt on her hair, how his lips caressed hers, how his love completed her, with warmth and fullness.

George thought about everything, too, and listened to the tires roll down the road and waited.

When she saw him, the terror in her eyes gave him joy he'd never known. It had been good before, but this was unparalleled. She was terrified.

Betty leaped for the door, but it was locked. She flew off the porch to run, anywhere, into the woods, down the road. Anywhere but here.

He grabbed her around the waist, picked her up and walked into the barn. She kicked, slammed her fists into him, clawed his face until blood ran, and he smiled. He loved it. He loved her.

Holding her under one arm, he cursed as she kicked and wiggled but managed to grab a rope from the wall and fling her to the ground so hard, the wind was knocked out of her. He tied her hands behind her back and dragged her to the center post.

Betty's brown face blanched a dusty gray as she gasped for air. Al had nearly died at this post at the hands of her own father. Did George know? Was that his plan? She stiffened her back and told him what he wanted to hear.

"Don't, George. I'll be good," she said. "Remember? You don't have to tie me up."

"But I want to, Betty. It'll be fun. Just you and me."

He yanked her to her feet and shoved her against the post, tying the rest of the rope around it. She could move, but she couldn't run away.

When he ripped her dress down the front and bared her breasts, she faltered in strength but refused to break. She stared into his eyes, daring him to make her close hers and shut him out.

No. No matter what he did, she wouldn't. Never. She'd watch every vile thing he did. She would force him to look into her eyes and see his evil reflected back at him. She would not bend. She stiffened her shoulders and thrust her breasts at him.

He pulled her body to his, let her feel his arousal, and ripped away the rest of her dress. His eyes traveled the length of her. He licked his lips.

It was harder to be courageous naked. She bent her knees in a fighting stance and tried to find strength enough to hate. When he ran his hands over her, she found it.

He glanced around the barn and saw what he needed. The riding crop. It danced in his hand as he flicked it back and forth, and Betty lifted her chin.

"Good, George. Make it easier for me to hate you." Her smile confused him.

The sting of the first touch of leather on her body startled her, but she could take it. She would. She watched his eyes glaze over and shimmer with the sick passion in his soul.

When the blood trickled down her belly, his joy exploded. He didn't know how much longer he could resist her. She needed him, too. He saw it in her eyes. They stared into his, begged him to take her.

Something was wrong. The chickens squawked, the heifer moaned, and Dog lay sleeping in the sun. Al tied the mare to a branch and went to look in the barn. Betty's eyes flickered to Al and quickly back to George.

Al flew to the house on silent feet, taking precious seconds to unlock the front door. She grabbed the rifle from its place on the wall, checked to make sure it was loaded, and was back at the barn in moments.

"George," she said at the door.

He turned toward her as Betty slid down the post, and Al pulled the trigger. She dropped the rifle and ran to Betty. Her fingers fumbled with the rope as she tried to untie her. "Hold still, girl."

But Betty kept turning, worried George would get up and attack them.

"He's dead, Betty."

"How do you know? You didn't look."

"I shot to kill."

"Oh, God. Oh, Lord."

"He needed to die."

Tears formed in Betty's eyes. Ones she wouldn't shed when he beat her. Ones she wouldn't shed when he violated her.

"God, now I cry."

"Go in the house, Betty. Wash up and put some salve on your cuts. Get dressed so we can go."

"Go where?"

"The hotel. I'll cover George and take care of the animals. Pack a bag," Al told her. "Wait. Don't wash up. Just put some clothes on and put these in a sack. Bring them." She held up the ripped dress lying bloodied by the center pole, the whipping post.

"Why . . . Oh. I see.

Betty looked at the body on the floor, the blood, the huge hole in his back where the bullet exited. It didn't look like the same person. Could this be the sick bastard who had brutalized her for years? This lump of flesh and bone lying on the floor of the barn? It was nothing, less than nothing, and would soon rot into the ground.

She felt sick to her stomach, but it wasn't for the man on the floor. It was for her friend.

"You won't go to jail, Al. He might have killed us both if you hadn't shot him."

"I know." But she didn't know for sure, and it wouldn't have made any difference in her decision to shoot George dead.

Betty climbed behind Al who urged Nag for a little more speed than she was used to. The lacerations in Betty's skin burned, and she felt blood still running when she moved. She tried not to groan.

"You okay?" Al asked.

"Sure."

They went straight to the stable and gave the mare to Edwin to rub down and feed. He saw the blood seeping through the fabric of her dress and turned his head away. He didn't want to pry.

Patrick was putting the finishing touches on the supper when they walked into the kitchen. He dropped the pot he had pulled from its hook, and it clattered onto the cupboard.

"What the hell? Abby! Get in here!"

He pulled out a chair and shoved Betty into it.

"Get some whiskey, Al. Bring the bottle."

"You okay, lass? Who hurt you? Abby said you were with Benjamin. Twasn't him, yes?"

"Yes."

"Benjamin did this?" The Irishman gave a guttural roar. His lips pulled back and showed his teeth. "We befriended him!"

"No. Yes, it wasn't him, Patrick. You confuse me."

"Ye wouldna lie for him."

"I *wouldna*. Geez, you've got me so addled I sound like you."

"Not such a bad thing, lass."

Al came back with the bottle, along with Shorty and Abby who poured liberal amounts for all of them. Bear followed to tell Abby not to rush. He'd take over the bar.

"We need the sheriff," Al said. "I killed George."

Shorty moved to her side, quickly for such a large man, and put an arm around her back.

"You're not serious," Abby said, but it came out a question because of the look in her eyes.

"I am. George is dead.

Betty tried to stand and sank back into her chair.

"She's telling the exact truth. George was whipping me. He'd hidden in the bushes by the house, and when . . . The short version is he stripped me, whipped me, and planned to rape me. I will tell Sheriff Hicks everything. This time. If I'd been more forthcoming long ago, Al wouldn't have had to kill anyone. I'm sorry, Al."

"George needed killing."

"I didn't clean up, so the sheriff can see the truth. Get him, please."

"I'll go," Shorty said. "You'll be okay?" he asked Al.

"I'll be fine."

"Where's George?"

"I left him where he fell, covered him with an old blanket. Don't know why."

Patrick followed him out to the stable where they talked while he saddled the gelding.

"Hicks may want to go get George first. I don't know," Shorty said. "See to it Betty stays as she is right now no matter how long it takes."

"Concerned about Al?"

"Sure. We don't know how Hicks will see it."

When Patrick went back in, they were sitting around the kitchen table.

"I have to set up the buffet," he said, and lifted the big pot of stew off the stove.

"I'll help." Al loaded several loaves of soda bread on a cutting board and followed him.

She came back for butter and a tray of bowls, shoved a hip against the swinging doors and left them again. Her face was set, her eyes bright, but tearless.

"I can do that, Al," Abby said, when she came back a second time. "Why don't you sit with Betty and let me help Da?"

"No. I'm fine."

"She's something." Betty twisted a strand of hair that had fallen over her face and staring at the doors Al had gone through. "Is she gonna be in trouble?"

Abby chewed her lip. She'd been wondering the same thing but wouldn't bring words to her fears. It wouldn't be fair if she went to jail for killing George. Al was right about one thing. He needed killing.

"We'll do everything to see that she isn't in trouble. Why didn't I think about this before? We need Samuel."

"What about Jesse?"

"Samuel is a criminal lawyer. He'll know what to do."

Abby stood up so fast her chair tipped over and crashed to the floor. Al poked her head through the door.

"You alright?"

"Yes. Tell Da and Bear I'll be gone for a bit. I'm going for Samuel."

He wore a shirt, no vest, no jacket. Abby stepped back when he opened the door, surprise widening her eyes.

"Wow. I wouldn't know you," she said, still panting and grasping at her chest. "You are earthly, after all."

"Abby, what are you doing?" He pulled her in and closed the door. "You shouldn't be here."

"I need you, Samuel."

His eyes lit, and the corners of his lips twitched. "I'm leaving that one alone."

"Seriously. Al might be in trouble, and I'll explain on the way. Okay?"

Samuel shrugged acceptance, slipped into his vest and jacket, and took her elbow to guide her down the steps and into his automobile.

"How'd you get here?"

"I ran."

"So, speak," he said, after he climbed in and they were rolling down the road.

"George Adams is dead. He was whipping Betty and going to rape her, again, and Al killed him. That's the short and sweet of it."

"Well, that is short."

"It's all I know."

"Let's leave it at that. I'll want to hear the story from Al and Betty, hopefully before Sheriff Hicks gets there.

Chapter Thirty-five

In a glance, Samuel's mind took in the situation in the hotel kitchen. Patrick ran in and out, dealing with guests who were finishing their meals. Betty sat in a blood-stained garment, obviously uncomfortable in the mess, her tattered dress on the table in front of her. Al sat across the table.

"Do you want to speak with them alone?" Abby asked.

"That's Al and Betty's call," Samuel said.

"We're family," Betty said. "All of us." She looked at Al whose dip of the head agreed.

They told the story, and Samuel asked clarifying questions which they answered. Their responses were confident and in agreement with each other. One time only did he hold up his hand to stop Al from speaking, when she said she intended to kill George.

"No, you didn't. You were stopping him from assaulting Betty and had to shoot when he turned and took a step toward you. Isn't that what happened?"

"Sure." Al knew Samuel was protecting her, but it galled her that she couldn't say George needed to die out loud. He did. Period.

"Isn't that what actually happened, Betty?" Samuel asked.

"Yes. Exactly. And you know that, Al. Whatever went on in your mind before the shot has nothing to do with anything. *That is* what happened." Betty stared hard at her friend, making her see what she saw.

The truth.

Sheriff Hicks and Shorty came in through the bar, and Shorty went to sit next to Al.

"Want privacy?" the sheriff asked, eyes on Abby, Patrick and Shorty.

"I'm not leaving again." Shorty's soft whisper held an aggressive edge that caused Abby's eyes to enlarge.

"Said this once already," Betty said. "We're family."

"I've heard what happened and will tell you Al acted in self-defense when she shot George." Samuel used his lawyer voice, and Hicks rolled his eyes and rubbed his chest. "Betty's wounds will verify George was in a murderous rage. Do you need to see her wounds as proof, or will Al's or Abby's word do?"

"Don't need to see all of them. One or two will do. I need to get on out to the farm. Take care of George. His mama's gonna take this hard."

Hearing his kind words for any of the Adams angered Betty, and she yanked the front of her dress open far enough that Sheriff Hicks could see several bloody whip marks. She pulled the skirt up to her thighs to show him the welts there.

"Enough for you, Sheriff?"

He turned his head, nausea building and acid burning in his chest. "Cover up. Damned man. Sick bastard. You?" he pointed at Al.

"No. He didn't get to me."

"Have Doctor Dan see to your wounds, Betty."

"I can look after them myself."

"No. Have Dan see to them."

"Oh." The look on Betty's face said she'd had enough. Now he asked for a physician to verify she'd been whipped. In case.

Sheriff Hicks said goodbye and suggested they find a place to stay for the night. He didn't want them at the farm while he investigated the scene of the shooting.

Patrick followed him to his buckboard.

"The lass wouldn't hurt a fly, Sheriff. Not less she had to. You know that."

"I don't know much of anything, Patrick. But I will after I take a look around."

George was definitely dead. Nothing he could do for him at this point. The bullet had entered his chest and come out his back like the women had said. He replaced the blanket and began his journey for evidence. The floor around the center post showed bloody blotches, as well as the post itself. Some old. Some new. He shook his head, remembering Al had been there.

He parted the bushes Betty had described and noted a large trampled area behind and in the middle where a flask had been tossed. He smelled whiskey when he unscrewed the cap and tucked it in a bag he carried for evidence.

Several other trampled places caught his attention, one under the living space window and one at the back of the house where he could see into the upstairs windows. He found another behind the barn where a crack between the boards revealed the milking area.

George had been a frequent visitor. It seemed unlikely another peeping Tom found Al's farm enticing. How many could there be? No, George had been waiting for Betty to be alone.

He went back for the rifle he'd seen in the barn and took it to the house. The door was unlocked. He stepped over Dog and made a quick tour of the place, noting the placement of windows in connection with the trampled grass and weed growth.

He left the rifle in the corner of the kitchen. He didn't need it, and who knew if the women would when they came home? There were other Adams men.

Hicks wondered why Dog hadn't set up a fuss. Back outside, he called to the animal who continued to snore. Damn dog was deaf. He tried to think of anything he'd forgotten to check out, anything to hold off getting George and taking him home but couldn't.

He struggled putting him in the wagon, but finally managed, having done it enough to know how. He covered George again, climbed up and clicked to his horse.

Emily saw the badge on the shirt in the driveway and the buckboard he climbed down from. She left the door open when she went out on the porch and down the steps, directly to the body lying in the back like she knew. She pulled back the blanket and collapsed into the dirt. Hicks tried to catch her, but couldn't. He knelt and wrapped both arms around her. His throat convulsed, grew thick. He wasn't cut out for this.

No woman should have to see her child dead. No parent, at all, but especially not women who carry them in their wombs, who give birth to them, suckle them at their breasts. Women who patch wounds and kiss scratched knees shouldn't see bullet holes that can't be mended, wounds that put their children in the ground.

"Where's your husband, Mrs. Adams? Where's Frank?"

"Montana. He's gone."

"Your husband is in Montana?"

"No. He's here. In the barn with Terry. One son left. That's all. One son," she wrapped her arms around her belly and moaned.

Sheriff Hicks had a dilemma. He didn't feel good about leaving her, but she needed Frank or Terry. Somebody.

"I'm going to help you inside, Mrs. Adams, and find someone to be with you. Can you stand?"

"I don't want to leave George. I can't. Please, don't make me leave him."

A young woman poked her head out the door. Hicks recognized Cecily and waved her over.

"Leave the young ones inside," he said, seeing them nearby and poking wary faces out the door.

"Stay with her while I find Frank or Terry, please," he said when she got there.

Frank bellowed in rage when Hicks found him and explained his son had been shot. Was dead. Without thought for his wife, he went into a horse stall and started to saddle a mare.

"This isn't gonna go unsettled, mister. You can bet your damned life on that. We've been pushed all we're going to be. That's for damned sure. He said he'd see us all dead."

Terry stopped his father's tirade by saying he'd go with him, but later. He took him by the shoulders and glared meaningfully at him.

"Shut up, Pop. You don't know what you're saying. Ma needs us now. Come on. We need to see to George."

Hicks became aware of the undercurrent of messages going from father to son, but he'd get to that later. At the moment, other things were more important.

Together, they took the body into the dining room and put him on the table. The men left him to be washed and prepared for burial by the two women.

That's another act they perform for the ones they love, Hicks thought. They're there at the beginning and at the end. They bring them into the world and prepare them for leaving it. He shook his head and rubbed his chest. He needed to retire, needed to be done with all this.

In the kitchen, Frank poured whiskey into several glasses. He shoved one into Hicks' hand. Terry grabbed another, gulped and poured again.

"Have a seat, Sheriff. We need to talk about who murdered my son." He kicked out a chair for the sheriff and sat across from him.

"Sit, son," he told Terry.

"The way I see it, he was killed in self-defense," Hicks said. "He was whipping a young woman, had stripped her naked, and was about to rape her. Another woman saw it happening and shot him as he headed for her with the whip." He pulled it out of the bag and showed it to them, still marked by Betty's blood.

"That's horse shit. George wouldn't do that. He can have all the female flesh he wants just by asking."

"He raped before. It's what got him in trouble in the first place. That's why he went to jail."

"Trumped up charges," Frank growled. "Court knew it. That's why they didn't keep him long."

Hicks watched Terry's studiedly placid face. He knew something he wasn't saying. Hicks watched while he told them the sordid tale.

"I saw where he hid so he could watch the women until he could get one alone. Grass and weeds were all trampled." He pulled the flask out of the bag by his chair. "Look familiar?"

Both men stared at the tin flask, and Hicks stuck it back in the bag knowing they'd recognized it.

"So, you're a mind reader?" Frank said. "You know what George was doing and thinking?"

Hicks blew out a puff of air. "No. Evidence and witnesses both speak. I put it all together and a story is told. That's all."

"You believe these women? Why? One of 'em killed my son. Why wouldn't she lie?"

"The bloody marks on one's body don't lie. He whipped her. He tore the dress from her body. I saw it."

"Stop!" Emily shrieked from the doorway. "Stop it, now! I won't hear anymore. My beautiful baby lies in the other room. Dead. Let him rest, I beg you."

Her weathered face had aged in the past half hour. Her hair hung limp and gray around it. Her shoulders stooped, and her step was weary.

Hicks' heart broke for her. He stood and offered her his glass. "Drink it, Mrs. Adams. I'll leave you alone with your grief. My condolences."

"Sheriff," she called as he walked toward the door. "George thought different than other boys. He always did. He wanted to be a man. Be big like his brothers and make his father proud. He couldn't. He didn't know how. And his father couldn't tell him how to be a man."

She looked at her husband, and her face crumpled. Hicks didn't see love in her eyes. It was something more, something bigger, something different that had grown in the forty or so years she'd cared for the man.

She hadn't carried him in her womb, but she had tended his injuries, his wounded heart, his weak soul. He'd been nurtured by her for all of their lives together. And she'd let him be *big* in his own eyes because he was in hers, larger than anyone, ever. He had power, and she gave it to him. It's what sustained him. But it wasn't love, not the kind he knew.

"He thought Betty was his. She's the woman, isn't she?" Emily said.

"Yes."

She put her hands over her face, and the wail that erupted from her came out a sob. "I'm so sorry. So sorry. He thought she belonged to him. I don't know why."

"Hush, Ma. Sheriff Hicks doesn't need to hear all that."

Hicks glared at Terry.

"If this comes to trial, and I don't believe it will, your mother will be asked to testify about what she knows. I think it's more than what she said. Isn't that right, Mrs. Adams?"

She didn't answer but turned away and went back to her dead son.

"Let yourself out, Sheriff," Terry said. "We're done here, but not with this whole business."

"Feels like a threat, Terry. I'm warning you to stay away from Betty Gerard and Al Tatum."

"Now *that* feels like a threat, Hicks," Frank Sr. said, rising from his chair to emphasize his words. He rose a head taller than the sheriff, but Hicks had been the law for many more years than he could count and knew a bully when he saw it. He also knew how to deal with one.

He smiled. He showed lots of teeth and punched the inside of his hat before putting it back on his head and cocking it to the side.

"It is. Be good boys, now, you hear?"

Frank snorted after Hicks left and poured another drink.

"Who the hell does that pipsqueak think he is coming in here and talking like that. Al Tatum, my ass. That little girl couldn't kill my boy. It was that Bear and you know it."

"Al can use a gun, Pop. She's been doing it all her life. I'm surprised she didn't kill her own pa with it."

"Bull. Abby's getting back at us for Frank leaving her. She put that Tatum girl up to it."

Terry eyed his father and wondered how much he should tell him about what they'd been up to. The tree crashing down in the road, narrowly missing Abby and her colored friends. The beating of Shorty and blaming it on the bootleggers. Bricks in windows. His face heated, and he fidgeted in the chair. Terry never squirmed – except for his father.

Frank slapped him on the back of his head. Hard. He saw blinking stars.

"What are you hiding, boy?"

"Nothing. I'm not hiding anything, but I don't think you should push the Sheriff – or Bear. You heard what he said."

"Get on out to the barn and finish the milking. I need to think." He saw Chunk and Bailey tiptoe by the dining room table and called to them.

"Get over there and look. It's a dead body. Your Uncle George. That's what happens when you let people walk all over you. Quit being sissies like your ma tries to make you be or you'll be dead, too."

Round eyes stared at their grandpa and swiveled to the body on the table. "Go on. Get on over there."

"Take the boys outside, Ceci. Help Terry milk," Emily said.

With one hand on each shoulder, Cecily guided them past Frank. One face turned to stare at him. The other watched the floor go by.

"Making damned girls out of 'em. You wait and see."

Chapter Thirty-six

After listening to Sheriff Hicks explain the evidence, the Lake County magistrate declared George Adams' death an act of self-defense which made most people breathe easier.

It infuriated Frank Adams. He strode down the streets of Idlewild boasting that it wasn't over. He harangued folks who stopped for groceries at Foster's store, and Joe's love of grizzly details and other people's troubles sustained and bolstered his babbling.

"I'll see my son's killer hang," he told Joe. "I swear, truth will tell."

"That'll be difficult," Jesse told him when he ran across him at Foster's, and Frank repeated his threat. "Michigan doesn't do capital punishment."

"They should," he barked. "Eye for an eye."

Jesse walked away, regretting he'd bothered to speak to him. He felt bad for the man but couldn't tolerate him. Frank Sr. knew everything about everything.

They buried George, and, for one reason or another, most of the town went to see his casket lowered into the ground. They kept their distance from the family, not wanting to intrude, but wanting to show respect.

The funeral hurt, tore at even hardened hearts. Everyone knew, through the magic of the grapevine, that George probably deserved to die, but still . . . He was one of their own, an Idlewild son.

Reverend Evans presided and sent George to heaven with fiery words of warning about lust and sin, about coveting and carnal acts of pleasure. Abby closed her eyes and wondered if the reverend thought pleasure led to an early, unnatural death, but whipping and bloody beatings were simply part of life.

"I can't tolerate that man," she whispered, and Samuel, who stood next to her, rolled his eyes.

"You'll damage your reputation," he whispered back.

"Already did that."

"True."

Abby let her mind wander, eager for the funeral to be over, to be away from her father-in-law's penetrating glare. Terry's, too. She'd tried to speak with Cecily, but the woman turned her head, grabbed her sons' hands and walked off.

"Please, I just want to say how sorry . . ." Abby called after her, but the words were ignored and never completed.

She couldn't get close enough to Emily to speak to her. Her husband and son kept her guarded, safe from interlopers like her. She understood, but wished it could be different, and wondered if Frank even knew about his brother.

Emily's back was straight, her chin high. Frank Sr. and Terry each held an arm, but Abby thought she didn't need them. She stood with her feet spread, solid, showing Idlewild she could withstand the trauma of burying her boy.

Frank said something to her, and she turned her head to look him in the eyes. She shook her head, mouthed, "No," and stepped away from him.

Emily held the first handful of soil, and she took her time spilling it. A stray Mallard flew overhead, honking a farewell, and she let her eyes follow it for a time before finishing her task.

Today, nobody was going to hurry her. Nobody was going to tell her what to do or how to do it. Nobody would convince her what was right or wrong. She already knew.

She let her eyes rest again on the coffin of her youngest son, and they softened. They shimmered with unshed tears. She rubbed a hand over her heart, fisted it like she would rip the organ from her body, and opened her hand over his grave. She dropped her heart and soul into the hole to be buried with him.

Emily knew she'd failed George. She hadn't been strong enough to stand up to her husband. She had loved and nurtured too much, stomped her foot too little. Had never slapped the flat of her hand on the table and said, "Enough!" Part of her went with George, and she would live and die with her failure. Remember it forever.

Abby watched, read her eyes and gestures, and respect for Emily Adams filled her heart. She hoped for a chance to tell her.

"You okay, lass?" her da asked, drawing her away from the mourners and toward the buggy.

"I am, Da. Just sad."

"Aye. To lose a child."

"What happened to George? What would make him do the things he did?"

Samuel helped her into their buggy and stepped back. "I have a couple of theories about that if you're interested."

"I am. Coming by?"

"I'll take that as an invitation."

Betty and Al, who'd been covering the hotel while Abby and Patrick went to the funeral, were ready to go home. They missed the farm. "We have animals," Al said.

Abby kicked the dirt. It had begun to snow, and, while it didn't collect on the ground yet, the world was a utopia of white purity. Light flakes skittered in exhaled breath and melted on noses.

The women sat astride Nag, Betty's arms wrapped lightly and comfortably around Al. Abby held the bridle like she could stop them from leaving by dragging the horse into the hotel with her.

Betty nudged her with the toe of her boot.

"Go on in, boss. We'll be fine, and you're freezing."

"Alright. Get home before dark. Lock your doors." Abby ran back inside and into the nearly empty bar. Samuel tugged an arm as she went by.

"Close up, Abby, and let's go for a ride."

"Better idea. Since it's just the five of us, let's do an early porch drink. I'll bring the lap robes, you fix the drinks."

"It's cold out, Abby."

"Little girl."

"How about we gather some chairs around the fireplace right here in the bar?"

"Deal. I want to hear your theories about... You know."

Between Shorty, Bear, Patrick and Samuel, they had the rocking chairs in front of the fire in an instant. Abby poured toddies, and the friends were seated and soaking up the warmth of the flames as evening fell to darkness. Phantom curled on Bear's shoulder, Cleo on Abby's lap, and orange Bob set up the loudest purr of all on Shorty's knee.

"This is nice. Why haven't we done this before," she asked.

"You needed me to guide you," Samuel said.

Shorty groaned, and Bear rolled his eyes. Patrick said, "And I'm a leprechaun."

Abby patted his hand. "Sure, Sammy."

"No. Not even my mother can call me Sammy."

"Sam-Sam?"

"I guess you don't want my highly educated theories," he threatened, raising narrow black eyebrows.

"I'd like to hear them," Shorty said. "Leave the man alone, Abby."

Samuel tapped a finger on the arm of his chair and tilted his head in thought. He pulled on his bottom lip.

"This is what I think. A need for power is magnified, even multiplied when one is continually stripped of it. It becomes an obsession and is exhibited in increasingly cruel and domineering ways."

"But why? And why cruel?" Abby asked.

"Psychologists claim it's because other, more natural expressions of authority, can't provide the psychological serenity real strength gives. The power of brutality substitutes because these people don't understand or possess inner strength, inner power."

"That makes sense, I guess. But why George? Why the Tatums? They're just lads," Patrick asked.

Bear wiped a hand over his eyes and down his beard. He'd seen strength. He *had* strength and knew it didn't come from a gun or a big mouth or a belt. It was quiet. Unassuming.

"Fathers," he said.

"All of them?" Patrick was a bit affronted. He was one.

"Not even a small percentage," Bear said. "Fathers who value their own authority above all else and fear it's loss. Fathers who give no power to their sons – or daughters. Who make all the decisions because they can't let go of control, like Frank Sr. who ruled as a dictator. Like Tatum who did the same but was cruel, as well."

Bear quit talking, and everyone knew he'd finished. Samuel suspected the man knew what he knew from experience.

The silence broke with the crackling of wood in the flames, the hiss of moisture escaping in smoky tendrils, and the hum of three felines. She sipped and pondered the fire, drawing comfort from the mesmerizing, flickering movement – gasped and sat erect.

"What?" Samuel spun toward her.

"I saw Cassandra in the flames, in the blue at the bottom where it's hottest."

"You saw Cassandra? Were her cats walking through the fire with her?" He smirked and raised an eyebrow.

"Don't be a brat. I did. I saw her."

"Maybe she appeared in the fire because we weren't outside, so she could wave her magic stick and give us prophecy," he said.

"Ye never know about the soothsayer. I wouldn't put anything past her or say she couldn't go where she wants." Patrick slapped his empty glass on the floor beside him.

"Refill, Da?"

"Thank you, lass. Then I'm for my room."

"Sit, Abby." Samuel stood and gave a perfunctory bow. 'I would *deem* it an honor to refill glasses." His eyes lit with fun, and his lips wiggled in suppressed laughter.

"More deeming," Shorty said. "You two *deem* more than anyone I know."

"Wonder what she wants," Abby said.

"Guessing you'll find out at tea tomorrow." Patrick took a couple sips of whiskey from the newly poured glass and headed upstairs with it. Shorty and Bear soon followed.

Abby wiggled one thumb in a circle around the other, hands in her lap and eyes on the fire. She wanted to look at Samuel to see if he fidgeted, but figured he wasn't. Samuel wouldn't fidget.

He pulled the watch from its pocket, flipped it open and shut, and returned it to its nest.

"I'm betting you don't even know what time it is," she said. His head spun toward her.

"What?"

"What time is it?"

He started to reach for the watch, and she stopped him with a hand on his when it landed on his vest pocket.

"Well?" she said.

"I was going to look."

"You just did."

"Oh."

"Were you saying you need to leave? Is that why you did that?

"No. I don't know why I did it."

"Hah! You do fidget."

"I do not."

He covered her hand with his, and his eyes darkened.

"Perhaps you bring out the worst in me, Abigail. Perhaps my mind becomes addled."

"Why?"

Samuel rested his head against the back of the chair and looked at her, at the multicolored flames dancing a rapid tango, and back to her. He liked the way her auburn hair reflected the fire and the way it crawled out of the ribbon trying to confine the mass at her neck. He liked the tilt of her head and the stubborn jut of her chin.

He liked her.

"Perhaps you make me something I've never been, and it's bewitching, and it actually *is* time for me to go. I know without looking at my watch; I'm fairly certain."

He stood and drained the glass. "I know the way out, Abby. Stay seated and relax."

She followed anyway. At the door, she tugged on his arm and he turned. She stood on tiptoe, brushed her lips against his and heard his groan of defeat. He tasted of whiskey and smelled of licorice. She kept him there while she moved her lips over his.

Too soon, he put his hands on her shoulders and held her back from him, brushed his fingers over her cheek, and she closed her eyes.

"You need to think, Abigail."

"I'm tired of thinking."

He pulled her close and felt her heart beat against his. He pressed his cheek against her hair, and it caught in the bristles of his late day beard.

"You're a trailblazer, Abigail, but you've not come up against this before. This is a battle you can't even imagine."

He stepped back and looked into her eyes. He saw what he'd been looking for all his life, and it pierced his heart. He turned and ran.

She watched him leave and kept watching until the sleek automobile faded from sight.

What had she done?

Al guided Nag straight to the barn without hesitation. She didn't want to think about what had happened inside and tried to drop Betty off in the yard, but the stubborn woman hung on.

"Get on with it, Al. I know what you're doing."

"You don't have to go in there."

"I surely do. So do you. It's where the heifer is. Where the chickens sleep. Nag, too. Think I'm going to forget it by avoiding where it happened?"

"No."

"Got over it before. I can do it again." She punched out a puff of air like her thoughts were nonsense and not worth the time of day. "Ain't gonna do it anymore, though. Thanks to you, Al."

Al didn't respond, and Betty worried she had offended her. She peered around Al's hair to see her face, see if she was angry, but she should have known better. Al's expression rarely changed with happy or sad, confused or indignant. She looked the same no matter what went on in her head.

"I'm sorry, Al. I don't know what it's like to . . . I don't know how you feel, and saying that was insensitive." She tugged at Al's shoulder. "It must be horrible for you."

"No. It's done."

"You saved me. Thank you."

"You're welcome."

Al punched the mare with her heels, gently, and she ambled in. The center pole had been washed clean of its dark smears, and the floor around it had fresh straw covering its bloody history.

Shorty, Al thought. He'd also tended to her animals while she and Betty had stayed at the hotel. No one would have noticed it on her lips, but a veiled smile hid there.

Betty rubbed the brush over Nag and gave her extra oats. Al pulled a stool up to the heifer and drew milk from her udders. It satisfied all of them. Her chickens gathered around, pecking and clucking, and Al filled her chest with the sweet scent of her barn.

Chapter Thirty-seven

Services at the hotel were easier than at private homes because they held it in the bar where room and chairs were available. They left them at the tables instead of moving everything, so it appeared as if people had wandered in for supper or a drink. It made Abby smile thinking of the folks who came there for church but had never stepped foot in the bar for anything.

The room filled, and Benjamin's fingers on the piano invited feet to move and bodies to sway. Muted chatter, people greeting people they hadn't seen since last Sunday, filled corners and empty spaces, making Abby's heart swell with -- something. Pride? Joy? Love?

The congregation wasn't everything she wanted it to be, but . . .

Shorty came in with Betty and Al. He'd been waiting in the stable to help them with Nag. He figured he should but didn't know how a man in love might act because he had no model to go by. He'd do anything for her. Carry her from her horse. Shield her from bullets with his body. Lay down in the dirt and let her walk on him to keep her feet from touching the ground. He chuckled, and she looked up at him.

"You'd not believe me," he told her.

"Why?"

"I was pondering what I'd do for loving you."

"And?"

"Anything."

"I believe you."

He pulled her against his side, but let her go before going in. He wouldn't sully Al's reputation. Time enough for hugs when they were married.

"Lovebirds," Betty said with a snicker, but her own heart beat a little faster when she heard the piano.

Eyes cast awkward glances toward Betty and Al. Everyone knew, but many couldn't find the words to breach the gap between knowing and talking about the whipping and the killing. They nodded and patted, threw out innocuous greetings and wishes for well-being and walked on. Al shrugged, and Betty grinned.

Bunny saw them from across the room and glided over, halted and let her eyes wash over them like a slow wave picking up and dropping information like pebbles in the surge. She put both hands on Betty's cheeks, held her still and looked her over from head to toe. She dipped her head once in approval.

"You could be my daughter," she said. "I'd be proud."

She turned to Al. She didn't touch her but stood close enough she could speak softly and be heard.

Al pulled inward, unsure of this imposing woman's intent. She knew Bunny Jackson by sight, knew she had a reputation in Idlewild for a couple of reasons – one as Cassandra's sister, but the other was the respect she had in the community. They looked to her for guidance. And they feared her.

Al tried to stand tall and lifted her chin.

"I once told Abigail we could never be kin, coloreds and whites. And we weren't friends because we could never truly know one another, our ancestral heritage began in a different world." She looked from Betty to Al and tried to keep her lips from trembling. "I was wrong. Friendship is stronger than race."

"Yes. It is," Al said and swallowed.

Bear and Abby watched the threesome from the bar. Abby worried since she'd been the recipient of Bunny's caustic tongue in the past, and both Betty and Al had been through enough. She breathed a relieved sigh when the faces showed pleasure and Bunny turned away.

"Happy?" Bear asked.

Abby gave a slow nod and looked around. Pastor Jenkins' big voice greeted folks. Children in their Sunday best tried to escape their mothers and fathers. Aunts and uncles or friends corralled them and dragged them to the corner set aside for youngsters. It was a family. In a family, everyone took care of the children.

Abby saw and sighed.

"Want one of your own?" Bear said.

"That's not likely."

Charity Evans threw open the door with a flourish, her blue cape flying in the wind. Behind her, Charles Chesnutt, ducked the wayward flaps of her fine wool garment. He grabbed for his hat as it flew, laughing and dancing around Charity in order to catch it. She got it first.

"How much will you pay for it, Charles?"

"For my own hat?"

"You know what they say about possession and . . . How many tenths of the law are necessary, Samuel?"

He stood just inside helping folks with their coats and trying to keep the wind from slamming the door against people.

"Leave me out of this, Charity. Charles, you're on your own."

"Men. I think I'll put a feather in it and wear it. I'll set a new trend."

"You do that already, Miss Evans," Charles said with an involuntary grin. They had gotten off to a bad start when they first met, but after getting to know her, he realized she wasn't a bad sort. She simply didn't think, not deeply or ostensibly, anyway.

Abby watched the interplay between the two and couldn't help the smile growing on her face.

"Yes," she whispered. "The foes have become friends."

She added Charity to the count and wished she could stop. Numbers didn't matter, but she giggled when it occurred to her it took some of the fingers of her second hand. More than five. That was good, wasn't it? An improvement, but not enough. She didn't want to call it good enough.

It would never be.

Pastor Jenkins called a song number to Benjamin whose fingers pounded out the chorus of *The Glory Song*. Folks sang where they stood, and, when the song ended, they found chairs.

Abby stayed by Bear at the end of the bar. She could see the reverend and watch the door for late comers. She closed her eyes while Pastor Jenkins prayed for the sick and hearty, for the sinful and sinless, for the living and dead. She thought of George in his grave and of Frank somewhere in Montana, and her eyes filled. She kept them closed, hoping the tears would be gone when she had to open them again.

The reverend hadn't completed his prayer for the universe and all its inhabitants when the door opened, and a gust hurled it against the inside wall. Samuel leaped to catch it, but halted in shock when he saw who entered.

She strode past him, past Abby, past the congregation, all the way to the front of the parishioners. She turned and stared, taking her time to let her gaze flow from table to table and over all the stunned and gaping worshippers.

She bowed her head for several moments, and, as soon as the reverend said *Amen*, she lifted her eyes to the back of the room. Silence penetrated their hearts and stilled their breath.

The first of Emily Adam's tears spilled from haunted eyes. She opened them wide, closed them, and tried again. She raised her tight fists and her angry voice. Fury and anguish twisted her face and lashed out at whoever would hear, whoever might understand, whoever had given birth and loved.

"This has to stop! It's over! It's done! This senseless hate and destruction, this slaughter of our guiltless children is going to stop!"

If silence could grow louder, it did. If the air in the room could dissolve into dust, it did. Emily's words created a vacuum, and no one wanted to be the first to disturb it . . . be the first to take a breath

When she could see through her tears, she threaded her way around the tables and over to where Al and Betty sat, her eyes on the young women.

Betty's wide eyes watched, and she nudged Benjamin who gladly gave up his seat.

Emily Adams found a place to worship in between the woman her son had abused and the woman who had killed him. She didn't turn to look at either of them when she took her seat, but faced forward and stared at Reverend Jenkins.

Tears still flowed, but she did her best to listen, to draw comfort from his words of praise, of admonishment, of glory. She had determined as she dropped soil and soul into her son's grave that the only real power existing for her from that day forward would be the Lord's.

This was the first step.

Because all eyes had been on Emily Adams, no one noticed Cecily standing at the back of the room, her sons attached to either hand, knuckles white. Their eyes were wide, not having seen so many colored faces together in one place at a single time. Their father's words of bigotry clouded their brains, and they clung to their mother's hands and were motionless.

"Four more," Abby whispered when she saw them. "Ten. I'll have to use my feet next time." She tried to pull in the grin stretching across her face but couldn't. Her heart was too full, too glad. Bear pulled on her arm.

"You're going to get a scowl from the pastor if you keep talking while he is."

"Sorry." She dropped her chin for a pious aspect, but her eyes were open and surveying the room.

The wind died to a balmy breeze before church let out, and folks shared a leisurely potluck lunch inside and on the porch. They talked with friends and caught up on family matters.

Abby made sure to meet with everyone, shook each hand and hugged each child. She felt the tug of connection, the pull of a particular string binding them to one another, and she dragged it around with her, guarding it, letting it trail inside the hotel and out on the lawn until the thread wove in and out and between so many people it became a tangled ball of human twine. The string was so tightly twisted, she believed, she hoped, that no one would be able to unravel who they'd become as a community, together.

Cecily, Bailey and Chunk hung at the outskirts of the throng of people. Abby headed for them as soon as she could. She hugged a stiff Cecily and dragged the boys off to play with the other children. She watched her sister-in-law's worried eyes trail the boys and settle there, wary and nervous.

"Thank you for coming, Ceci," Abby said when she came back without the boys.

"Emily made me. I don't understand, but she insisted. Terry is furious. Frank Sr. is living in the barn."

Abby could only nod. She knew the Adams home must be in turmoil but could do nothing to fix it. Time and thought might.

"Sorry," she said. "I wish you knew how much."

Abby waited for Emily who had eased her way over to Cecily. Her mother-in-law didn't look like the woman she knew, the one who hovered over her with flour dusted hands or sizzling iron skillet, back when she'd married Frank and was the ruling matriarch. She was smaller, bonier, and the skin on her frame seemed too large to cover her fragile bones.

"Thank you so much for coming, Mrs. Adams," Abby said, reaching for the older woman's hand.

Emily let her take it and hold it, but it seemed to be an effort not to snatch it back and hide it in the folds of her dress.

"It's what should be. Will be."

Abby's head dipped in sorrow. Emily's words were solid, even determined, but, at the same time, they were lifeless and dead. The hollow sound made Abby think of George's grave and the sight of his mother wanting to go with him.

She wrapped her arm around Emily's shoulder, and they stood together, let the sun slant its rays over them, warm them. They didn't speak. Words wouldn't help or heal. She didn't pull away from Abby's one-armed embrace, and the proximity gave something to both of them – a sense of calm which towered over what they had expected or even hoped to find together.

Emily's head swung like a pendulum on a large grandfather clock, smooth and slow, steady, as she took in the people milling about the yard in front of the hotel. Her hand went to her mouth, and breath blew through her fingers.

"Are you alright, Mrs. Adams?" Abby asked.

"I will be. Just takes a little getting used to. But I'll be fine, I vow."

"These are my friends."

"I know that, Abigail."

Abby's eyes closed and her knees might have buckled a bit when she saw Sue and Sally marching their way. She loved them, but, this once, hoped they would move on by.

No luck. Sue labored up to them, purple evening gown bouncing over all her luscious rolls, and stuck out her hand.

"Mrs. Adams. You probably don't know me, but I know you. Pleasure to meet you in person."

Emily threw back her shoulders and declared it was her pleasure, as well. Abby expelled hot, relieved air. She wondered how it hadn't burned her lungs as it waited to exit.

Sally raised herself to her full six feet and waited for Emily to offer her hand.

"Lovely gown," Emily said as she extended it. "Wonderful, bright red to match this autumn day."

"Doesn't it? Thank you. Sometimes everyone needs a little color to make life more interesting. More rewarding."

Sally's lush lips twitched at the corners, and Abby couldn't tell if she had made a meaningful pun or a slip of the tongue. She'd know for certain if it had been Sue, but Sally?

"My condolences for the loss of your son, Mrs. Adams. I can't begin to feel your grief but believe you've taken a first and most meaningful step today." Sally continued to hold her hand.

It appeared to Abby if Emily wanted to retrieve it, she'd have to yank it back.

Sally patted the hand. "I've not known the loss of a child, but I've known sorrow. I've never talked about it with anyone, ever, but if you wish help in your grief, I am here for you. I would share with you."

Abby's mouth hung open. She was stunned – by Sally's eloquence and by her revelation. Had she made it up? Was it a bad joke? It certainly didn't seem to be. Before Abby could close her mouth, Sally released Emily's hand and glided away, Sue rolling along behind her and trying to catch up.

Betty and Benjamin strolled across the grass to greet Mildred and James Gerard, her parents. He intended to ask for Betty's hand, and his own fidgeted behind his back. He never got the chance.

Mildred chewed a thumb nail, and Betty knew the sign. Her mother was upset.

"What's wrong, Ma?"

James wove a hand under his wife's arm to draw her away from the crowd. He didn't trust the volume of Mildred's voice if she got going on what stuck in her craw. Betty followed them.

"That woman thinks it's okay to stroll in here and rant at us? The woman whose son violated you? Over and over? Would still be doing it if . . ."

"Ma. Stop. Hush."

"I will not! She thinks dead is the worst thing that can happen to a body? It isn't, and you know it, Betty. Dead isn't worse than rapes and beatings. Not worse than living in fear every day and knowing you can't do anything because your rapist is a white boy."

James dragged her to their buggy, shushing and patting her shoulder. He gave Betty a grimace that was half sorrow and half apology.

"We'll come out, Pa. Benjamin wants to talk with you."

His lips split in a grin. "The answer is yes, son. Absolutely, yes."

"How do you know what he wants?" Betty stuck out a hip and put a fisted hand on it.

"Saucy wench. Course I know. But right now, I need to get your ma home." Betty walked with them, leaving Benjamin behind to wait for her.

"Let it go, Ma. Abby believes our all-mixed-up church is the answer, and I kinda do, too. We can't love the Lord together and hate each other at the same time. Try it, Ma."

Mildred's grim lips and firm jaw said she didn't want to hear any of it.

"Think about it, please? You see Abby there every Sunday. That doesn't hurt, does it?"

"Doesn't it?"

"Please, Ma. Think about Al. And Abby. And me. Please."

Chapter Thirty-eight

The last Chautauqua fell in late December and celebrated Christmas soon to come.

Snow covered the ground, and, somehow, it felt warmer outside than when the bare grass was painted white with frost. Lanterns lit all four corners of the pavilion, and a nativity scene decorated the ground in between it and the lake. A frosty moon lit the manger, as it must have when the baby Jesus lay there. The scene mesmerized. Fingers and toes warmed at the bonfire, and a tall pile of wood stacked nearby meant it would last all weekend.

Charles Chesnutt gave the keynote address and read a selection from his collection of short stories, *The Conjure Woman*. Because his negro characters spoke in dialect, a few people were offended by the language, and some didn't even understand. His *Uncle Julius* stories told of the psychology and social consequences of slavery in complex ways many didn't appreciate until much later – after they had mulled it over. Charles wasn't afraid to use the means available to him in order to tell the tale and make a point.

"I'm surprised he hasn't been lynched," Samuel said to Abby.

Her head spun to glare at him. "Don't say such a thing. That's terrible."

"No. What's terrible is that it's true. I think what saves him is most folks don't understand his work, and they don't want to take the time to – or admit to it."

"That's true. And I'm trying, but it's complicated. He's too smart."

"Not for a smarty pants."

Samuel didn't smile, but his eyes danced with warmth and his mustache twitched. Abby could tell he was enjoying himself.

"It's a commentary on Antebellum society," Bear said.

Both heads swung to him.

"I didn't know you'd read his work," Abby said.

"I did."

"You are something, my friend."

"And I'm impressed." Samuel noted Bear's quiet eyes, his noble and immobile expression.

What else did the man hide behind his scarred beard and taciturn demeanor? He'd never know unless Bear wanted him to. No one did. But the man was unquestionably formidable, and Samuel knew it without knowing why.

Phantom snaked through the crowd and clawed his way up Bear's leg. He held a hand to the back of the cat's head to give him some leverage for the climb, and he curled around Bear's neck like a fox stole.

"Traitor," Abby said, rubbing a finger under the cat's chin.

With growing excitement, Abby watched musicians set up instruments and music stands for Buddy Black's band. She wanted to dance, wanted to one-step again like Samuel had taught her, and her feet tapped in anticipation. She didn't care if she shouldn't. She *would* dance, convention could be damned. She thrust her shoulders back and tossed her head.

"Who'd you just wallop?" Samuel asked.

"What are you talking about?"

Bear chuckled. "You did, Abby. He's right. You punched somebody."

"I did no such thing." She crossed her arms and blushed when she snorted, prompting a chuckle from Bear. It escaped without intention or prior notice, and she hated it, but couldn't stop the crass noise. She usually followed it with a stomp of her foot. Some lady she was.

"Fibber," Bear said.

"Dissembler," Samuel said.

Bear looked sideways at him, raised an eyebrow and went back to watching the workers set up the band. In moments, Buddy was fingering the strings of his guitar. A clarinet, two trombones, and a coronet wailed the New Orleans jazz he'd invented.

When Buddy traded his guitar for the coronet, the music took over every breath and heartbeat. It rushed through the bloodstream and moved feet and arms and bodies. Abby had to dance. She turned to Bear and Samuel.

"Okay, you're both right. I punched anyone who told me it wouldn't be right for me to dance. So, you wanna?"

She held her hands out to both men. Bear backed away, and Samuel took her hand and put his other at her side. Her feet didn't touch the ground, and her lips didn't quit grinning. Her heart pounded with joy.

When that dance finished with a flash of leg, they waltzed, and Abby floated, her arm on Samuel's broad shoulders, his hand on her back. Scandal would follow, and she didn't care. She wanted to dance – and she did. Her eyes were green fire, her smile showed big, white teeth, and she didn't try to cover them with her hand.

Church was scheduled under the pavilion as long as the weather held, and it did. Chairs filled quickly, but the bonfire had been rekindled, and standing folks gravitated there. They could get warm and stare into the fire during Reverend Jenkins' sermon and be happy they weren't looking at the flames of hell.

Abby stood on the porch and counted. She couldn't help it. Ten, and even worse, they'd lost Mildred and James Gerard. They hadn't attended services since Mrs. Adams became a parishioner.

Benjamin's auto pulled up and dislodged Al and Betty who leaped up the steps.

"Your ma coming today, Betty?" Abby asked without any confidence in the answer.

"Yes. In fact, here they are." She glanced sideways to see Abby's reaction.

The Adams' buggy pulled up to the pavilion. James Gerard climbed out of the driver's side and went around to help the others: Mildred, Emily, Ceci, Chunk and Bailey.

Abby's jaw hung. Her head swung to Betty. "What . . .?"

Emily slipped an arm through Mildred's and they walked together to seats near the front, leaving the rest to follow or go where they chose. Cecily and the boys went to the bonfire, and James found Samuel still setting up chairs near the back. Abby closed her mouth and found her tongue. "What happened?"

"Charles Chesnutt happened."

"Explain."

"He came out to the house yesterday. He knows a lot of stuff."

"Yes, he does, but what did he do?"

"He asked Ma if she believed in human liberty, if she believed that all of us are equal. And then he said, 'So, do you not believe in the 'Good Book?'"

Abby's eyes widened at his brashness. Mildred was a solid church goer. "Did she throw him out?"

Betty shook her head.

"Well, then, how . . ."

"He went outside and brought in Mrs. Adams," Betty said, and began to tell her what and how it all happened.

"I don't blame you, Mrs. Gerard," Emily had said. "I would hate me, too. I hated you for having a beautiful daughter – not that her beauty is an excuse for George's behavior. It isn't. I just used it as one."

Mildred sat silent at the kitchen table. No expression. No words. Her lips were a gray slash across her face as Emily continued to speak.

"You *should* hate me, because I knew long ago what he'd done to Betty. Yes. I'm going to use her name even though I know it bothers you, and I don't have the right to have it on my tongue. Betty is a wonderful, strong woman. You have reason to be proud. I don't. I'm ashamed – of my sons, but mostly of myself, for not raising them to be strong, virtuous men. I'm asking your forgiveness, and I know it's presumptuous. It's easy to ask and not easy to give. I know that, but I'm asking anyway."

Mildred didn't respond. Her hands knotted together where they lay on the table, her pulse throbbed at her temples, and her nostrils distended. She wanted to hit the white woman sitting in her kitchen asking more of her than she had to give, more than she'd already given. She wanted to knock her chair over and stomp her face bloody like they'd done to Betty.

Emily knew the toll she exacted, could see it in eyes filled with fury. "I'm sorry," she said. "I'm so very sorry. Please tell me. What can I do?" Tears ran down her cheeks, and she didn't bother to wipe them away.

"Why are you doing this? Why are you here? You took my daughter. Why are you trying to take my church?" Mildred said, anger bubbling inside her, a volcano ready to erupt.

Emily sat back in her chair. She wanted her words to be right, to be accurate. She owed honesty to this woman. When she found the answer, she leaned forward, made a steeple out of her forefingers and prayed she would be heard.

"It's the building blocks, Mrs. Gerard. I'm tearing down the old blocks so we can build again, this time with blocks glued together with mortar made of esteem. I'm asking you to do the same. It's not easy, I know. Ask Mister Chesnutt. He'll explain. Please? Get to know me. Let me know you."

Mildred's breath blew long and harsh. It came from somewhere deep in her gut, and it wasn't one of relief, but of angst laced with anger.

"You have two grandsons."

"Yes. Chunk and Bailey. Why?"

"They gonna play with *my* grandsons?"

Emily sat upright. She hadn't considered that, and it showed.

Mildred scoffed. "Course not."

"Wait. Yes," she said, suddenly sure of herself. "They will. And they'll start at church."

Mildred gave a slow, tired nod. It felt like she was throwing away the rod making her back straight, keeping her upright, but it was only her rage she discarded. She rubbed a forefinger under her nose, squeezed her nostrils and squinted her eyes closed.

"I'm not sure of any of this, but I'm tired of hating you. I'm tired of being afraid, so . . . I'll be there at church. Can't say I am forgiving you, because I just don't know. We'll have to see about that part."

Emily bolted out of her chair, happy to have made a minute step of progress.

"I'll pick you up tomorrow in my buggy. It's big, and we'll all fit. I'm so happy, Mildred. You don't know. You just don't know what . . . My sons . . . You don't know."

Tears filled her eyes and she tried to swallow them back, but they were happy tears. She was on her way to making George's mistakes her own and finding *his* forgiveness.

Porch chairs made a half circle in front of the fireplace. Their runners creaked awkwardly on the wooden floor until people found the revered rhythm. Patrick stoked the fire, adding more wood than required, but it was early. Folks would likely be here for a while.

Abby brought a tray of hot toddies and set them on the low table in front of them. She took one for herself and a seat next to her da.

"I miss my loon," she said. "And my owl and my raccoon and my opossum and my bat and my Cassandra. I miss the porch."

"Not *your* porch? Isn't it yours, too? It's cold out there, lass."

She stared at her da with eyes of love, never more so than during times of turmoil, and turned to Charles. "You were wonderful this weekend, in so many ways. Thank you."

His handsome face, highlighted by the fire, looked tired. He felt his years after engaging with an audience, after trying to share what he believed. It taxed him because it meant so much.

"I'm old."

Charity tapped his shoulder and batted her eyes, much like she'd done on the first night they met at the bar and she'd tried to pick him up.

"You're a spring chicken," she said. "And a chicken. Walk me home when I leave?"

Charles didn't answer, but he didn't say no. Abby's eyebrows raised – happy they were friends. Nice people, she thought.

"Shorty instructed me to say he and Al are, uh, engaged is the term, I think," Bear said.

An eruption of hand clapping bounced off the walls and echoed in the empty bar.

"Damn good news," Patrick said. "Love both the lad and the lass. He's not taking her from my kitchen, is he?" Fear supplanted his joy.

"Not that I know." Bear shrugged. "I gave you all I was told to give."

"What's going on with all the love around here?" Abby said. "Betty accepted Benjamin's proposal, too."

Voices were low, compliments of the hectic Chautauqua, little sleep, and high emotions. Peace settled in each breast, and each mind found places to go in memory of the day and yesterday and on to making tomorrow's.

Charity stood, and Charles followed. Bear and Patrick said goodnight. Samuel turned to read Abby's thoughts. Did she want him to leave so she could go to bed? Did she want him to stay?

"Stay," she said. "I want to sit on the porch wrapped in a woolen blanket."

"Did you read my mind?"

"Maybe. Will you join me?"

Samuel smirked, refilled their drinks, and took them to the porch while Abby found a couple of heavy blankets. They met at the far end where shadows melted into the darkness. He covered her with one of the blankets she'd brought, tucked her in and handed her a hot toddy.

"I should tuck you in, Samuel, but then you'd have to get up to re-tuck me."

Her lids were heavy, and she dragged them open. It had been a long week.

"I think I can tuck myself. Enjoy your porch time."

"I am. Thank you."

Her loon gave a last moan and lifted from the lake. Abby knew he was leaving for the winter, and she said a silent goodbye. Warmth gathered at her throat, wet and threatening.

"What's wrong with me, Samuel? My loon is making me cry."

"I don't think it's the loon."

"Then what?"

She spotted Cassandra off to the right, her walking stick poking in the snow-damp edge of the lake. Her clowder marched in step as if they were soldiers.

"Who is she, Samuel? How does she know what she does?"

"What does she know? Things you don't?"

"I think so. At least, it sure seems like it."

Cassandra turned to them, waved her stick and bowed, bending low enough her hair dragged the ground. She stayed so long, Abby began to worry, but, when she stood, the moon's beam lit her face. It wore a smile and an invitation.

Abby would visit her tomorrow.

TO MY READERS

I am happy to share my work with you and hope you enjoyed *The Whipping Post* and all my fictional and real characters. It is my dream to cause some laughter along with a little serious contemplation. The more I create events and characters who lived (or could have lived) in Idlewild, the more I am forced to think about oppression in all its forms, about the harm it does, not only to recipients of subjugation, but to persecutors – the bullies.

I have confidence in the ideas of Charles Waddell Chesnutt; esteem has healing power, and I believe familiarity and knowledge build esteem. It's a cycle we need to promote.

Go to www.julisisung.com for news. If you leave your email, I will let you know when the sequel is available.

Made in the USA
Lexington, KY
07 November 2019

56527234R00249